SAVING GRACE

Jennifer H. Westall

Book 3 in the Healing Ruby series

Saving Grace/ Jennifer H. Westall. -- 1st ed.
ISBN 978-0-9908759-9-4

*To my son, Brody
because you're just that awesome.*

Rejoice not over me, O my enemy;
when I fall, I shall rise;
when I sit in darkness,
the Lord will be a light to me.

—Micah 7:8

Ruby

January, 1937

To be honest, I didn't give much thought to choosing a name for myself. In fact, during those first days and nights rattling around on the Southern Pacific's Sunset Line, I'd have to say I spent most of the time in a daze. My head still pounded from my most recent concussion, and my stomach swam each time the train took a curve. First Alabama, then Mississippi slid past the dirty window. I hardly noticed much of anything until Henry and I reached New Orleans a couple of nights after beginning our long journey to California. It hit me then that I was in one of the exotic cities I'd dreamed of visiting since I was a little girl.

But running for your life puts a different perspective on dreams.

We'd put nearly two whole states between me and Alabama's electric chair, and still it didn't seem far enough. I didn't dare suggest we spend even one night in New Orleans as Henry handed over our tickets to be inspected for what had to be the twentieth time. As the steward moved away from us, I rested my head on Henry's shoulder. His muscles relaxed beneath my cheek.

"I'm so sorry, Rubes," he said, lowering his voice. "I wish I could afford one of them sleeping cars. You must be exhausted."

I gave his arm a little squeeze. "I'll be all right."

"I promise once we get a good ways through Texas, we'll stop and sleep a night or two."

Lifting my head, I met his tired eyes, and I thought of Mother. My half-brother, James, had my daddy's eyes, just like I did. Dark, fierce eyes. But Henry, always the one to be different, had the same eyes as Mother. Gentle, hazel warmth that glinted with mischief. Only now they were weary, sagging with days of unrest and worry. I wished I could change things.

"I brought something for ya," Henry said. I sat up as he pulled up his bag from beneath his seat. "I figured on waiting to show ya, but now seems like as good a time as any."

I waited for him to dig to the bottom of the bag, gasping when he pulled out Daddy's Bible. "Henry...how did you get this?" Tears welled in my eyes, blurring my vision.

"Mother was all right with me having it since you were...well, since she thought you were gone. I knew it meant a lot to you, so I packed it up." He smiled at me like he was right proud of himself. "I was able to get some other things for ya when Mother wasn't looking. Your brush and a few of your clothes. And this."

He showed me the bag, and I tugged on the white fabric inside. I pulled it out, treasuring the softness against my hands and the tiny, beautiful red roses. "My dress," I managed to whisper.

"I figured you wouldn't want to leave that one behind."

I couldn't help but remember the smile on Daddy's face when I'd opened his Christmas gift to me so many years ago. I hadn't realized it would be the last Christmas we'd spend together. By the time it was warm enough for me to wear the dress, it had been for his funeral. My chest grew heavy with the memories.

"Henry," I said, "maybe there's another way."

He laid his head back against the chair and let out a sigh. "Rubes, we done been over this a million times. This is the only way you don't end up dead."

"But, if I explain everything—"

"To who? The sheriff? The judge? And what're you gonna tell 'em?"

"The truth. That I had no idea what Roy and the others were going to do. That—"

He dropped his chin and eyed me. "You know that ain't the truth that's gonna free you. That truth is long gone."

I placed the dress back in the bag and turned my gaze toward the window, knowing full well I couldn't tell the whole truth. Even Henry still didn't know everything. Besides, that would mean putting Matthew at the center of a whole heap of trouble, and I just couldn't bear the thought of him going to jail too.

"Seems to me that's what got you in this mess to begin with," he said. "The time for truth-telling is passed. Now we just have to make the best of a bad situation. Everyone thinks you drowned in that spring. No one's hunting you. This is our best chance."

Once again we'd arrived at the same conclusion. Fleeing across the country. Starting over. Burying my identity along with my secrets. It was a strange sensation to be dead to everyone I knew. There was an exhilarating freedom in it that left me wracked with guilt. How could I let Matthew believe I was dead? Henry and I had gone round and round about it. Tell Matthew. Don't tell Matthew. In the end I couldn't bring myself to put his future in jeopardy. I loved him too much to condemn him to, at best, a life of lies and hiding. He deserved so much better than that.

As the train rocked and rattled beneath me for another sleepless night, and another long day, I couldn't stop thinking of everyone I'd left behind. Would they ever forgive me if they knew the truth? Was there a way to ease their pain without risking too much? What kind of life could possibly lie ahead?

Daddy and Mother had done it. They'd abandoned everyone they knew and started over in a new town, burying their own heartache and secrets when they'd buried Grace. Daddy had lost his wife. Mother had lost her best friend. And James, just a baby, never even knew his real mother.

I wondered, had Daddy felt like this? Wracked with guilt and shame for running away. Like, just when he'd been put to the test, he'd failed. Like I'd failed. I knew deep inside myself, that by going on the run I wasn't just leaving behind my home and my family, I was also leaving my faith. Because when it came down to it, if I truly believed all I claimed to believe, I'd face execution with peace in my heart, like Daniel before the lions.

But I had no peace. All I had inside of me was fear. Fear for Henry. Fear for Matthew. Fear of what more could possibly happen. And now, all I had left in the world was Henry.

I was still pondering all this the next evening when I dragged my tired body off the train in some tiny Texas town in the middle of the desert. I followed Henry across a dusty road toward a hotel, the wind whipping my dress around my legs. It was all I could do to keep my feet moving. I didn't even bother to take notice of the name of the hotel. I thought it might have started with an "H." The Holland, maybe.

An older man in a faded cowboy hat greeted us at the front desk. I let Henry take care of all the arrangements, keeping my head down. My heart thudded when the cowboy asked for our names. I glanced up to see him holding a pen over a large ledger.

"That'll be one dollar for the night. Can I have your names please?"

Henry shot me a nervous glance. "Ah, Graves. Henry Graves. And this is my cousin—"

"Grace," I blurted out. "Grace..." I needed a last name. "Miller."

Henry raised an eyebrow at me, but he didn't show any other sign of surprise. He handed over the money, picked up our bags, and nodded his head toward the stairs. "Well, come on, Grace. Let's get some sleep."

CHAPTER ONE

Matthew

November 20, 1941

My first glimpse of paradise came after nearly three weeks at sea. I'd boarded the *SS President Coolidge*, a converted luxury liner, in San Francisco surrounded by cold drizzle and uncertainty. Rumors were rampant, and I figured we were headed for the Philippines, but once we'd left Hawaii, there'd been no doubt as to our destination. Tension between the U.S. and Japan was escalating by the day, and I was only a small drop in the sea of soldiers being funneled to the Pacific Islands.

All morning I'd watched the land draw closer, smelled the sweet aroma of coconut mixed with salty air. As the ship cut a path through the Straits of San Bernardino, I joined Doug Watson and Hank "Cam" Cameron on the port rail. Doug and I had been together for over a year, working with the Corps of Engineers on a couple of different dams in the southwest. We'd known with the rising unease around the world, it was only a matter of time before we were sent overseas. I'd expected somewhere in Europe, but it was clear when our unit was told to report to San Francisco that we were headed somewhere in the Pacific. We'd met Cam on the ship. He was barely five feet seven, but he talked like he was eight feet tall. He'd nearly gotten himself into a couple of scuffles

5

early on, and Doug had come to his defense. Cam had latched onto us for the rest of the voyage.

I'd been anxious over heading out to sea at first. For nearly five years I'd maintained an infrequent correspondence with Henry Graves, and last I'd heard from him, he was flying P-40s in the Philippines. I'd spent those years putting as much distance between Cullman, Alabama and me as I possibly could. The thought of running into Henry, however remote, gave me pause. It had taken everything I had, all the discipline the Army could teach me, to train my mind to let go of Ruby. It had taken so long to accept she was really gone. Sometimes, if I closed my eyes for a moment, it felt like she was still right next to me.

Now, as we passed countless islands dense with palm leaves, white beaches, and coves full of bobbing fishermen, I could do nothing but think of Ruby. She would've loved this. Adventure. Exotic lands. I pictured her lying on the grassy slope of my parents' home as I'd sulked beside her in my wheelchair. She'd poured out her dreams of adventure to Mary and me nearly every day when we were kids. That seemed like a different lifetime now.

"What did I tell you, boys?" Doug spread his massive arms out toward the islands slipping past. "Ever seen anything like it?"

"Still would've rather stayed in Hawaii myself," Cam said. "That's where all the action's gonna be. The Japs ain't gonna care about some islands in the middle of nowhere. Bet they try to hit Pearl Harbor first. Man, I'd love to go head to head with a Zero."

Another soldier to Cam's right dropped his head back and laughed. "Oh, please! The Japs can't even make planes that can fly high enough for you to worry about. And besides, I hear they can't hardly see through those slanted eyes of theirs."

Cam's chest bowed out. "Them Japs ain't got enough guts to attack us. Besides, we'd kick 'em back to kingdom come in less than two weeks."

I exchanged a look with Doug, who rolled his eyes. We'd debated the Japanese position during the three-week voyage, more out of boredom than conviction. I was fairly certain, as was every other soldier who jumped into the conversation, that the Japanese might have the desire to attack us, but knew better than to provoke the U. S. into war. Doug had other ideas, but I chalked it up to a boyish fascination with battle.

"Well, it's definitely the most beautiful place I've ever seen," I said. "Middle of nowhere works just fine for me."

We continued to chew on the rumors and possibilities of the future over the next few hours as we headed north across the Philippine Sea. The sun hung low in the sky by the time we entered Manila Bay. To our left lay dense jungle and mountains. A sergeant, who looked like he'd seen many more years of service than any of us, nodded toward a tadpole-shaped island jutting out of the water to our right. Along the beach I could make out several twelve-inch guns pointed toward the mouth of the bay. "That there's Corregidor. The Rock. Guarantee you there ain't no ships getting under them guns." He pulled his cigar out of his mouth and pointed to the opposite shore where the jungle spread up and over the mountains. "And that there's Bataan. Definitely don't want to get stationed in that mess. Malaria will get you long before any Japs."

I knew it would still be several hours before the ship docked, so I decided to head below deck to get a little sleep. "I'll catch you boys later."

I made my way down to the bunks spread throughout the lower decks and found the group where Doug and I slept. Squeezing into the lowest bunk, I grabbed a notebook and pen. I'd been avoiding writing this letter for nearly a month, but now that I'd arrived safely, I knew it was only right to let Mary know where I was. I pulled her latest letter from the back of the notebook and read over it again so I could address her questions.

Dear Matthew,

I hope this letter finds you well. I'm sending it to the last known address I have for you in the hopes it will reach you in time. It's been nearly two years since I've heard from you, despite the several letters I've sent. I can only pray you've been able to bury all the anger of the past, and that you've found happiness wherever you are.

Unfortunately, Mother's health has continued to deteriorate, and Dr. Fisher says it's just a matter of time before we lose her. Andrew and I have moved into the house with her and Father, which makes caring for her easier. Rebecca loves toddling around the huge rooms, listening to her voice echo. Ellis chases her around while I tend to Mother. You really should see her, Matthew. She could use an uncle who can relate to her rebellious spirit. I'm expecting another baby in February, so of course, I'm exhausted. But we're happy most of the time, and I think having Rebecca here is good for Mother, even though she sometimes mixes up our names.

Mother's asking for you nearly every day. Won't you come see her before it's too late? I know you're determined to pretend Father doesn't exist, but does that mean the rest of us have to suffer as well? I miss you so much. Please tell me there's hope for us to be a family again.

Your loving sister,
Mary

I felt as awful reading it the second time as I had the first. I hated hurting Mother and Mary, but I was just as determined now as I was when I left that I'd never go home again. The intensity of my anger and pain may have dulled over the years, but not my resolve. Not when Father had practically ensured Ruby's conviction and death sentence. Still, it was only right to let Mary know where I was and that I was all right. So I put pen to paper.

Dearest Mary,

I do miss you and Mother deeply, and I'm sorry for the pain I've caused you both. I hope one day you'll be able to forgive me. Although I can't return home, I can tell you that I am doing well. The Army has sent me to the Pacific, where I will be working on runways and construction. I don't know how long I'll be here, maybe a couple of years. Please don't worry about me. Just know that I'm well. Pay no attention to the rumors of war. We are far from danger here. I'm sorry I won't make it home to see Mother. Tell her I love her, and give her a kiss for me. I know that isn't nearly enough, but it's the best I can do for now. Take care of my precious niece. I received your pictures, and she looks exactly like her beautiful mother. I'm sure I'll see her someday. I pray your new baby will be healthy and beautiful as well.

Your Loving Brother,
Matthew

I debated on writing a letter to Henry to let him know I'd arrived in the Philippines. A small voice in the corner of my mind whispered thoughts of healing and redemption, that bringing me here was part of God's plan. But for what purpose I couldn't imagine. Henry would want to meet, and I wasn't sure I was ready for that. I had appreciated his company so much, even leaned on him, in the days following Ruby's death. And I'd written to him at first, as he'd asked. But letting go of Ruby and moving on with my life had meant drifting apart from Henry as well. Our letters had grown less frequent, and I didn't even know if he was still stationed on the islands.

I put away my pen and notebook and closed my eyes. It was for the best. I was spending the next two years in a tropical dream, and I was determined to soak up every moment. The fact that Ruby's brother might be nearby meant nothing.

Ruby

November 21, 1941

I stepped into the waiting room of the San Gerardo Medical Clinic and glanced around at the small, brown faces looking up at me expectantly. The clinic was nothing more than a ramshackle house that was in the process of being converted into a medical facility, one tiny room at a time. The waiting room had only needed a bit of furniture, so it didn't show the same signs of ongoing repair as the rest of the house.

"Frances Mercado?" I called.

Frances weaved her way from the front window through the crowded room toward me, offering a bashful smile as she neared. She'd been in to see the doctor a few times in the year I'd been working as a nurse at the clinic. I led her down the hallway to what had once been a bedroom. In the next room, Mrs. Vega's baby was still screaming. The doctor had given him a start when he'd tried to examine the baby's nasal cavity, and he hadn't stopped crying since. I closed the door to muffle the wailing as Frances took a seat on the bamboo chair beside the exam table.

"How are you today?" I asked, getting my notepad ready.

She tucked her legs beneath her and squeezed up her shoulders. "I am okay," she said in a thick Tagalog accent.

I took a seat opposite her. "How is your family doing?"

"They are okay."

"How about your sisters?"

"They are okay."

She wouldn't look me in the eye for long. That wasn't unusual. She was only fifteen, and even though she'd warmed up to me a little more each time she came in, she still kept her eyes glued to the floor.

"Can you tell me why you're here today?" I asked.

She squeezed her shoulders up again and shook her head. "I told Father I was not feeling good this morning. He sent me here."

I offered my warmest smile, even though my blood was heating up. "Same as before?"

She nodded.

"All right, then. I'll check a few things, and Dr. Grant will come examine you."

I checked her blood pressure and heart rate, which seemed fine. I made a mental note of the bruising around her upper arm. Then I excused myself and went across the hall to the other exam room, where the Vega baby had finally stopped crying. I poked my head around the door.

"Frances Mercado is ready for you next."

Mrs. Vega had gathered her things, so I pushed the door open wider to let her out. She kissed my cheek as she passed. "Dear Miss Grace. You are too thin. Come to my house and let me cook for you."

I couldn't help reaching out for the baby on her shoulder, rubbing his back gently. "How about Tuesday?" I said.

"Oh, that is wonderful! Come after your work is done. And bring your doctor friend. He needs a good meal too, no? You both work too hard." She continued patting the baby on the back as she walked down the hallway. "I see you both on Tuesday."

I turned back into the empty exam room as Dr. Joseph Grant looked up from his notes. His dark eyes seemed troubled. "Frances is next? How is she?"

"She seems all right," I said. "A few bruises on her upper arm. And she says she has the same thing again."

He sighed and ran a hand through his thick black hair. Then he stood, towering over me, and gathered his notes and pen. I followed him into the room with Frances and stood near the door as he took the seat across from her, rattling off questions in Tagalog. I knew enough of the words to understand that she was suffering with another bout of venereal disease.

Frances covered her face while Joseph gave her a thorough exam. I thought I saw a tear escape from under her arm, but she said nothing. Afterward, she sat on the side of the table, her arms wrapped around her stomach. She asked how long she would have to wait to be well enough to work.

He handed her several sulfa tabs and lowered himself to her eye level. "You have to give it at least two weeks. Three is better."

She nodded, but I knew she'd be lucky to have two days before she had to work again. She slid the sulfa tabs into the pocket of her filthy dress. "Thank you," she said, standing.

He nodded, met my gaze briefly, and then stepped out again. I knew it wouldn't do any good to say anything to Frances, but I just couldn't help myself.

"Why do you do this?" I asked. "You don't have to."

She shook her head. "You do not understand, Miss Grace. I must get money for family to eat."

"There has to be another way. You could work as a *lavandera*—"

"No. Father says I must have a soldier boyfriend. I must do it. He will get angry. I must keep clean and make soldiers happy."

"No, you don't have to do that. God will provide for you and your family. You just have to trust Him."

"Grace," came Joseph's deep voice from behind me. "We have patients waiting, and I'm sure Frances needs to get home to her family."

I stepped aside and let Frances pass through the door, shaking my head. "There has to be something more we can do for her," I said.

He stepped into the room and let the door close. "You know as well as I do there's nothing more we can do. Her father is going to get every peso he can for her."

"Why doesn't she just leave?"

He looked at me over the top of his glasses. "She has a thirteen-year-old sister. She doesn't want this life for her. She thinks if she brings in enough money, then her father won't make her sister 'get a boyfriend' too."

My stomach rolled, and I wiped my hand across my forehead. "How can a father do that to his own daughter?"

"Things are very different here than in the States, Grace. It's accepted...even expected. It's how they survive. We have to do the best we can to help them."

I couldn't see how giving out a few sulfa tablets and sending her back into the same life was helping at all. "What are we even doing here? How are we helping these people?"

His expression softened. "Listen, let's do all we can for the people here today. Let tomorrow worry about itself. No more anguish over what you can't control. In fact, why don't you let me take you out tonight? You need to relax. We'll go to that place you love, with the dancing."

I let out a long sigh, trying to breathe out my frustration. He smiled down at me with an affection I'd been trying to discourage for months. "Dr. Grant—"

"Joseph."

"Fine," I said. "*Joseph*, I don't think it's such a good idea for us to go out together."

"Yes, yes. I know. You've said all this before. But that didn't stop you from having dinner with me until recently. What's changed?"

"You changed. You've made it very clear how you feel, and I've made it very clear how I feel—"

"Then there's no misunderstanding," he said. "We're just two friends getting dinner and having a nice evening."

"I can't tonight, anyway. Henry is coming into town, and I said I'd have dinner with him."

"Great! The more the merrier. Let's all go."

My mouth fell open, and I stammered to think of an excuse. "I...I don't..."

"Just say yes, Grace. Let's just have a good time. We both need it. Come on."

I crossed my arms over my chest and finally relented. "All right, fine. But I'm not dancing with you."

Matthew

A perfect cloudless sky rested over Manila when we disembarked the ship and headed over to Fort Santiago to get our assignments. Manila was like nothing I'd ever seen before. I'd had no idea what to expect, but I was taken completely by surprise at the modern city before me. Traffic jammed the roads, and men in white suits bustled along sidewalks in every direction. We passed theaters, museums, clubs of all sorts, and upscale hotels.

Beside me, Doug pointed out the Manila Hotel, practically sparkling against the deep blue sky. "I heard that's where MacArthur lives. Has a whole floor to himself."

I didn't much care where Douglas MacArthur was headquartered. Opinions on the general ran from admiration to downright disgust over his handling of the veterans back in the early thirties. I landed somewhere near disinterested respect. So I nodded and feigned a small amount of interest.

We arrived at Fort Santiago where we were informed we'd be heading north later in the afternoon to Clark Field. There was just enough time to grab some lunch at a nearby restaurant before we loaded our gear on a truck. Once again I was amazed at the high energy of the city. The streets were filled with the clip-clop of small ponies pulling coaches in and out among the honking taxicabs. And every few feet we passed a cart or wagon where we were bombarded with calls to "buy, buy, buy!" It all flew past me so quickly; I was barely able to comprehend what kind of strange place I'd landed on.

But not all of Manila was so modern, or so appealing. Once the truck crossed over the Pasig River, it was clear we were headed through the rougher side of the city. The streets were still crowded, but mostly with the smaller, darker-skinned Filipinos. The dilapidated buildings looked ready to fall in, and the entire place smelled like manure. I sat back in the truck and covered my nose, eager to get out of the city.

Clark Field, which was situated in a huge plain in the Pampanga Province, was only about an hour northwest of Manila. Piling out of the truck, I got my first full view of the airstrip and surrounding base. Bungalows lined the runway, and what looked like part of a golf course spread out west of the airfield. Surrounding the vast plain lay several mountain ranges just begging to be explored. The place looked more like a vacation spot than a military base.

Our group gathered near the main runway to meet our direct supervisor, Major William Hart. He was an imposing man, well over six feet tall, but his baby-faced features undermined his gruff exterior. We gave him a proper salute, and he got right down to business.

"Gentleman, you are here to facilitate the construction of barracks, as well as to maintain the newly built runways for the B-17s. As you can see, we are in the process of a steady build-up of planes and airmen here. You'll be assigned to houses nearby, but things may be crowded for the time being. I suggest storing any of your nonessential items in Manila if you return soon. Do your job, keep your nose clean, and you should enjoy your time here."

After pointing out the mess hall, the theatre, and a few other essential buildings, we were assigned housing. Doug, Cam, and I grabbed our bags and made our way across the runway toward the bungalows.

"Want to head into the city this weekend?" Cam asked.

"I'm in," Doug said.

"Maybe," I said. "Let's see how things go."

Doug huffed. "That means it will just be the two of us. The Monk here doesn't go for anything fun."

I ignored the nickname and kept walking.

"What?" Cam said. "You don't even want to go out for a few drinks? Maybe meet a few pretty girls?"

"Nah," Doug said. "He'll work extra shifts before he'll head out to have some fun."

We came to the bungalow where I would be staying. I wasn't eager to continue the conversation, so I bid them goodbye and walked up the steps into the screened-in front porch. There were two bamboo chairs on each side, with a small bamboo table between them. I knocked on the door and pushed it open. "Hello?" I called.

I stepped into a common room that contained a larger bamboo table and six chairs, a sofa, and a small coffee table with a radio. Voices came from upstairs, and within a few seconds, three men were jogging down them toward me. The first to reach me was a tall redheaded guy who looked like he'd been attacked by freckles. He stuck out his hand and gave me a firm handshake.

"How's it going? I'm Jim Harris."

"Matthew Doyle."

Another guy stepped around him with a pockmarked face, but a friendly smile. "Gene Wallinksi."

The third guy down the stairs shook my hand, but he took a moment to look me over. He was of average height, but quite muscular. "Albert Frost. You just get in?"

"Fresh off the boat," I said.

"You a pilot?" Albert asked.

"Engineer."

"That's perfect," Jim said. "Maybe you can rig something up to keep the geckos out of my stuff."

"Geckos?" I looked around more closely, and sure enough, geckos were all over the place. A few hung from the ceiling; more were crawling along the baseboards. I gave an involuntary shudder.

"Don't worry," Albert said. "We've tried to convince him that the geckos are good, but he's still freaked out by them. They eat the mosquitos and other critters, so *most* of us don't mind having them around." He pointed up the stairs. "You can take the empty cot upstairs. We're heading over to the golf course. Want to come?"

"No thanks. Maybe next time." I wanted to get settled and spend some time gathering my thoughts about what lay ahead.

Albert shrugged. "All right. Suit yourself. Supper's at eighteen hundred. Oh, and don't mind the little brown people. They all work here. You can chip in a few pesos every week to hire them. Two houseboys: Basa and Dima something-or-other. They'll keep your shoes and room looking ship-shape and bring you drinks or whatever else you need. Then there are two ladies who do the washing: Miss Halina and Miss Una. Very friendly. Just leave your laundry at the end of your cot, and they'll take care of it for you. Oh, and Roberto does all the cooking. He's amazing. Just don't watch him cook it. You'll never eat again."

"Great," I said. "Anything else I should know?"

"Just relax and have a good time. Duty here is light, and there's plenty to keep you occupied afterward." Jim glanced over at the other two and laughed. "Just stay away from the seedy side of Angeles and Manila. The hookers in that part of town will send you to the infirmary faster than you can say, 'Thank you, ma'am.'"

They had a good laugh as they headed out the door. Once it closed behind them, I was completely alone. I threw my duffle bag over my shoulder and trudged up the stairs. There were two bedrooms, each with two cots inside. Each cot had a metal closet at the head and a footlocker at the foot of the bed.

I lugged my bag over to the empty cot and took in my new bedroom. It was nothing special, but the view of the mountains was something else. I made up my mind to go exploring the next few days after my duties were completed.

Taking a seat at the end of my cot, I reached into my duffle bag and pulled out my Bible. I set it on the small bamboo table near my cot. It was all I needed to make this little part of the world home. At least for now. I closed my eyes and dropped my head.

Lord, thank You for bringing me here to such a magnificent place. Grant me wisdom and courage. Teach me to have the kind of faith Ruby had. Help me to live out the life of service she should have. Please, forgive me for my doubts. I don't deserve Your blessings, but I thank You for the love You've shown me. Thank You for Your mercy and Your grace.

CHAPTER TWO

Ruby

November 21, 1941

I had come to particularly enjoy a little place on the roof of a quaint hotel near the bay. They had a beautiful view of the ships, and an orchestra that wasn't so loud I couldn't think straight. It was a perfect place for me to enjoy the evening. Not so much for Henry. He preferred a modern band with sounds to which he could swing his lady friends around.

"How 'bout we head over to the Jai Alai after this?" Henry said, setting his beer on the table and sliding his arm around Janine Langston's neck. She was a nurse over at Sternberg, the base hospital, and she'd been sweet on Henry for nearly two months now. I wondered if Henry even realized what his flirtations were doing to her. She seemed like such a nice girl. I'd hate for her feelings to get hurt.

"That sounds like fun," Janine said, her blue eyes lighting up. She looked over at Natalie Williams, another nurse whom I'd met only once before. "You game?"

Natalie, resting her chin in her hand and looking utterly bored, rolled her eyes. "Sure. Anything beats this dump."

19

Natalie made me a little uncomfortable 'cause it seemed like every time I glanced her way, she was studying me, and I wasn't overly eager to socialize with her.

"I think I'll head home when we leave here," I said. "I have to work tomorrow."

Henry glanced over at Joseph, who was finishing his second beer. "Come on, Doc. She can stay out a little longer, right? I mean, it's not like she needs to be there at the crack of dawn."

Joseph shook his head and chuckled. "You're talking to the wrong person. She has the day off tomorrow. Just can't get her to actually take it."

"You should've joined up with the army nurses," Henry said. "They don't work half as much as you do, and they actually get paid."

Joseph worked his jaw muscles, but he didn't say anything. I didn't respond either. Henry knew exactly why I couldn't be an army nurse. I'd barely been able to get away with faking a few unofficial documents to get on the boat to the Philippines. The army would have figured me out for sure.

It was no matter. Henry barely noticed my silence. He winked at Janine and invited her to dance. Together they jumped up and disappeared into the small crowd near the orchestra. When I turned back to the table, Natalie was scrutinizing me again. The hair on my neck prickled.

"You seem so familiar to me," she said. "Have we met before? I mean, before I came to Manila."

I shook my head, my stomach flipping. "I don't believe so."

She didn't look convinced. "Where did you say you were from?"

"Georgia," I answered quickly.

She shrugged and leaned back in her chair, flipping her hair over her shoulder. "I suppose you must favor someone then."

Surely I was just being paranoid. After years of secrets, it seemed to come with the territory. Still, I was ready to escape the conversation. "How about that dance?" I said to Joseph.

His eyebrows shot up, and his deep brown eyes lit up. "Really? I thought you said—"

"I changed my mind."

He jumped up and took my hand, leading me out onto the balcony where the music wasn't so loud. He pulled me around in front of him, sliding his arm around my waist and smiling down at me. Despite myself, I had to admit he was quite handsome. He swayed me gently as the music flowed around us, and I became acutely conscious of how close we were. I hadn't felt that way since...

An image of Matthew looking down into my eyes, leaning in to kiss me, sent a stab of pain through my chest. Where was he right at that moment? Was he dancing with someone too? Had he forgotten me after nearly five years? I should've hoped for his happiness, but a tiny part of my heart still clung to him. I wondered if it always would.

Joseph squeezed my hand as we turned toward the view of the bay. "You all right? You don't seem to be enjoying yourself. Is there something on your mind?"

Part of me wanted to confide in him. He'd been such a good friend the past year. Joseph was the son of a wealthy U.S. businessman and a poor Filipino girl. He'd been raised in the States by his father, given up by his mother for a chance at a better life, and had returned to his native country at the age of twenty-eight to find her. When they were at last reunited, she'd been in poor health, so he'd decided to stay and care for her, along with others trapped in the slums of Manila. I'd heard about his efforts to provide the poor Filipinos with medical care at the church he and I attended, and when I'd asked if I could help, he'd looked at me like I was crazy.

"You want to help care for poor patients in the worst part of the city who most likely can't pay?" he'd said. "You could make a lot more money in the newer sections of Manila."

"I don't need the money," I'd answered.

Joseph had waited for further explanation, but I'd learned to reveal as little as possible about myself. Eventually he'd agreed to let me work as a nurse, and we'd butted heads amiably ever since. But he never pushed to know more about my past, as if he sensed that it was a place I couldn't go. As I danced with him on the balcony, I realized I felt more comfortable than I had since going on the run.

I smiled up at him in return, hoping to ease his concern. "I'm good. Just a little tired."

"Is there anything I can do to help you enjoy yourself? You seem distracted tonight."

Again I was reminded of why I didn't put myself in these positions. I'd once believed with all my heart in telling the truth, a lesson I'd learned in my early teens. I was a terrible liar, and I truly believed it dishonored the gift God had given me. But ever since the trial—in fact, ever since I took the blame for Chester's death—it seemed like my life was wrapped up in one lie after another.

And like my uncle Asa before me, I'd lost that precious gift somehow.

I didn't want to lie to Joseph, but there was no truthful answer I could give. So I shrugged and tried to smile. "I was just thinking about all the work that needs to be done at the clinic tomorrow. The kitchen needs a thorough cleaning, and I need to go through the sulfa supply—"

"Stop worrying over the clinic," Joseph said, frowning. "And the patients, and their sisters and parents and grandmothers, for crying out loud. You work like you're paying penance or something."

My cheeks warmed. Was I that obvious? "I don't believe in penance," I said as blithely as I could. I even managed a smile.

"Could've fooled me, Sister Grace." He grinned down at me for a long moment. Then, stopping our momentum, he grew serious. "God loves you just as you are. You don't have to earn it."

"I know. I just want my life to mean something...to make a difference. I need to help. It's the only time when things make sense."

He leaned toward me, sending a wave of fear through me that he might kiss me. But Henry swept past and spun me away. My breath caught as I righted myself without falling on my rear end. "Henry!"

He laughed and called over to Joseph, "I'll bring her right back!"

Henry continued to whirl us away from the small crowd until we could speak privately. "What gives, Rubes? You look miserable tonight. Doc giving you a hard time?"

"No, just...I guess my mind keeps wandering."

He frowned. "No mystery where it's going."

"Have you...heard from him?"

"Look, I know it hasn't been easy to leave everything behind, but look around at where we are. Would you have ever imagined us, you and me, off on such an adventure? This place is right out of a magazine! I got houseboys shining my shoes, *lavanderas* washing my clothes, and a pocketful of money every month to treat my ladies to some fine times, even after I fork over a third of it to you. Every day is like a dream here. You just gotta let yourself enjoy it."

He spun me around again, and I couldn't help but laugh. "Some things never change."

"Look, if I can arrange for Mike to take us up in his plane again, will you forget this nonsense about working yourself to death, and come with us tomorrow? We have some great fun planned before I head back to Clark."

I rolled my eyes, aware of exactly what he was doing. "You know me too well."

"Come on," he insisted. "I bet if you flirt with Mike a little, he'll let you fly it yourself for a while."

"Oh, all right," I said, unable to pass up the chance to fly. "But I'm not flirting with that ape you call a friend."

The next afternoon I stood off to the side, waiting for Mike to complete the check of his Stearman biplane at Nichols field, just south of Manila. He'd somehow saved enough money during his year and a half in the Philippines to buy it from a retiring doctor who'd used it to fly to patients in more remote locations on the island. The plane was Mike's pride and joy, and he kept it in mint condition.

I avoided making eye contact with him as he went through a detailed inspection. Mike had been out for my attention all morning on the golf course, and I'd about kicked Henry in the rear for bringing him along. But I supposed it was the friendly thing to do if I wanted him to take me up flying.

Mike Sawyer had been friends with Henry since before we left the States, so I was used to his open flirtations with me. They'd played baseball together in the minor leagues back before they both decided to take to the air. Only difference was that Henry was determined to be a fighter pilot, while Mike wanted to do battle with the sea as well as the enemy. On most days, Mike was manning his seaplane for the Navy, a large PBY that looked to me like it might snap in half in a strong wind. On top of that, it didn't coast along a runway, but across the top of the water. I got seasick just thinking about it. I wouldn't go up in that thing if it were the last plane on earth.

It was Mike who'd first written to Henry describing the paradise atmosphere in the Philippines, and Henry had figured it was the perfect place for us. He'd said it was so far away from our troubles that we might just be able to live there forever. And I had to admit it did my mind good to distance myself from all those terrible events. So I had that to be grateful to Mike for, but there was no way I'd ever let him in on my secret.

"Well, that should do it," Mike announced as he came along beside me. A bead of sweat trickled out of his dark hair and ran down the side of his cheek. "I reckon she's ready."

Henry clapped his hands together. "All right, then. Get this baby in the air! And this time, Grace, maybe you can manage to complete a turn without dumping Mike out of the plane."

I snapped my head around to glare at Henry. "I didn't dump him out of the plane!"

Mike laughed and put a hand on Henry's shoulder. "I 'bout did fall out, I swear!"

I crossed my arms over my chest and waited for the two of them to stop laughing. I knew I was having trouble making turns, but they didn't have to make such a fuss over it.

"Come on," Mike said, strolling over to help me climb into the front seat.

I secured my goggles and safety straps. Henry jumped up on the wing and grinned at me over the side of the cockpit. "Don't be nervous, Rubes," he said quietly. "I seen you conquer things much scarier than this before. You can do it."

I thanked him with a smile. Then he jumped down and called out to Mike, "You ain't gonna let her take off or land, are ya?"

"I don't feel like dying today!" Mike shouted back from behind me.

"I can do it!" I shouted back. "You two just watch. I'll show you."

Mike's chuckling voice came through my headset. "Don't worry, Grace. We're just teasing. You're doing a fine job. Henry's right proud of ya."

I wasn't quite ready to let go of my pride and admit it, but I was afraid they were right. Still, I'd dreamed of flying for as long as I could remember, and I was determined to get the hang of it. Flying was the closest I came to being truly free.

We coasted over to the runway, pausing to check the signals. Mike switched into teacher mode, going through the steps of taking off with me again. I nodded along as I mentally pictured each step he was taking behind me.

"You want to try it on your own today?" he asked.

"Yes!" I said, with a little too much enthusiasm. "If you think I'm ready." I wasn't so sure I was ready, but I wasn't about to tell him that.

"Only one way to find out."

I said a quick prayer in my head, opened up the throttle, and held on-to the stick as the plane began to coast down the runway. Wind whipped and whooshed around me, and as the plane tilted up, my stomach dropped. Within seconds we were up, gliding toward a brilliant blue sky. Mike whooped and hollered into my headset. I relaxed my death grip on the stick, and let the joy of the moment sink in.

"All right, level her off some," Mike said as we reached ten thousand feet.

I pushed the stick forward a bit until the horizon spread out before me. "Where are we heading today?"

"Just keep her level for now. We'll try a right turn once we get clear of Cavite."

I trimmed the plane so it would essentially fly itself, while I took in the glory of the day. With the bay to my right, and the luscious, green mountains beyond, I imagined soaring off into the clouds that rested around the tops. Up here, away from my daily struggle to atone for my sins, I could let go and simply be with God. I imagined Him just above me, His invisible hand resting beneath the plane, and began to feel at peace.

"Great job keeping the attitude of the wings straight. You ready to try that turn?" Mike broke through my thoughts.

"Absolutely."

"Let's talk our way through this, okay? Let's give some pressure on the right pedal as we push the stick right. That's it."

I pushed the pedal and the stick, but as usual, I struggled to grasp a feel for just how much rudder I needed. The left wing tilted up, and for a split second, the plane moved left. Then it banked right, and headed into the turn.

"Good girl," Mike said. "Come off the aileron and start to level her off."

I pushed the stick back to the left, dropping the left wing. But as usual it was too much, and I overcorrected, swinging the right wing up. As I tried to level each swing, I seemed only to continue its momentum.

"Come on, Grace" Mike said. "Loosen up. You're holding on too tight and trying too hard to be perfect. Ease her into the turn, and ease her out of it."

I let out a deep sigh as I felt the pressure on my hands of Mike taking control of the plane from behind me. I let go and the plane leveled off. "I should be able to do this by now!"

"You'll get it. Like I said, just relax. You have to let yourself feel the plane beneath you. Become part of the plane. Don't fight against it."

"That sounds all well and good, but I can't seem to get this plane to see eye-to-eye with me."

He chuckled and turned us away from the water, heading north along the coast and back toward Nichols Field. "Let's give it another try."

I gritted my teeth and took hold of the stick, determined to make a smooth turn. "All right, I'm ready."

"She's all yours."

I slowly pressed the stick to the right, and the left wing rose up. The plane dipped left again, and I let out a frustrated moan.

Matthew

After getting settled into the house Friday evening, I somehow let Doug and Cam talk me into going back to Manila with them on Saturday to store some of their extra belongings. At least, that was the story they used to get me to go along. I knew what they were really after, especially once they made it clear we wouldn't be returning until the following day. Jim Harris had a car, so he volunteered to drive us, and before I knew it, I was crammed into a '38 Chrysler convertible along with Doug, Cam, Jim, and Gene.

It was a nice day, with a rich, blue sky set off by the vibrant colors of the tropics. I didn't mind the drive so much since it gave me a better look at my surroundings than I'd gotten from the truck coming in. We sped through the run-down section of town, with Jim honking the horn at the slow-moving carts in the road. Once we crossed over the Pasig, the streets were jammed with taxis and carriages, so Jim was forced to slow down.

We checked in at the Manila Hotel, grabbed a bite to eat, and found a storage facility for the few items Doug and Cam had crammed into the trunk. It was pretty pitiful. Hardly worth the money for the storage room, but they insisted it was necessary. So I went along with the facade.

After a tour of the various entertainment spots available, the guys settled on the Jai Alai club for the evening's amusement. I wasn't too keen on a rowdy evening, but I had to admit the native sport played at the club interested me. So I decided to do my best to enjoy the outing.

When we left the hotel that night, Manila had transformed into a hub of electricity. Music poured out of various clubs and restaurants. Soldiers and sailors lined the streets, exotic women on their arms, as they moved from one spot to the next. We turned onto Taft Avenue, lined with its beautiful acacia trees, and I could see the lights of the club as we approached. It was the most striking building I'd seen yet.

The four-story cylinder-shaped entrance, lined with glass, reflected the lights of the city, making it sparkle in the night sky. Patrons lined the street to get in, already having a good time as they waited. We found a parking spot and eventually made our way inside, which was just as impressive as the outside. A large arena housed the jai alai courts, a game featuring two white-suited players whipping a ball against the wall with a curved scoop attached to the arm.

I followed Jim and Gene, who obviously knew exactly where they were headed, upstairs to a balcony with tables already filled with groups of partiers. Jim leaned over and spoke into the ear of a Filipino boy in a white jacket, slipped a few bills into his hand, and turned back to our group as the boy took off.

"It'll just be a minute," Jim yelled over the noise. "You fellas in a betting mood tonight?"

I most definitely was not, but it was clear I was in the minority. As I watched, dozens of Filipino boys in the same white jackets flitted between the tables and the betting windows. The noise of the game, the fans cheering, and people laughing surrounded me, but all I could hear was Ruby's voice as she'd smiled at me one afternoon, nearly ten years before, as I'd held a basketball in my lap. In my mind, all I saw was her shining face against the deep blue Alabama sky.

"Want to place a bet that I can make it?" I'd said.

"I don't gamble."

"Too much sin for ya?"

"Nothing to wager."

Would I ever make it through even one day without missing her? I had to get a grip. Had to find a way to move on. Just then, the boy returned and gestured toward a table near the front of the balcony. When the other guys moved in that direction, I noticed the group at the next table over, and a familiar face came into view. Henry threw his head back and laughed. His arm was wrapped around a young woman, and she gazed up at him as if he was recounting a captivating tale.

I froze where I stood, conflicted on the course to take. I could go over and speak to Henry, but would it dampen both our evenings? Or worse, would I see how easily he'd forgotten his own sister, who had adored him like the sun? I couldn't stand the thought of watching Henry enjoy himself so freely, as if the world hadn't become a completely different place as it had for me.

Instead, I grabbed Doug's arm and nodded toward the bar behind me. "I'll join you in a little while, all right?"

Doug's eyes narrowed. "Come on, man. Don't be a Fuddy-Duddy. I know this isn't your kind of place, but loosen up and have some fun for once."

"I'm not a Fuddy-Duddy. I just need a little space. That's all."

He sighed and shrugged his shoulders. "Whatever you say, man."

As Doug walked away, I turned and headed over to the bar, grabbing a seat near the end. The bartender made his way over, and I ordered a beer. I'd never been one to drink much, but I could use a little help shutting out the past. So I downed the entire bottle as soon as it arrived and ordered another. The alcohol went to work quickly. And within a few minutes, another distraction offered itself up in the way of gorgeous, big brown eyes smiling at me from the other side of the bar.

I smiled back. She leaned over to the woman seated next to her, mouthing something near her ear. Then she stood and weaved her way through the crowd, around the edge of the bar, until she was standing just behind me. A sweet, rosy smell settled around me as she called out to the bartender.

"Jones! Can I get a gin and tonic over here?"

She squeezed between me and the guy next to me, reaching her slender arm across the bar to retrieve the glass. Her smile held my attention, keeping my eyes from wandering to ungentlemanly places. "Hi there," she said with a southern twang that reminded me of home.

"Hi yourself," I said. I slid a bill over to the bartender. "Let me get that for you."

"I haven't seen you in here before," she said. "You just get off the boat?"

"That's about the way of things. How long have you been here?"

"Oh, about nine months. Where ya from?"

"Alabama. You?"

She smiled and took a long sip of her drink before answering. "Tennessee. Up around Nashville."

"Well, we're just about neighbors then. I knew I recognized your accent. I almost moved to Nashville once myself."

"Honey, you didn't miss out on anything, trust me. I couldn't wait to get out of there."

"I know what you mean." I downed the rest of my beer and stood, tired of yelling over the noise. "Say, you want to go for a walk? I can't hear nothing in here."

"Sure. Just a minute." She took another long sip of her drink before setting it on the bar. "I'll just grab my purse."

She glided back through the crowd, a graceful sway to her slight body. I made my way toward the exit, keeping one eye on her as she stopped at a table and gathered her purse. It was the same table where Henry sat. He didn't seem to notice as she left, and he never looked my way. Relief washed over me. I put a hand on her back and guided her toward the stairs. I definitely needed to get out of there.

We made our way out of the club and strolled down Taft Avenue toward the bay. I realized I hadn't even asked her name, so I finally introduced myself.

"I'm Natalie," she said. "Natalie Williams. I'm an army nurse over at Sternberg."

"And how do you like the military life?" I asked.

She shrugged. "It's all right here. Lots of things to do outside of the job. And it gave me a chance to get away from home, find some adventure. You know?"

I shoved my hands in my pockets. "Yeah, I can understand that for sure."

We curved around onto the next street, and I spied a small grassy area with a few palm trees and a bench. I pointed across the street and asked her if she wanted to sit for a while. She agreed, and we laughed as we dodged honking taxis to cross.

When we were seated, she rested her elbow on the back of the bench and propped her chin in her hand. She looked over at me with an invit-

ing smile that warmed my insides. "How about you? Where are you stationed?"

"Up at Clark for now. I'm with the Corps of Engineers, so we go
wherever there's work to be done."

"An engineer. You must be very smart. And an officer, too, I see."

"Just a Second Lieutenant. Barely qualifies."

She batted her eyelashes coyly. "So, you're a good ole southern boy,
huh? It's nice to spend some time with a man with manners." Lifting her
face, she reached her hand across the top of the bench, running her fingers along the collar of my shirt. "But you know, we're a long ways from
the fine southern tradition of courtship."

My insides stirred, even with my surprise at her boldness. "Natalie,
you are a very attractive young lady, but…I don't…I'm not looking for a
relationship—"

She giggled, covering her mouth with her other hand. "A *relationship*?
You really are a good southern gentleman!"

Heat rushed up my neck and cheeks. "Yes, ma'am. And I ain't
ashamed of it."

She scooted closer, taking my hand in hers. "Oh, no! You shouldn't
be. In fact, it's quite refreshing. Ever since the officers sent their wives
and girlfriends back home to the States, they've been as eager
as…well…you get my meaning, I'm sure."

I couldn't deny some sense of eagerness in my body, but it didn't
override my good judgment. Still, my hand warmed where she continued to hold onto it. I felt the need to get moving again. "Would you like
to walk a little more?" I said. "Maybe check out the bay for a while?"

She grinned and seemed to study me with amused curiosity. "Why
not?"

We stood and continued along the sidewalk a block further, this time
with her hand tucked into the crook of my elbow. It felt good, but at the
same time, not quite right. Maybe moving on with my life would feel
weird for a while, but I resolved to give it my best effort. Ruby wouldn't

want me to be alone the rest of my life, and I didn't want that either. Fact was, I didn't know what I wanted. But it might feel nice to explore my options.

Natalie and I continued our stroll toward the bay, getting to know each other more. She told me about leaving home when she was just sixteen after her mother died. She'd worked her way through nursing school and joined the Red Cross simply because it was about the only job available. She'd jumped at the chance to come to the Philippines after hearing about the tropical paradise from a friend.

"Has it been everything you wanted?" I asked.

"Oh, I suppose," she said. "Honestly, the work doesn't appeal to me so much. I don't particularly enjoy dealing with blood and vomit and such. But everything else has been a dream. The dances and parties! There's always something exciting going on here."

We'd reached the end of the road where it ran into the Manila Hotel. We headed around to the large deck facing the bay, where in the moonlight I could make out the hulls of sunken Spanish ships in the sand just down the beach. When we reached the edge, I stopped and marveled at the beauty of the city and the bay. I'd never been anywhere like this before in my life, and I took a moment to soak it in.

Natalie slipped her hand into mine. "It's pretty amazing, isn't it? Nothing like home?"

"You read my mind."

She smiled up at me, and without thinking, I slipped my arm around her waist and pulled her body into mine. I kissed her gently at first, trying to shut out the memory of Ruby's lips on mine. Natalie responded with eagerness, wrapping her hands around my neck.

I allowed myself to feel the heat flooding my body for only a moment. The rush was both intoxicating and alarming. I pulled my face away from hers and dropped my hands from her waist. But she continued to hold onto my neck, and I became aware of her chest pressed against mine. I gently gripped her hips and moved her back a step.

"I'm sorry," I started. "I don't usually do that."

"Maybe you should."

I couldn't help but chuckle. "You're just a lovely little ball of trouble, aren't you?"

She laughed with me for a moment. "Maybe. I guess you'll just have to find out."

"I reckon I will." I took her hand and kissed the back of it. "Can I see you again sometime?"

She grinned mischievously. "Again? We haven't finished this time yet."

CHAPTER THREE

Matthew

December 8, 1941

Natalie and I made plans to see each other again the following weekend, but it wasn't meant to be. The next Monday, Colonel Maitland, the commander of Clark Field, called a meeting of all the officers. I admired Colonel Maitland greatly. Though he was a famous pilot in his own right, and quite imposing as a person, he was also down-to-earth. When he spoke to us, his voice was calm, but confident.

"From this point on, Clark Field is on a war footing," he said, pacing slowly in front of the group. "All leave is cancelled until further notice. Even travel to Stotsenburg must be reported and approved. Every plane will be armed, and every bomber fully loaded. When your crews are patrolling the China Sea, they are to attack any ship that fails to respond properly. Likewise, they are to engage any plane that does not respond properly." He stopped pacing and faced us with a grave expression. "These are serious times, men. You are officers, and leaders. Act accordingly, and set a good example to the men in your charge."

Most of the men, including myself, took the announcement with a modest amount of concern. But other than the canceling of leave, things didn't change too much. Doug and I helped to build revetments, large arching structures covered with earth and brush that could conceal an entire plane. We also built one of the dummy planes designed to look like a large B-17. It was mostly made out of plywood, but the pilots told us that, from the air at least, they couldn't tell the difference between the dummy and the real thing.

With nothing much to do in the evenings but hang around the airfield, speculation became the major pastime. I wasn't too nervous, myself. Neither were most of the others. We figured that even if the Japs did have the nerve to attack the U.S., we'd make short work of them.

I gave my rifle and pistol an extra cleaning, but that was about it for my preparations. Doug and I continued our engineering duties, and everyone else returned to theirs too. I did notice an increase in activity around the base, such as new foxholes being dug, more frequent patrols, and a general sense that our duties carried much more weight than they ever had. All around us were the indications that war was approaching, but the bubble of paradise had blinded us all to the seriousness of our situation.

That all changed the morning of December 8.

I was eating breakfast with Jim and Gene when Albert burst through the front door with more excitement in his expression than I'd ever seen. He panted like he'd been running. "They did it! The dirty Japs attacked Pearl Harbor!"

"Someone's pulling your leg," Jim said. A lieutenant colonel from Texas, he was the highest-ranking officer among us. Surely he'd know better than anyone if anything like that had happened.

"I swear!" Albert insisted. "A whole bunch of Jap planes bombed Pearl Harbor and Hickam Field just before oh eight hundred Pacific time. About oh two hundred for us."

"I don't believe it," I said.

"They sunk the *Arizona!*" Albert wasn't exactly given to fits of excitement, so I was beginning to get concerned.

We all looked at each other as if we were waiting for someone to make a decision. "I just can't imagine it," Gene said. "With all the planes we got at Hickam, the Japs wouldn't stand a chance. You must've gotten some bad information or something." Gene was a first lieutenant with the 19th bomb group, and I gathered he took his job as navigator quite seriously. Late in the evenings, he'd lie on his cot studying maps of the Pacific, especially the island of Formosa just north of the Philippines. He'd go on and on about how nerve-wracking it was to know such a large force of Japanese planes was within striking distance of his precious B-17 bombers. I figured if anyone would know about the Japanese positions, it would be Gene.

Albert ran a hand through his hair and shook his head. "I think this is for real, fellas. I got it straight from my commanding officer. And he got it from headquarters."

"Well," I said, pushing away from the table. "I reckon we'd better get over there and see what we can find out."

We gathered our gear and were out the door in a flash. As we crossed the field, I watched what appeared to be the same activity as every morning—fighters from early morning patrols coming in, and others taking off for reconnaissance missions. Soldiers were pouring out of the barracks and heading for the mess hall, laughing and carrying on. And in one group of pilots I caught sight again of Henry. This time he saw me too, and his face registered surprise.

"Matthew Doyle!" he said, coming over to greet me. "What in blazes are you doing here?"

I smiled and shook his hand, waving for the others to continue on without me. "I got here a few weeks ago with an Engineering battalion. Been wondering if we'd run into each other. I wasn't sure if you were still stationed out here." The white lie barely registered in my conscience as it slipped off my tongue.

Henry looked much the same as he always had; a bit more tan than I remembered, but I imagined that could be attributed to the tropics.

"Yeah, I been here over a year and a half now." He pointed toward a group of P-40s. "Mine's the one that barely limps down the runway. Been hoping to get a new one. I keep hearing there's replacements on the way, but I reckon everything's a mess now if the reports about Pearl Harbor are true."

"You heard?"

"Yep. It's all anyone's talking about in the mess hall. Don't make any sense to me, though. If the reports are to be believed, then we're at war. And if we're at war, I'd think we'd be hearing official word about it and getting orders to prepare for a fight."

"That's true. I'm just on my way to see what I can find out at Headquarters."

Henry rubbed the back of his neck and seemed to contemplate his next words. "Hey listen, we should get together and talk. Soon. Especially if...well, if we're really at war. That kind of changes everything, I reckon."

"Changes what?"

He glanced down at his watch. "Look, I got to run. We've been ordered to do some flights around the area to keep an eye out for the Japs. Can I meet up with you afterward? Say, eleven or so? We'll get some lunch and catch up."

"All right. I'll see what I can find out. I'll meet you back here, and we can go eat over at my place. We've got a fantastic cook."

"Sounds good," Henry said. Then he jogged across the field toward the group of P-40s. I hoped he didn't want to talk about our families, or worse, about Ruby. I didn't have any idea how I would handle that, but maybe he had something else on his mind.

When I reached engineering Headquarters, I found several of my fellow officers, including Doug, gathered around a radio on Major Hart's desk. They all leaned in as the voice coming through from Manila gave an update on the situation in Hawaii:

Just before 8 A.M. Honolulu time, Japanese carrier planes attacked the U.S. naval base at Pearl Harbor, sinking four battleships. Complete numbers of the dead and wounded are unavailable at this time, but the situation is grave.

"*Four* battleships?" someone said. "How? What in the world's going on?"

He was promptly hushed by several others as the updates continued. The *Arizona* and the *Oklahoma* had been sunk, and nearly every plane at Hickam Field had been destroyed. My stomach knotted. There was no way the Japs would bomb Pearl Harbor and then completely overlook our fleet in the Philippines. They'd be coming for us soon. But how soon?

"What do we need to do?" I asked Major Hart. "This means we're at war, don't it? Do we have orders?"

Major Hart, who'd been seated atop his desk, stood and faced us. "I haven't received any official orders as of yet. Until I do, we get this place as ready as we can. Make sure to have your gas mask on you at all times, along with your helmet and pistol. Gather your men and get every set of hands possible to start digging foxholes and trenches." He pointed at Doug. "Lieutenant Watson, you and your men check all the revetments and make sure they're ready for the planes. Things may get hectic around here this morning, gentlemen, so keep your men calm and focused on the task at hand. Let's not speculate too much beyond what we know. Dismissed."

Ruby

When I heard about the bombing of Pearl Harbor on the radio, it shook me to my core. I hurried through the streets past people who were busily stacking sandbags, taping up black curtains along the windows, and digging trenches right in their yards. My heart raced from my hurried pace, as well as my fear. When I reached the clinic, I was surprised to find it empty. Not a single patient in sight.

I found Joseph seated at the kitchen table, leaning close to the radio in front of him. He glanced up at me, his face mashed into a frown. "Have you heard?"

"Yes," I said, taking a seat across from him. "What's the latest news?"

"Four battleships sunk. Thousands dead or wounded. Most of the planes destroyed. It was...a massacre."

"How could this happen?" I asked, more to myself than to him.

"I don't know. I thought...I thought we were prepared for this."

We sat there in silence for a while, listening to the horrifying reports coming in. I closed my eyes and prayed as hard as I could for the people suffering in Hawaii at that very moment. I couldn't imagine the terror they were feeling.

Joseph's hand closed around my own, and I opened my eyes. "Do you have somewhere safe to go?" he asked.

"What do you mean?"

"Somewhere with more shelter than that hut you're staying in. You need a place you can go that can withstand an attack."

My stomach clenched. "You don't think...they won't come here. Surely not. America will declare war. We'll respond and attack them before they can attack us here. Why, I bet we're already on full alert and getting planes in the air." That made me think of Henry, and my fear doubled.

Joseph shook his head and squeezed my hand. "Grace, this island is the next largest military target in the Pacific. We are not safe here."

I pulled my hand out from under his and closed my eyes again. *Lord, please be with Henry. And please keep us all safe from attack. Put your arms of protection around this place, around Henry.* I thought of the reports of the horrible things the Japanese were doing to the people they conquered in China. It was too gruesome to be real, and yet I'd seen the images of the dead, mutilated bodies...thousands of them. I repeated my prayer.

When I opened my eyes, I met Joseph's gaze. "They're going to need our help. The soldiers. The hospitals. We should find out what we can do." Just then the radio announcer broke into our conversation.

Japanese bombers have been sighted in northern Luzon. Camp John Hay near Baguio has been bombed, and there are reports of Japanese planes headed toward Clark Field. We have no further information at this time.

My breath caught. "They're already here."

Matthew

An eerie bustle settled over Clark Field. No one really knew what to do; just that they should be doing *something*. I supervised my group in digging several trenches around headquarters and two of our revetments, and even jumped in there and helped dig. I reminded my men of their responsibilities, and encouraged them to keep an ear to the wind and an eye on the sky at all times.

At one point, something must have happened because all the P-35s, P-40s, and B-17s took off in a frenzy. I thought for a moment a few of them would crash into each other, having never seen such a frantic display. So I ran to headquarters to see if there was any word. There I found Major Hart standing outside the building, looking up into the sky with his hand shading his eyes.

"What in the world's going on?" I asked.

"Beats all I ever seen," he said. "There was a report of a Japanese raid coming and everything was ordered off the field immediately. Pilots scrambled everywhere. I think a few of the guys in the 19th even got left on the ground."

We stood there, dumbfounded, looking north in search of approaching planes. But the skies remained clear. After a few minutes, Major Hart shook his head and turned to go. "Best get back to work. Won't fend off any attacks by standing around."

I spent the rest of the morning with one eye on my work and one eye on the sky. Just after 11 A.M., the planes that had been evacuated returned to refuel. I met Henry soon afterward, and we walked across the field to the row of officers' houses.

"Where are you staying?" I asked.

"I'm bunking with several fellas in the pursuit squadron down at the other end of the runway. Used to be housing for families, but after they shipped all the officers' families back to the States, they moved a bunch of us in to clear out room in the barracks. We were the first ones to get moved, so we got the big nice house on the end. Have to share it with nine other fellas, though."

I showed Henry into our house and introduced him to Jim and Albert, who were sitting at the table with the radio tuned to a Manila station. When Henry shook hands with Jim, they looked at each other in curious recognition before figuring out they'd played a few rounds of golf together earlier in the summer.

"You're friends with Mike Sawyer, right?" Jim asked.

"Sure," Henry said. "We run around together from time to time."

"Yeah, you played in the minors back in California together."

Henry rocked back and forth on his heels and grinned. "Yeah, for a while. I tried to make it to the majors, but just couldn't catch a break."

Roberto brought out a plate piled with rice, fish, and various fruits. We took our seats around the table and dug in. Between bites, Jim peppered Henry with baseball questions while Albert and I sat silently listening.

"You miss it?" Jim asked.

"Nah," Henry said. "This is the life here. Got money in my pocket, servants at my beck and call, and I get to fly an airplane every day. Not to mention all the beautiful women. I can't imagine ever wanting to leave."

I glanced over at Albert, who was staring at Henry in disbelief. "Don't you have family back home?"

"Well, sure." Henry's eyes darted over to me. "But that doesn't mean I can't enjoy myself here. They're getting along just fine without me."

Albert shook his head and pushed away from the table. "I got some things to take care of. I'm sure my wife and daughter will be alarmed at the news of Pearl Harbor. Best let them know we're still all right here." He stomped up the stairs.

Henry looked at me as if to ask what his problem was, but I shrugged it off. "He actually likes his family."

He was quiet for a moment, and the air between us seemed to thicken. Eventually he leaned back in his chair and sighed. "So, I was saying earlier that I had some things I wanted to talk to you about. Can we uh...go out on the porch for a bit?"

"Sure," I said, though I wanted to just say goodbye.

Henry shook hands with Jim, and we stepped outside, leaving the door ajar so we could hear any important radio bulletins. "All right, let's have it," I said.

Henry walked over to the edge of the porch with his back to me. I could tell he was uneasy, and steeled myself for the ache that would surely split me open at the mention of Ruby's name.

"Listen," he started. "I'm really sorry about the way things went down when...well, after we left Cullman. I always meant to stay in touch better. Things got so crazy, and I...I wasn't exactly sure where you were. Didn't figure you'd want me writing to your parents."

"No," I said. "Definitely not."

He turned to face me and leaned back against the railing of the porch. "Things haven't been easy for any of us. I didn't want...What I mean is..."

He couldn't seem to finish a sentence. What could be so hard to say to me? "Hey, that part of my life is over. There's no need to dwell on it anymore. I'm doing all right."

"I see that. I just mean to say that things change over time, and what you try to do sometimes...to make things right...sometimes you just mess things up worse."

My gut wrenched as I thought of Ruby pushing me up from the abyss of Cold Spring, saving my life, giving up hers. I'd wanted so badly to save her, but I'd killed her instead. "Henry," I said, my voice cracking. "I know what I did was wrong. I've beaten myself up for it over and over. I've replayed that day so many times, wondering what I could have done differently—"

"I ain't talking about that," he interrupted. "Not about you, anyway. It was me. I messed things up."

I was so confused, but before I could press him further, I heard the strangest thing on the radio. Stepping back through the doorway, I looked over at Jim. "Did he just say what I think he said?"

And then the announcer said it again.

I repeat: As we speak, Clark Field is under attack.

Jim burst out laughing and shook his head. "I wonder if the folks over in Hawaii are sitting around their radios thinking everyone's lost their minds. Maybe it's all one big hoax."

I stepped back onto the porch and walked over beside Henry. "You see anything?" We searched the clear blue sky, seeing nothing but a few stray clouds. "Clear as a bell out here," I called back at Jim.

Henry turned to me again and took a deep breath. "I don't know how to say this, or even if I should say anything." He rubbed his hands over his face. I wished he'd just spit out whatever he needed to say. Then, at last, he met my gaze. "Ruby's alive."

But I didn't register his words, 'cause right then, all I saw was a brilliant white light.

***

The first explosion sent me flying into the air. I blacked out. As soon as I awoke, my ears ringing, I tried to orient myself. My head ached. Blood seeped from my nose.

I'd landed in what remained of our living room. The front wall had been blown down, and flames licked everything around me. Another explosion rocked the ground, followed by another. I pushed pieces of wall and furniture off me, rolled onto all fours, and vomited. Albert came stumbling down the stairs, which remarkably were still intact.

As I coughed and tried to catch my breath, Henry crawled out from beneath a pile of debris about five feet away from me. "You all right?" I called.

He nodded, coughing violently. More bombs exploded, sounding as if they were further away. Albert grabbed my hand and pulled me up. "Where's Jim?" he said.

Before I could respond, another bomb hit nearby, sending debris and shrapnel flying around us. I dropped to the floor again and covered my head. Water shot out of the burst pipes, drenching me and everything around me. Henry and Albert stumbled toward the back of the house. I pushed myself up to run for it.

"Matthew! Help me." Jim's voice came up from beneath the rubble.

I flung away as much as I could until I reached him. "Albert! I found Jim! Help me get him outta here!"

I uncovered him enough to pull him free. As Albert arrived at my side, we both froze. Shrapnel had ripped a gaping wound across Jim's abdomen. Another explosion sent us into action, and we picked up Jim as carefully as we could. We carried him out of the back of the house to the foxhole in the backyard, one concussion after another shaking the ground beneath us. Henry helped support Jim while I climbed down into the hole, then they handed Jim down to me.

"I forgot my medical bag!" Albert yelled over the constant bombardment. "I'll be right back!" He ran back toward the burning house and disappeared inside. Henry lay flat and covered his head while the ground continued to tremble.

"Get inside!" I yelled.

"No! I have to get to my plane and get in the air."

"Are you crazy? You're going to get yourself killed!"

There was a momentary pause in the explosions, and Henry jumped up. "If I can get in the air, I can shoot 'em down. Better than getting blown up down here!" He met my gaze. "Take care of yourself, Matthew."

And then he was gone, racing across the yard toward the airfield. I tried to focus on helping Jim. Blood gushed out of him, and his intestines had spilled out of the wound. My stomach lurched.

Albert jumped into the foxhole and came over to us with his bag. He looked Jim over, and even he turned a shade of green. Our eyes locked, and he shook his head. Then he reached into his bag and pulled out a shot of morphine. "Here ya go," he said. "This'll help the pain until we can get you to the hospital."

Jim looked up at me with glazed eyes, his freckles livid against his pale skin. "How bad is it? I can't look."

"You'll be all right. Just hang in there." What else could I say? I closed my eyes and prayed God would ease his pain. When I opened them again, he was dead.

Albert and I huddled in the foxhole for a while. Time seemed to stop moving. Waves upon waves of bombs exploded across the airfield. I clutched my head. My ears hurt. My eyes ached. My stomach rolled. Then came a break in the bombing. Cautiously, Albert climbed out of the foxhole with his bag.

"Where are you going?" I said.

"I need to see to the wounded."

I watched him run toward the airfield as well, leaving me completely alone. My ears ringing, I climbed out of the foxhole and made my way through smoking debris to the edge of the airfield, where I got my first glimpse of the devastation. Everything was on fire—the planes, the hangars, the barracks, even the grass. Huge craters spread over the runway. Worst of all was the number of bodies: some lifeless, others moaning and crying out. But before I could grasp the full measure of what had happened, I heard the hum of approaching planes.

As I took off running for the foxhole again, the rat-a-tat of machine gun fire split the air. I dove into the foxhole and closed my eyes. "God, have mercy on us," I prayed. I tried to think of a coherent prayer, but all I could manage was to repeat my pleas for mercy, over and over.

The Japanese strafed the entire base for what seemed like an eternity. And all I could do was sit there like a coward. Beyond the tree line, I watched as swarms of Japanese fighter planes dove down, some as close as tree-level, and laid a pattern of bullets across the site. Men scrambled to the anti-aircraft guns, blasting away until a spray of bullets took them out. Then another man would jump to the gun, blasting furiously at the diving planes.

I gathered my courage and ran for the field. I had nothing but my pistol to shoot, and as ridiculous as it was, I opened up everything I had at any plane coming close to me. At times, it was as if I could see their faces sneering down at me. Maybe it was useless, but at least I wasn't cowering in a foxhole.

I was going to fight to the end if I had to.

CHAPTER FOUR

Ruby

December 8, 1941

I had to get to Henry, but I had no idea if that was even possible. Joseph suggested we go to Sternberg hospital on the army base in Manila. We could offer our services and possibly get more information about what was going on. It was the safest place to be if the city were to be bombed, so we gathered some of our meager supplies and headed for Sternberg.

Joseph tried to catch us a cab, but it was useless as every vehicle was occupied. The burst of car horns punctuated the packed streets, and the locals rushed every which way as they hoarded any supplies they could get their hands on. We finally waved down a small buggy being pulled by an even smaller pony. The elderly Pilipino man gestured toward a rickety wooden seat.

Joseph held out his hand to me. "I think this is the best we're going to get for now."

I took his hand and climbed inside, setting the bag of supplies on my lap. Joseph climbed in next to me, and the whole buggy leaned alarmingly to his side. We exchanged nervous glances.

"Where you go?" the old man asked, grabbing the straps beneath the pony's head.

Joseph answered in Tagalog, and the man nodded and tugged on the reins until the pony took a few steps forward. I felt sorry for the poor animal. It seemed as though it might collapse at any moment. "You know," I said. "It might be faster if we just walk."

Joseph grimaced as he looked at the crowd. "Maybe. But it's still probably safer to stay aboard in this mob."

It was no more than three kilometers to the base hospital, but getting through the crowded streets was nearly impossible, especially once we crossed over the Pasig River. I held onto the side of the buggy as it swayed back and forth with each step of the pony. Finally reaching the main entrance to the hospital, we jumped out of the buggy. Joseph gave the man several pesos and his eyes widened. He grabbed Joseph by the arm, speaking rapidly in Tagalog. Joseph shook his head and responded. As we disembarked and ran up to the front doors, I asked what the old man had said.

"He was very grateful. Wanted to know if he should wait out here for us. I told him we wouldn't need him."

I took a quick moment to thank God for putting me in the company of someone who knew his way around the city and spoke the language. I would've been lost and in a panic were it not for his steady thinking.

When we reached the front desk, no one was there. We searched the hallways nearby with no luck. I wondered if this was a bad sign. Maybe they knew an attack was imminent, and had already taken shelter.

"Let's try the cafeteria," Joseph suggested. "It's about lunch time."

He scanned the walls until he found a sign pointing us in the right direction. We hurried along the hallway with our meager supplies still bouncing around in the bags hanging from our shoulders. Rounding a corner into the cafeteria, I saw a group of nurses and doctors all huddled around the same table.

"Come on," Joseph said, waving a hand for me to follow him.

We joined the group encircling the table, and from their midst, I could hear the crackling sound of a radio. An announcer was reporting on the most recent information coming out of Pearl Harbor. The death toll was still climbing, now in the thousands, and many more were buried inside the sunken ships. I covered my mouth and for an instant, I remembered nearly drowning in my own watery grave. Panic rose up in my throat, and I let out a gasp.

Joseph put his hand on my shoulder. "You all right?" he said, close to my ear.

I nodded, unable to form any words. The news continued to worsen, with the announcer then reporting that Clark Field was under attack at that very moment. I took a few steps backward and fell into a chair, burying my face in my hands.

Oh Lord, please be with Henry. Give him Your protection. Please, keep him from harm.

I moved my hands away from my face to find Joseph kneeling in front of me. "Can I get you some water or something?"

I shook my head. "I'm just worried about Henry."

"You're so pale. Let me get you something. Have you eaten at all today?"

"No, really. I'm fine. I just need to find a way to get to Henry."

It was then that I saw Janine in the huddle around the table, so I jumped up and tried to get her attention. Our eyes met, and she waved, then made her way through the crowd to us. She took the chair next to mine, and held my hands in hers.

"Oh, Grace," she said. "I'm so glad to see you. You must be so worried."

"Have you heard anything?" I asked.

She shook her head. "We have a meeting in five minutes. Hopefully, I'll find out more."

"How are you holding up?"

She took a shaky breath and sat up a bit straighter. "I'm all right. I'm trying to only think about doing my job." Her eyes welled up, even as she did her best to stop them. "I mean, he's not...we aren't even officially together or anything, but if he's hurt...or worse..."

My chest tightened, and I tried to reassure us both. "He'll be all right. He's a good pilot, and he knows what he's doing."

She squeezed my hand and stood, swiping at the corners of her eyes. "I'll come find you as soon as the meeting's over." She joined the other doctors and nurses as they left the cafeteria, leaving Joseph and me alone.

I hated feeling so helpless. I'd never been one to sit around and wait for something to happen. "I'm going to go find some way to help out around here," I said.

Joseph stepped back as I moved past him and out the door. I heard his footsteps running after me. "What are you going to do?"

I shrugged. "Don't know. But I'll do *something*."

I went back to the nurse's station at the front entrance. This time Natalie was seated there, with a phone to her ear. As I approached, she explained into the receiver, "No ma'am, I don't have any more information at this time." She put the phone down and glanced up at me. It rang again. She held up a finger.

"Hello, Sternberg Hospital. How may I help you?" She dropped her forehead into her hand. "No, I don't have any information on that right now...Yes, we are aware of the situation...No, I don't have any information." She hung up, but before she could say a word, it rang again.

She gave me an exasperated sigh. "Can I help you?"

"I want to volunteer for something. Who should I speak with?"

"Everyone's in a meeting right now. If you'll take a seat, I'll be with you shortly." I started to protest, but she picked up the ringing phone and went back to explaining to yet another caller that she didn't have any information.

I wasn't eager to stand around and wait, so I headed down a hallway to my left. Joseph came along beside me. "Now what are you doing?"

I made a right turn and found a large room with about twenty beds spread out in rows. Only about ten were occupied. "I reckon I'm going to see if these people need anything."

Matthew

An unnatural silence filled my ears once the attack ended. It lasted for only a few moments before the cries for help, the moans, and the screams pierced my consciousness. I ran along the crater-strewn runway, reaching the group of planes, but couldn't get close because they were all on fire. Bodies littered the earth around them. In a couple of planes, I could make out the forms of bodies in the flame-filled cockpits. My nostrils filled with the acrid smells of gasoline, charred metal, and burning flesh.

My body shook with coughing spasms as I searched the area, looking everywhere for Henry. Another soldier, bloodied but on his feet, joined me in checking for survivors. I felt every wrist I came across for a pulse, checking dog tags when the body was beyond recognition. Some of the injured stumbled around in a daze, and I did my best to help them. We needed a transport to the hospital.

About thirty feet away I saw a truck with the back end blown off. But all four tires were still on it. I sprinted over and climbed into the cab, finding the key in the ignition. I turned it. Nothing happened. Turned it again. Still nothing.

I dropped my head and prayed. *Lord, you gotta get this truck cranked. Please help us!* Then I tried again, and the engine came to life. Jumping out of the cab, I helped the other soldier load the wounded into the back. But I still hadn't found Henry, so I went back to the part of the wreckage I hadn't searched yet.

As I kicked away burning debris, I heard moaning from beneath a pile of rubble a few feet away. The other soldier and I worked to uncover the man below, tossing aside part of a wing, a tire, and a good deal of lumber. When I finally uncovered him, I saw it was Henry, and my heart sank. He was bleeding from nearly every part of his body, and his right calf muscle gaped open.

"He's alive!" I said. "Let's get him loaded on the truck and get to the hospital!"

I ripped off my shirt and tied it around his leg to try to staunch the blood flow. We carried him over to the truck and carefully loaded him into the back. Then we climbed into the cab, and I made a beeline for the hospital.

Thankfully, Stotsenburg was only a couple of miles away, but when we arrived, it was in chaos. Bloody, mangled bodies littered the grounds. A medic helped us lift Henry out of the cab and place him on a stretcher on the lawn. I stood over Henry, watching as a young woman nearby examined one patient after another. She worked her way over to us and gave Henry a quick once-over. She gave him a shot of morphine and redressed his leg in gauze.

"Is he going to be all right?" I asked.

She looked up at me with frightened, wide eyes. "I don't know. We're doing all we can. He needs surgery."

She stood and called over to a couple of soldiers toting a man on a stretcher toward the entrance of the hospital. "Hey! This one needs to go to surgery." One of them, a large man smeared with blood from head to foot, nodded at her. Then she turned to me. "You okay? You need treatment?"

"I'm all right. Is there anything I can do to help?"

"Yes, you can help carry these men to the tents and operating rooms." She hollered at another soldier standing nearby who looked dazed. "Hey! Sir! Can you help?" He nodded, so she waved him over. "Take this man to the operating room. Just follow those two."

She turned and pointed at the two soldiers she'd called to before. They were just heading up the front stairs. I bent over Henry and picked up the corners of the stretcher where he lay motionless. The other guy, still looking dazed and a bit frightened, bent over and grabbed the other two corners.

"Ready?" I said.

He nodded and started walking. We carried Henry up the stairs and through the front doors. Broken, bloody bodies lined the hallway. I kept moving, following the two men in front of us. As we turned down another hallway, the smell of burned flesh mixed with the sickening sweet smell of blood hit me full on, turning my stomach.

At last we came to a room busy with a doctor and two nurses working on three patients simultaneously. One of the nurses pointed at the doorway. "Put him in the hall," she said, barely taking her eyes off her most critical patient. "We'll get to him as soon as we can."

We laid Henry on his stretcher on the hallway floor next to another patient. I wondered if there was any way he'd be seen before he bled out. I could only hope the meager dressings would hold. I stuck my head back into the door and spoke to the nurse who'd directed me. "Miss? How long until he can be cared for?"

She handed the doctor an instrument and answered again without looking at me. "We're overrun. We're doing the best we can."

I leaned over Henry and prayed, feeling helpless to do anything else. Fretting over him would accomplish nothing. So I headed back down the hallway and onto the lawn. I carried four more stretchers into the hospital before another nurse stopped me in my tracks.

"What's your story? You look like you need to get that checked out."

"Get what checked out?" I asked.

She pointed at my chest, and I looked down. My undershirt was covered in blood. At first, I wasn't sure if it was my own or that of the men I'd been carrying around. I realized my undershirt had holes in it. And the legs of my pants were ripped to shreds. I could see tiny fragments of metal imbedded in my arms and upper torso.

"I never felt a thing," I murmured in surprise.

"Come on," the nurse said. "Let's get you patched up."

She led me to a tent where several medics were cleaning out wounds that weren't life threatening. I waited on a gurney until one was able to carefully pick all the shrapnel out of my body. He rinsed each wound, bandaged me up, and pronounced me "ready for service."

"What does that mean?" I asked.

"It means you should return to Clark. Try and get some rest."

I thought that was the most ridiculous thing anyone had ever said to me. *Rest?* There'd be no rest, no place to lie down, no comfort. Maybe ever again.

Ruby

Joseph and I spent the next thirty minutes walking from bed to bed, speaking with the gentlemen who were recovering from various procedures. Nothing too serious—an appendectomy, a hernia, a couple of broken bones, and some other minor surgeries. All the patients were stable, but I brought them water and fluffed their pillows. What they each wanted most though, was information.

"What's the latest at Pearl Harbor?"

"Any reports of bombings on Luzon?"

"I'd sure like to show them Nips just what we're made of."

We answered what we could, letting them know they'd be taken care of as soon as possible. Every once in a while I glanced over at Joseph as he checked a chart or listened to a patient's heart. He'd give me a small smile. We weren't doing much, of course. But it felt better to move, to do some small task that took my mind off Henry.

Natalie and another nurse I didn't know walked in a bit later. They looked at us with surprise, and Natalie pointed a finger at me. "What are you doing in here?"

I tried to explain. The one I didn't know seemed sympathetic. But Natalie's face wrinkled into a frown, and she said she'd have to call her supervisor, Mrs. Fincher.

"Great," I said. "That's exactly who I want to speak with."

She shot a suspicious look over at Joseph. Sending the younger nurse to find Mrs. Fincher, she proceeded to check on the patients as if she thought we'd harmed them in some way. Within a few minutes, the nurse returned, followed by a woman whose appearance suggested she must have been in her fifties, and yet she moved as though she were twenty years younger. I sensed her commanding energy as soon as she entered the room, and I liked her immediately.

"And who might you be?" she asked, approaching me swiftly as if she had a million other things to do.

"I'm Grace Miller," I said, extending my hand. "I work as a nurse over at a clinic just north of Binondo. I want to volunteer."

"You're American, right?" I nodded, as she looked me over. "Where did you do your training?"

"I haven't been to nursing school. But I've worked with doctors since I was sixteen. I've delivered countless babies, assisted in minor surgeries, and—"

"I'm sorry," she said, cutting me off. "We have protocols and proper procedures here you couldn't possibly learn in a matter of days. We need experienced nurses, preferably surgical nurses."

I glanced at Natalie, who had a satisfied glint in her eyes. "Mrs. Fincher," I said. "I respect your decision. But if things get as bad as it looks like they might, I have a feeling proper procedures will fly right out the window. You're going to need help. Maybe I haven't been to nursing school, and maybe I don't have the book learning you do, but I know I can be of assistance."

She lowered her chin and peered at me over the rim of her glasses. "You may be right on that count." Her gaze travelled over to Joseph. "And what about you?"

Jumping into action, he came beside me. "I'm Joseph Grant. I run the clinic where Grace and I work. I have a medical degree from the University of Virginia School of Medicine."

She studied him closely. "You're Filipino."

"Yes, ma'am," he said.

"You speak Tagalog?"

"Yes, ma'am."

She shook her head. "There's no time for formalities here. Come with me, and I'll see what we can do with the both of you."

Natalie's mouth dropped open as Mrs. Fincher turned on her heel and marched out the door. Joseph and I glanced at each other and then ran to catch up with her. She turned down several hallways until we reached what appeared to be a break room. It was smaller than the cafeteria, with light streaming in through the huge windows. Small tables were set up around the room, along with a sofa in the middle.

Mrs. Fincher snapped around to face us. "As you suspected, Miss Miller, things are more serious than we first anticipated. We've received word that our military bases north of here are receiving heavy bombardment. Fort Stotsenburg is overrun with casualties from Clark Field. They're requesting help."

"I'll go," I said.

She raised her eyebrows. "Maybe you should let me finish. We're putting together a team of nurses and doctors to travel in convoy to Fort Stotsenburg in less than hour. We'll need help to fill their duties here."

"With all due respect," I said. "I'd like to go to Stotsenburg."

Joseph's hand slid over the top of my shoulder. "Grace, I know you're worried about Henry, but Stotsenburg's going to be right in the thick of things. You should stay here where there's more protection."

"Mrs. Fincher, are there only going to be military personnel in this convoy?" I asked.

"No," she said. "There are a few civilian nurses going, some local Filipino nurses."

"Then I'd like to go too."

She thought it over for only a few moments. "All right then. Let's get you some supplies. Dr. Grant, considering your qualifications and ability to speak with the locals, we'd be best served if you could remain here."

He gave me a sidelong glance. "I'll do whatever is needed."

***

While Joseph and I helped load medical supplies into the convoy trucks he tried several times to convince me not to go, but I refused to even consider it. "I *have* to find Henry," I said. "And I have to do everything I can to help those boys up there."

As enlisted men continued shoving the supplies onto the trucks, Joseph grabbed my elbow and pulled me off to the side. "There are going to be plenty of men here who will need tending to as well, you know. There's already rumors of an invasion force landing in the Lingayen Gulf." He leaned toward me and lowered his voice. "The Japanese are coming. And they are brutal, Grace. They will show no restraint just because you're a woman. In fact, that seems to increase their brutality. You know what they did to the women in Nanking. I couldn't stand...If they hurt you...You need to get somewhere safe."

His concern for me was touching, but I knew what I had to do. "Joseph, you've been so kind to me—"

"No," he said, shaking his head and stepping back. "Don't start telling me goodbye."

"I have to go."

"No, you don't."

Behind me, a corpsman announced the bus was leaving. I reached out and took Joseph by the hand. "Listen, I don't have time to explain everything right now. But...Henry...he isn't my cousin. He's my brother. And he's all I have left in the world. I have to go to him."

"Your brother? Why would you—"

"I have to go. There's no time to explain. Please, take care of yourself. Thank you for giving me the chance to work at the clinic."

I let go of his hand and ran toward the bus. I could hear him calling out to me over the motors of the bus and trucks, but I refused to look back. I jogged up the steps into the bus and made my way toward the back. Glancing around, I spotted Natalie's disapproving face, and was relieved to see Janine seated across from her. Janine's eyes widened when she saw me.

"Grace! How did you get on here?"

I took the seat next to her and smiled over at Natalie. Her mouth pressed into a thin line, like she was trying to smile but couldn't. "I talked to Mrs. Fincher and told her I wanted to go. She said some other civilian nurses were going as well, and I wouldn't take no for an answer."

"You must be insane," Natalie said. "Mrs. Fincher practically had to threaten me with a court-martial to get me on here." She shook her head and turned her gaze out the window. Her face was pale and her eyes looked red, as if she'd been crying.

"I volunteered too," Janine said, pulling my attention away from Natalie. "I don't know what I was thinking, I mean, I know how dangerous it is. I...I just...I have to see Henry."

The bus lurched into motion and wound its way through the streets of Manila. Traffic had only gotten worse since I'd arrived at the hospital that morning, and we made slow progress until we reached the city limits. Toward the front of the bus, more than twenty soldiers kept a watchful eye on the sky, and I couldn't help but search for Japanese planes myself. But the sky was as clear as any other day in the tropics.

Once we left the city, the convoy was able to cover ground more quickly, so I closed my eyes and prayed for safety. *Lord, please be with all the boys who've been injured today, both here and at Pearl Harbor. Be close to Henry. Keep him in Your right hand, protecting his body and mind from all the danger surrounding him. Give him the peace of knowing that You are with him always.*

I prayed the same thing over and over, until I drifted off to sleep with the rocking of the bus, my forehead pressed against the back of the seat in front of me. I wasn't sure how long I dozed, but I awoke when the bus jerked to a stop. The driver opened the door and jumped out. Night had fallen, and we'd stopped under a canopy of jungle trees covering the road, so I couldn't see the sky. Were we under attack?

"Where are we?" I asked Janine, as if she'd know any more than I did.

A serviceman turned around in his seat. "We're getting close now."

"Then why are we stopping?" Natalie asked, her voice high and tight.

"Do you smell that?" I asked Janine.

A pungent stench filled the bus. Smoke mixed with other chemical smells—burning rubber, oil, and metal—settled in the air around us. The driver came back onto the bus, and word spread back to us that debris littered the road ahead. As we inched forward, I gazed out the windows at smoldering jeeps, felled trees, and even a large chunk of an airplane. I tried not to imagine Henry in the cockpit of a fiery plane, crashing to the earth.

Since none of the vehicles were traveling with their lights on, we moved at a snail's pace, heading in the general direction of a flickering orange glow ahead. Murmuring filled the bus as we passed Clark Field.

"The place is demolished," one man said.

Planes and buildings still burned, casting enough light to take in the destruction. Tanks circled the runway, their guns pointed to the moonless sky. To my left, I noticed propellers and tires flung into trees. The bus hit a crater, and Natalie yelped. I grabbed Janine's hand and squeezed it. "I'm sure Henry's all right," I said, more to myself than to her.

We pulled away from Clark Field and headed into the darkness. Fort Stotsenburg lay a few miles ahead. Murmuring from the passengers turned into concerned questions as the bus slowed to a halt and the driver got to his feet. "Everyone just stay seated and quiet for now, please."

He climbed out and went to stand in front of the bus, while we sat in uncomfortable silence. When the driver returned, he moved the bus along slowly, dodging craters the size of small ponds along with the debris. He stopped again and repeated the same procedure of standing in front of the bus.

"What's he doing?" Janine asked.

The medic in front of us turned around again. "The guys up front say we're having trouble locating the hospital in the dark."

At that, the driver came back on board, his face stricken. "We're here. Let's get the supplies unloaded as soon as we can and get them inside."

The servicemen let the nurses off the bus first, and we huddled together beside the bus. I couldn't make out much. There was a hazy smoke around everything, and I couldn't see more than several feet in front of me. I turned to Janine.

"How do we even know we're in the right place?" I asked.

She turned her head, searching. "I don't know."

"Wait," said Natalie, her voice breaking. "Listen."

Horror spread across each woman's face as we registered the sounds. Wailing, moaning, crying. The sounds of desperate pain came from beyond the haze. That was how the driver knew we were in the right place. He'd followed the screams.

***

Before the bus was even unloaded we went to work, making our way across the grounds toward the main hospital. The smoke parted to reveal bodies everywhere, all of them writhing and calling out for help.

Medics and nurses moved among them, assessing who was critical and who could wait. I didn't envy them that job.

Once inside, it was clear the fort's meager hospital was never intended to treat even a fraction of this many wounded. Men lay on tables, gurneys, even the floor. The smell of burned flesh, blood, and sweat was overwhelming and my stomach turned over. I'd seen suffering before, and I'd seen my fair share of blood, but this...this was like nothing I could have imagined.

If only I hadn't lost my gift. If only I could somehow pray over all these men and stop their bleeding. Why was I even here? I didn't belong in this chaos! I had no idea what I was doing. My heart raced. My eyes watered. I had to get myself under control.

I closed my eyes for one momentary prayer for courage and peace. And then I set to my work. I cleaned out ghastly wounds, administered morphine, and checked each patient I saw carefully for signs of shock. At first, my legs were weak, and my hands shook, but after a couple of hours, I became numb. The cries blended into one nauseating moan in the background, and I was able to focus on the task at hand.

I was nearly to the point of feeling confident on my feet when I looked up to see Henry being prepared for surgery. I dropped the pan of bloody bandages I'd been carrying and ran to his side. The doctor and nurse attending to him looked up at me in confusion.

"This is my brother!" I screamed, without thinking. I bent over him and called to him, but his eyes didn't open. I glanced down at his wrecked body. Bullet wounds and shredded flesh; the calf muscle in his right leg spilling out of a gaping wound. I turned to the doctor, who'd already begun removing the bullets.

"Can you save his leg?" I asked.

The doctor glanced up. "There's no time. I either take the leg now and he lives, or I patch him up and he dies from infection."

"But the bones are still intact. Can't you at least try?"

"The blood flow is compromised." The doctor's expression indicated he was at his wits' end. "I don't have time for a lengthy surgery when there are dozens more men whose lives are hanging by a thread. Now get back to your job."

"Please, Doctor," I begged over the commotion. "Just look closely. Don't take his leg if you can save it."

He sighed, keeping his eyes on his patient. "Please just let me do my job."

I backed away, unable to resume my task. All I could see was Henry as a kid, chasing after me in the yard, playing basketball with me as we were losing our home, swimming with me in the creek. He was the only person in the world who knew me. He was the thread keeping me tied to the earth. I prayed with all I had for God to heal him. Then I prayed for the doctor, that he would take the time to save Henry's leg.

When I opened my eyes, the doctor was examining the leg. He glanced up at me, frowning. "Look, I'll do what I can, all right? I'll stitch up the muscles and hope the blood flow stays intact. You'll have to keep an eye on it, though."

I nodded, unable to say anything with the knot in my throat. I turned back to my duties, thanking God for hearing my prayer. It was hard to concentrate, but I managed to get through the night without losing my mind. And the surgical team only lost seven men out of all those who'd come through. There was much to be thankful for.

By dawn, I was so exhausted that I feared I might fall asleep standing up. I located Janine, and told her about Henry. We found him recovering in a room full of patients who'd lost one or more limbs. We checked his sutures, checked the color of his swollen leg and foot, and tried to clean away the mud and blood still caked to his body. He never stirred, which worried us both.

"He's been through so much," Janine said, a tear slipping down her cheek. "His body just needs to recover. He'll be all right."

It seemed as though we were taking turns reassuring each other. "Want to grab a bite to eat?" I asked.

She wiped her brow and tucked strands of greasy hair back under her cap. "I guess we should. I could use a bath. And some sleep."

Slowly we made our way back outside to a makeshift mess hall set up in one of the tents. Exhausted nurses, medics, and other staff moved through the tent in a dazed, bloody procession. A few nurses who'd been on staff during the initial bombing replayed the previous day's events. I could hardly imagine the terror of hiding under a table as bombs dropped all around me.

I ate what I could stomach, and then Janine and I returned to the hospital. We were both afraid of another raid, and decided it was best to seek shelter inside. Several other nurses were headed to a bunker underneath the pharmacy, but when we reached it, the putrid smell was more than I could bear.

"I'm going to get some fresh air," I said after only a few minutes. "I don't think I can take this."

Janine, her body leaned back against a wall, was already half asleep. She mumbled a response I didn't understand.

Outside again, I took the chance to find a quiet place to pray, opening up all my fears from the previous night, and thanking God for getting me through it. I brought to my mind as many faces as I could remember of the men I'd treated, and I prayed for their healing. And I laid my heart bare as I prayed for Henry. Then, as I closed my prayer, I thought of Matthew, so far across the ocean, away from all this suffering and anguish. I ached for him so much; it nearly overwhelmed me. And I couldn't stop myself from sobbing. I wondered what he was doing at that moment. And I wished that somehow, I could tell him all that was in my heart.

CHAPTER FIVE

Matthew

December 9, 1941

I barely slept a wink the night after the attack on Clark Field and Stotsenburg. By nightfall, almost everyone had evacuated into the cover of the jungle. Seemed like there was more safety in numbers, so I joined up with the 200th Anti-aircraft unit to make camp. It was a restless night for all of us as we kept a watchful eye on the sky for parachutes.

At dawn, I decided to try to salvage what I could from our bungalow. I returned to its burned out shell, and was able to retrieve a blanket, my knapsack, and a few essentials. Amazingly, my Bible lay unharmed next to a pile of debris. I picked it up and thanked God for protecting me, sliding it into the knapsack for safekeeping.

Next I caught a ride over to Fort Stotsenburg to see about Henry. Along the way, I thought back on our conversation just before everything had gone haywire, wondering if somehow I'd misunderstood him. He was trying to tell me something about Ruby. My brain kept forming the words, "Ruby's alive." But that was impossible.

I tried not to worry over it on account of there being much more pressing issues, like surviving another attack, which would most certainly come. Maybe Henry'd be awake, and he could explain what he'd been trying to say. Then I could make sense of it all and put it behind me.

When I arrived at Fort Stotsenburg, it was still smoldering. The small hospital had spilled out onto the grounds, and the nurses and doctors moved around the tents in a daze. Most of them were covered in blood. I stopped a young nurse as she passed me and asked if she knew where I could find Henry Graves.

She shook her head. "Sorry, fella. I don't hardly know where I am, much less where someone else is." She wiped her hand across her brow before pointing across the grounds. "There's some doctors and nurses eating breakfast over in the mess hall. You can ask around there."

I thanked her and headed in the direction she'd pointed. I quizzed the other doctors and nurses I passed along the way, but none of them were able to tell me where I could find Henry. I wandered through tent after tent, checking endless cots for a familiar face. Nothing. Then I headed through the rooms of the hospital. I was about to give up when I found him lying on a gurney in a room full of broken, decimated bodies.

Some moaned as they moved around. Others were as still as death. When I reached Henry, his eyes were open, but he didn't seem to see me. I leaned over him and laid a hand on his arm. "Henry? You all right?"

Slowly he turned his head to me and a smile tugged at his lips. "Matthew. You made it. I didn't see you for a while. Thought you might've drowned."

Drowned?

"No, I'm all right," I said. "I found you near your plane—"

"I can't lie to you," he said. "I found Ruby. I wasn't gonna tell you, 'cause Ruby don't want you getting into trouble with the law. And I thought it would be safer for her if nobody knew."

"You're not making any sense," I said.

"You nearly died trying to save her. You deserve to know." Henry winced. "My head hurts. And my leg is throbbing like crazy. Where is this place?"

"Henry, what's the last thing you remember?" His eyes glazed over, and he stared at the ceiling. "Henry?"

After a heart-stopping moment where I thought he'd crashed, Henry blinked and brought his gaze back to me. "I don't think I can go back down to the woods like this. You'll have to get Ruby and get her out of town. She's a little banged up, but I think she'll be all right. We were going to take a train out to California. You two should go on, and I'll meet you out there."

I put my hand on his forehead. He was burning up with fever. I glanced around for a nurse or doctor. "Miss?" I called to a nurse who was checking a patient across the room. "Can you come take a look at my friend here?"

After she'd taken a few steps, she stopped and stared at me. "Matthew?"

My brain finally kicked in, and I realized it was Natalie. I straightened and came around Henry's gurney to meet her. "Natalie, what are you doing here? I thought you were at Sternberg."

"I was, but they sent me up here." She hesitated before wrapping her arms around her waist. "I'm so glad you're all right. I was so worried about you."

"Yes, I'm fine. But would you mind taking a look at my friend here?"

She nodded and moved around me. "You know Henry?" she asked, glancing back at me over her shoulder as she checked his vitals.

"Yes," I said. "We grew up together."

She held his wrist in her hands, counting to herself, then placed it down and glanced at me with a puzzled look. "That's funny, I thought he said he was from Georgia. But then again, I might not have paid much attention. He's been dating another nurse at the hospital. That's how I met him." She leaned forward to tighten the covers around Henry, and placed the back of her hand to his forehead. "He's got a fever." She moved the blanket covering his legs, and I got a view of the damage as she looked over the wound. "Doc tried to save his leg, but it's not looking good. Probably have to remove it later today if it's getting infected."

"He don't seem right in the head," I said. "He's talking about things like he's in the past."

"What do you mean?"

"You know, he's talking about things that happened years ago as if they were happening right now."

Natalie frowned and covered his leg again. "I'm no doctor, but he's probably in shock. I think we all are, to be honest. I'm sure he'll be all right."

Henry moaned, so I stepped closer to him and leaned over him. "You need something?"

"You gotta find Ruby. She needs help."

I glanced over him at Natalie. "See what I mean? Ruby's been dead for five years."

But before she could answer, the stomach-lurching sound of the air raid pierced the air, and Natalie's face drained of all color. Her eyes shot open. "Oh no! They've come back!"

My heart thundered in my chest. Frantically, I searched for shelter, but there was none. An explosion sounded outside, followed by a tremor in the walls. Natalie screamed. Patients hollered all around us.

"Get me outta here!"

"It's the Japs again!"

I grabbed Natalie by the hand and pulled her into the hallway, tucking her beneath me as we crouched against the walls. The explosions came over and over again. The walls shook, and dust filled the air. I coughed and sucked in dust. I could feel Natalie sobbing against my chest. I squeezed her tighter and did my best to keep her calm.

"It's going to be all right," I said between blasts. "We're going to be fine."

I had no idea if I was right. But at least this time I wasn't out in the open.

Ruby

I had found my way to a quiet part of the grounds, away from the devastation and agony, when I heard the whine of the air raid siren. I'd just been in the middle of thanking God for His protection, when I realized I was nowhere near any foxholes or shelter. I looked up in time to see planes high above, approaching from the north in large V formations. And below them floated small strips of silver, glinting in the sun like confetti. My heart raced, and I ran for the empty swimming pool nearby. Just as I jumped into the deep end and slammed my body against the wall, an explosion rocked the ground beneath my feet. My screams were drowned out by the next explosion, and the next, and the next.

My head bounced off the side of the pool, and my throat stung. I could barely breathe. *Lord, please help us! Protect Henry...the nurses, the doctors, the patients...Have mercy!*

The bombing lasted several minutes, and then a painful silence came over everything. My ears rang, and I thought for a moment I might vomit. I dropped to all fours, heaving. Then I heard an ominous buzzing sound in the distance. Planes approached again, this time much closer to the ground than before. Dust flew up in the air as the rat-a-tat of bullets grazed the grounds. I pressed myself flat against the wall again just before they hit the empty pool, sending shards of concrete flying.

I screamed again, and continued to pray and call on Jesus's name. I tried to control my panic, but it felt like my heart was going to burst right out of my chest. Finally, the strafing ended, and I collapsed onto the floor of the pool. I breathed in and out, in and out. I was still alive.

Climbing out of the pool on shaky legs, I ran toward the hospital, rounding the corner to another awful scene. The fires that had burned out in the night were blazing again. Smoke poured from vehicles, buildings, and tents, and the smell of burning rubber and metal filled the air. Men screamed for help from all directions as they writhed in pain.

I took a look at the hospital building, and it seemed to be unaffected. At least I knew Henry was safe. I ran for the tent closest to me, horrified by the number of bullet holes in it. Staff came in from all directions, and everyone set to work again as if the night before had never happened.

As I grabbed as much morphine as I could carry, I thought about Jonah from the Bible. He'd run away from God's plan for him, and God had chased him down with a terrible storm on the sea, eventually sending a great fish to swallow him whole. I couldn't help but wonder about my own running over the past five years. Was God chasing me down with a war? Were the Japanese a great fish that would eventually swallow me up?

Matthew

Once the bombing ceased, I sat down on the floor and pulled Natalie against my chest. She continued to sob, and I did the best I could to calm her. "It's all right," I whispered into her ear. "It's over now. They're gone." I repeated myself over and over, until she finally quieted. But her body still shook as though she were freezing.

I held her against me another minute, rubbing my hands along her arms to try to soothe her. The quivering subsided, and she wiped her tears from her face, smudging dirt across her cheeks. "Thank you," she croaked. "I'm sorry. I'm such a wreck."

"Hey, it's okay," I said, reaching up to wipe the dirt away. I held her cheek in my hand and smiled. "Nothing to worry about. I think we're all terrified." I leaned over and kissed her forehead. "Why don't we go check on the patients?"

She pushed herself up as I did, and we went back into the hospital room. Except for a few whimpering patients, all was fine. I checked on Henry. He hadn't moved an inch. Natalie checked the other patients until a doctor popped his head through the door and told us they needed all available hands outside. We ran through the hallway and into the chaos that awaited on the lawn.

Natalie gripped her stomach as a gurney went by with a bloodied body sprawled across it. "I don't know if I can do this again," she said.

"You can," I answered. "Just do your best. That's all anyone can ask."

"Thanks," she said, waving as another nurse motioned for her to follow. "I'll find you when we get done."

I waved in return, then jumped into service as I had the previous day—carting injured bodies to various tents, cleaning up debris, and putting out fires. My body ached with exhaustion, and my stomach cramped with hunger. I did what I could to move from one job to the next so I wouldn't think about it, and sometime late in the afternoon, I was finally told I could rest.

I wandered toward the tent I believed to be the mess hall, and gobbled the plate of food being offered, not even registering what it even was. I dropped my head onto the table for a moment, just to feel my eyes close. A moment later a hand rested on my back, jolting me awake. I shot up, causing Natalie to yelp beside me.

"Matthew! Sheesh!" she said.

My heart pounded against my chest. Where was I? Reality flooded back in like a terrible wave. I took a few deep breaths to get control of myself. "Sorry about that. I must've dozed off."

"I can't blame you," Natalie said, turning to her plate. "I'm not sure I'm actually alive right now." She picked at her food.

My stomach growled watching her. "You need to eat all that," I said. "You never know when the food might get scarce."

She pushed the plate in front of me. "Take it. I can't. I think I'm going to be sick."

"You need some fresh air," I said, wrapping an arm around her waist and lifting her up. "Come on. Let's walk for a bit."

She moved beside me out of the tent and across the lawn toward the nurses' quarters. "Would probably do you some good to wash up." I said. "You'll feel loads better."

"Can't say I'll smell any better."

I smiled at her as she went through the opening in the tent. "I'll wait around out here. Unless you want to get some sleep? I should probably get back over to Clark soon anyhow."

She rubbed her hands together, her face ashen. "I'll just wash up for a minute and come back," she said as she receded into the darkness of the tent.

I walked a few feet away and found a spot against the stone wall of the hospital to lean against. I sat down in the grass and rested my head back, feeling the rays of the sun warm my cold fears. *Lord, thank You for your protection, yet again. I pray You'll be with Henry and heal his broken body. I pray You'll help us all find the courage to beat back this approaching evil. And Lord, I pray I would honor You with my words and actions. Forgive me for my fears and doubts. Forgive my unbelief.*

I must have dozed off again, because this time I awoke to a gentle shaking of my shoulders. I opened my eyes to see Natalie kneeling in front of me. She managed a weak smile. "Time to wake up, soldier," she said.

I pushed myself to my feet and admired how nice she looked. "I think your color's finally returning."

She stood and touched her hand to her cheek. "Well, a little touch of rouge never hurt anyone."

I started to comment that she looked lovely despite her surroundings, when my heart nearly stopped beating right there and then. I had looked up just in time to see a young woman walk across the lawn and head for the nurses' tent across from where I stood. She moved exactly like Ruby. Her frame was Ruby's. Her face was Ruby's.

"Matthew?" Natalie spoke to me, but I couldn't take my eyes from the woman.

I strode across the grass to the opening of the tent, arriving just as she did. I didn't believe it was actually her. Surely I was imagining the woman standing close enough to reach out and touch?

Ruby was dead. Buried at the bottom of Cold Spring. But there in front of me, frozen just as I was, stood Ruby Graves.

Ruby

My mind and body completely spent, I was headed to the nurses' quarters when Matthew Doyle stepped right in my path. I stopped and stared at him, not believing what was in front of my very eyes. And from the expression on his face, he was thinking the same thing.

"Ruby?" he said, as if he didn't trust his own voice. "Is it really you?"

I opened my mouth, but my voice wouldn't work. It was as if I'd swallowed cotton, and I could think of nothing to say. Panic rose inside of me, and for a second, I considered running away. But where would I go? And besides, he'd seen me. There was no more hiding this from him.

He shook his head slowly. "Surely I'm dreaming...or something."

"Matthew," I managed somehow. "You're here." I swallowed. "How?"

"Then it is you. You're...*alive*." His hand went to his forehead, and his gaze dropped from me to the ground, and back up at me again.

"What's going on?" a female voice said. Natalie stood to my right looking between us, seemingly as puzzled as we were.

Matthew didn't seem to notice her. He only stared at me. "How is this possible? You're supposed to be...You let me think you were dead all this time? Why?" When I couldn't answer, he took a step toward me. "*Why?*"

I glanced at Natalie, whose interest in the conversation sent a jolt of fear sparking through me. "I can't," I started, turning back to Matthew. "I mean, I can explain, but not like this. Can we take a walk?"

His face flushed red, and he pressed his mouth into a hard frown. "You let me believe you died! That I...that I *killed* you! What kind of person does that?"

"Matthew, please," I begged quietly. His voice was rising dangerously, and people were beginning to look at us. "Let me explain."

"What's to explain? I understand everything. You took your chance to escape and didn't care enough to even let me know you were alive. You know, if you didn't love me, all you had to do was say so. You didn't have to punish me!"

With that, he turned and stormed away. I started to run after him, but Natalie's expression stopped me cold. Her eyes were wide, and her mouth had dropped open. She lifted a finger at me. "Your...your name's not Grace Miller. You're that girl. I knew I recognized you."

Matthew was now pacing back and forth across the parade grounds, shaking his head and muttering to himself. Should I go to him? Should I just run as far away from this place as possible? But there was Henry...and now Matthew knew I was alive. I had to face this.

I took a deep breath and tried to dissuade Natalie from her conclusions. "No, no. I am Grace Miller."

She shook her head and took a step back. "He called you Ruby. I heard him." She pointed toward the hospital. "And Henry. He said something to Matthew about finding Ruby. He meant you." She narrowed her eyes at me. "His name's Henry Graves. And you're Ruby Graves."

Matthew sat on the ground now, resting his elbows on his knees and his head in his hands. I had to go to him. Even if Natalie knew who I was, I had to explain things to Matthew. And then I'd run if I had to. I stiffened my spine and faced Natalie with as much confidence as I could muster.

"I have no idea what you're talking about. Excuse me."

I pushed past her and walked calmly over to Matthew, taking a seat in the grass beside him. I had no words to soothe the pain he was in. But I had to try to make him understand the truth of what had happened.

"Matthew? Can I please explain?"

He dropped his hands from his face, anger still pouring out of him. "Sure. I'd love to hear this."

"I never meant to hurt you. Please, if you hear nothing else I say right now, you have to hear this. I would *never* hurt you on purpose."

"And yet, you did."

My throat ached, and my eyes began to well up. I had to find a way to make things clear. "Listen, I had no idea what was going on at first. A man, an old hermit who lived in the woods near the spring, he found me unconscious and took me to his cabin to try to help me. I had a bad concussion and a fever for days. All I wanted was to get to you. To make sure you were safe. But I was out of my head."

"Are you still out of your head?" His dark eyes bore into mine, pained and accusing.

"No."

"Then explain to me, how once you were no longer *out of your head,* you couldn't let me know that you were all right." He didn't even give me a chance to answer. "Do you know what kind of hell I've been through, Ruby? I thought I killed you. I thought you were dead because of my reckless actions."

"I'm so sorry," I said, unable to hold back my tears. "I wanted to tell you. Henry and I talked about it over and over."

"Henry." He dropped his head. "That's right. He knew you were alive too." Then he looked back up at me with another wave of disbelief. "Every letter he wrote me was a lie. He stood there with me at your grave...at your *grave*...and lied to me."

I put a hand on his arm, but he jerked it away. "We wanted to tell you. Both of us wanted to tell you the truth. But I was so afraid you'd be putting yourself in danger. That if we were caught, you'd go to prison for helping me. I couldn't do that to you. And Henry was afraid that if you insisted on going with us, we'd be more conspicuous. He said we'd tell you when we got settled somewhere, and it would be safer for all of us. But then—"

"Then what? You forgot? You were just so happy without me you didn't want me anymore?"

"No!" I reached for his arm again, grateful he didn't pull away this time. "But then you joined the army, and I knew you couldn't just drop everything and come to us. I prayed about it and prayed about it. And I thought that if you were happy, if you'd moved on, then I should give you the chance to have that life. I didn't want you to have to look over your shoulder like I do every day."

He shook his head and dropped it back into his hands, saying nothing for several agonizing minutes. I prayed God would give his mind peace and clarity. That he could see my heart and its intentions. His body gradually shifted from rigid anger to melted defeat. And when he looked at me again, I could see that I might never gain his forgiveness.

"You gave up on us. On me. I guess I deserved it—"

"No—"

"Let me finish," he demanded. "I need to say this. And then I need to go back to Clark and figure out what's next. Our lives are hanging in the balance right now, and it's probably not the best time to figure all this other stuff out. But I want to understand. I want to see the truth for what it is. And the truth is that you couldn't believe in me. You couldn't trust my love for you. That I would do anything I could to protect you and keep you safe."

He took a deep breath and turned to face me, bringing his hand to my cheek and looking at me with moist eyes. "But I have to thank God that you're alive. Whatever it means. Even if it means we were separated. I am grateful. I'm confused. I'm hurt. But I *am* grateful."

His thumb swiped away the tears that wouldn't stop. Again I couldn't find my voice, because somewhere deep inside of me, I knew he was right. I *had* doubted him. I *had* doubted his love for me. And I had made the worst mistake of my life, in so many, many ways. How would I ever make this right again?

CHAPTER SIX

Ruby

December 9, 1941

As darkness fell over Fort Stotsenburg, I sat by Henry's side watching him breathe. His condition hadn't changed much, and his leg was terribly swollen. But the fever worried me most. When the doctor came by to check on him, he said Henry would need further surgery, so they were sending him to Manila as soon as possible, along with some other patients in similar predicaments. I prayed God would allow him to keep his leg, remembering the terrible time Daddy had after losing his, and when no one was looking, I even spread a little extra sulfa powder on the wound.

At one point, I realized there were no nurses present, so I took the opportunity to tell Henry what happened earlier. I didn't know what I was hoping for. Maybe that he'd open his eyes and tell me how silly I was being. That Matthew would forgive me in time, and I just needed to be patient. But I wasn't so sure I had time.

"Someone knows who I am," I said quietly. "And I can't figure out what to do. I need you to wake up and tell me what to do." He didn't stir. "Should I run? Maybe find a local family willing to help me hide until the war's over?"

I imagined him sitting on the side of the bed, his cocky grin reassuring me that he would take care of everything. "Rubes," he'd say. "Don't worry. Everything'll be fine. We'll go up into the mountains or something and hide out for a while." But he was in the army now. We couldn't just take off like we used to. I'd have to find a way to face this without running. At least for now.

I took his hand, hoping to feel his fingers tighten around mine. "I can't leave you here. Not when you're in such bad shape. But maybe I can go to Manila with you. Maybe Joseph can help us. He has family here."

"Planning your escape?" said a voice from across the room. I turned and saw Natalie moving toward me. "I figured you'd be in here." She stopped by Henry's bedside opposite from me. "Looks like your partner in crime can't help you right now."

The hair on my arms prickled, and I felt a sudden chill. "I have an aunt," she said. "She's a bit crazy, and tends to get overly dramatic. But she does love a good story. She came up to visit us this one time right around Christmas 'bout five years ago. I remember 'cause I was about to graduate from high school. And she spun a whopper that day."

Natalie leaned on her hands onto Henry's bed, looking at me like she was about to share the juiciest story she'd ever heard. "See, she lives in this little town in Alabama just outside of Cullman. Hanceville or something like that. She's widowed, which has made her even crazier, I say. Anyway, she runs a boarding house for young women just getting started in the world."

My stomach grew nauseous as I realized exactly who her aunt was. *Ms. Harmon.* She'd kicked me out of the boarding house as soon as I'd been arrested. I did my best to look like I had no idea whom Natalie was speaking of, but I'd never had much of a poker face.

"She said," Natalie continued, lowering her voice, "that one of the girls who'd been living with her had been arrested for murder. Said the girl had a Negro boyfriend, and when they got caught, they killed the poor fella who walked in on 'em."

I swallowed the bile rising up in my throat. "Sounds terrible."

Natalie cocked an eyebrow. "I'm sure it does."

"And you think...you think that I'm that girl."

She leaned back and crossed her arms over her chest. "Oh, I know you are. I seen a picture in the paper Aunt Celia brought with her. Read the article and everything. Like I said, I knew I recognized you. Just took me a while to place you."

I didn't want to lie anymore, and it didn't seem to be working anyway. But I knew in my gut I shouldn't trust Natalie. "Listen, I can explain everything. It's not what you think at all. That newspaper told all kinds of lies just to sell papers. None of it was true."

"You didn't kill that man?"

I paused, my instincts to protect Samuel still as strong as they'd been five years before. "He attacked me. Twice. He beat and raped a friend of mine, and then he came after me. I was defending myself."

As my words registered with Natalie, I thought I saw a glimmer of something—if not understanding, then perhaps pity. "Jury didn't believe that," she said, her brown eyes burning quizzically into mine.

I dropped my gaze and fought back my desire to run. It was time to stop running. "It's a long story to explain, but the jury was fixed. Matthew can tell you. It was his father that did it."

I saw another flicker of something in her eyes, felt a shift in her attitude toward me. She dropped her arms and leaned toward me again. "What's your relationship to Matthew? Are you two involved?"

"He is...a very dear friend. We were involved for a short time during my trial, but..."

"He thought you died. I heard him say it."

"Yes."

She studied me for a while longer, and all I could do was wonder what she was thinking, what she was deciding about my future. Eventually she sighed and looked over at Henry, then back at me. "I have a good mind to turn you in."

My stomach knotted. "Natalie, we're in the middle of a war. And all I want to do is help Henry and the other brave boys here survive this thing the best they can. I don't know what would come of your turning me in. But I know if you decide to keep quiet, and let me do my job, I'd sure be indebted to you."

She waited, a hint of a smile on her lips. "Well, I reckon there's nothing to be done with you way out here in the middle of this mess. So I won't say nothing."

"Thank you so much—"

"But you mind yourself," she said quickly. "And stay away from Matthew. He's a good man that don't need to get tangled up in your lies. Besides, he cares for me. I can see that. And I don't want him worrying over you."

A stab of pain shot through my chest. *Matthew cares for her.* He was involved with Natalie, and Natalie knew who I was. I had no choice at the moment, not if I was going to stay with Henry. Maybe, given time, I could figure out how to get away once Henry was well. And maybe someday, Matthew would forgive me.

"All right," I said. "I understand. Thank you for not saying anything."

She let out a sigh like she was relieved, and then put on a weak smile. "Well then, I'm glad that's settled. I better hurry on off to get some rest. And you should too. No telling when there will be another raid."

As she headed for the door, I felt compelled to try one last time. "Natalie," I called. She turned and faced me. "I swear. I am not a murderer."

She glanced around the room and lowered her voice like we had some big secret between us. "Okay. Whatever you say, *Grace.*"

Matthew

December 11, 1941

I returned to my duties at Clark Field with all the strength I could muster; doing my best not to think on everything I'd learned. The Japs contributed their part to my efforts, bombing us each day around lunchtime. I was grateful that they seemed to have turned their attention on the airfield, and Fort Stotsenburg was left mostly untouched. We moved our decoy planes every day, and every day the Japs took the bait. They'd bomb those poor decoys to kingdom come while the few remaining planes that were operational were safely tucked away in our revetments. Afterward, we'd fill in the new craters and smooth them over, then move the decoys once again.

General Wainwright, the commander of the I Philippine Corps, sent some observation crews into the mountains to our northwest. They'd signal at the first sight of the Japanese bombers, and with so much advanced notice, we were able to reduce the casualties to virtually zero. It wasn't much, but by reducing our casualties and drawing their bombs away from our planes, we felt like we were doing all we could, while the Japanese wasted their ammunition on us.

We gathered around the radio twice a day to listen to what was going on in the world. President Roosevelt's speech before Congress was especially inspiring for us all. We came to the conclusion that we'd dig in and hold our position as long as we could until reinforcements could arrive, which we had no doubt were already on their way.

We were so busy that I didn't get back over to Fort Stotsenburg until a couple of days later. I caught another ride to the hospital and walked the grounds until I found Ruby in one of the tents for less serious conditions, visiting with each patient to ask them if they needed anything. I walked over to her and put my hand on her elbow.

"When do you have a break?" I asked.

She looked genuinely surprised to see me. I reckoned I couldn't blame her after the way I'd left the other day. "I'm on my break now," she said. "Why? What's going on?"

"Can we talk?"

Her eyes darted around the tent. "I suppose."

I strode out of the tent and headed for the parade ground again. But she called out from some ways behind me. I stopped and turned around.

"Um, do you mind if we talk over here?" She gestured toward a small utility building behind the hospital. I shrugged and followed her lead.

Once inside, she closed the door, and the heavy, damp air grew twenty degrees hotter. "Why don't we leave the door open? It's like an oven in here." Not only that, I could barely see her with the little light provided by the sole window to my right.

She pushed the door slightly ajar. "Any better?"

"Not much."

"I'm sorry. I just thought we might need some privacy."

I leaned back onto a table, folding my arms across my chest. In the light streaming through the cracked door, I could see she was filthy and exhausted. Memories of the girl I'd known many years before, who'd picked cotton till her fingers bled just so her family wouldn't starve, flooded my mind and a pang of regret shot through me. Hadn't I started us on this path of mistrust all those years ago? I'd turned my back on her, and then she'd done the same to me. Did that make us even somehow? I needed to understand everything that had happened, but I had no idea where to begin.

"How's Henry?" I asked, figuring it was the easiest place to start.

"He's not improving much, but it doesn't seem to be getting any worse," she said. "The doctor's making plans to send him to Manila for more surgery. The infection's the first priority though. He's in pretty awful pain. I'll probably go back to Manila with him and the other patients."

"How soon?"

"Couple of days."

She was so matter-of-fact, so unemotional in her answers, that I was beginning to think she hadn't wanted to see me again. Maybe it was best to leave well enough alone. I'd ask what I needed to know, and finally close the door on that part of my life for good.

"So, I understand you and Natalie Williams are seeing each other," she said, breaking into my thoughts.

"What? Who told you that?"

She didn't answer. Just pushed the door open for a moment, glanced out, and then let it swing back to slightly ajar.

"Look, can we just speak frankly here? I really need some answers. The whole truth. Not that thing you do where you stop talking and just wait for me to move on."

"All right." She said it as though it were so easy.

"You've been with Henry all this time? Every time he wrote me? From Texas? From New Mexico? San Francisco?" She nodded after I named each city. "Why didn't you let me know you were all right?"

She sighed and gripped her hands together. "We both wanted to tell you. But every time he wrote it down, he said it made him nervous. Like he was handing over the evidence against me. He couldn't bring himself to send it, so he'd tear it up, swearing that next time he'd explain everything. Then once you joined the army, he definitely didn't want to send it. He figured with everything going on in the world, the army would be reading your letters. It just...went on like that for years. And then you stopped writing altogether. I told myself you'd moved on, and you had a life of your own. And that it would be cruel to...to..."

"Tell me the truth?" She met my gaze with such despondency; I almost lost my willpower right there. But I shored up my defenses quickly. "Was it because you didn't love me? Or was it because you were angry at me?"

She shook her head. "No. Nothing like that."

"Then what? 'Cause none of this makes a lick of sense, Ruby."

"I don't know what to say. I'm sorry. I'm so sorry." A small tear eased its way out of the corner of her eye and rolled slowly down her cheek. "What I did was unforgivable. I don't blame you for hating me."

Hating her? I knew I could never hate her, but what I felt was so mixed up inside me, I couldn't make heads or tails of it. "Look," I said. "None of that matters right now. I mean, it does, but it don't. You know?" I gestured toward the chaos beyond the door. "I mean, we're trapped on an island in the middle of a war zone. Our problems are minuscule compared to the families of those men who died the past few days. Or the soldiers who can't walk anymore. Their lives are turned upside down."

"You're right," she said. "We have to stay focused on our jobs."

I pushed away from the table and straightened. "Good. Then it's settled. No more talk of the past. You do your job, and I'll do mine. Agreed?"

"Agreed."

Ruby

December 12, 1941

I made it my goal to think only about the things I could control. I could get a man more morphine to dull his pain. I could hand a doctor a scalpel or check sutures for signs of infection. I could wrap a blanket around a shivering body in shock. I could sit next to Henry, clean his wounds, and try to lift his spirits. Those tasks became lifelines for me. Because when I stopped, when I allowed myself to drift into thoughts of what might lie ahead, fear slid into my heart and mind like a snake, whispering that I'd brought all this on myself.

Seeing Matthew again and aching to be in his arms had reminded me of all I'd left behind. The hole I'd tried so hard to fill had been exposed, and all I knew to do was to work desperately to fill it in again. So even though I was so tired I could hardly stand without getting light-headed, I threw myself into my duties. When my shift was over, I grabbed a bite to eat and offered to cover for another nurse who seemed to need a break. And as it happened, Natalie seemed more than willing to take me up on the offer.

In the early morning hours before my shift started the next day, I went to check on Henry's progress. Janine and I alternated sitting with him through the night if he was in pain, sleeping in a chair beside his bed. It did my heart a world of good to know she was caring for him with just as much dedication as I was.

That morning I walked into the hospital room to find Janine resting her head on the bed next to Henry's leg. She held his hand in hers, and she appeared to be sound asleep. I walked over to her and gently rubbed her back until she stirred.

"Morning," I said. "You look wiped out. Is everything all right?"

"He had a bad night," she said. "He hollered out several times like he was having nightmares. Then his leg went to hurting so bad I couldn't stand it. I didn't know if he was reliving the injury in his nightmare, or if he was actually in pain." She leaned back in the chair and rubbed her eyes. "Once I held his hand and started talking real easy to him, he settled down and went back to sleep."

I lifted the blanket and looked over his bandages. The infection appeared to be fading, but he was still struggling with pain. I covered the leg and turned to Janine. "Dr. Henderson says they're transferring patients to Sternberg tomorrow that need more surgery. I asked if I could go with them."

"I suppose that's a good thing," she said. "But I can't help but wonder what's going to happen to all of us."

"I'm sure there are ships and planes on the way here as we speak. We'll get this turned around in no time."

"I sure hope so. The bombs, day after day—they wear on my sanity. I keep waiting for one to fall right on me."

I could see her eyes welling up. This was precisely the kind of thinking I had been working so hard to avoid. So I did what I could to change the subject. "I want to thank you for taking such good care of Henry. I had no idea he meant so much to you."

Her cheeks warmed, and she turned a fond gaze on his sleeping face. "I can't seem to help myself. I mean, I know he's gone out with a lot of girls, and he probably doesn't feel the same way about me, but there's just something about his spirit that calls to me."

"I know what you mean," I said. "Seems like all my best childhood memories are wrapped up in something to do with Henry. He always knew how to make me laugh whenever I got into trouble, which was quite often. But he also knew when to take my hand and tell me everything was going to be all right." I couldn't help but think back on the day of Daddy's funeral, when I'd felt like the earth might swallow me whole. Or the day we'd packed our things to leave the only home I'd ever known, and we'd played in the creek all afternoon. He'd held me together.

"Grace?" Janine said. "Henry's been saying things. Things that don't always make sense."

My stomach knotted. "Like what?"

"Well, he'll ask for Ruby sometimes. Or maybe Rubes? I'm not too sure. But...is he talking about you?"

Lying had always made me sick to my stomach. I hated it. I looked down at Henry and tried to figure out what he might say, resolving myself to yet another lie. "My name is Ruby. Grace is my middle name. People back home call me Ruby, but not since we left." I figured that was better than admitting I'd just picked out Grace as an alias on a whim.

She looked up at me with a curious expression. "Are you two really cousins?"

"No." I sighed, afraid my secret would spill out around me like the milk from a shattered jar. Messy, and rotten. "He's my brother."

"Then why—"

"Listen, there's a whole long story there that isn't all that interesting. I don't think now's the time to get into it."

"Hey, everyone has a past. Some aren't so pleasant. If you don't want to tell me, then I understand." She didn't look like she was buying it, but thankfully she didn't press the matter. "What about that fella I saw you talking to the other day? It looked like a pretty intense conversation."

I shook my head and pushed down the ache rising in my throat. "That's another long story."

"Sounds like you have some interesting stories to tell," she said, lifting a curious eyebrow.

"You have no idea."

Matthew

Major Hart called another meeting and informed us that Germany had now declared war on the United States. That seemed to energize most of the guys. I reckoned they hoped to get their chance to take on the Nazis, but Doug and I both realized this was bad news.

"If we get pulled into conflict with Europe, then there won't be any reinforcements to send here," I said in a low voice.

Doug leaned onto his elbows and shook his head. "Surely there's already some help coming this way."

"Not if they get rerouted."

"So we're sitting ducks."

Major Hart dismissed the meeting and everyone filed out except Doug and me. I'd already completed my assignment for the day, so I approached Major Hart as he perched on the edge of a desk and asked for a few extra hours leave to head over to Fort Stotsenburg.

"I don't see why it would be a problem, Lieutenant," he said.

Doug snickered from behind me. "He just wants to get in some *alone* time with his girl while he still can."

Major Hart lifted an amused eyebrow. "Is that so?"

"Actually, sir, I need to see if I can find a safe place for a woman I'm concerned about. I've heard some Filipino workers say their families are heading up into the mountains to wait out the war."

"She local?" Major Hart asked.

"No, American. But not military personnel."

"You know, the army allows officers to send their wives home," Major Hart said, lowering his chin and eyeing me. "But that assumes you want to marry her. And that there's transportation off the islands."

I wasn't sure how to respond. "Thank you for the advice, sir."

Major Hart nodded once and went around to the other side of his desk, where he pulled out a drawer and dug out a set of keys. "Here," he said, tossing them at me. "Take my car. And good luck." Then he winked at me. "Take your time. Might be the last chance you have for some female company for a very long while."

I ignored the mischievous look from Doug and wasted no time getting over to the hospital. I was banking on Ruby getting a break soon, and if not, that someone might cover for her while we took a drive. I found her sitting outside a tent, nursing a small cup of water. She looked especially tired.

"Afternoon, Ru—Grace," I said. I still couldn't get used to calling her that. "I was wondering if I could get you to take a ride with me?"

Her hand shielded her eyes from the sun as she looked up at me. "I can't. I have to get back to my shift in a few minutes."

"Can someone cover for you?"

"Everyone else is just as overworked as I am. I can't ask them to give up their rest for me."

I was certain she regularly gave up her own rest for others, but just as I was getting ready to argue the point, another nurse approached us with a curious smile on her face. "Hi there," she said. "Who might you be?"

Ruby jumped up from the overturned bucket where she was seated. "Listen, I can't go anywhere right now. Please excuse me."

The girl smiled and grabbed Ruby's arm. "Sure you can." Then she looked back at me. "Lord knows she needs a real break."

"You think someone would cover for her for a while?" I asked.

"Sure! Any of the girls would be happy to do it. She's generous enough with her help. You two run along, and I'll see to getting her covered."

"Janine—" Ruby protested.

I took her elbow and didn't let her finish. "No arguing. This is important."

She pressed her lips together, looking over my shoulder at Janine. I tugged her away before she could mount any further objections. When we reached Major Hart's blue Plymouth convertible, Ruby stopped in her tracks.

"Wait, is this *yours?*" she asked.

"No, just on loan. Come on, get in."

"Where are we going?"

I climbed behind the wheel. She stood by the passenger door like she didn't quite trust me. "Don't worry. I'm not kidnapping you or anything. We'll be back in a few hours." The thought flashed through my mind that the last time I'd driven her anywhere, we'd ended up crashing into a river, and nearly drowning at the bottom of a freezing spring. I supposed her hesitation was warranted.

She pulled open the door and climbed inside. I turned the key, and the engine roared to life. I relished the strength under the hood for a moment. I was going to have to get me a convertible when I got back to the States.

Dust trailed along behind us as I drove down a winding road that led into the mountainous jungle. I stopped once we'd reached a secluded area where I was sure we wouldn't run into any other people. Then I turned off the engine and prepared to do battle.

"So what's this all about?" she asked, the engine having barely stopped.

"I want you to let me make some arrangements."

"What kind of arrangements?"

I pointed toward the mountains. "Some of the Filipinos I work with are heading into the mountains to wait out the war. They're good people. They'd keep you safe."

She shook her head before I'd even finished. "I can't leave Henry."

"Ruby, you're not trained for war."

"Who is? This isn't something any of us are really ready for. But I've kept up just as well as anyone else. And I won't leave Henry."

I hadn't actually believed I'd convince her, but at least I had tried. So now, it was on to Plan B. I released the wheel and reached under the seat beneath me. "I figured you'd say that." I pulled out a sock, and then pulled out the pistol I'd stuffed inside it. "I want you to take this."

Her eyes widened. "What? No—"

"Yes, Ruby. Just listen to me. You have to be able to protect yourself."

"But I've never even shot a gun!"

"That's why I brought you out here. I'll teach you. It ain't too hard. Just aim and squeeze."

She shook her head. "No, no, no. I help people. I help them recover from bullet holes. I don't put bullet holes *in them*."

I took a deep breath and set the gun on the dashboard, trying another approach. "Can't you please just listen to me for once? You're leaving with Henry to go back to Manila tomorrow. I'm sure we'll be evacuated soon, too. I won't be able to protect you. I need to know you'll be all right. I need to be able to do my job without worrying about you." Her eyes softened, making my heart thump to life. "Ruby, if the Japanese invade, they'll head for Manila. And they don't have one ounce of mercy. You know what they do to women, don't you?"

The mere suggestion of the Japanese soldiers' brutality made the blood drain from her face. "They don't call it the Rape of Nanking for nothing." I'd once seen the pictures in the newspaper and read the report of the thousands of innocent women and children who were tortured and killed.

"I know about it," she said quietly.

"Then you know why I have to do this. I can't even think of anything like that happening to you." I gripped the steering wheel until my knuckles turned white. "I've been praying about things a lot the past couple of days. It's been real easy to put all the blame for my pain on you, but the truth is: I failed you after the trial. I couldn't understand what you were trying to tell me about trusting God, about stepping out of the boat and going to Jesus despite the storm around you. I almost lost my faith completely. But I think I understand things better now. And I'm not trying to force something that isn't God's plan. So just give me this *one* thing. Let me teach you how to shoot."

She nodded. "All right. I'll do it."

Victory.

***

I didn't have any targets with me, so I had to improvise. I dug around until I found a couple of shirts in the Major's trunk. I bundled up a bunch of palm leaves and tied the shirts around them. Then I waved at Ruby as she leaned on the car. "Come on over here."

I set up the targets on the side of a slope and started her out about ten yards away. I showed her how to grip the pistol in both hands, how to line up the sight on the end. Then I stepped around behind her. "Now, hold it out in front of you with your arms straight. Good. Now, when you fire the gun, don't try to anticipate the recoil."

"What do you mean?" she said.

I reached over her right shoulder and pointed at the back of the gun. "Most people start thinking about how the gun's going to jerk up or back when it fires. So they tighten their muscles to keep it steady, but you wind up pulling it off target. Just make sure you breathe; then squeeze the trigger with a slow, steady pull. Go ahead and give it a try."

She locked her elbows again, and I pulled my hand away. I could see the sight moving all around. She squeezed the trigger, and it clicked. "How was that?" she asked.

"Not bad. Your aim's a little unsteady, but you'll get better. Want to try it with a bullet?"

"Sure."

I loaded the gun and handed it back to her. "Keep the muzzle pointed down until you're ready to shoot. *Never* point that thing at anyone or anything you're not willing to kill."

She looked up at me with incredulous eyes. "I...I don't think I can kill anyone."

"You might surprise yourself if your life's in danger."

She turned back to the target, and I stepped behind her again. "Breathe, then squeeze."

The gun swayed a little, and then she snapped the trigger back. A loud boom echoed off the mountain. She hadn't even come close. She lowered the gun and turned around. "That was terrible. I could tell."

"Just relax. Remember to take a breath, and pull the trigger with a steady squeeze."

She fired the gun five more times with the same result, handing it back to me empty and frowning like she did when she was determined to win an argument with me. "Load it up and tell me what I'm doing wrong."

I couldn't help but grin as I slid six more rounds into the revolver. "You're still anticipating the recoil."

She took the gun and turned her back to me. Her shoulders rose and fell with her breath. Then she straightened her arms and shot again. This time dirt kicked up just above and to the right of the shirt. "That's better," I said. "This time, try to pull the trigger two times, quickly."

SAVING GRACE | 95

She did as I said, hitting around the shirt. Her arm dropped, and she let out a frustrated sigh. "Why am I so bad at this?"

I turned her shoulders around until she faced me. "Listen, I've never seen any obstacle you couldn't conquer. Apparently, even death. You can do this."

She cracked a small smile. "Well, I guess it's a good sign that you can joke about it. Does this mean you forgive me?"

"Let's not push it."

She frowned. "In all seriousness, I'm never going to get this. At least, not in the short time we have."

"You can do this, " I said, stepping just a bit closer. "Just breathe. Clear your mind."

"I can't."

"Close your eyes. Shut out everything. Even me. Breathe in. Breathe out." I slowly turned her so she faced the target and moved behind her again. Lowering my voice, I spoke into her ear. "Breathe in. Breathe out. Now open your eyes, find the target, and squeeze."

She raised her arms and squeezed the trigger in perfect sync, blowing a hole through the shirt. She fired it twice more, emptying the chamber. Then she turned to me with a triumphant smile. "I did it! That worked!"

"Great job," I said, taking the gun as she handed it back. "I knew you'd get it. Just breathe and squeeze."

She looked up at me with so much joy that I couldn't help but smile back. Warmth spread through my chest, and I almost reached for her. *Almost.* I forced myself to step back and cleared my throat. "Want to try a few more rounds?"

"Sure," she said.

I loaded the gun once more, and she emptied it into the shirt. Then she shot four more rounds, loading it herself. I was pleased that she'd gotten as much as she could out of one session, so we packed up and headed back to Fort Stotsenburg.

Ruby was quiet as I drove, mostly looking away from me and out into the jungle. I couldn't read her anymore. I didn't even know her anymore. And that thought sat in my chest like lead. When we were in sight of the fort, she finally spoke.

"Why did you do this?"

"Do what?"

"Take me out shooting. I thought we'd decided to just *do our jobs.*"

"And I intend to do just that," I said as I brought the car to a stop about thirty yards from her tent. "But no matter what's happened between us, I can't send you off into Manila defenseless against the Japanese. It just ain't in me to do that."

In silence we climbed out of the car and closed the doors, then she looked at me with a sad sort of smile. "Thank you."

And with that she trudged across the grass toward her tent. But about halfway there, she stopped and stared at an approaching figure who must have said something to her. As the person stepped out from behind a tree, I could see it was Natalie. I couldn't hear her, but Ruby said something in reply. Then Natalie turned and headed for me.

I realized I'd completely forgotten about her in the past few days, and I felt terrible for it. Especially when she approached me with such a weary, but happy smile. "Wow!" she said. "Nice car!"

"Thanks, but it's not mine."

She walked around the front, admiring it as she dragged a finger across the hood. Then she came over next to me and rested her back against the side. "Man, what a crazy few days it's been here," she said. "I guess Clark's been busy too."

"Very," I said, taking a quick glance toward the nurse's tent. Ruby had turned to watch us, and I felt a sudden sense of control.

Natalie shifted her body toward mine, walking her fingers up the buttons of my shirt. "Sure would be nice to relax for a while. I'd give just about anything to be back on the beach with you."

Nothing inside me moved for this girl, except maybe pity. But my anger at Ruby had not subsided, and that moved me instead. I found myself slipping my arm around her waist and pulling her in for a kiss, letting my frustration drive my lips into hers. She gripped my shirt, pulling just as tightly.

When we separated for a moment, I asked if she wanted to go for a drive. "Sure thing, soldier," she said with a smile.

As she walked around the front of the car, I took another quick glance toward the tents. Ruby was gone.

CHAPTER SEVEN

Ruby

December 13, 1941

I tossed and turned all night, failing to fall asleep before it was time to leave for Manila. No matter how heavy my eyes were, when I closed them, I was confronted with images of bloody limbs being sawn off, men crying out in pain, or Matthew leaning down to kiss Natalie. My body would jolt, waking me repeatedly throughout the night. When I stood from my cot, it was still dark outside, and my head pounded. The earth swayed beneath me. I was exhausted and filthy from head to toe. I desperately needed a bath.

I gathered my helmet and the blanket I'd been issued. Then I considered the gun still stuffed inside the sock Matthew had given me. I hadn't wanted it at first, for many reasons. It seemed so contrary to my call to help people. But I had to admit a large part of me enjoyed learning to shoot, especially once I caught the hang of it. So I stuffed it inside the blanket and walked over to where the bus was being loaded down with supplies. I stepped inside, but didn't see any patients. A tall, haggard-looking fellow who seemed to be in charge barked orders as men flung boxes onto the bus. I didn't exactly know how to tell what rank someone was, so I just said, "Excuse me, sir?"

He didn't hear me. Or he simply chose to ignore me. I went back down the steps to stand beside him. "Excuse me, sir. Is this the bus headed to Sternberg?"

"Orders have changed," he said abruptly. "You all are taking the train down to Manila because the roads are so jammed up with people trying to get in and out of the city. Get on the bus, and it'll take you over to the railroad car."

He didn't miss a beat jumping right back to ordering his men around. I figured it was best to stay out of the way, so I found a seat on the bus and waited quietly. But the horizon was already starting to turn silver, and I was afraid we were going to get caught in a bombing raid if we messed around much longer. Another nurse, who I thought was named Laura, climbed on board, along with a medic. I smiled at them both the best I could, and I reckon their returned half-smiles were about the best they could manage too.

The bus rumbled along the road for a couple of kilometers until we reached the train station. I climbed out and could make out the shapes of patients on gurneys being lifted into two boxcars. Stretchers had been placed on racks secured to the walls of the boxcars, and men were stacked three stretchers to a rack. I found Henry in the second car, strapped into the middle section of a group of stretchers.

"Hey, you ready to get a move on?" I said.

He grimaced at me with bloodshot eyes. "Rubes, I'm so glad to see ya. My leg...it don't feel right. I know it's messed up bad. Are they gonna take it when I get to Manila? I don't want to lose my leg. I can't end up like Daddy."

I checked his pulse and his temperature. "You'll be just fine. I'll get you something to help with the pain. Just hang in there, all right?"

I found another boxcar with supplies, and asked for a few doses of morphine for the patients in pain. Then I went back and gave Henry a dose. Once he was taken care of, I walked around to the other men, checking to see if they needed some as well. Most were already in drug-induced sleep, but one soldier was curled up on his side in a ball, facing the wall. I sat with him a few minutes, but he resisted all offers of help, not even turning to speak to me.

After much scurrying around, securing patients to their stretchers and getting supplies loaded up, we finally began moving toward Manila. By that time, the sun was much higher in the sky than it should've been, and I was more than just worried about an attack during our journey. I was certain it was bound to happen.

I tried not to dwell on it too much as we passed through the countryside. I thought of the time when, as a young girl, I had hopped a train between Hanceville and Cullman just so I could help out at the soup kitchen with Matthew. That had been one of the most exhilarating experiences of my life. I remembered sitting on the edge of that boxcar with my legs dangling out, dreaming of seeing the world. Now, as I stood in the middle of a boxcar full of shattered men, I wished for that carefree feeling of possibility. So many lives had been shattered in just a few short days.

The train jerked, the brakes squealing. I stumbled to the open door to figure out what was going on. People ran from the train in all directions, and the sound of the distant buzzing that had haunted my nightmares as well as my days, turned my stomach. I looked north, and sure enough, a large formation of Japanese planes, in their familiar V pattern, were approaching. Behind me, men shrieked to be let out of their stretchers.

"It's them!"

"Let me out of here! I ain't dying strapped to a stretcher

The man in the back of the car who hadn't turned to look at me earlier now looked around the boxcar, laughing hysterically. My head spun as my heart pounded away. What was I supposed to do?

"Ruby!" Henry called. "Cut me loose!"

The medic who'd been in the car with me came over from the door, raising his hands to calm everyone. "No one is going anywhere. You all need to stay in your beds."

Several of the men swore and kept thrashing at the belts holding them to the stretchers. The buzzing grew louder and louder, filling my head with searing pain. I went over to Henry and did the only thing I knew to do. I took Henry's hand and knelt beside him, praying as loud as I could over the hum of the planes, which were nearly on top of us then.

"The Lord is my rock, and my fortress, and my deliverer; my God, my strength, in whom I will trust; my buckler, and the horn of my salvation, and my high tower. I will call upon the Lord, who is worthy to be praised: so shall I be saved from mine enemies."

I said the verse again, louder this time, feeling its power work peace through my mind. I repeated it a third time, and realized when I'd finished, that the screams around me had been replaced with silence. I stood and looked around. Every man in the car—the patients, the medic, even the young man who'd been laughing—was looking at me with wide, disbelieving eyes.

Then I realized why it was so quiet. The planes were gone.

***

The rest of the ride into Manila was quiet. The men lay on their backs without a word. Some of them moved their lips with their eyes closed, as if they were praying. I went around, checking to see that they hadn't reinjured themselves, and that they were secured in their stretchers. Each man looked at me in varying degrees of fear or amazement, but I couldn't figure out why. Did they think my prayer had somehow kept us safe? I had no way to know, but still, I rode the rest of the way near the open door so I could keep an eye on the sky. I didn't see any more planes, but what I did see was just as terrifying. Black smoke rose from Manila in waves.

Once we arrived at the train station, Henry and the other patients were loaded onto ambulances and carted through the city. I rode with the nurses and other personnel in the back of a truck along roads jammed with Filipinos trying to get into the city, as well as those trying to get out. People pushed carts loaded down with belongings, children, and the elderly. Buildings burned. Bodies were strewn in the streets. Every urge within me wanted to jump out of that truck and do everything I could to help these poor people, but I sat frozen to my seat.

When we neared the hospital, a hazy smog hung over everything. People seemed to be coming to the hospital from all directions—sailors, soldiers, and civilians. The patients we'd brought with us joined the parade of casualties. I stayed with Henry as a couple of enlisted men took him down a crowded hallway and set him on the floor in a room that was already bursting at the seams.

I touched one of the men on the arm, and he turned to me with weary eyes. "Do you know when a surgeon might be able to get to him?" I asked.

He sighed and tossed up his hands. "I can't say. As soon as possible."

One of the army nurses came into the room and began checking patients. She looked as drained and shell-shocked as the nurses up at Fort Stotsenburg. I went over to her and did my best not to interrupt her work. "Excuse me, do you know where I could find Mrs. Fincher?"

She nodded, but continued counting the pulse of the man's wrist she was holding. When she finished, she took a quick glance at me. "She's managing the operating rooms. We're overrun."

"I'll see if I can find her," I said. "I'll be back to help out as soon as I can."

I followed the signs to the operating rooms and found Mrs. Fincher giving out orders to nurses and service men as they passed by her with stretcher after stretcher. I pushed through the crowd and got as close to her as I could. "Mrs. Fincher," I called from across the hall. "I'd like to volunteer, if you'll have me."

"Goodness, I don't remember your name, but yes, I believe we can use you. Do you have any surgical experience?"

"Not much. Mostly wound care and recovery. And my name's Grace."

"That'll do." She pointed to a hallway off to her right. "We need help treating the burn cases. Go down this hallway and take a left. Follow it to the end. You'll know when you're in the right place."

"Is there somewhere for me to stay here at the hospital?"

"Nurse's quarters are in the back near the gardens. If you can find an empty bed, you're welcome to use it."

I thanked her, following her directions and turning left, heading down another long hallway. I wondered how in the world I was going to find my way back to Henry, or to the nurse's quarters for that matter. Then I realized why she'd said I would know when I was in the right place. The moans and cries were unmistakable. But worse than that was the nauseating stench of burned flesh.

As I neared the end of the hallway, I saw men and women lying on gurneys on both sides of the hall. One Filipino lady held a young boy of about three in her arms, and she looked up at me with anguished eyes. "Can you help, please?"

I tried to soothe her with a smile and looked down at her wounds. Her arms were charred and peeling away in blisters, the whiteness of bone clearly visible against blackened flesh. "Let me see what I can do."

She stepped into my path, pleading as though she thought I was her last hope. "No, not for me. See?"

She held the unconscious boy out to me, and I could see his lips were blue. I went into the room to my left, searching frantically for a doctor. "This child out here needs help, now!"

The room was filled with singed bodies wrapped in bandages. A doctor across the room looked up from his patient, and I saw the familiar eyes of Joseph Grant. "Grace!" he called. "I'll be right there!"

I turned back to the mother and held my hands out to her. "May I take him?"

She grimaced as the boy rolled limply across her injured arms and into mine. I laid him on the gurney she'd been sitting on and checked his vitals. His breathing wasn't right. I put my head on his chest and listened as best I could over all the wailing and commotion. His heartbeat was faint.

When I straightened, Joseph came along beside me. "He needs oxygen," I said.

Joseph grabbed the nearest oxygen tank and strapped the nasal cannula into the boy's nose. We waited for what seemed like an eternity and I wished, not for the first or even hundredth time, that my healing gift had not deserted me. I could feel the boy's mother pacing behind me as his life drained away. His whole face was turning blue. The oxygen was doing nothing. I turned to Joseph, hoping he'd have answers. "What now?"

He glanced sideways at the mother and lowered his voice. "I don't think there's anything we can do. He isn't going to make it, and there are urgent cases in there."

"We can't just give up on him! What about a stimulant?"

"The needle's six inches long. If I miss his heart by even a hair, it'll kill him anyway. I don't mean to be cruel. If you can think of any other way—"

"Alcohol!" I shouted.

"What?"

"Alcohol is a stimulant. Is there any around?"

His eyes widened. "You might be on to something." Then he ran down the hallway and disappeared.

I turned to the mother and tried to reassure her. "He'll be right back. What's the boy's name?"

"Paolo," she said, her voice breaking. She came to his side and took his hand, stroking the back of it.

"I'm Grace," I said. "Would you like to pray with me until the doctor gets back?" She nodded her head, so I closed my eyes. "Lord, please be with little Paolo and his mother. Let us find a way to save him. Give us peace of mind and wisdom."

"I found some!" Joseph called as he ran back toward us holding up a bottle of whiskey. He handed the bottle to me along with some gauze and a container of sugar.

I dipped the gauze in the whiskey, followed by the sugar. Then I inserted it into the boy's mouth. By this time, he was seriously blue, and my heart raced with fear. I begged God for the whiskey to work, and I took the mother's hand in mine. We watched anxiously as the boy sucked on the gauze, lightly at first, but then stronger and stronger. His color began to return to normal, and I nearly jumped up on the gurney to shout praises.

I took the mother's hands in mine and shared her grateful smile. "Now, let's get you taken care of too."

I walked over to a supply cabinet and grabbed what I needed to clean her wounds. When I returned, she was seated beside Paolo with tears streaming down her face. I thought for a moment he'd worsened, but she was smiling up at Joseph as he spoke to her in Tagalog. I irrigated the burns on her arms, surprised by her ability to withstand the pain she must have been feeling, before spraying tannic acid over them and dressing them loosely.

"Thank you," she said, looking between Joseph and me.

I gave her a quick hug, taking care to avoid her bandages. "You'll both be good as new. God bless you."

Joseph turned to head back into the room where I'd found him. He pulled his mask down and wiped his arm across his brow. "I'm so glad to see you. Can we talk later?"

"Sure. I'm going to try to find a bed in the nurse's quarters when I'm done here. Just come find me."

"Will do." He pulled his mask back up and sped away to the next patient crying out in pain. And I continued on down the hallway, one patient at a time, irrigating, spraying, and praying for relief.

***

After hours of working the burn ward, my body and spirit were completely spent. I found Joseph and asked him to help me find the nurses' quarters. He led me through the maze of hallways and out to the garden area. I was shocked to see patients lined up, even out in the gardens. Men lay on blankets, stretchers, even doors that had been torn from their hinges. I stopped on the sidewalk, but Joseph put an arm over my shoulder and kept me moving. It was impossible to help everyone. Eventually we reached a set of small cottages with porches.

"Why don't you find a bed and get cleaned up," Joseph said. "I've got a few things for you. I'll go get them and be right back."

"All right. Thank you for the help."

The first cottage I entered was full, with belongings stashed under each of the six beds. The second was full as well. I met another nurse named Theresa who kindly told me I was welcome to share her bed if I couldn't find another. I was about to get discouraged when I entered the third cottage. A girl about my age was buttoning up her uniform and gave me a tired smile as I came in.

"Can I help you?" she asked.

"I'm Grace. I'm a civilian nurse. Volunteered to help out. Mrs. Fincher said I could stay here if I could find a bed."

"Nice to meet you, Grace. I'm Sharon. I believe the bed over in the corner's free. The nurse who was sleeping there was sent up to Fort Stotsenburg several days ago."

I thanked her and went over to the bed, dropping my helmet onto it. I wanted a shower so badly, but I had no soap, no clean clothes. I turned back to Sharon. "Would you happen to have a bit of soap I could use?"

"Why, sure!" She dug into a small case on her bed and handed me a bar of soap and a bottle of shampoo. "Listen, I have to report back on duty. I'll see you later."

"All right. Thank you again."

The door clapped shut behind her, leaving me alone for the first time in what felt like years. I went into the bathroom and started the water. Then I pulled off the filthy uniform that I'd been wearing since the first night I'd arrived at Fort Stotsenburg. It smelled just awful, and I didn't think I'd ever get the stains out. I'd have to ask Mrs. Fincher if there were any extra clothes I could use.

I stepped beneath the tepid water and closed my eyes, relishing the water running over my skin. I watched as days of grime, blood, and horror washed down the drain. And in that moment, I couldn't control my emotions anymore. I dropped my face into my hands and sobbed.

When eventually I emerged from the shower, I felt as though I could sleep for days. I went to pick up my filthy uniform, dreading the stench of it, when I realized it was gone. In its place on the bed was a dress—my dress—from my things at the cottage where I'd been living the past year. Then I noticed the suitcase at the end of the bed. It was my suitcase. I opened it up to find several of my dresses, some undergarments, stockings, and another pair of my shoes.

Joseph.

I pulled several items out; so grateful to see the dress Daddy had bought me for Christmas when I was thirteen. And beneath that was Daddy's Bible. I held it to my chest, thanking God for this small blessing. Then I put on the dress that had been laid on my bed, repacked my things into the suitcase, and did my best to tame my tangled wet hair.

Stepping over to the phone in the cottage, I called the nurse's station. A voice as drained as my own answered. "Can you tell me if Henry Graves has been into surgery yet?" I asked.

"I'll check. One moment."

As I waited, I heard a knock on the screen door. Joseph peeked in. "Is it all right to come in?"

I covered the receiver with my hand and motioned for him to enter. "Just trying to check on Henry."

He took a seat on a bed across the room from mine, propping himself against the wall. He pulled up his long legs and rested his elbows on his knees, closing his eyes and waiting.

The voice came back on the other end. "Is this Grace?"

"Yes, were you able to find out anything on Henry?"

"Mrs. Fincher wanted me to let you know that Henry is in a stable condition. He hasn't been in for surgery yet. I'm afraid our surgical teams have been slammed. I'm not sure when they'll get to him."

"Oh," I said. "Well, thank you."

"Grace? Do you think you'd be able to take a shift tonight? We could use some extra hands?"

"Of course."

"All right. Come in at eleven, then."

I hung up the phone and went over to my bed, dropping onto it so hard I was afraid I'd broken the springs. I glanced over at Joseph, who hadn't moved. "Thank you for getting my things from my house. Especially my daddy's Bible. That means the world to me."

He opened one eye. "Wasn't any trouble." Then he closed it again. "Good thing I went when I did. It's been leveled by the bombing since then."

I was so tired I couldn't sit up any longer. I stretched out on the bed facing Joseph, my whole body aching with fatigue. "I could sleep for days, maybe even through the bombs."

He was quiet for a good minute, so I thought he might have fallen asleep. Darkness crept in around me as well.

"So your name's not Grace Miller," he said, startling me back to consciousness. "Is it Ruby?"

I couldn't read his expression. Maybe because we were both too tired. I nodded. "How did you know?"

"You said Henry Graves was your brother. That Bible there has a family tree in it. Henry Graves has only one sister listed."

"I see." I didn't know what to say. In a matter of just a few days I'd managed to undo years of secrets. I'd lost my ability to control my tongue, and if I wasn't careful, it was going to cost me.

"Kinda makes sense, I guess," he said. "I heard him call you 'Rubes' a couple of times. Never thought much of it till now." He lifted his brow like he was waiting for me to fill in the details, but I kept quiet. "Why all the secrecy?"

"That's a very, *very* long story. And frankly, I've never told it to anyone. I don't intend to start now."

"You don't trust me? Come on." He shook his head. "What? Are you a criminal or something?"

"Or something."

He held my gaze for a while, and I could see he was trying to work things out. Somewhere in the back of my mind, I knew this was the beginning of my undoing, but I was tired of lying. I was tired of everything at that moment, actually. I began to drift again.

"You could tell me," Joseph said. "I wouldn't judge you."

"I can't."

"Ruby, I'd protect you."

Hearing him say my name sounded so strange, and yet, it was also comforting. Like coming home. I looked over at him once more, and I could see the ache in his gaze that I'd known was in my own many years before as I'd looked on Matthew. Loving someone who didn't love you in return was about the most awful feeling in the world.

"Joseph, listen. I'm in love with someone. Have been since I was thirteen. I can't imagine I'll ever love anyone else. Don't waste your affection on me. You don't even know me."

He let his head drop back against the wall again and closed his eyes. I figured we were done talking, so I closed mine as well. A heavy fog of sleep moved over me, but I heard him mumble before it claimed me for its own.

"I would...if only you'd let me."

CHAPTER EIGHT

Ruby

December 23, 1941

The next several days blended into a dizzying period of time without measure. The mornings began with an early breakfast in the mess hall, followed by checking in on patients admitted the previous day and night and releasing those able to walk unassisted. All this needed to be accomplished before lunch at eleven. Because after lunch, the chaos started anew.

The Japanese bombed Manila, the docks, Cavite Naval Base, and Nichols Field every day between noon and one. They attacked like clockwork, with virtually no American planes to deter them, no anti-aircraft guns to reach them. The best we could do was take shelter and ride it out. Patients well enough to move were placed in slit trenches dug all around the hospital. Those that couldn't move hung on to their sanity as the earth shook, lights flickered, and the walls rattled.

When the bombing was over, the rest of the day shifted into a frenzy. New casualties would flood the wards. Surgical teams worked long into the night under blackout conditions to save as many as they could. What amazed me through all of this was the total commitment from the personnel, from the motor pool to the mess hall, from the orderlies up to the surgeons. No one slacked off for a moment. No matter how exhausted we were, each person filled their role with everything they had.

At night, when I was able to grab a few hours of rest, I cried out to God on behalf of the men, women, and children I'd served that day, but I also thanked Him for the opportunity to be part of such an amazing group of people. And then, in the quiet, I prayed He would restore my gift. I longed to be able to stop the suffering surrounding me. If only He'd work through me again, maybe some of them could be saved. But the gift of healing remained a distant memory.

Once, about five days or so after I'd arrived at Sternberg, I went to check on Henry and found Janine standing beside his bed. He'd finally been able to get the surgery he'd needed for his torn ligaments, and the doctor had removed some lingering shrapnel that had been giving him terrible pain. So Henry was sitting up, flirting just like his old self, when I came in.

Janine smiled at me and gave me a hug. "Oh, Grace, it's so good to see you."

I returned her embrace. "It's good to see you too. When did you get here?"

"They shipped us down yesterday. They're clearing out everyone from Fort Stotsenburg. Word is the Japs have landed in Lingayen Gulf. They're marching south."

This wasn't unexpected news, but it was frightening all the same. "How long do we have until they reach Manila?"

"About a week...maybe a little longer," Henry said. "Depends on how determined they are to get here."

"Manila's been declared an open city," Janine said. "All military personnel are being moved. I heard we're all headed for Bataan."

"The jungle?" I asked. "Why can't they just evacuate us out of the Philippines altogether? The jungle's the worst possible place to send sick and injured men."

Henry, with an unusually serious dimeanor, met my gaze. "The Japs got the islands surrounded. Ain't no one getting in, or out of here. Bataan is just a way to hold out until reinforcements come."

I did my best to ignore the twist of fear worming into my heart as I pictured the Japanese soldiers marching in our direction.

"Probably best to focus on our jobs here until we know something definite," Janine said with a bit of forced cheer. She looked down at Henry and smiled. "Speaking of which, do you need anything before I get back to my duties?"

He held out a hand. She took it, and he pulled her closer. "Just a kiss before you go?"

She giggled and kissed him on the forehead. "That'll have to do for now."

He threw up his hands in protest. "Well, for Pete's sake, I can get one of those from just about any of these nurses around here."

She pointed a reprimanding finger at him. "You better watch it. I'll have Mary Alice give you a sponge bath."

Henry glanced over at the large, abrasive nurse checking on a patient across the room. His face contorted. "Oh, no. Please. Anything but that."

Janine turned to go, so I said goodbye to Henry and walked with her for a piece. "I think I'll head out to the garden for some fresh air," I said. "I'll see you later."

"Hold on just a minute," Janine said, grabbing my arm and pulling me to the side of the hallway. She reached into the pocket of her coveralls and pulled out a slip of paper. "Right before we were evacuated, your friend Matthew found me and asked me to give you this."

I took it and stared at it for a moment. "Was he...was he all right?"

"Seemed to be. I think he was being moved out as well." She frowned. "Say, tell me something. You two seem to mean something special to each other, but I heard Natalie talking about him like they're together. What's going on there?"

I didn't have an answer, at least not one that I could explain. "It's a little complicated."

She shrugged. "Well, it's none of my business. I better get to work. See ya."

"See ya," I said.

I turned and hurried through the halls and out into the garden, where I found a bench and tore open the letter before I'd even sat down.

Dear Ruby,

I feel terrible about the way we left things. I always hated being mad at you, and hated it even more when you were mad at me. I've been praying for understanding, that God would allow me to see things through your eyes. I know in my heart you didn't mean to hurt me. I just can't seem to get past my own pride. This whole world's a mess right now, and I don't know what the future holds. We're being moved to Bataan, but I don't know exactly where yet. Please stay safe. I can't make heads or tails of things, but underneath my pride and anger, even when I wish I didn't, I know I still love you.

Yours,

Matthew

Relief washed over me, and I held the letter to my chest as I thanked God. Matthew was safe. He still loved me. This at least, was a beginning.

I made my way to my quarters to get some rest before the evening shift. When I walked inside and went over to my bed, I noticed a dress laid out that wasn't mine. Other personal items—a brush, makeup, bobby pins—were spread across the bed as well. Before I could figure out whose they were, Natalie appeared in the bathroom doorway with a towel wrapped around her.

"Grace?" she said. "What are you doing in here?"

"I was going to rest a bit before my shift. When did you get back?"

"You're working *here?*" she asked, as if it was the most absurd thing she'd ever heard. "I suppose with things the way they are, they have to get help from wherever they can find it."

I slid Matthew's letter into my pocket as she walked over to the bed and sat down, rubbing a towel against her short hair. "Oh, you wouldn't believe the time I've had. After they *forced* me to go up to Stotsenburg, which might as well be the front line, and I nearly died trying to save those boys' lives, I come back here and find out they just *gave* my bed away. I've got nowhere to sleep, and I'm exhausted!"

"Oh, was this your bed? I had no idea. I'm sorry. You can have it back."

She smiled up at me. "Oh, thank you so much. I suppose those are your things I moved." She pointed next to the bed where my belongings were haphazardly strewn against the wall. "It really is very kind of you."

"Of course," I said, gathering my things in my arms. "I'll just find another bed." I was willing to do just about anything to keep her quiet and happy for the time being, at least until Henry was well enough to help me figure out what to do.

December 24, 1941

The following day was Christmas Eve, and though some of the staff and patients tried to make it festive, most of us were too drained to make merriment. That morning, I was called into a meeting with Mrs. Fincher and Dr. Stimson, who'd been coordinating the non-military volunteers. There were a few other nurses and doctors present, and when Joseph came into the room, he immediately frowned at me.

"You look terrible," he said. "Long night?"

"Something like that." I hadn't been able to find another empty bed, so I'd found a cot and set it up in the garden near a large palm tree. My neck was stiff, and my eyes ached.

"Do you know what this is about?"

"Probably the evacuation. Janine said they're moving everyone to Bataan."

Joseph scratched at the short beard he'd grown over the past few weeks and looked out the window to his left. "Things could get even worse around here when the Japs show up. We should think about a safe place to go. Maybe the mountains with my mother's family."

"I don't want to leave Henry."

He lifted an eyebrow. "Henry may be forced to leave you if the military is evacuating the city."

I thought about that as Mrs. Fincher and Dr. Stimson closed the door to the meeting room and faced all of us with grim expressions. Janine had been right. It was about the evacuations. After confirming that the army and navy were moving all staff and military patients to hospitals being set up on Bataan, Mrs. Fincher explained that any remaining American citizens were being encouraged to stay put, since Manila had been declared an open city. I was certain the Japanese wouldn't care what the city declared. They'd consider it an American military position, and treat it as such. I was shocked MacArthur would be so naive.

"Although we respect the advice," she continued, "those of you in this room have been extremely helpful, going above and beyond to serve your fellow countrymen, and we would like to offer you the chance to continue in that service if you so choose. We'll begin the evacuation process tomorrow. Take some time to think it over, but not too long. And no matter what you decide, the United States of America thanks you for your sacrifice."

There were a few questions, but neither Dr. Stimson nor Mrs. Fincher had much in the way of details. It was a pretty straightforward choice. Evacuate, or take our chances with the Japanese.

By the time we sat down for the late-afternoon mess—a valiant but inadequate attempt at Christmas dinner—I'd decided to evacuate with the army nurses, since it was my best chance to stay near Henry. There was no guarantee we'd be sent to the same location, but at least we'd be moving in the same direction. Joseph was still on the fence, unsure about leaving his mother.

"Do you really want to risk being captured by the Japs?" Henry asked.

Joseph pushed soggy roast potatoes around his plate with his fork. "No, but I don't want to leave my mother to the same fate either."

"Didn't you say she has family that's going into the mountains? Could she go with them?"

He shrugged, but before he could answer, the air raid siren went off, and we all jumped up from our chairs, that familiar lurch of fear in the pit of my stomach threatening to bring back my Christmas dinner. Janine supported Henry as he hobbled across the cafeteria and out the back door to the trenches in the garden. Joseph and I followed close behind, helping Henry and Janine down before jumping into the next trench over.

"Some Christmas, huh?" Joseph said, once we were settled.

Two other nurses and an orderly slipped into the trench beside us. I sat on the ground and waited for the concussions to begin. Joseph scooted over next to me, pressing his shoulder against mine. "I've decided to stay here in Manila."

"What?" I said, jerking my head around to meet his gaze. "That's crazy. You'll be taken prisoner."

"I'm not a combatant."

"That won't matter."

He took a deep breath. "They need doctors to stay with the patients that can't be moved, and I need to make sure mother is safe. If she goes with her family into the mountains, then I'll get out of the city too."

I heard the roar of planes cross over the area. Most likely they were headed for Cavite and Corregidor, but it was unnerving all the same. Joseph looked down at his hands as he rubbed them back and forth. I couldn't think of anything to say. I understood his reasons for staying, but I was afraid for him. I tilted my head to the side, and rested it against his broad shoulder. He was strong and intelligent. He could take care of himself.

When the bombing finally ceased, we climbed out of the trench and helped other patients out as well. Joseph helped Henry to a bench, and we all gazed at the sky for a few minutes, unsure it was really over. "Joseph has decided to stay," I said, hoping the others could talk him out of it, even if I couldn't.

"That's crazy," Henry said. "You should get out while the getting's good."

"I understand what I'm signing up for," Joseph said. "I'll stay here and look after the patients left behind. I'll be fine. God will protect me." There was a long silence, filled with all the words we couldn't or shouldn't say. Then Joseph smiled down at me. "Stay safe, all right? Thank you for all your help at the clinic, for being a shining light of God's love, and for making me smile every day."

He leaned over and kissed me on the cheek. Then he excused himself and left. I watched his departing back for a few moments, wishing I could change his mind. When I turned back at Henry and Janine, they both averted their eyes. Henry cleared his throat.

"Well, we better get you back to your room," Janine said to him.

"I reckon I'll see you ladies on Bataan, then," he said with a smile.

I tried to smile for his sake. "Don't try anything ridiculous while we're gone now. I'd hate to have to come back here and rescue you."

"No need to worry, little Rubes. I'll be as good as new before you even get to your new jungle hospital. You need to quit worrying about me and figure out how you're going to fend off the monkeys and lizards."

Janine shook her head. "I don't know how you two can take this so lightly. I just can't stand the thought of leaving you behind."

I took her hand and offered a gentle smile. "It's just our way, I guess. Try not to worry. God will keep us all in His hands, and we just have to trust in Him."

She didn't look too certain as she looked over at Henry. "I'll write to you, even though I don't know how you'll get my letters."

"You take care of each other," Henry said, winking at Janine. "You're my best girls."

She leaned in and kissed him, her face flushing red. He slid his hand around her neck and held her there for a moment longer, resting his forehead against hers. For a brief second, I saw real concern on his face. I dropped my gaze as they whispered to each other. Then I gave him a last hug before Janine helped him up to walk him to his bed.

It would be another night on the cot in the garden for me, and I had a sneaking suspicion I'd better get used to sleeping underneath the stars.

December 25, 1941

The next afternoon, Janine, Natalie and I gathered our things and boarded a truck that took us down to the docks. There we joined sixteen other army nurses on the *Mc E. Hyde*, which would ferry us across Manila Bay to the Bataan peninsula. Mrs. Fincher kept the girls moving along, and the ship shoved off just after sunset. Cavite and other installations in Manila burned bright enough that some of the girls read books or newspapers along the way. I joined some of them along the port rail, watching the shoreline grow farther and farther away.

"Do you think we'll make it across the bay before the Japs get us?" one of the girls muttered to no one in particular.

Janine shot me a nervous glance. I was certain everyone on board had already wondered that, but mentioning it out loud seemed to be asking for trouble. I decided to try to change the subject. "What do you think the hospital will be like where we're going?"

"I imagine it will be like most hospitals," Natalie said. "Though it's not nearly far enough away from the bombs. I thought for sure they'd be getting us out of here by now." She lifted a shaking hand to light her cigarette.

"Say," Janine said, pointing out over the bay. "Wonder why we're heading toward Corregidor? I thought we were going to Bataan."

I followed her finger, and sure enough, the front of the boat was pointed straight for the tadpole-shaped island that guarded the mouth of the bay. "Isn't there a hospital in the underground tunnels?" I said. "Maybe there's been a mistake. Maybe we've been assigned there."

We speculated on our destination for a while, Natalie telling us she'd heard the supplies on Corregidor could last three years. "I certainly hope we won't need them for that long," I said.

Sometime around ten, Mrs. Fincher called us all together near the back of the boat. "Now ladies, we'll be stopping at Corregidor for the evening in order for supplies to be loaded to take with us to the hospital on Bataan. So if you'll just make yourselves comfortable and get some rest, you'll be fresh for the trip tomorrow."

I had to admit I was disappointed. It sounded like Corregidor offered more in the way of protection and provisions. I leaned into Janine and whispered into her ear. "I hope for all our sakes this war is over soon. Surely there's a military convoy on the way with reinforcements? I mean, this is the United States Army, for goodness sake!"

"From your lips to God's ears," Janine replied.

After breakfast the following morning, I leaned onto the starboard rail and stared out across the bay at the dense Bataan jungle spreading up over the mountains. It didn't seem too far, perhaps within swimming distance, if necessary. That only gave me a small amount of comfort from my thoughts of a Japanese attack. I was keenly aware of the fact that the final leg of our trip across the bay would take place in broad daylight.

As the boat churned through the water, I pulled Matthew's letter out of my pocket and read it again. *He still loved me.* I held onto that grain of hope as I closed my eyes and prayed once again for his safety. But while I was deep in prayer, his letter was rudely snatched from my hands.

I opened my eyes to find Natalie shaking the paper at me. "What are you doing with a letter from *my* boyfriend?" she yelled.

My mind whirled. "What? Your boyfriend?"

"Yes! You...you said I could trust you. You said you'd stay away from him. I believed you!"

"Wait, Natalie," I said, trying to understand and calm her at the same time. Other ears were beginning to perk up. "There's nothing to get upset over."

"Nothing to get upset over?" she cried incredulously, holding the letter up in front of her. "He says he loves you!" She threw her hands up and shouted even louder. "You lied to me!"

Heat rushed up my cheeks. Three other girls peeked around the front of the boat at us and whispered to each other. I had no idea what to do. If Natalie snapped, and told everyone who I was, would I be arrested? Sent to a military prison to ride out the war? I couldn't fathom what might happen to me.

"Listen, I didn't lie. Matthew and I agreed to only focus on our jobs. I had no idea—"

"You must have done something, tricked him somehow with your lies."

"No—"

"That's all you do is lie, isn't it? Does he know who you really are? He mustn't if he thinks he loves you!"

I could hear murmuring behind me. I had to get this under control. I lowered my voice. "Natalie, I promise. I haven't answered the letter. I haven't encouraged Matthew in any way. I have stayed away from him, and I didn't lie to you. You *can* trust me. What do I have to do to show you?"

The fury in her eyes cooled, and she too looked around to see the curious faces watching us. She looked down at the letter, then back at me. Slowly, she ripped the letter to shreds and dropped the pieces over the side of the boat. Then she took a step toward me and lowered her voice as well. "I don't know what to believe. But you'd better stay away from Matthew."

She brushed past me and went to the back of the boat, where several girls pulled her aside. I had to wonder what she might say. I was going to have to figure out how to get away from Natalie as soon as possible, and in the meantime I'd have to do my best to steer clear of her altogether.

By the time we docked at a wharf on the peninsula, not a single girl on the boat had spoken to me. They had, however, been speaking *about* me. I caught several disapproving shakes of the head, and dozens of harsh stares. I waited with a few other girls to retrieve our suitcases. Most had left theirs behind to be unloaded with the supplies, but I couldn't take the chance of getting separated from my cherished memories, or Matthew's gun.

As I came out from the storage room and headed out to the gangway, I heard several girls gasp and scream. I jerked my head in the direction they were pointing, back across the bay. My heart raced to life when I saw planes bearing down on our position.

I yelled to the girls in front of me. "Let's move!"

We ran down the gangway, along the dock and onto the sand. Girls scrambled everywhere, diving into foxholes and behind trees or bushes. I scanned for a foxhole, but the few I could see were full of terrified, screaming bodies. I heard the zip of bullets hitting water.

Oh God, save me!

I spotted a large fallen tree, so I dropped my suitcase and ran across the sand, launching myself over it. I shoved my body up against the trunk amid a cacophony of screams, gunfire, and explosions. Within minutes the planes were gone, but I huddled against the tree, unable to straighten my shaking body. I concentrated on breathing until I felt steady again. Then, bracing my arms against the trunk, I pushed myself up to standing.

The first thing I noticed was the boat ablaze in the water, tilted to one side, and sinking. Slowly, the nurses came together in a huddle on the beach and watched it drop beneath the surface. "Did everyone make it off the boat all right?" Mrs. Fincher shouted. "Let's take a head count."

"All our things!" someone wailed.

"My clothes!"

"My mother's earrings!"

I walked over to my suitcase where I'd dropped it in the sand. A single bullet hole had pierced the top right-hand corner. Dread filled me as I peeked inside, checking Matthew's gun. The barrel had been badly dented, and would be of no more use to me now than a blunt instrument. It was disappointing for sure, but thankfully, Daddy's Bible and my dress had survived.

December 27, 1941

After spending the night at a staging area a few kilometers from the wharf, we loaded our weary bodies into another truck. Luckily, seventeen doctors and thirty medics and orderlies whose supplies were not sitting at the bottom of Manila Bay joined us. At least we wouldn't be showing up to the hospital completely empty-handed. Then we made the trek to what was called Jungle Hospital #2. I wasn't exactly sure where the first hospital was located, but one of the medics in our group said it was near Limay. "Won't last long there," he said. "The Japs are bombing all around that area."

As the trucks bounced along the road, I couldn't help but worry about Henry, Matthew, and Joseph. What if Henry was sent to the other hospital? What if Joseph was captured? What if I never saw Matthew again? My thoughts swirled in all different directions, and try as I might, I couldn't quiet my fears, even with prayer. My head knew God was in control and that I shouldn't fear for them, but my heart felt like lead in my chest, weighted down by what-if's.

The trucks pulled off the main road at kilometer 162.5 and headed straight into the jungle. The ride became even more jarring, and several times we had to stop for men to cut down dense underbrush ahead of us.

During one of our stops, I scooted over toward Janine and asked her how she was holding up.

"All right, I suppose," she said. "As long as I don't think on things too much. I just pray Henry's all right."

"I'm sure he is. The Japs don't know what they're getting into if they try to take him. He'll have them all charmed into surrendering within a day or two."

She let out a half laugh, half sob. "You're probably right there." She sniffled and swiped away a stray tear. "What about you? Are you doing all right? Some of the girls were talking about a fight between you and Natalie."

"Oh, that was nothing. Just a misunderstanding. There's much bigger things to worry over, I reckon. I keep telling myself that God holds us all in His hands. Our lives. Our deaths. Worrying don't add a thing to my life except trouble. But I can't seem to chase it away."

The truck lurched forward again, and we continued into the jungle for another hour, creeping along at a snail's pace. By the time we finally stopped for the last time and unloaded, it was nearly dinnertime. I climbed out of the back of the truck and stretched my aching legs and back, before joining Janine and the other nurses as they clumped together beside the trucks. I realized that every man in the small camp had stopped what he was doing, and was now gaping at us as if we were standing there as naked as the day we were born.

Most of them mumbled to each other, but a few were less discreet about their displeasure at seeing us. "Nurses? What in Sam Hill are we supposed to do with a bunch of women?"

"Well, if you don't know the answer to that one…"

Several of the men chuckled, and then they all went back to their business. Most of them kept glancing at us though, shaking their heads and commenting to their buddies.

"…shouldn't be allowed…"

"Can't fight a war with women around! They got no training for such things."

"Now I'm gonna be worried about protecting them instead of killing dirty Japs."

Mrs. Fincher stepped in front of us, thrusting her chest out. "Ladies, gather your things and follow me." She turned on her heels as well as any soldier, and we fell in behind her. Most of the girls kept their heads high as they walked through the makeshift camp. I couldn't help but notice that nothing in the camp looked remotely like a hospital. In fact, it didn't look like much of anything, except jungle.

We wound our way through dense trees, bushes, creepers, and clumps of bamboo until we reached the bank of a river. A group of seven or eight men were leaning on tree trunks, waiting for us. They didn't look too happy to see us either. One of them, a husky fellow with a cigarette hanging from his mouth came over to Mrs. Fincher and took up a wide stance, crossing his arms over his chest.

"We're here to help you girls set up. We got some cots and a bit of rope. But that's about it for now. We sent for the engineers, but they ain't showed up yet."

"We'll make do," Mrs. Fincher said. "And we appreciate the help." She turned to face us. "Girls, let's do what we can to get set up quickly so these men can get back to their jobs."

The husky one looked a bit surprised by her brisk commands. He turned back to his men, and they went to work setting up cots in rows of six. Then they strung up a few feet of rope between the cots and the vague path leading back to the main camp. The few of us who had made it off the boat with a suitcase or two hung up our clothing to provide a sense of privacy, though in reality there was none. The only thing I refused to hang up was my white dress with the roses. That, I kept stored away.

Lastly, the men dug three holes in the ground for latrines. I could see by the looks on the girls' faces that we all had the same idea. *Mortifying.*

As the men were finishing up, I happened to be putting my things on a cot near a tall, lanky fellow who was tying a rope around a palm tree. He was filthy from head to toe, just like the rest of us, and his scraggly beard must have itched him, 'cause he kept scratching at it.

"Is there anything else we can do to help?" I asked.

He pulled the top tight before turning to look at me. "Just stay out the way as much as you can, I reckon."

"You know, we don't actually *want* to be a burden. We just want to serve as best we can. Just like the rest of you."

His gruff frown eased a bit. "Well, there ain't nothing to be done yet, anyhow. There ain't a single tool in the whole camp. Whoever picked this place out forgot to tell the engineers or the supply depot. Looks like we'll be building a hospital with our bare hands."

"God will provide. That's what my mother would say, anyway."

He shook his head and chuckled. "Lady, not even God can find this place. We're on our own."

The men wished us well and headed back through the trees. I went with Janine and the rest of the nurses to the river, hoping it was deep enough to wash up. We found a beautiful little spot with large rocks that provided a bit of a pool. Vines and shrubs hung around the river, giving us a modest amount of seclusion. At that point, I didn't care much about modesty any longer, and it seemed, neither did the other girls.

We removed the dingy coveralls, stripping down to our underwear, and waded into the cool, rolling water. I eased across the rocks and found a spot a few feet deep where I could lower myself almost completely under the water. I leaned back against a rock and closed my eyes, letting my thoughts wander back to the creek where I'd played with Henry as a little girl.

Lord, please keep Henry safe. I know he's in Your hands. If it's Your will, please bring him here and not to the other hospital. Please keep Joseph safe in Manila. And please be with Matthew, wherever he might be. I pray you'll watch over him, and that someday, somehow, You'll heal his broken heart. Please for-

give me for my fear and doubt. Forgive me for hiding for so long, and for not trusting in You. I promise I'll do everything I can to make things right. Just...please...send your Spirit....speak to me again. I ache to hear Your voice. And lastly, Lord, I pray you'll bring peace to Natalie's heart. Help her to see the truth.

I kept my eyes closed, hoping for the still, quiet whisper that filled my thoughts when I was younger. But all I heard was the chattering of the other girls. My chest grew heavy, and I did my best not to cry. Why wouldn't God speak to me anymore? Why couldn't He forgive me?

I opened my eyes and saw Natalie talking in hushed tones to three other nurses around her. They all looked over at me, and then went back to talking. I sat up and began rinsing my face and body, doing my best to ignore the dread creeping into my heart. I scrubbed away the dirt and grime of the past few days. Whether God would speak to me or not, I'd have to do everything I could to keep Natalie quiet. Even if that young man had been right, and I *was* completely on my own.

CHAPTER NINE

Matthew

December 27, 1941

I stood on the western bank of the creek that snaked along beside our camp at Cabcaben, looking through a break in the dense mangrove trees at the sky across the bay turning various shades of pink. If I were standing there at any other time, even just a few weeks before, it would have been a beautiful sight. But the once pristine skyline I'd observed on the *President Coolidge* as it had sailed into Manila Bay was now black with smoke. The Japanese continued to bomb it to pieces every day. I'd heard from a first lieutenant in communications that the nurses were being evacuated to various jungle hospitals on Bataan and Corregidor, and I prayed with all my heart that Ruby had been evacuated with them.

Of course, she'd never been one to do anything the way I thought she should. She'd have some valiant reason to stay behind no doubt, some poor soul who needed saving. Perhaps if I hadn't been so harsh with her, or if I had tried harder to convince her to go into hiding... I had to chuckle to myself before the thought took hold. She wouldn't have done what I wanted her to do, no matter the circumstances. If I'd learned any-thing from my experiences with Ruby, it was that my best course of action was to pray. So I bowed my head, closed my eyes, and searched for God's presence in the turmoil and doubt surrounding me.

Lord, I know You are with me every second of every day, just as You've been with Ruby all this time. Keep her safe. Help me to forgive. Give me peace as I work to save the lives of as many of my brothers as I can. Give me courage to face the enemy when the time comes. And may I honor You with my life, or my death, whatever Your path may be.

I opened my eyes and soaked up the peace that came over me. When I felt ready, I headed across the stream and up the path to the camp I shared with members of the Navy engineers, other army engineers, a few pilots who'd lost their planes in the bombings at Clark Field, and a communications unit who'd set up a station near the airfield we were building for the fighter planes and bombers that were expected to land soon all over the Bataan peninsula.

I found Doug seated on a large rock outside our tent. He puffed on a cigarette and stared off into the jungle. "You all right?" I asked.

"Oh sure," he said. "Just watching a monkey run off with my lighter. I'm thinking about shooting him when he comes back around." He peered up at me. "You get things straightened out with God today?"

"I reckon."

"So is He gonna get us some reinforcements up here and wrap up this war in a few days?"

"I don't rightly know. He don't exactly listen to my suggestions about things."

He pushed himself up, groaning with the effort. "Well, let's head over to the communications station and ask 'em if they know anything. I'm sure they don't, but it'll give me something to complain about."

We made our way along the path that wound down toward the main road where the radio had been set up. A fellow by the name of Ron Gunner was manning the radio. He was another displaced pilot who'd been conscripted into a job he'd never been trained for. But like most everyone else, he was picking it up fast. Doug and I found Ron sitting under a group of mango trees, listening intently to the radio.

"What's the news?" Doug asked.

Ron held up a finger and leaned in closer to the speaker. I couldn't make out a darn thing. Just sounded like waves of static. But he seemed to hear something exciting, as his bushy eyebrows shot up like a rocket. "Some guys over at Navy headquarters are saying there's a convoy heading this way. I've been trying to get details."

"I wouldn't hold my breath," I said. "There's been a convoy on the way for over a week now."

Ron pulled his headset off his ears. "I'm just telling you what I heard."

"All I know," Doug said, "is that MacArthur better get this mess organized and figured out soon. I'm so hungry I could eat a carabao all by myself. The filthy animals."

Ron laughed and shook a cigarette from the pack he'd pulled out of his pocket. He placed it on his lips and then offered the pack to me. I waved him off. "No thanks."

"You don't smoke?" He looked downright shocked. "Well, I don't think I ever met a soldier that didn't smoke."

I tapped my chest. "Well, now you have. T.B. when I was in high school. Nasty stuff."

Ron grunted and offered a cigarette to Doug, then pocketed the pack and whipped out a lighter. "Say, you boys heading over to the hospital nearby? I heard they're asking for engineers to help out for a couple of days."

"We're fixing up the revetments over by the airstrip," Doug answered.

"You say it's a hospital?" I asked.

He nodded. "Got a bunch of doctors and nurses out there with no actual hospital put together yet. There's a crew of Navy and Army engineers heading over there at first light."

"You know where it is?" I asked.

"Sure! It's only a couple of kilometers from here."

I nodded at Doug. "We're volunteering to go. I need to see if Ruby's there."

Doug frowned but didn't protest. I hadn't said much about Ruby, but I'd made it clear I felt responsible for her. "I reckon we ought to go find the Captain and see about joining up with 'em," he said.

We both reached down and shook Ron's hand before heading back into the jungle. I couldn't help but get my hopes up, even though I knew it was a long shot. I kept up a silent string of prayers all the way back to base camp, hoping I'd be able to find Ruby. I had to make things right with her. I had no idea what that meant for us. Still, a man could hope, and in this situation, it was about *all* a man could do.

December 28, 1941

The next day Doug and I joined three trucks of engineers and rode two kilometers along the coastal road to what was supposed to be the location of a hospital. But it would've barely qualified as a rudimentary camp. The trucks themselves hardly made it through the heavy jungle foliage. Once we arrived at the campsite and unloaded, I immediately scanned the groups of tents for the nurses. But I couldn't see any females at all.

"This is going to be a hospital?" Doug asked.

I took in the scant number of small tents with groups of doctors, medics, and orderlies seated together on the ground. They were eating from mess kits, which meant they hadn't even set up a kitchen yet. I knew food would be a top priority. "Looks like we'll be starting from scratch."

As the rest of the engineers unloaded the tools and equipment we'd brought, I stepped over to a group of scraggly medics nearby just finishing up their breakfast. "Any of you fellas know where the nurses are?"

Every one of them chuckled. "You just got here! Already looking for a good time?"

My face heated up, causing more laughter. He pointed with his fork. "I believe they set up quarters over by the river yesterday. Shouldn't be too far to walk."

I thanked him and rejoined Doug, who was listening to Captain Prescott get an earful of information from a haggard-looking group of doctors. Prescott nodded and frowned, holding up his hands to silence the men. "All right, all right. I can see for myself there's a load of work to be done right away. Let's get a preliminary plan in place and get moving. This place'll be overrun with patients before you know it." He turned to face the group of engineers behind him. "Men, let's get the equipment in order immediately. I want to have a meeting with the entire camp— doctors, nurses, staff, everyone—at oh nine hundred." He pulled a gold watch from his breast pocket. "That's in twenty minutes."

I took the opportunity to slide away and search for Ruby, heading in the direction the man had pointed earlier and literally stumbling onto a path that snaked through vines, creepers, and bamboo. After a few minutes of walking, I heard the splashing of water, and the higher pitch of female voices. Up ahead of me was a string of women's clothing blocking off a section of jungle. I noticed several nightgowns among the clothing, and feeling uneasy, I realized I was most likely intruding into their personal space.

I cleared my throat and called out, "Excuse me, ladies?"

The chatter stopped, and six female faces appeared over the top of the skimpy clothing barrier. When they saw me, several of them smiled.

"My goodness, I wasn't expecting company."

"Better liven up, girls. We got a fella calling."

"Why, I haven't even combed out my hair properly!"

I smiled back at them and shoved my hands in my pockets. "I'm look- ing for a friend of mine. You ladies wouldn't happen to know anyone by the name Grace Miller, now would you?"

Another face popped up. It was Natalie, and my stomach knotted. "Matthew? Is that you?" she said.

Her face disappeared, and she hurried around the barrier. The joy on her face only increased my anxiety. I did my best to hide it. "Why, Natalie! I had no idea you'd be here. What a pleasant surprise."

She threw her arms around my neck, so I hugged her in return. "I was so worried about you!" she said. "I thought for sure they sent you off somewhere dangerous, and I might never see you again. Are you here to help with the hospital?"

"Yes. I came with some other engineers to get things set up." I stole a quick glance around and didn't see Ruby. But I did notice several pairs of eyes on us from around the barrier. "Listen, can we talk for just a minute? Somewhere a little more...um, private?"

She looked back at the other girls and giggled. "Excuse us, ladies. We need to be *alone*."

We walked several feet away into the brush and stopped behind some large palm leaves. I knew this wasn't going to be fun, but I needed to be honest with her. I'd avoided going back to Stotsenburg in the hopes that she'd forget about me as time wore on. But I could see from the expression on her face she was expecting much more.

When we stopped walking, she slid up against me and kissed me before I could say a word. I did my best to be polite and let her finish. Then I pulled her shoulders back and forced a smile. "I, uh, wasn't expecting to see you."

Her expression fell. "Well, you seem almost disappointed."

"Listen, I need to be honest with you. I don't think we're...well, wanting the same things. I wasn't looking for anything serious, and when I met you, I had no idea...I mean, Ru—Grace and I have this history, and I had no idea she was here. And I need to get things straightened out with her before I can...I mean, I thought she was dead. I never..."

My garbled explanation was going terribly; I could tell from the tears welling up in her eyes. But to Natalie's credit, she seemed to be making the effort to take the news well. "I understand," she said. "You need time to properly end things with Grace. You never closed the book with her, and you don't want to start anything new until you've done so."

I ran my hand through my hair and rubbed the back of my neck, trying to think of a better way of saying this. "Sort of," was all I could manage. "I just…is Grace here?"

"Sure," she said. "But I haven't seen her this morning."

"There's a meeting for the whole camp starting in a few minutes. I really wanted to talk to her beforehand. Looks like it'll have to wait."

"Maybe she's already there," Natalie said. "I'll walk with you."

I paused, knowing I should try one last time to make sure she understood. "Natalie, I hope you know I never meant to lead you on or anything. I really do like you—"

"Hey, I understand," she said. "Everything's crazy right now. I don't know how anyone's thinking about anything but surviving at this point. You get things straightened out with Grace. I'll be here when you're ready." Her gaze was steady and I could only hope she'd taken in what I'd said.

We walked back to the path, where other nurses were making their way to camp. I kept an eye out for Ruby as we walked, but I didn't see her. Natalie walked beside me, filling me in on their trip across the bay. I only half listened, until she got to the part where their boat was bombed. I stopped and stared at her in shock.

"Did everyone make it off the boat all right?" I asked.

"Oh yes. We all just made it into foxholes. But most of our belongings went down with the ship. I'm afraid I don't even have a dress to wear, or my letters from my family, or…anything."

Her voice cracked, and I instinctively put an arm over her shoulder. "I'm so sorry. But I'm sure everything will be all right soon."

"I don't think it will." Tears slipped down her cheeks, and she swiped them away. "I think…we're all going to die out here."

"Come on," I said, pulling her into a hug. "Don't think that way. We have to stay positive."

As I hugged her, I glanced around over the top of her head, and finally I saw Ruby. She walked out of the brush from the same path Natalie and I had just come from. She must've been only a short distance behind us. She stopped when she saw me, a flash of relief coming over her face.

I let go of Natalie. "I'm sorry, but I just saw Grace. I really do need to speak with her."

Natalie sniffed and nodded. I started toward Ruby, but already her expression had changed. As I neared, I realized she was looking past me, back at Natalie, and her eyes told me everything. I'd already hurt her, and I hadn't said a word.

**

"I'm so glad you're here," I started, but before I could get anything else out, Captain Prescott called everyone to order. I lowered my voice to a whisper. "I really need to talk to you."

Ruby crossed her arms and turned to her left to face Captain Prescott. "Not now," she whispered.

"I need to apologize. I shouldn't have acted the way I did back at Fort Stotsenburg."

She didn't say anything, just stood there staring at Captain Prescott as he commended the leaders for picking a spot so well hidden. I did my best to listen to him as well.

"It's important for everyone to remember that we're all in this together," he said. "Each and every one of you will be called upon to perform duties you may not be familiar with or trained in. But we must do our best to support one another and to learn from those with experience. There's no telling how long this hospital may be necessary, so we will approach it from a standpoint of providing what's needed at the present time, with preparation for the near future to the best of our ability."

I leaned toward Ruby and whispered, "Are you angry with me?"

She shot me a hard look, leaving no doubt things were not settled between us. "I'm trying to listen."

"I'm trying to apologize."

"Fine. Apology accepted. Now hush."

I turned my attention back to Captain Prescott as he made it clear that the first order of business would be to establish a passable road so that supplies, equipment, and food could be brought into camp immediately. A team was assigned to the bulldozer we'd brought with us from Cabcaben, along with a group of Filipino men brandishing long bolos.

"Did you get my letter?" I tried again.

She nodded.

"And?" I couldn't believe she was being so difficult.

She sighed and turned a stony expression toward me. "I got it. Thank you."

"That's all you have to say?" It was becoming increasingly difficult to keep my voice at a whisper.

"Now is *not* the time for this." Her eyes darted past me again in the direction of where I'd left Natalie. And it hit me that she'd probably seen us hugging. Combined with the kiss she'd most likely seen at Stotsenburg, it was no wonder she was angry. I reached for her elbow, but at my touch, she took a step away from me. Frustration surged through me. I had no choice but to direct my attention back to Captain Prescott.

"The second order of business will be to secure the supplies and food necessary to sustain the staff as well as the flow of patients that will undoubtedly be streaming into the hospital." Prescott pointed to a man standing to his right, whom I hadn't noticed previously. "Sergeant McMillan here is the supply officer, and he'll be leading a small team of volunteers back into Manila today to secure as many supplies as possible before the Japanese are able to confiscate everything." He narrowed his eyes as he looked around the camp. "Any volunteers?"

A few hands went up. I glanced at Ruby again, still refusing to acknowledge my existence. What was going on with her? I'd never known her to hold a grudge with such coldness toward me. Even when she hadn't trusted me, she'd always been kind.

Prescott was still searching the camp for volunteers, so I stuck my hand in the air. He nodded as he pointed at me. "All right then, Lieutenant Doyle."

This time, Ruby whirled round to face me. "What are you doing?"

I dropped my hand, satisfied I at last had her attention. "So now you want to talk to me?"

She frowned, and again she glanced over at Natalie. "Is that why you volunteered? To get my attention? That would be just about the dumbest thing you've ever done, Matthew Doyle. And that's saying a lot."

She turned away from me again, pretending to listen to the next item Prescott was covering. But I could tell she was upset. Her whole body was rigid. I decided to wait until the meeting was over, and maybe then I could try again. Prescott concluded his remarks with the third item of importance for the day: setting up a mess area. My stomach couldn't agree more. A delivery of supplies and food was expected from the Medical Depot at any time, and he asked if anyone had any cooking experience. A few volunteers raised their hands and were swiftly put in charge. Their faces gave away their surprise, prompting another reminder of every man's duty to serve the best he could. Then he turned to the group of nurses, most of whom were gathered off to my right.

"Ladies, I believe this would be an area where your skills would be most appreciated," Prescott said with a smile.

The girls didn't betray the anger I was sure flashed through most, if not all, of them. A few of them lifted their chins in defiance at the suggestion they would best serve in the kitchen, but that was the extent. Even after a male voice nearby muttered loud enough for everyone to hear, "Ain't having no dames fooling around with my mess hall."

Prescott ended his remarks with the announcement that mess would be served at sixteen-thirty, and to expect further instructions from our staff sergeants and other leaders later in the day. Then we were dismissed to begin our duties.

Ruby turned to leave without a word, so I marched to catch up with her. "What is going on with you?" I demanded.

"I don't know what you mean." She continued moving quickly toward the area where the men put in charge of mess were gathering.

"You know exactly what I mean. I'm trying to apologize and make things right with you. And all you can manage is to give me the cold shoulder. This isn't like you."

"Maybe you don't know me anymore."

"That's apparent."

We reached the group, so she finally stopped and faced me. "Look. I appreciate the apology. And I understand why you were angry. But as you can see, there are much bigger things going on around here besides you and me." She darted a glance at the other nurses approaching. "Can't this wait?"

"Sure," I said with as much sarcasm as I could. "I'll just catch up with you later."

I took a few steps away before she called my name. When I turned around, I almost thought I saw genuine concern in her face. "Please be careful," she said.

Then without another word she turned to a nurse who came up beside her and began talking. So that was it. All I'd get before heading out on a dangerous mission was *be careful* as an afterthought. How could she have changed so much? How could she have so little regard for me?

I stomped away and found my group, trying to shut out thoughts of Ruby. I noticed Doug had joined the circle and tried to smile at him. "Didn't see you volunteer," I said.

"Wouldn't miss out on this fun, especially if you're going." He nodded in the direction I'd come from. "You talk to your girl?"

"I guess you could say that."

"Worried about ya going, huh?" He winked as if the whole thing were funny.

Right then, Sergeant McMillan began going over the plans for getting into the city. I had to push aside my confusion over Ruby. Whatever was bothering her would have to be worked out later. I might not be experienced with combat, but even I knew the situation would be made even more dangerous if I was distracted.

***

The road along the coast was jammed with trucks, soldiers, civilians, and carts loaded down with supplies, all heading in the opposite direction from us. It took forever to move even one kilometer. The plan was to arrive in Manila early enough to beat the midday bombing raid, but by the time we reached the edges of the city, I could see two large V formations of bombers approaching from the north and west.

The truck pulled over in what was barely more than a shantytown, filled mostly with dilapidated shacks leaning into each other as if they too were seeking shelter from the bombs. McMillan came around behind the truck and ordered us all out.

"Find a trench and cover your heads best you can!" he yelled.

We scrambled in several directions as bombs hit the ground in the distance. I ran down a street, realizing the explosions were rapidly approaching me. As one hit a few streets over, my knees buckled, and I stumbled several feet before tripping over a large mound of clothing. I hit the dirt and rolled, coming to my feet again. Looking back at where I'd fallen, I could see it wasn't a pile of clothes I'd tripped over, but a corpse. Well, half of one anyway. The lower extremities were missing, with entrails dragging in the dust. I nearly retched, but another concussion knocked me over. They were nearly on top of me.

I pushed myself up and ran around the last house on the street. I had no idea where Doug was, or anyone else for that matter. But I finally spotted a trench behind the house I'd just rounded. So I ran and dove into it, crashing into bodies already inside. There were screams, and hands grabbed me. A fist punched me in the gut. I sucked in a breath and doubled over.

Voices above me argued in Tagalog. Then large hands grabbed my shoulders and righted me. I looked into four sets of dark, frightened eyes staring back at me as if I were the one attacking them. I put my hands up and yelled over the thunderous crash of another bomb.

"I'm sorry! I don't mean any harm!"

Across from me, two young Filipino girls, who couldn't be more than twelve or thirteen, bent over with their hands clasped tightly against their ears. I took a step backward until my back rested against the dirt wall behind me, and I too did my best to shut out the chaos of the bombs.

When it was finally over, and the planes were completely gone, I climbed out of the trench and reached a hand down to help the others out. The small older man, who I assumed had been the one to punch me, gripped my hand and pulled himself out. Then we both reached down to pull out the girls and their mother.

We stood there for an awkward moment staring at each other, before the father stuck out his hand. "Sorry," he said. "Thought you might be Japanese."

I shook his hand and smiled, rubbing my stomach where it still felt a bit nauseous. I thought it was a stretch to confuse me with a Japanese soldier, but I decided not to push it. Fear did things to the mind. "It's all right. I'm sure I startled you."

His eyes darted to the girls, who were dusting off their tattered dresses, though I didn't think it was doing much good. His shoulders drooped, and he took a step toward me and lowered his voice. "You...have money? If you like..."

His voice trailed off, and he glanced again at the girls. An uneasy feeling swelled in my gut, and it had nothing to do with the aftereffects of the punch. I shook my head. "No, no."

"You pick whichever you like. A few pesos."

I couldn't bring myself to look at the girls again. I felt into my pockets and found a few coins. I placed them in the man's hand, closing mine around his. Then I looked him in the eyes. "You have beautiful girls. Keep them safe."

His eyes welled up, and the lines around his mouth deepened with his frown. "I have nothing else to give."

"Then give me your prayers, and that will be plenty."

I nodded to the girls' mother and headed back the way I'd come. The truck was just where we'd left it, and the men in our group were already climbing inside. Doug was visibly relieved to see me. "Thank God! I lost track of you there. Where'd you go?"

"I jumped onto a nice Filipino family in a trench. Scared the daylights out of all of us."

Slowly the truck made its way through the empty streets of Manila. Each time I saw a mangled corpse lying by the roadside, I wondered why no one had come along to claim it and bury the body. As we passed the charred remains of a church, I noticed a sign hanging on what was left of the gate.

BE CALM. STAY HOME. YOU ARE AS SAFE THERE AS ANYWHERE.

That sign stuck with me. Rather than making people feel safe, it was a cold reminder that there was no place of safety. No hiding from the bombs that fell daily. All anyone could do was pray for mercy. So as we made the final turn into Sternberg Hospital, that was exactly what I did. I prayed for mercy.

When the truck came to a stop, we hopped out and received a brief reminder of the supplies and equipment we were to search for inside.

McMillan kept his remarks short and to the point, reminding us several times to grab every ounce of quinine and iodine we could find. Then we divided into four groups of three men, and went about scouring the hospital.

The entire building was empty; deserted halls leading to vacated rooms. I searched for supply closets, gathering what I could into boxes and transporting it out to the waiting truck. On my third trip out, there was another truck waiting. By the sixth trip, there were two more trucks, four in total. One of the groups of three was sent over to a supply depot to load up food.

We worked quickly, barely speaking. The eerie silence of the hospital only intensified my suspicions that the Japanese were close at hand. All I wanted to do was find what we needed and get out of there as quickly as possible. As I raided another supply closet, I heard an incredulous voice behind me.

"What in God's name are you doing?"

I whipped around to find a tall doctor blocking the doorway with his arms folded over his chest. He wore no insignia, so he couldn't be military. He stared down on me through his glasses like I was stealing food from starving children.

"I'm here with a group of doctors and staff from one of the jungle hospitals being set up. We're in need of supplies." It struck me that this man might very well be pilfering supplies himself. "Just who might you be?"

He stepped back from the doorway and lowered his arms. "I'm a local doctor. Name's Joseph Grant. I've been helping out around here the past few days."

"Are you an American?"

He nodded. "Missionary."

"You look...I thought you might be Filipino." I'd never seen a Filipino who was as tall as myself.

"That too. It's a long story."

I definitely didn't have time for long stories. "Look, I have to get these supplies loaded. Mind giving me a hand?"

He held out his arms and I threw a couple of boxes on them before leading him out to the waiting trucks. Once the supplies were loaded, I stuck out my hand. "Thanks for the help. You want to come with us? We're going to need more doctors, I'm sure."

Just at that moment, an explosion a few miles away caused me to nearly jump out of my skin. I ducked and covered my head till I noticed Joseph chuckling. I stood again and asked what was so funny.

"It's just the army blowing up ammunition and secret documents and such. I saw them getting ready to do it a while ago."

"Why are they blowing up perfectly good ammunition?"

"To keep it out of the hands of the Japs, I suppose. I hear they'll be here at any moment. You boys better get moving."

The other trucks were about full, and the fourth truck had arrived from the depot stuffed full of canned food. "Come on," I said. "Come with us. You don't want to be here when the Japs overrun this place. They'll never believe someone with your height is Filipino."

He glanced around and shrugged. "I might just take you up on that. Nothing more I can do here. Can't be any more dangerous in the jungle."

"Then it's settled. You're coming with us."

CHAPTER TEN

Ruby

December 28, 1941

By mid-afternoon we'd managed to cobble together a workable mess area, although we had no stove as of yet to cook anything. A group of men made a run to the Bataan depot and brought back some tables and chairs. It wouldn't be enough, but at least it was a start. The Filipinos made quick work of the underbrush, creating a small clearing with adequate cover beneath the trees for us to set up.

Trucks were coming in and out of the area all day, and every time a new one showed up, I ran to see if it was Matthew returning from Manila. Each time it wasn't, my heart grew a little heavier with worry. I tried not to think about the danger he was facing, instead focusing on the tasks at hand. But it proved difficult. I found myself mumbling prayers throughout the day.

I felt just awful about treating him so coolly that morning, but Natalie had been watching us the entire time, and I didn't dare risk upsetting her again. It was best for now to keep my distance.

As I was setting up the last few chairs, a truck arrived with supplies and equipment from Corregidor, along with a stove. Sam Lewis, a first lieutenant who'd done some cooking during his training back in the

States, was put in charge of mess, and he eyed the stove with skepticism. "Now, I don't have a great deal of experience, but I do know one gasoline range isn't going to cook enough food to feed the personnel we got here, much less the patients once they start arriving."

I was standing just behind Sam, watching as a wiry soldier hooked up the stove. I'd had about enough of his negative attitude and his comments about how inadequate everything was. "Come on, Sam. Have faith. If God could feed five thousand men with only a few fish and some loaves of bread, surely He can feed a few hundred."

Sam turned around, his black brow pushed down into a frustrated glare. "That's all well and good for Sunday school, but this is war. You ever been starved half to death?"

"Yes," I said. "As a matter of fact I have. And I've seen first-hand how God provides in times of trouble."

His eyes widened a bit. "Well, I suppose we'll find out soon enough. Gotta have mess ready in a couple of hours. I don't suppose you know how to make biscuits for several hundred people?"

I wasn't about to lose face, so I tipped up my chin. "I can certainly handle it."

"Great! Then you and the ladies get busy with biscuits and tea while I throw together a slumgullion stew. We'll be a regular five star establishment before we know it!" He went over to a pile of equipment and began tossing around large pots. Sam's sarcastic tone still irked, but I did my best to ignore it.

I turned to Janine and a couple of other girls standing beside me. "Mind helping me with the biscuits?"

Janine shrugged. "Might as well. We'll get fussed at no matter what we do anyway. Especially by Mr. Grumpy Pants over there."

She nodded her head toward Sam, who was now loudly complaining about the lack of food available to him. I turned back to Janine and asked, "What in the world is slumgullion stew?"

She wrinkled her nose. "It's just a stew thrown together with whatever's available. I imagine it'll have a bit of canned meat, rice, some canned vegetables if we're lucky."

Natalie scrunched up her nose as well. "Sounds perfectly awful."

The other nurses agreed, but we decided to make the best of it, since the men would expect us to complain. We set to work gathering all the ingredients we needed. I thought back over Mother's recipe for biscuits, did some math in my head, and tried to get the amounts right. As we mixed up the dough, each girl seemed to feel compelled to tell me how her mother had made biscuits, how this one ingredient or that way of kneading made all the difference in the world. We were a little low on lard, and it was hard to manage the large amount of dough we were working with. The first batch of biscuits came out hard as rocks.

Sam took a break from his stew to taste one and frowned as soon as it was in his mouth. "Thought you said you knew how to make biscuits."

"I do!" I said. "Just haven't figured out how to make a large batch. I'll get the next one right."

"Don't matter much to these fellas anyhow," he said, shaking his head. "They're so hungry they won't notice. Don't worry yourself over getting 'em perfect. Just get 'em done."

We finally got the process down well enough to turn out enough biscuits for the camp that were just a bit softer than rocks. They weren't anywhere close to the light, buttery bread my mother had made, but I didn't hear too many complaints.

While we were serving the staff in two shifts, since there wasn't enough room for everyone at once, another convoy of trucks rolled up. I stepped where I could see the men unloading, relieved when Matthew jumped down from the back of one of them. All I wanted to do was run to his arms, but I held my ground. Instead, it was Natalie who greeted him.

He smiled down at her, that same smile that had done me in so long ago. My stomach knotted watching him hug her. When she stepped back, he scanned the camp until he found me. I waved, and decided welcoming him back couldn't be enough to raise Natalie's ire.

As I walked toward the trucks, another familiar face rounded the end of the truck. "Joseph!" I yelled. Then I did break into a run.

"Grace!" he exclaimed with a huge grin. "I was hoping to find you here."

I threw my arms around his neck, thinking of nothing else but how glad I was that he wasn't in the hands of the Japanese. "I'm so glad you're all right."

He held me close and kissed the top of my head before letting go. I stepped back and looked over at Matthew, whose face was frozen in a deep scowl. In fact, his whole body was rigid as he regarded Joseph with both anger and curiosity. Beside him, Natalie looked on with an expression of pure enjoyment.

I instinctively put another step between Joseph and myself. "Matthew, this is Joseph Grant from Manila. We—"

"Yes, we've met," Matthew said, coming over to us with Natalie still in tow. "But how do you two know each other?" His eyes moved from me to Joseph, and then back to me.

"I worked as a nurse in Joseph's clinic. He's a missionary, and we went to the same church." Then I looked up at Joseph. "How do you and Matthew know each other?"

Joseph smiled awkwardly. "I caught him raiding a supply closet at the hospital and thought he was stealing. Once we got everything straightened out, I volunteered to help."

"But I thought you were going to stay in Manila and care for your mother?"

"She went into the mountains with her family, and I stayed behind to help transfer patients."

"Do you know what happened to Henry?" I asked, forgetting the awkward tension for a moment. "Was he still there?"

Joseph put a reassuring hand on my shoulder. "He was evacuated just this morning."

As soon as Joseph touched me, I could sense Matthew stiffen. I did my best to keep things light and friendly, but my stomach tightened.

"Joseph, this is Matthew. He's…he's the one I told you about. We've been friends since I was a girl."

"Well, *Grace*," Matthew said. "We've been a little bit more than friends."

He shot a strained smile down at me. I took a quick glance at Natalie, who slipped a possessive hand around Matthew's arm. He didn't seem to notice. Behind me, I heard a loud clanging and Sam calling for the second shift of diners. I was relieved to have a distraction. "You boys hungry? I hear we're having slumgullion stew. Sounds like an adventure for your taste buds!"

Matthew gave Joseph another hard look before nodding his head. "I'm famished."

Matthew

January 5, 1942

Over the next few days, everyone in the camp worked from sunrise to sunset to get the hospital in working order. There was no time, or energy for that matter, for much conversation, so I decided to focus my efforts on my work rather than looking for opportunities to speak with Ruby alone. Besides, she was *never* alone. She ate with the nurses, sometimes that guy, Joseph, and she worked tirelessly. Actually, it was a small comfort to realize that at least that much remained the same. Ruby worked harder and with more stamina than anyone I'd ever known.

The fact was, just about everyone in the camp was working themselves to the bone. And the accomplishment was nothing short of a miracle. Within a few days, the dense jungle location had been transformed into a hospital with roads, a mess area, supplies, and transportation for patients. We'd created a ward with a few hundred beds, covered by a canopy of palm leaves, vines, and creepers as perfect camoflauge. Head-quarters were established, along with general quarters for personnel, and I had worked with other engineers to create a water filtration sys-tem using the Real River, providing the entire camp with clean water. In fact, we were able to divert the water in such a way as to create an island effect for the nurses' quarters, giving them even more privacy.

We built a fully functioning operating room, wired and camouflaged so surgeries could be performed while under blackout. It was almost immediately expanded. And a particularly brave young medical officer had made a daring run to Fort Stotsenburg to retrieve a field sterilizer, without which the doctors wouldn't have been able to perform even the most basic surgeries. He'd returned in a mad dash just ahead of the ap-proaching Japanese. All around me was the very evidence that kept my hopes high we would eventually win the war. Americans didn't know how to lose.

But all of this, combined with our rations being cut in half, started to take its toll. And the frustration of watching Ruby, day after day, keep her distance from me, barely looking at me, was maddening. I tried to tell myself it was just because she was working so hard, but even that didn't hold water. She had time to chat with Joseph.

I had decided I couldn't stand that guy. The day after he arrived, some Filipinos from a nearby village came to offer some help. Joseph, who naturally spoke their language, was able to communicate the needs of the hospital quite well. That same day, and all the days following, a multitude of Filipinos built furniture and other essentials out of bamboo that surrounded the camp. The beds, tables, chairs, medicine cabinets, even the flooring in the operating rooms were made from bamboo. Jo-seph was a hero. Of course he was.

A week after arriving, most of the engineers were heading back to Cabcaben and other airfields nearby, with a few staying at the hospital to help with more minor construction tasks that remained. I'd had about enough of being mostly ignored by Ruby, and hounded by Natalie, so I decided to join the fellas returning to their posts. The trucks were scheduled to pull out shortly after mess, and I debated with myself on whether to attempt once more to figure out what was going on with Ruby. After going back and forth on the matter, I decided it was worth one last shot.

After getting my food, I found her seated near a group of nurses, but still a few chairs away. She looked up at me as I stood across the table from her, and I saw how deep her weariness went. She gazed past me with bloodshot eyes that didn't seem to register who I was.

"Can I join you for a few minutes?" I asked.

She nodded and chewed a forkful of rice. I slid into the chair across from her, eager to finally speak with her, but suddenly losing all train of thought as soon as I took a couple of bites of food. Hunger seized my body. I wolfed down the rice and canned meat, and shoved a biscuit down so fast I didn't even taste it. Once I finally came up for air, I saw her plate was empty as well.

I leaned onto my elbows toward her. "Ruby, I don't understand what's going on with you. The only thing I can figure is that you never wanted me to know you were alive, and you wanted to move on with your life without me in it, and somehow I've messed up your plans. Is that it?"

She glanced around, almost like she was afraid someone was watching her. "No, that's...that's not it at all. I'm just so tired all the time. And there's so much to be done. I can't think about you and me right now, okay?"

"But you can think clear enough to speak with Joseph?"

"What? No, you don't understand."

"Then make me understand."

Another glance around. "I can't."

"Okay, I *know* something is wrong. And it's got nothing to do with being tired. Why do you seem so nervous when we talk?"

She rested her forehead in her hands, staring down at the table for a long moment. When she looked back up at me, I could see she was struggling with a truth she didn't want to tell. I knew that look on her face. I'd seen it over and over after she'd been arrested, until she'd finally told me the truth about Chester's death. Ruby was the worst liar in the world. I had no idea what she was keeping from me, but I saw it was tearing her up inside.

I reached across the table and took her forearm in my hand. "Hey, listen. You don't have to explain anything to me right now. I know you're tired. I know something is eating at you. But I've also learned that you won't tell me nothing till you're good and ready. So I won't push. Just tell me something though, are you involved with Joseph?"

She shook her head, and relief flooded through me. Whatever else might be wrong, I could face. Ruby with another man...that would rip my heart out.

She jerked her arm away from my hand and sat up straight as several other nurses joined us at the table. And then Joseph took the chair next to her. He eyed me with a hint of suspicion. The feeling was mutual. But before I could say anything, Natalie dropped into the chair on my left.

"I am so tired, I don't think I can swallow one bite," she said.

Ruby gathered her plate and stood to leave. "Are you finished already?" Joseph asked her.

She looked down at him, and then she looked at me. "I'm flat out exhausted. I'm going to bathe and lie down for a while."

"All right," Joseph said. "I'll check in on you later."

My stomach clenched. Maybe Ruby didn't have feelings for him, but he clearly had feelings for her. He watched her walk away, and then turned back to me with less effort to hide his distaste for me. "Is she all right?" he asked.

"I reckon," I said. "She didn't say a whole lot."

Natalie dropped her fork onto her plate and gripped her stomach. "Oh, my stomach is cramping from this terrible food," she moaned. "I'm so hungry I can barely stand it. Then I come here and have to eat this stuff."

"Be thankful for what you have," I said, barely making the effort to control my disdain. "Who knows how long it's going to last."

She looked alarmed by this thought and went back to shoveling her food. I had to meet up with the convoy leaving the camp soon, so I gathered my plate and dismissed myself from the table. Natalie gripped my arm. "You'll come say bye to me before you leave, won't you?"

My instinct was to say no, but at that moment a terrible thought entered my mind. Something inside of me said, *at least she cares...*

"Sure, darlin'. I'll come say bye to you."

Ruby

January 26, 1942

For the better part of a month, caring for the patients pouring into our hospital from the surrounding areas consumed nearly every moment of my days. That was true for everyone though, and amazingly, morale stayed high. Soldiers came to us every day, some of them merely boys, who had lain where they'd fallen for days before being discovered and brought to us for treatment. By that time, their wounds were decaying from infection, infested with maggots, or worst of all, bubbling with the horrifying effects of gas gangrene. They came to us with broken, ravaged bodies, and yet their spirits remained hopeful. I made it a point to smile at each face I greeted, and I was greatly surprised by the number of wounded who returned that smile.

We continued to expand the hospital, adding new wards every few days, and by the end of January, we had over two thousand patients scattered throughout numerous open-air wards, which provided beds for anywhere from two to six hundred men. With only a staff of forty-three army nurses, twenty-one Filipinos, and eight of us civilians, we kept up a rotation that burned up every ounce of energy in our calorie-deprived bodies.

I spent each day going through my duties with a singular focus: to pour everything I had into keeping each patient in my care alive. I bathed them, cleaned their burns and lacerations, packed the wounds with sulfa powder, and changed their dressings with as much care as I could. Some of the poor men needed morphine just for the removal of bandages. The blood-caked dressings were practically glued to the raw flesh, causing some of the soldiers to pass out from the pain.

Nights were the worst. Even if you weren't on duty, which itself was quite a challenge under the blackout conditions, no one slept well. The local Filipinos had fashioned cots that, under different circumstances, might have been quite agreeable. The bamboo frame was supportive, and the rice-stuffed mattress was comfortable enough. But nearly every night I was awakened by the chatter of monkeys, or a rat crawling across my feet, or the yelp of someone else being assaulted by a nighttime critter. Thankfully, early on, one of the girls remembered that putting the legs of the bed into cans of water would keep ants from climbing up and terrorizing us in the night.

By the third week of January I had settled into a routine, and finally felt as though I were getting a decent handle on my duties, when Natalie approached me one morning with a request. We'd both been so busy, I hadn't seen much of her, and I'd nearly forgotten all about her knowledge of my past. But something inside of me snapped to attention when she dropped into a chair across from me at breakfast.

"Ruby, I need your help," she said, looking at me with bloodshot eyes. "I can't do what Mrs. Fincher wants me to. I just can't."

"What do you mean?" I asked.

"She moved me to the gas gangrene ward for this week."

I could immediately understand Natalie's distress. Every nurse dreaded that assignment. Gas gangrene wasn't your everyday, run-of-the-mill infection. It was its own special brand of torture for soldiers. Had been for centuries. The bacteria worked its way deep into the muscle, where it destroyed blood and tissue as it gave off a sickeningly sweet aroma. The name came from the tiny gas bubbles it left behind. If not treated properly, the disease spread, causing entire limbs to swell to four times their normal size. Many limbs were simply amputated.

I actually felt sorry for Natalie, despite our disagreements. "How can I help?" I asked.

"I don't think I can do it. Just thinking about working with the...the wounds, makes me nauseous. And the smell! Every time someone has come into the operating room with that stuff, and that odor filled the room, I have vomited. Every time!"

My stomach felt a little queasy just listening to her. "I don't know, Natalie. Seems only fair for every nurse to take her turn. I did a week already, if you'll remember." I'd volunteered for the first week, preferring to jump into the most difficult assignment while I still had my strength.

"I know, I know. And I wouldn't ask normally. It's just that I just haven't been feeling so well lately. I think I might be coming down with malaria."

"Have you been taking your quinine every day?"

"Yes, but...I just feel sick all the time. I'm so drained! I can't keep this up."

"All right," I said. "I'll switch with you, but just for today." I hated the thought of going back to that ward, but a small part of me hoped that if I helped her out, she'd be more inclined to keep her mouth shut about me.

She smiled and thanked me. "Ruby, you are the best!" I felt my face go rigid, and she must have noticed too. "Oh, I mean Grace. I'm sorry. I mean, *Grace*, you're the best."

I should've known better. One day turned into two. Two days turned into three. And before the week was out, I had done her entire turn in the gas gangrene ward. My dreams were haunted every night, what little I slept, by men crying out, "Just take it off!" as they flailed monstrously swollen limbs at me. I was grateful when that week was finally over, and grateful to be done with Natalie.

But, as it turned out, she had only just begun.

February 8, 1942

As January came to a close, the fighting near the tip of the Bataan peninsula intensified as the Japanese bombarded Mariveles in an attempt to cut off supplies from Corregidor to the south of us. We heard many first-hand accounts of the terrifying dogfights between our boys and the Japanese Zeros from the injured, but it felt like we got a front row seat to the fighting as well. The falling shrapnel from the nearby antiaircraft guns was as much a danger to us as the Japanese.

By early February, nerves were shot. There were bombings throughout the day and night, and planes flew directly over us, firing bullets and sending large chunks of metal into our midst. One medic had just left his bed when a large, burning chunk landed right where he'd been resting. One of the cooks in the third mess area was killed when a stray bullet struck him in the head. Everywhere I went—the ward I was assigned to, the mess area, or my bed—I was always aware of the nearest trench. We all were.

The thing was, I could handle the constant threat of injury or disease, or even hunger. I could handle being completely drained of energy. But what I struggled with daily, the thing that kept my spirit in turmoil, was the acute absence of God's presence when I prayed.

Every night, I went to a quiet spot along the river and poured out my heart before the Lord. I prayed for the men I'd nursed that day, for my family back home, for Henry's safety, for Matthew's safety and peace of mind. I called out in agony, begging God to send me some small sign that He was with me, that He'd forgiven me for my fear and doubt over the years. But the night remained still, with only the chatter of monkeys and the songs of crickets and frogs as my answer.

"Why?" I sobbed one night, as I peered up through a break in the jungle canopy. "Why won't You come near? I need Your comfort and reassurance. I've tried so hard to pour every ounce of my being into caring for the sick and injured. I've told You I was sorry for running away, for lying to everyone, and for doubting Your plans for me. I'm so sorry. Please, just send Your spirit. Speak to my heart again. Even if You don't restore the gift of healing, please just speak to me. I'm desperate for You. Only You."

I leaned against the rock behind me and covered my face, crying until I had nothing left. There were no answers, no quiet words of comfort or scriptures brought to my mind. Once the tears let up, I pulled myself together and headed off to bed for another restless night of tossing and turning.

The next day was Sunday, and I'd been looking forward to it all week. A small chapel had been built out of bamboo, and we were having our first worship service that evening after mess. It put a little extra energy into my day, and I was able to forget the loneliness of the previous evening.

"You're awful chipper today," a patient named Thomas White said, as I tugged gently on the dressing around his upper arm. It had been amputated a few days before.

I smiled at him as he looked up at me through a morphine haze. "God is good."

He shook his head. "God took my arm."

"That's true, but He gave you your life."

"For now, anyway."

I hummed a hymn as I checked his sutures and changed the dressing, and he joined in every once in a while. As I finished up, I placed my hand on his chest and closed my eyes. "Lord, bless Thomas. Heal his body, and his spirit. Give him peace, and let him know that he belongs to You forever."

When I opened my eyes, Thomas was asleep, his remaining hand resting on mine. I gently slid my hand away, and waved at Sandra, the nurse who was supervising my assigned ward. She waved back, and I headed for mess area #2. It was closest to our quarters, and all the nurses not working ate there together. On my way across the camp, I saw Joseph come out of the brush from the direction of the gas gangrene ward. His expression was grim until he saw me, and then he smiled. I waited for him to catch up and we walked the rest of the way together.

"You looked perplexed," I said. "Everything all right?"

"Just thinking about the gangrene cases. I've been over there all week trying to figure out a better way to treat them since we've run out of antitoxin."

"Any ideas?"

"Nothing substantial yet. But those poor fellas deserve some relief."

I agreed, but I also needed a change in subject before eating, so I asked if he was going to the worship service that evening.

"Oh, certainly. I wouldn't miss it."

"Good," I said. "We'll go together."

I tried to keep the conversation up as we waited in line. This was the worst part of mess. My mouth would water and ache, knowing it was about to be fed. But my stomach would roll with nausea, knowing the same dismal food would be waiting for me: carabao meat, rice, tomatoes. When I finally got my plate and took a seat between Joseph and Janine, I said a quick prayer thanking God for the food, but I couldn't say I meant it very much.

Just then, I saw Matthew seated on the other side of the clearing beside Natalie. He leaned toward her and spoke something in her ear, and she chuckled. What was he doing back here? I glanced down at my plate and picked at the gray meat. So much for enjoying the evening.

To make matters worse, halfway through the meal bombs exploded close enough to send everyone scrambling for trenches. Joseph helped me and then Janine climb down into a nearby trench, but then he stood off to the side while the bombing continued.

"What are you doing?" I shouted. "Get in a trench!"

"It's not that close," he said. "I'm making sure no one steals our food while you're hiding."

I shook my head and said a prayer for his safety. "Sometimes he can be such a pain in my rear," I said to Janine.

She grabbed my arm and pulled me down, covering her head with her hands. We leaned into one another as we rode out the concussions for the next several minutes. All the while, I could see the top of Joseph's head stationed near our table.

CHAPTER ELEVEN

Matthew

February 8, 1942

As the bombing drew closer, I helped some of the nurses climb into a trench. I'd planned to stay outside the trench to give all the girls and patients room, but Natalie clung to me harder with each concussion, and she refused to get inside without me. It was annoying, but I realized the girl was genuinely terrified. Her entire body shook, and tears streaked her grimy face.

"Natalie," I said as gently and sternly as I could. "You need to get into the trench, honey. You'll be safe in there."

She squeezed my arm so hard I was sure the circulation was cut off. "I can't. I can't let go."

I scooted her closer to the side, and several of the other girls reached up toward her, trying to convince her to get in. She looked down at them and then back at me. Then she shook her head and closed her eyes. I took a quick glance around to make sure the women and patients were all taken care of. Across the clearing, Joseph stood above the trenches on that side as if he were guarding them.

Everyone was as secure as they were going to get, so I sat down on the side of the trench and pulled Natalie down with me. "Come on," I eased. "I'll get in with you."

She lowered herself beside me, and we scooted into the trench together. Once settled, I slid down the wall, and pulled Natalie under my arm. She shook as if she was freezing, and buried her face into my chest. I did my best to keep her calm, but with every explosion, she jumped and sobbed.

"It's going to be all right," I said. "Come on. Those aren't nearly close enough to hurt any of us."

"I can't...help it. I...can't stop...shaking."

I held her a little tighter and spoke quietly into her ear, hoping to take her mind off our surroundings. "Tell me about your family back home. You're from Nashville, right? What kind of place was it where you grew up?"

She looked up at me like I was nuts. "Home? It was...just a...normal place."

"A farm?"

"No, a place in town." She shuddered again. "A big white house with...a fence around...and a huge oak tree."

"Did you have brothers and sisters?"

"Two sisters, but they were much older. From my father's first marriage."

"Were you close?"

"No," she said, her shuddering finally slowing. "They hardly ever came around. They said my mother was crazy, and they didn't want my father to marry her."

I chuckled, trying to lighten the mood. But a bomb hit close enough to send dirt and debris into the trench, and she nearly jumped out of her skin, stifling a scream. I squeezed her close again, and went back to talking as quickly as possible. "They thought she was crazy, huh? What was she really like?"

SAVING GRACE | 163

"She actually *was* crazy. Well, at least, I heard the doctor tell my father something like that when I was little. I mean, some days she was amazing. We'd get all dressed up and go out on the town, and she'd take me to the most expensive shops and buy me any dress I wanted. Then she'd take me for ice cream, and we'd laugh until our stomachs hurt."

"That doesn't sound too crazy."

"Well, other times, she'd lock herself in her bedroom for days, sometimes weeks, and I could hear her crying. My father had no idea what to do with her. He just took off when she was like that, so I had to take care of her."

Another concussion sent her face back into my chest, and she shook there for a minute. I rubbed her back and waited for her to calm again. "That must've been real hard on you. Taking care of your mother at such a young age."

"It was. That was one reason I wanted to get out of there so badly. Especially once Mother died, and Daddy went crazy too."

The bombs had stopped, and so had her shaking, but her tears still flowed. I wondered if asking about her family had been a mistake. I stood and pulled her up, keeping my arm over her shoulder. Her legs still seemed wobbly. I helped her over to the side of the trench, and one of the other nurses helped pull her out. As I climbed out, I surveyed the damage. A few overturned chairs mostly, and some ashen faces, but the bombs had not been close enough to do any real damage.

I was thankful then that the other nurses came forward to take charge of comforting Natalie. It gave me a chance to help straighten things up, plus I admit I felt suddenly out of my depth, as if I'd inadvertently uncovered something rotten from her past. We cleaned up our plates from dinner. No one spoke much for a few minutes, but gradually chuckles returned to conversations, and before long, everyone was talking and laughing normally again. I glanced over at Ruby, who'd climbed out of a trench on the other side. She met my gaze, and held it for a minute. Something in her eyes grabbed me, as if she longed to speak to me. But it was fleeting, and she turned away.

Natalie slipped her hand around my elbow, appearing from nowhere. "Thank you for keeping me calm," she said. "I'm sorry I was so difficult."

I patted her hand. "Don't worry about it. I'm sure you weren't the only one who was afraid."

"Want to go for a walk?"

I dropped her hand and took a step away from her. "Nah, I'm heading over to the chapel. I think the service is starting soon."

"Oh," she said, her face falling into a frown. "That's right. That was why you came in the first place."

"You, uh...you want to come?" I had to admit, a small part of me hoped she'd say no. But guilt shot through me. Didn't everyone deserve the comfort of the Lord right now?

"Ah, I think I'll head back to the river to clean up," she said. "I'm still feeling a little woozy."

I said goodbye and headed over to the small chapel that had been set up recently. The chaplain, Sergeant Watters, called it the Church of All Faiths. There were a few rows of bamboo benches, a bamboo altar, and a couple of foxholes nearby. As we gathered together, most of the men sat on the ground up front, the women on the benches in the back. I stood behind the benches and kept one eye on the sky, the other on Ruby seated several rows in front of me.

Sergeant Watters made a few announcements, his soft voice barely carrying to the back. He concluded with a gentle admonition. "You fellas make sure to scatter if the Japs come back. Let the women take the foxholes."

Then he swung his arms up and led us in a few hymns. We stuck to the familiar since no one had a hymnal. 'How Great Thou Art' and 'Holy, Holy, Holy' were easy enough for most. Then Sergeant Watters read from Second Corinthians a lengthy description of all that Paul suffered in the name of Christ, from beatings to shipwrecks, to imprisonment. Hunger. Thirst. A list every one of us could feel in our own bodies.

He concluded with these verses from chapter twelve:

"And lest I should be exalted above measure through the abundance of the revelations, there was given to me a thorn in the flesh, the messenger of Satan to buffet me, lest I should be exalted above measure. For this thing I besought the Lord thrice, that it might depart from me. And he said unto me, My grace is sufficient for thee: for my strength is made perfect in weakness. Most gladly therefore will I rather glory in my infirmities, that the power of Christ may rest upon me. Therefore I take pleasure in infirmities, in reproaches, in necessities, in persecutions, in distress for Christ's sake: for when I am weak, then am I strong."

Sergeant Watters closed the Bible and looked around at those gathered before him with a sad sort of smile, placing his fist over his heart. "Young men and women, you are in the midst of great persecution, both of body and spirit. Do not lose heart. Your Father in Heaven knows of your pain, your hunger, and your fears. Give your cares to Him daily, and He will guard your soul. I cannot stand before you and ask you to be glad over your sufferings, but God tells us to rely on His strength when we are at our weakest. And we can know that we have a mighty warrior on our side."

"Amen," resonated around the chapel, accompanied by several nodding heads. I hadn't yet felt the suffering many of the patients here had; especially those too sick or injured to make it to the chapel. But I had a strong suspicion that my time was coming. And I had to wonder if I had what it would take to keep my faith intact in such circumstances.

As everyone stood to leave, Ruby turned and once again made eye contact with me. She glanced around before making her way through the benches to the back where I still stood. I could see she'd been

166 JENNIFER H. WESTALL

fighting off tears, perhaps from the chaplain's message. I ached to wrap my arms around her. Why was she still so distant?

"I was surprised to see you," she said. "Are you staying for a while?"

I shook my head. "Just came for the service. I'm heading back to Cabcaben in a little while."

"Oh." She looked around again. What was with her nervousness all the time? It was like she was afraid someone was watching her.

"Ruby, why can't you talk to me? Why can't we work this out?"

She rubbed her hands together. "I promise, it's nothing to do with you. I just..."

"Just what?"

She looked around again. "I better go. I have to report back to my ward in a few minutes."

I sighed and rubbed my palms against my eyes. "All right. I'll be back again next Sunday. Can we please talk then? We can go somewhere quiet. Just the two of us."

"M—Maybe. I really do have to go."

She scurried away before I could say any more. I was about to turn to go, when I caught Joseph's eye from across the chapel. He raised his hand toward me and began walking in my direction. "Hey, Matthew," he called. "Wait up."

"I have to get over to the truck," I said. "It'll have to be quick."

"I'll walk with you, then," he said.

"All right."

We walked a few paces, and at first he seemed unsure of what he wanted to say. But he didn't take long to get pretty direct about things.

"It upsets Grace when she sees you. Why is that?"

"Maybe you can tell me. She isn't really saying much to me."

"How do you know Grace?"

I eyed him sideways, deciding caution was best. "We know each other from back home."

"Then you know her? I mean...you actually *know* her?"

The tone in his voice gave me pause. What had Ruby been telling this guy? "Yeah, I know her. What about it?"

"I'm just worried about her. Something doesn't seem right with her. I mean, she's always been quiet about her past, but she's never hesitated to speak up and put me in my place. But recently she's just completely withdrawn. And like I said, she gets upset when she sees you."

I stopped and faced him, tired of all the intrigue of the past weeks. "Look, just tell me straight up what your relationship is with Grace. Are you two...together?"

"No," he said.

"But you would like to be. Am I right?"

He sighed and rubbed his hand over his brow. "Look, all I know is that something's wrong. I thought you might know what it is, but I guess you're as clueless as I am."

"Seems that way."

"Well, I'll let you get going. Sorry to have bothered you."

I shook the hand he offered and took off for the truck waiting at the main hospital. Part of me was begrudgingly impressed that he cared enough about her to know something was off. But that small part was quickly beaten down by the part of me that had no intention of sharing her with anyone else. I was done with being in the dark. Come the following Sunday, Ruby and I were going to get all this mess straightened out once and for all.

Ruby

February 12, 1942

In my assigned ward Thursday morning, I could hardly stand on my own two feet for more than a few minutes. I'd never been so hungry, so weakened, and so pathetic in my entire life. On Monday morning, Natalie had sat down across from me, looking so sickly I actually felt bad for her. She made a pitiful effort to be friendly for about two minutes, and then she just outright asked me to give her my breakfast. My meager, tiny, less-than-five-hundred-calorie breakfast. After another cut in our rations, we were down to only two meals a day. One thousand calories to live on, and she wanted half of them. I must've looked at her like she was downright crazy.

But then she sat up straighter, looked around at the other nurses taking their seats nearby, and said, "Why, *Ruby*, that's an amazing story." She leaned in a little closer. "All that running from the law must make a girl pretty desperate."

I had pushed my tray over to her and hissed, "Just this once."

But she and I both knew it wouldn't be just once.

Without my breakfast each day, I barely made it to four-thirty mess before I crashed completely. I told Natalie that if she insisted on starving me to death, she'd have no one else to get food from. Defiantly she'd shove another bite of my breakfast in her mouth. But she'd left me the toast.

Back when my family was working as sharecroppers, I'd just *thought* I knew what it was like to go hungry. I'd lost weight, and my stomach had cramped most days. But this was something else entirely. All I could think about was food. Steak. Bacon. Eggs. Pie. Carrots. Peas...The obsession wouldn't stop.

Every time it seemed that I couldn't bear it a moment longer, I'd think about Jesus out in the wilderness, fasting for forty days. At least I had one meal to look forward to.

I turned my attention off food and went back to caring for the patients in my ward. I stopped after every four men and sat down for just a moment to replenish my energy. During one of my stops, I saw a young sergeant looking at me with a concerned expression. "You all right, Miss Grace?"

I nodded, ashamed at my weakness in front of these brave men. That very sergeant had had both of his legs removed at the knees just the day before, and here he was, worried about me. I pushed myself up to standing, determined to go at least five or six more men before resting again. But the rush of planes overhead sent the leaves above me waving in all directions. Two or three more swooped down low, and gunfire broke out. A bomb exploded so close, I heard nurses and patients screaming in fear.

I dove under the closest bed and wrapped my hands around my head. Several more explosions shook the ground, and I could've sworn I was lifted off the ground a bit. *Dear God, have mercy!* My heart pounded in my ears nearly as loudly as the gunfire above me. With a crash, a large chunk of shrapnel fell through the trees about thirty feet from the ward, ricocheting into branches and thudding to the ground.

Peering out from under the bed, I saw that same sergeant looking down at me. Our eyes met, and I realized he had no way of taking cover. He was just lying in that bed, exposed to whatever may fall upon him. What was I doing? Wasn't I the same person who'd run across the Calhoun's field with a tornado coming right at me? I'd been terrified that day too. But I'd realized God was calling me into the storm, and that even if He took my life, there was no place I'd rather be than in the storm with Jesus.

I crawled out from under that bed and went right back to doing my job. I was still that same girl; I just had to choose to go into the storm. I wasn't going to hide anymore, wasn't going to run. And as the bombs continued to fall, I continued to check dressings, administer morphine, and offer encouragement to those men.

When the raid finally stopped, I allowed myself to take a seat for just a few minutes. Several of my patients offered me smiles, and one sent me a thumbs-up. I smiled and relished the respect in their eyes. In fact, it was nice to respect myself for a change.

And right there I decided that life was just too precarious to waste time being afraid. I'd give Natalie some of my food, 'cause even I could see the girl's health and peace of mind were hanging on by a thread. But there was no way I was going to lose Matthew again. If all we had left together was the time it would take for the Japs to overrun us, then I wasn't going to waste another minute of it appeasing Natalie.

Matthew

Cabcaben was the only airstrip on the Bataan peninsula without a single airplane. Not one. But we maintained the field and revetments with no doubt that U.S. planes were soon to come. So one evening after mess, when I'd made my way from camp back down to the field, and I heard from Ron that planes were expected that evening, I couldn't help the relief and joy that came over me. And I wasn't alone.

The ground crew seated around in small groups throughout the bamboo thickets buzzed with excitement. It was getting dark, so I couldn't make out who was speaking, but I listened as they shared their elation with one another.

"Hey, Frank! That confirms that rumor we heard from the Navy 'bout the convoy coming!"

"How many planes are on the way?"

"Don't know."

"Boy howdy! Things are gonna start turning around now!"

It took several minutes for the excitement to die down, and conversation turned to MacArthur. Some of the fellas seemed bitter, reveling in rumors of MacArthur cowering in the tunnels beneath Corregidor, even using his nickname, Dugout Doug. Others still clung to their faith in him, defending his decision to send untrained Filipino units to face the Japanese onslaught on the beaches of Northern Luzon. I couldn't care less about MacArthur. He might as well be on the moon for all the good it did us each day.

While another fella was speaking, we heard the low rumble of planes in the distance, and everyone fell silent, probably out of fear at first. But as that beautiful sound grew louder and closer, we knew they were American. Then we jumped up and ran for the airstrip. I watched and listened with my heart racing. As I peered into the dark sky, a plane appeared from the south toward the bay. The lights flashed. The runway lit up with the pitiful field lights we'd installed.

The plane descended like a dark, gliding bird, touching down and rolling to a stop. Then another plane appeared from the same direction. The ground crews ran to the first, rolling it into a revetment as the second landed, followed by a third. Another fella standing next to me cursed and shook his head.

"They're just old P-40s! What good's that gonna do anybody?"

As it turned out, the planes were beat-up P-40s that had survived the attack on Clark Field and had been in service over at Bataan airstrip, just three kilometers away. And although it was nice to know there'd finally be some defense at the Cabcaben field, my hopes for a turning tide were dashed. I returned to camp with a heavy heart, wondering if we truly were on our own. What if America *never* sent help? What if *no one* was coming?

I crawled under my mosquito net onto my cot and lay there for hours, unable to sleep, yet exhausted in body and spirit. My stomach cramped with hunger. My skin itched from relentless bug bites. And my chest ached every time my thoughts turned to Ruby. I lay there that night and thought of home. I thought of Mother and Mary, of the beautiful niece I'd never met, and I wondered if I ever would. *I might actually die in this jungle*, I thought. *Even the sight of Father would be more bearable than this.*

I wanted to pray, but I couldn't put words to my feelings. My spirit cried out to God, begging for help and understanding. I could feel the ache leaving me and floating up to heaven, and I knew He heard my wordless cries. *Guide me, Lord,* I finally managed. *Fill me. Anchor me. You are my rock and my salvation. But I am sinking. Please, give me some sign of hope.*

I managed a small amount of fitful sleep that night, and awoke the following morning to the blasts of bombs a few kilometers away.

Antiaircraft guns exploded, and bullets streaked across the sky. My head pounded. I couldn't even manage enough fear to climb out of my cot and take cover. I just lay there and listened to the sounds of our approaching doom.

When it was over, I made my way to the mess area and found Doug waiting in line. "Rough night?" he asked.

"A bit."

"I heard about the planes."

I nodded. "Not sure what good three measly planes will do, but it's three more than we had yesterday."

"That's the spirit," he said.

We inched through the line, grabbed our meager breakfast, and headed for a bamboo table on the west side near a group of palm trees. I stopped in my tracks when I saw Henry Graves seated at the table, cutting up with the pilots who'd arrived the night before. He must've been telling a whopping good story, 'cause they were enthralled as he finished with an explanation of how he'd outwitted a Jap scout.

I dropped my plate onto the table just as the others burst out laughing. When he saw me, Henry eased himself up and thrust out his hand. "Well! If it ain't Matthew Doyle!"

I shook his hand and couldn't help but smile back. "My, you're looking better than the last time I saw you."

He pulled up his pants leg and showed off the bright pink scar that was still healing along his calf. "Gonna be a beaut!"

I introduced him to Doug and they shook hands. "Where'd you come from?" I asked.

"Aw, I been down at the beach with the 200th Coast Artillery ever since I could walk. They had me spotting enemy and friendly planes for a while, but seeing as how we ain't got hardly any friendlies left, they sent me this way to find some more useful work. But what I really need to do is get back in a plane, like these fellas!"

They made a rousing noise in support of his declaration, and Henry grinned from ear to ear. How could he be so happy? Did he have no idea what was going on around us?

I dropped into a chair as the three pilots said their goodbyes and headed for the airfield. Then I shoved the tiny breakfast into my mouth. It was gone way too quickly, and my stomach growled for more. I'd about had all I could take, and I flipped my fork onto my plate with a huff.

"What in God's name are we doing here, anyway?" I said. "So what if the Japs get the Philippines? What difference does it make?"

To my left, Doug stared at me like I'd lost my mind. Across from me, Henry's playful smile faded from his lips. They looked at me and at each other with the kind of awkwardness that comes when a teacher asks you a question that you don't know the answer to, in front of the whole class.

Then, as if he hadn't heard me at all, Henry leaned across the table and lowered his voice. "Say, you two want a real treat? Come with me."

I wasn't in the mood for playing around, and I told Henry as much. But he wouldn't take no for an answer, so Doug and I followed him into the dense part of the jungle to the south of camp. I noticed his limp, but I also noticed that it didn't seem to slow him down much. In fact, he crept through the dangling vines, the thick bamboo shoots, and mango groves with an agility that surprised me. How did he have so much energy?

Once we were away from the noise of camp, he looked back at Doug and me and motioned for us to keep quiet as we followed, not that we were making any noise anyway. Doug gave me a quizzical look, and I shrugged in response. What else was there to do at the moment? We tiptoed through the brush a few feet behind Henry until he froze. He motioned for us to stay still. Then he pounced on a huge lizard I hadn't even seen beneath a palm tree.

A thick tail thrashed around his arms as he turned around and held the creature out proudly. "Now we can feast!"

Doug bunched his face up. "Ugh, please don't tell me you plan on cooking that poor thing."

"I most certainly do," Henry said, shifting his hold on the lizard's neck then flinging it around in a quick, fatal circle. "Just like a chicken!"

"You're...serious?" I asked.

"I make a mean iguana stew."

My stomach cramped again as if to remind me that I was in no position to be choosy. "All right then, let's make some stew."

***

Turned out, iguana stew wasn't half bad. And with Henry around to capture the smaller, more interesting critters roaming through our camping area each day, my stomach eased up a bit. Not only that, having Henry around brought a lift to my spirits as well. We reminisced over strange stews and rice mixed with chewy meat that I didn't dare ask about. We talked about playing ball together back in high school, games we remembered, players who'd impressed us, Alabama football, and professional baseball. It made home seem a little more real, a little more attainable.

On Saturday evening, after we finished listening to the radio program from San Francisco, we sat around with Doug shooting the breeze for a while, speculating on what was to come from all this. As darkness fell, Doug bid us goodnight, and Henry finally put on his serious face. He leaned forward onto his elbows and lowered his voice.

"Listen, I gotta apologize for the way I handled everything with Ruby. I know I could've done better by you, and for that I'm truly sorry. You gotta know she never wanted to hurt you, and she loves you like crazy."

My heart thumped a little harder in my chest. "I have to be honest, I didn't take the news so well. And I was pretty upset with both of you for a while. But once I thought about it, I realized that I probably would've done the same thing. And I'm grateful to you for getting her out of that danger."

"Looks like I brought her to a whole other kind of danger, though. I have to admit, this wasn't one of my best plans."

I managed a quiet chuckle. "No, I reckon in hindsight, it was a pretty poor plan on all our parts." We settled into quiet contemplation over that for a few minutes before I spoke again. "You want to go see her? I'm heading over to the hospital tomorrow afternoon."

"Yeah, I'd like that."

I felt better after clearing the air, and that night I was able to get a decent amount of sleep. Henry and I set out the following day for the hospital, catching a ride with a truck taking supplies in that direction. We bounced along the road with our eyes on the sky, but we didn't spot any Japanese planes. I realized that the Japs hadn't bombed us at all that day, which had to be a first. Maybe that was why I felt more at peace. Or maybe it was reuniting with Henry. Could've been a combination of factors. But as we arrived at Jungle Hospital #2, I felt for the first time a sense of hope that things might just work out all right for all of us.

We climbed out of the back of the truck amid a cloud of dust and made our way toward the mess area where the nurses usually ate. It wasn't quite time for mess yet, but I was hoping to talk to Ruby beforehand and finally straighten out all the vexation between us. I walked around a couple of wards, trying not to look too closely at the broken men scattered about. They didn't even have a tent over them. Just jungle covering and mosquito nets.

Henry stopped to shake hands with someone he knew, so I turned to look around for Ruby. The hospital had grown so large; I wasn't sure where to look for her. While Henry laughed with the fella behind me, I stopped another nurse walking by that looked familiar and asked her if she knew where I might find Grace Miller. She shrugged her drooping shoulders and pointed east. "I think she's over in ward twelve today. But I'm not sure."

She wiped her hand across her brow, smudging a little dirt on her forehead, and made an attempt at a friendly smile, which I appreciated. "Thanks," I told her. "How much longer till dinner?"

She glanced down at a thin silver wristwatch. "About thirty minutes."

I turned and tugged on Henry's sleeve. "Let's get moving."

Henry said goodbye and fell into step beside me. "It's a cryin' shame what's happening to these boys. I had no idea there were so many."

"I don't understand this myself," I said. "I know God has a purpose in everything, even the things we don't understand, but this is...this is so far beyond my comprehension."

Henry dropped his head as we made our way past several more wards. I hadn't seen him look so serious in a long time. But his face lit up when Ruby called out his name and took off running toward us. She flew into him, throwing her arms around his neck, crying and laughing at the same time. He swung her up off the ground and held onto her for a few minutes while her sobs continued. I couldn't help that part of me that ached for her to be so happy to see me too.

She finally released him, and dove right into questioning him on where he'd been and how his leg was healing. He filled her in, just as he'd done for me. Then Janine came running to him as well. She was a little more reserved than Ruby, but it was clear she was thrilled to see him. He wrapped an arm around her shoulder and winked over at me. "If you'll excuse us for a few minutes, we need to get reacquainted."

I smiled in return and watched them head behind the records shack. Giggles floated out from behind the wall before it went quiet. I turned to Ruby, who still held her smile, but for the first time I actually *saw* her, and it was frightening. Her face was pale, and her eyes had dark circles beneath them. Her coveralls hung so loose on her that it looked more like her shoulders were a set of hangers. She didn't look well at all.

I stepped a little closer and put a hand on her shoulder, feeling the bone like a small baseball in my hand. "Ruby, are you okay?"

She didn't pull away, which I'd half expected. Instead, she let out a deep sigh as if she'd been punctured. "I'm just so tired," she said. "I can barely hold myself up."

"Let's go find a place to rest," I said.

"No, I have two more patients to finish up with. Then I can break for mess."

"Can we please go somewhere quiet and talk as soon as you can? It's important."

She met my gaze, but dropped her head quickly and looked around. "I want to talk to you too. Just...not here." She spoke as if she were arranging some secret meeting, as if she were afraid of something. *Or someone.* "Do you know where the dental clinic is?"

I nodded, trying to remember where we'd built it.

"Go through the small grove of mango trees off to the side, and then follow the small path that winds back toward the river. Wait for me on the path."

"Sure, but why all the secrecy? What's going on?"

"I promise, I'll tell you everything. Just meet me there in ten minutes, okay?" Her eyes darted around again. I was starting to get nervous myself.

She hurried back to her ward, and I headed off in the direction of the dental clinic. I hadn't made it far before I heard the familiar voice of Natalie calling out to me from across the clearing. I stopped and turned toward her as she made a beeline for me. She was the last person I wanted to see at the moment.

"Matthew! When did you get here?"

"Just now," I said. "I've got a few things to take care of before mess."

"Oh, well stick around this time and let's do something. One of the medics set up a real wood dance floor just yesterday and we're gonna be playing some music this evening."

I forced a smile and pulled my arm out from under her hand. "Well that sounds swell. I don't think I'll be able to make it tonight, though. Maybe some other time, all right?"

Her expression fell, which made me feel like the biggest jerk. Hadn't I already told her I wasn't ready for any kind of dating? Why couldn't she just accept that? "Listen," I said, glancing down at my watch. "I gotta run. I have a meeting I need to get to. I'll see you later."

I strode away as quick as I could so there'd be no doubt as to my intentions.

CHAPTER TWELVE

Ruby

February 15, 1942

I kept an eye out for Natalie or any of her friends as I made my way through the camp toward the dental clinic. I hadn't seen her since breakfast that morning, but she had a knack for showing up whenever Matthew was around. I stood next to the building trying to look like I had a reason for being there; taking one last sweeping gaze around to make sure no one was watching, I ducked into the mangroves.

When I stepped out onto the path, Matthew was pacing a few feet away. My heart skipped and sped up, just like it had done so often before. I waited for his pacing to turn him back in my direction, and when he faced me, I tried to think of where to begin.

"Thank you for meeting me," I said. "I'm sorry about all this."

I thought at first that he was angry, but I realized his pacing was out of worry. He looked absolutely stricken. "Ruby, you don't look well. Are you sick? Are you hurt? What's going on? I don't understand why you've been so distant and cold. I don't understand anything that's going on."

"I guess I have a lot to explain."

He came to me and took my shoulders in his hands. "Look at you. You're wasting away. I can feel your bones. Aren't you eating?"

I was so tired, and he was so near. Without any thought, I leaned into him and rested my head on his chest. He wrapped his arms around my back and supported me. It felt so wonderful; I didn't want to move. As he spoke, his voice rumbled through his chest. "Talk to me, please. I need to know what's going on."

My knees were about to buckle. "I need to sit down."

He lifted me into his arms like a child and carried me off the path to a large boulder. Carefully he lowered us both to the ground, leaning his back against the boulder and pulling me into his lap. I had no energy to resist, and I didn't want to. I sat across his legs and rested my cheek on his shoulder. My eyes were so heavy, and his body was so comforting. He stroked my arms and kissed my forehead, and all I wanted to do was sleep right there until all the madness was over.

Through the haze of my thoughts, I heard him praying over me, asking the Lord to give me strength. His words spread like a warm blanket over me, and I loved him more in that moment than I ever had. Then my eyes closed and I drifted off to sleep.

I had no idea how long I slept there in his arms, but it was the most peaceful rest I'd had in years. I awoke with a sense of clarity that had been sorely missing since the first bombs hit Clark Field. Lifting my head from his shoulder, I met his gaze. Matthew's eyes searched mine, and he slid his hand from my shoulder along my neck and up to my cheek.

"I've missed you so much," he whispered.

As he touched his lips to mine, joy spread through me like fire. Finally, after being shattered for so long, my heart was full. I sank deeper into his kiss as he slid his arms around my back and pulled me tighter against him. It was so wonderful to be so safe and so loved, that I didn't want it to end. But eventually he pulled his face back from mine.

"You ready to talk to me?"

I nodded. "I'll do my best."

"Why have you been pushing me away? Are you angry with me?"

"No. It's just…"

"What?"

I gazed up at him and wondered how much I should say. "If I tell you what's been going on, you have to promise you'll listen to me, and do what I say. You can't go running off half-cocked and cause a scene."

"Ruby, I can't promise I won't get upset. But you can trust me."

"Remember when I accidentally spilled the beans about Chester attacking me? You remember how you handled that?"

He leaned his head back against the boulder and looked up at the sky. "Yes."

"And you remember when I told you about what happened between Chester and me in the barn? About Samuel being the one who killed him? How you promised me that you wouldn't tell anyone?"

"Yes."

"And what did you do?"

"I told Mr. Oliver." He straightened again and looked on me with a hint of righteous indignation. "But you should've told him the whole truth from the beginning. Maybe we wouldn't have gotten into such a mess."

"You know why I couldn't do that. But listen, the point is if I tell you things, you have to keep your cool."

He grimaced, but then agreed. "All right, then. Tell me everything, and I'll be as cool as can be."

I doubted that, but it was time to explain everything, whether he kept his promise or not. I couldn't bear this anymore alone. "You know that girl, Natalie?"

Matthew's head dropped back against the boulder again. "Ruby, I'm so sorry about getting involved with her, but you have to know I never had any interest in her. Not really."

"I believe you," I said, though the image of him kissing her still stung. "But that's not what this is about."

He straightened again. "It's not?"

"No. You see, while we were at Fort Stotsenburg, Natalie overheard you call me Ruby. And she'd mentioned before that I seemed familiar to her. Well, it turns out she's from Nashville, and her aunt is Ms. Harmon."

"Who?"

"You remember. The older lady who rented the room to me in Hanceville. She kicked me out when I got arrested."

Understanding dawned in his expression. "Oh, Ruby. Natalie knows who you really are, doesn't she?"

"Yes, and at first she threatened to turn me in." His face reddened, but to his credit he didn't interrupt. "I tried to explain to her that I was defending myself and that Chester had attacked me. She said she wouldn't say anything, and I thought if I just kept my head down and did my job quietly, I could disappear again when this was all over. But, then...then she told me to stay away from you."

"She what?" He sat up straight as a board, nearly bouncing me out of his lap. I scooted off him and stood, 'cause I could see he'd need to pace this news out. Sure enough, he jumped up and went to pacing, huffing like an angry bull. "She told you to stay away from me?"

"Yes. She said you were a good man, and shouldn't be mixed up with me. And at the time, I had to agree with her. I didn't want you to go down with me if something happened."

He stopped and rubbed the back of his neck, doing his best to stay calm. "So that's why you acted the way you did. You were pushing me away to protect yourself. And I just kept coming at you. Has she threatened you again?"

I hesitated, knowing this was the moment of truth. I took a deep breath, and decided I was done lying. "She made it clear she'd turn me in if I didn't give her my breakfast every morning."

He stared at me wide-eyed, looking me over again. "Oh, Ruby. And you did, didn't you? That's why you're so...weak."

I nodded. "But I'm not letting her have her way with me anymore. I mean, I don't care so much about giving her some food. I've gone hungry before, and I can survive it again. But I'm done giving her my joy. I'm done with giving her you."

He stepped over to me and cupped my face in his hands. Then he kissed me, filling my cup again. "We'll figure this out together, all right?" he said. "I swear. I'm not losing you again."

Matthew

It was all I could do to keep myself from marching right over to Natalie and giving her a piece of my mind. But I realized that Ruby was right. Every time she'd confided in me, I'd blown it. Well, I couldn't admit that I blew it when I told Mr. Oliver about Samuel—I'd still do the same thing given the chance. And it had felt good to deck Chester after what he did to Ruby. But my actions had affected her ability to trust me, and I needed to stop taking matters into my own hands when it came to her. So I fought my instincts and kept my cool just like I promised.

Ruby and I agreed that we needed to think on things and come up with a plan we both agreed to. She could point the finger at me all day long, but if she was being honest, she'd see that she was always just as stubborn and determined to do things her own way as I was. But I didn't point that out since she seemed so willing to solve this problem together.

Instead, I kept my focus on her immediate needs, which was food first, and possibly medical attention. I kept my distance after we came out of the jungle, but I kept a close eye on her to make sure she went to the mess area to eat. There was no sign of Natalie, and as far as I could tell, even though Ruby must have been starving, she only picked at the rice and tomatoes.

As I was getting ready to leave with Henry, Natalie appeared, walking over to us as we were helping to load medical supplies onto the truck that was our ride back to Cabcaben. She smiled at me, which made my stomach swim. I had a good mind to tell her to buzz off, but I'd promised Ruby not to act any differently with her until we decided on the best course of action. So I forced a smile in return.

"Are you leaving already?" she said, pushing her lips into a pout.

"Sorry, but we have to get back to camp while it's still daylight."

"But I didn't even get to spend any time with you."

I glanced over at Henry, who threw a crate onto the truck without looking at us. But his eyebrows shot up all the same. "Listen Natalie, I'm sorry about missing you today. I really am. I'll be back soon. You keep working hard, you hear?"

She wrapped her arms around her stomach. "I try, but I just don't feel so well. I think I'm coming down with malaria."

Good, I thought. *That should keep you away from Ruby.* But then I felt a sting of guilt—a small one—that I was glad she was sick. Although I'd felt sorry for Natalie after hearing about her unhappy childhood, and it certainly explained her neediness, my pity for her had dwindled to nothing. I loaded another crate onto the truck, and turned back to Natalie with an attempt to seem disappointed.

"Looks like we have to get going. You take care. I'm sure you'll be all right."

She stepped over to me and slid her arms around my waist. I wanted to rip her arms off me, but I focused on keeping my voice steady rather than thinking about her taking Ruby's food. I pressed my hands against her back, pretending to hug her. Then I released her after a moment and headed for the back of the truck, climbing inside and giving Natalie a wave. She waved back and stood there watching the truck until we turned onto the main road.

I sat across from Henry in the truck, waiting for him to lay into me, but not one word passed his lips during the ride back to camp. It only took a few minutes to cover the couple of kilometers, and once we arrived, we started unloading the crates of supplies straightaway. Only then did Henry break his silence.

"So what's going on with you and that other nurse?"

I knew we'd need some privacy for this conversation. "Why don't we take a walk so I can explain everything that Ruby told me today. You need to know what's going on."

A flash of worry crossed his expression. "Is she in trouble?"

I jerked my head toward a path that led down to the airstrip, and Henry followed me. As we walked, I told him all about Natalie, how I'd met her when I first arrived on the island and gone out with her once. I admitted I'd handled it badly when I'd found out Ruby was alive. I told him how needy Natalie had been ever since the bombing began, and hinted that there might be reason to believe she wasn't entirely sound of mind. And I filled him in on everything Ruby had told me earlier that day. Henry walked along beside me in silence. When I finished, he came to a standstill and considered the situation for a minute.

"What do you think we should do?" he asked.

"I told Ruby I'd think on it and talk to you about it. We want to make sure we all agree to a solid plan."

"My first thought is to get her out of there. We could flee into the mountains, maybe. Hide out until all this conflict is over."

I'd thought of that several times already. "You think some locals would take her in? How would we protect her if the Japanese overrun the place?"

"I'll go AWOL. I can make it look like I was ambushed and killed or something. I'll just be one of the many other soldiers missing in action. I can keep us fed."

"No," I said. "I'll go AWOL. I'm not getting separated from her again."

Henry wandered along the path for a moment, absently scratching at his face. "There's got to be a better way. I wonder... Maybe...no. There's Mike. But I'm not sure where to find him."

I reached out and caught his arm. "Hey, what are you thinking?"

"I know this guy who flies PBYs for the Navy. In fact, he was giving Ruby flying lessons—"

"Wait, you're telling me Ruby's flown a plane?" It seemed surreal that my little girl from Hanceville had commanded an aircraft. But then again, why should I be surprised?

"Sure thing, in fact he's taken a real shine to her—his favorite pupil." Henry grinned, but my glare stopped that line of conversation in its tracks. "Anyway, the P-40 pilots I was talking to the other day mentioned that some planes and a couple of subs have made it through the blockade to Australia. Maybe Mike can get us word if he hears of another plan to get people out."

"That's not much of a plan. And how would we even get her on a plane or sub?"

"She's a civilian. That works in her favor."

I shook my head. "That's not enough."

"If she was sick enough, they might go for it."

We needed something stronger. Something the army would definitely act on. A policy that would ensure her safe passage. And I knew exactly what I had to do.

Ruby

February 20, 1942

The next several days were much better, even though I remained weak from hunger. I gave Natalie most of my breakfast each morning, and then I did my best to keep up with my duties in the ward. Whenever I struggled to stay on my feet, I thought of Matthew's arms around me, and I prayed for his safety. I'd thank God for leading us back to each other, and I'd ask for mercy from all the doubt and fear that had controlled me. I'd pray for God to fill me with strength to make it to the afternoon, when I could eat my full meal and go to the river to bathe.

Late that Friday morning, a patient placed a note in my hand as I checked his blood pressure. I looked at him curiously, and he gave me a wide smile. "What's this for?" I asked.

"Just read it." He winked at me, and I wondered if the morphine was making him goofy. "I didn't write it. Believe me, if I had written it, I'd have been much more romantic. But another nurse gave it to me and told me to make sure I gave this to you when you came by."

I smiled down at him before opening the small piece of paper.

Report with Miss Langston after supper to her new assignment.
Dr. Samuel Abner

It took a moment for me to realize the note was a message from Matthew. There was no doctor by that name at this hospital, and he'd chosen names that would only be meaningful to me. I grinned to myself at the thought of seeing him again, and I was able to finish my duties that day with only a few breaks.

At supper I found Janine seated alone, so I sat across from her and shoveled my rice and carabao meat into my mouth. I wasn't sure how to begin, but I was desperate to know if we were meeting Matthew later, so I bit the bullet and asked.

"Do you know what's going on?" I asked.

"What do you mean?" Janine kept on chewing without looking at me.

"Do you know about the note I received earlier today?"

"Something about a new assignment. Yeah."

I leaned over the table and lowered my voice. "Is it Matthew?"

She glared at me and told me to shush. But I could see something glinting in her eyes. I clamped my mouth shut, and waited impatiently for her to finish her food. Tonight was a treat for some reason, as we also had canned peaches. The slight amount of sugar was enough to send my blood racing through my body. We cleaned our places, and quietly made our way back to the nurses' quarters. The long walk was agonizing, but I figured it was important to follow Janine's lead, especially when I saw Natalie sitting on her cot, filing her nails just across the small clearing.

Calmly, Janine gathered her soap and a clean cloth, her usual items for bathing in the river. So I gathered mine as well, no trace of excitement visible on my face. We made our way down toward the bank, but before we got there, we made a right turn and began heading upstream. We climbed over roots and rocks, curved around vines and foliage, and eventually came to a place where a large tree had fallen across the water. Janine stopped there and leaned against it. As exhilarated as I was to see Matthew, I was about out of energy.

At that moment, Henry and Matthew emerged from across the river and crossed the fallen tree to our side. They jumped down, Henry with a triumphant smile. "See," he said. "Told you my best girls would be able to follow instructions."

"Yeah, yeah," Matthew said with a chuckle. "Now scram."

Henry slipped an arm around Janine. "Come on, baby. Let's give these two some alone time."

They walked further upstream, but I could hear Janine's giggles drifting along with the river, so they couldn't have gone too far. I didn't have time to think about it much, because soon Matthew had me wrapped in his arms, and the only thing that mattered was soaking up every second with him. After a few moments of tender kisses and whispered greetings, we made our way to a few rocks along the riverbank. I took a seat, and Matthew pulled a small handkerchief out of his pocket.

"Take this," he said.

I unwrapped it to find a few morsels of what appeared to be roasted meat. "What is it?"

"Don't ask. Just eat all of it. You need your strength."

I picked over it, wondering just what kind of creature I was feasting on. "How did you get this?"

"Your brother's pretty ingenious when he wants to be."

I chewed on one of the morsels. It was stringy and tough, but not so bad I couldn't swallow it. "Thank you," I said.

He stood next to me while I finished it, then tucked the handkerchief back into his pocket. "I'll bring you as much as I can whenever we come. I think we can get over here at least two or three times a week. Can you meet that often?"

"I think so. The last week, we've been finishing our duties a little earlier. Seems like the Japs have stopped bombing nearby for some reason."

"They have. I'm sure they're just regrouping for something bigger, but while it lasts, I'd like to see you as often as I can. Henry and I think we may have a way to get you off the island."

I grimaced. "So you told him? About Natalie?"

He nodded. "He took it better than I did. But we both agree it's not safe for you to stay with the army nurses any longer than you have to. So he's getting a message to some guy he knows that flies PBY planes for the Navy."

"Mike?"

Matthew's brow shot up. "That's the guy. I gather you were acquainted?"

"He was teaching me to fly."

He chuckled and shook his head. "You'll never cease to amaze me, Ruby Graves. Anyway, there's no plan in place yet, but there's rumors that some PBYs and a sub have gotten through the Jap blockade, and they may be sending more soon. We're going to do everything we can to make sure you're on one."

Then it dawned on me what he was really saying. "Just me? What about you? What about Henry?"

He didn't answer at first. Just came over and took a seat beside me, leaning forward onto his elbows like he'd been carrying a heavy load and needed a rest. I laid my cheek on his shoulder and thought about what that would mean. Could I really leave them behind in this awful nightmare? After being apart for so long, the thought of leaving Matthew here nearly split my chest wide open.

"I can't do it," I said, hearing my voice crack. "I couldn't leave you again."

He let out a deep sigh and straightened with a sense of confidence. "Let's not worry over it until it's a real option. We're in God's hands, and He already has the perfect plan in place. We just need to be patient and have faith."

I met his gaze, surprised by his steady, calm assurance. "You've changed so much. Where did all this faith come from?"

Matthew smiled. "You, of course. You showed me the way, and God took my hand. It's all from Him."

I had no idea what to say. I was overcome with guilt at how much my faith had wavered and wondered if I should mention my own fears that God was ignoring my prayers, having taken away my gift. And yet, here I sat beside the boy I'd loved for the better part of my life on the other side of the world from where we'd begun. Was redemption still possible? I had to believe it was.

"Listen," he said quietly. "I came here to talk to you about something else also." Breaking off, he rubbed his hands together for a moment. "I think...I think we should discuss our future."

"It's so hard to even imagine the future. I can barely think about tomorrow."

Matthew's leg bounced up and down and his nervous energy spread to me. What was going on in his head?

"You know," he said, "I've loved you for so long. I know I was pretty stupid about it when we were younger. I handled things all wrong back then. And I sure made a mess of things after the trial. I take full responsibility for that." With visible effort, he stopped bouncing his leg and turned slightly to face me. "But I want you to know, I aim to be a better man from now on. The kind of man you can depend on. The kind of man you can trust with your life." Looking deep into my eyes, he reached over and took my hands in his. "Ruby, I love you with every-thing that I am. And I always will, no matter what. And for some crazy reason that don't make a lick of sense, you love me too."

I realized my heart was pounding, and my palms felt hot and damp. "Well, you haven't always made it easy."

He lifted his hand to cup my face. "I know. And I'm sorry. But all that's over now. I promise you, nothing will come between us again." At that, Matthew touched his forehead to mine and whispered, "Ruby, will you marry me?"

I was overwhelmed with so much joy and love; I couldn't find my voice. All I could do was nod and kiss him, tears spilling down my cheeks.

"Is that a yes?" he asked.

"Yes."

"You're sure?"

I kissed him again. "*Yes.*"

"'Cause you know, you told me once that you wouldn't marry me if I was the last man on earth."

I leaned back and laughed. "By the time we get off this island, you just might be."

He stood and pulled me into his embrace, wiping my tears as we laughed and teased each other. It was the way we always should have been. From the time we met, until that moment, we had spent the better part of ten years in some kind of conflict. And even though we still hadn't found a place where we could love each other in peace, we'd found peace in that moment. And I never wanted it to end.

***

On Sunday, I sat through the chapel service next to Joseph with so much on my mind I could barely pay attention, especially with Matthew stand-ing behind the benches. I was giddy with happiness when I thought of marrying Matthew, but I also knew I'd be hurting Joseph, and some small part of me felt I owed him an explanation. But what could I say? Matthew and I had decided that we needed to maintain our secrecy for the time being, so telling Joseph was out. But I felt I had to say something.

When the service ended, I pulled him aside and asked how he was doing. He seemed taken by surprise. "I'm doing as well as can be expected, given the circumstances."

"Have you made any progress with the gas gangrene cases?"

He eyed me suspiciously. I couldn't blame him. In my weakness and exhaustion, I had practically ignored him the past two weeks. "We're definitely onto something. I think we'll start seeing a more rapid recovery soon with a new technique one of the doctors over at Jungle Hospital #1 has been employing."

"That's wonderful." I glanced over at Sergeant Watters, who was deep in conversation with Matthew. "Um, Joseph, I need to explain...something. But I'm not sure how."

He waited for me to say more, but I was stuck. I threw my hands up in exasperation. "I'm going to marry Matthew," I blurted out.

His eyes widened. "Did you say *marry* him?"

I looked around quickly to make sure no one was listening and made a point to lower my voice. "I wasn't supposed to tell anyone, but I wanted to be honest with you. I know how you feel about me, and I didn't think it was fair to keep it from you."

"Hey, you've been extremely fair and honest with me. I never expected to...well, to convince you to love me. And I can accept that." Joseph's expression was pained. "But, are you sure about Matthew? Every time he's come around, you seem upset."

"It wasn't Matthew upsetting me. It was someone else, which is why we're keeping the wedding quiet for now. I hope you'll understand."

His expression softened. "Of course. You can trust me. My lips are sealed."

I stood on my tiptoes and kissed his cheek. "Thank you."

I took a quick peek at Matthew, who was frowning over at me. His gaze followed Joseph as he walked away, and I could tell I'd have to explain some things. But I'd spotted Natalie approaching from across the camp, and I was determined not to watch her flirt with Matthew. So I headed back to the nurses' quarters with Janine.

Later that evening, I went to the river with Janine to wash away the grime of the day, and we huddled together on a rock away from the other girls. Janine was all smiles, and after I'd announced my news and went on and on, whispering my hopes that Sergeant Watters would agree to marry us, she leaned toward me with a twinkle in her eyes.

"Henry and I are getting married too!" she confessed, barely containing herself.

"Really? Oh, Janine, that's wonderful!" I threw my arms around her neck and laughed as we almost tumbled off the rock into the river. "This means we'll be sisters," I said.

Janine's blue eyes settled into a serious expression. "Now, we have to keep our cool. It's all supposed to be secret, which I think makes it even more romantic!"

I wasn't sure about the secrecy adding any romance, but knowing Janine would be part of my family warmed my heart. I'd missed everyone from back home so much, especially little Abner. Even thoughts of James, as sour as he could be, brought an ache to my chest when I prayed for him nightly.

"Has Henry told you...about...well, about me?" I asked shyly.

She dropped her gaze to the water below, growing quiet. "He said you were convicted of murder, but he told me what really happened. I'm sorry you had to go through all that. It must have been a nightmare."

Having another person know my story was unnerving. I wanted to trust Janine, especially now, so I thanked her for understanding. "I just hope we can keep Natalie from wrecking everything. She's determined to make me miserable."

"She doesn't look well," Janine said. "I think she's coming down with all kinds of stuff. Which serves her right, if you ask me. But maybe her illness will keep her out of your business for a while."

I wouldn't wish malaria or any of the other jungle maladies on Natalie, but I had to admit, I was hoping she'd be too preoccupied to care much about what I was doing.

Janine and I finished bathing and snuck away up the river to meet Matthew and Henry at our usual spot. When we came around the curve in the path, the guys were seated on the end of the fallen tree trunk, their legs dangling off as if they hadn't a care in the world. Matthew's smile spread over his face, sending my stomach topsy-turvy. I smiled in return, and he hopped down.

"Hidey," he said, planting a kiss on me before I could respond.

"What did Sergeant Watters say?" I asked.

"He took a little convincing, but he agreed to marry us, all of us, right here next Friday evening. And he agreed to keep it under wraps for now. Just wants us to make it official when we aren't in a war zone anymore. You know, with the licenses and all."

Janine pulled away from Henry long enough to share a bouncing hug with me. "We're going to get married together! Can you believe it?"

I laughed and let the joy of the moment erase the years of fear and running that had consumed me. Here, among my future family, I could simply be Ruby. And it was heaven. Matthew wrapped his arms around my waist and smiled down at me, sending waves of happiness through my heart.

When Henry and Janine stole away for a little while, Matthew and I found a spot to sit near the river. He took off his boots and rolled up the legs on his pants. Then he groaned as he slipped them into the cool water and lay back to rest his head in my lap. I nibbled on the strange-tasting meat he'd brought this time and ran my hands through his hair with my free hand.

"I think we should live in Australia," he said out of the blue. "If you get on a plane or sub out of here, they'll take you to Australia. You can wait for me there, in Melbourne, and I'll come find you. Then we can get a ranch or something. Live on our own, with no worries over the past." He looked up at me then. "Just you and me...and three or four little boys to drive you nuts."

I nodded and kept on running my fingers through his hair. It was nice to imagine the two of us together like that, living in peace. So I let the dream settle around me, let myself dwell there in our imaginary home, with our imaginary boys. And for a little while longer, we kept the real world at bay.

CHAPTER THIRTEEN

Ruby

February 27, 1942

I stood as still as possible, trying to keep my stomach from turning completely inside out while Janine pinned up the last few strands of my hair. We'd managed to sneak away from the nurses' quarters with my dress stuffed inside my coveralls, and hairpins, a brush, and a small amount of makeup in my pockets. It was the first time I was glad for the oversized coveralls the army had issued me.

But as Janine finished up and looked over her work, I couldn't help but feel absurd standing there in that beautiful dress Daddy had bought me all those years ago, my hair and makeup done, and my feet stuck into my huge brown army boots.

"I look ridiculous," I told her.

Janine glared at me like Mother used to when I complained about dressing up. "You look beautiful. Trust me. He isn't going to be looking at your feet." She straightened and tossed her hair about her shoulders. "Now, how about me? Should I put my hair up?"

Her soft brown curls had turned to straw, like everyone else's had. There was nothing to be done about it. But for someone who'd been

197

living in the jungle for two months, she looked lovely. "Leave it the way it is," I said. "You've fussed over it long enough. Let's do this."

Smiling, she nodded and smoothed her hands down the dress she'd borrowed from another nurse with the excuse of impressing her boyfriend. It hung on her like she was a skeleton, but her face glowed with excitement. I imagined anyone else who saw us would feel sorry for us, but I was the happiest I'd been in years.

Janine whistled, her signal to Henry that he was to come around the opposite side of the boulder behind which we were hiding. Janine listened for his response, and she stepped around the right side, while Henry came up on my left. He smiled at me and kissed me on the cheek.

You look amazing, little Rubes," he said. "Love the boots." He chuckled, and I slapped his arm. "You sure about this?"

I nodded. "You?"

"Oh yeah." He clapped his hands together and rocked on his heels.

"She's amazing, Henry. A good friend. And she loves you like crazy."

He stopped rocking, and his expression grew serious. "I didn't think it was possible for me to love someone like this. I mean, I know I like to play around and everything, but Janine…she's different. She takes care of me like I'm the most important person in the world, but then she turns around and calls me out when I'm a fool. No one's ever treated me like that. I can't imagine my life without her now."

I took his hands in mine and looked up into his eyes, which were shining with joy. "Henry, thank you for taking care of me all these years. For watching out for me, and keeping me laughing, even when there was nothing to laugh about. You're the best big brother a girl could ever hope for."

His smile fell. "I know you wish it was Daddy here with you, but it's an honor to give you away." My eyes welled up thinking of Daddy, but of course, Henry couldn't let the moment pass by without making me laugh. "Anyways, I was getting tired of supporting you." He winked at me. "'Bout time someone took you off my hands."

I slapped his shoulder and laughed with him. Then Janine's whistle signaled that she and Matthew were ready to begin. Henry took my hand and tucked it into the crook of his elbow. "Shall we?"

"We shall."

Stepping around the boulder, we made our way through vines and palm leaves until we came to a small path that led back to the river. Matthew and Janine came to stand beside us. I only caught Matthew's eye for a moment before he turned to face the river and Sergeant Watters waiting beside it.

Sergeant Watters beamed at the four of us, then began to sing, his voice filling the small clearing with a deep power that filled my spirit to overflowing. As he sang, we slowly made our way toward him, turning to face each other during the final verse.

"Amazing Grace, how sweet the sound
That saved a wretch like me.
I once was lost, but now I'm found
Was blind, but now, I see.

"Through many dangers, toils, and snares
I have already come
'Tis Grace hath brought me safe thus far
And Grace will lead me home.

"The Lord has promised good to me
His Word my hope secures
He will my shield and portion be
As long as life endures.

"When we've been there ten thousand years
Bright shining as the sun,
We've no less days to sing God's praise

Than when we first begun."

As I faced Matthew during the final verse, I was overcome with joy. He looked at me with so much love I couldn't tear my eyes from his. I knew tears were streaming down my face, but I didn't care. I only wanted to be with him forever.

"Who gives these women in marriage?" Sergeant Watters broke into my dream, but I still couldn't look away from Matthew, and he never looked away from me as he said, "I, Matthew Doyle, as her friend, give Janine Langston to be married."

Then Henry squeezed my hand. "I, Henry Graves, as her brother, give Ruby Graves to be married."

Henry released my hand, and I stepped over to Matthew. He took my hands in his, and gazed down at me. Warmth spread from his hands to mine, up through my arms, and throughout my entire body. In his face I saw my past, my present, and my future, all mingled into one breathtaking smile.

As he repeated the vows, I had to squeeze his hands to make sure this was all real. "I, Matthew, take thee, Ruby, to be my wife, and before God and these witnesses, I promise to be a faithful and true husband." He held out his hand, and Henry placed a ring in his palm. Matthew slid it onto my finger, the ring so large it would surely fall off if I ever dropped my hand to my side. Then he smiled at me again. "With this ring, I thee wed, and all my worldly goods I thee endow. In sickness and in health, in poverty, or in wealth, until death do us part."

Somewhere in the distant part of my mind, I heard Henry repeating the same vows to Janine. I gazed up at Matthew's shining eyes. He winked and then whispered, "You okay?"

I must have looked a fright. A wrinkled dress that was ten years old, stringy hair falling out of its pins, army boots, and tear-streaked makeup. But Matthew looked down at me like I was the most beautiful girl in the world, only making my eyes fill up again. I managed to nod.

Then it was my turn. "Ruby," Sergeant Watters said. "Repeat after me."

I swallowed, and did the best I could. "I, Ruby, take thee Matthew, to be my husband, and before God and these witnesses, I promise to be a faithful and true wife."

It was at that point that panic shot through me. "I don't have a ring."

Matthew stuck out his hand again, and Henry placed another ring in his palm. I broke my gaze with Matthew for a moment to turn and look over my shoulder at a grinning Henry. "Where did you—"

Matthew turned me back to face him and put the ring in my hand. "Come on," he said. "Worry about that later."

I took the ring and slid it onto his fourth finger. It was a better fit, but still a bit large even for him. Sergeant Watters began again, and I repeated the rest of the vows.

"With this ring, I thee wed, and all my worldly goods I thee endow. In sickness and in health, in poverty, or in wealth, until death do us part."

I hadn't wanted to say the part about death. With so much suffering around us each day, I was afraid to even mention it. But Matthew had insisted on keeping everything as traditional and official as possible, so I'd gone along with it. In the end, the statement came and went along with the others, and I forgot all about it as soon as Sergeant Watters pronounced us husband and wife.

Throwing my arms around Matthew's neck, I kissed him like it might be the last. He pulled my waist into his and kissed me in return, until Sergeant Watters cleared his throat. Matthew smiled down at me before turning to thank Sergeant Watters. They shook hands quickly while I turned to Janine and hugged her neck.

When we pulled apart, I could see she'd been crying too, and we had a good laugh at each other. As Sergeant Watters headed back toward camp, Henry wrapped an arm around Janine and swept her into an embrace.

Matthew's arms slid around my waist from behind, and he rested his chin on my shoulder. "You ready to do a little bit of hiking?"

I giggled as his scruffy beard tickled my neck. "Sure," I said, laughing. "But it's not too far, is it?"

He turned my body into his, kissing me deeply. "No, Mrs. Doyle," he breathed, sending chills down my arm. "It's not too far."

Matthew

I lay on the blanket I'd spread beneath a canopy of palm leaves, watching the sunset paint the sky. My arm was tucked tightly around Ruby's waist, her back against my bare chest. I rested my head in my hand and looked over her shoulder as she ran her fingers up and down my arm. It had been so easy to get lost in these moments together and forget about the horrors taking place nearby. For a little while, we were just two people all alone in the world, becoming one body, one heart.

All I could do was think about how long I'd waited to get to this very day. How many times had I dreamed of holding her, only to awaken to a world where she was gone? Some part of me wondered if this too was a dream. If so, I hoped I'd never awaken.

I kissed her bare shoulder and turned her onto her back. She smiled up at me, sending heat through my body again, despite feeling completely spent. "What are you thinking about?" she asked.

I leaned down and kissed her nose, then her cheek, her ear. "That I can't believe this is real. That after all the time I spent dreaming of you, you're really mine."

She pressed her hand against my cheek. "I don't deserve you. Not after everything I did. I should've never left."

I pressed my finger to her lips. "Shh. None of that matters now. All that matters is that we're together." I leaned down and spoke into her ear. "And you know what the best part is?"

"What?"

"Now, you have to do what I say."

"Excuse me?" Her grin betrayed her lame attempt at anger.

"It's in the Bible. God says so. You have to submit to me."

"I see." She narrowed her eyes. "I should've known you had an ulterior motive. Well, you can forget that." She moved to stand up, but I rolled her onto her back and gently pinned her beneath me. She yelped and giggled.

"Oh, no you don't," I said. I touched my lips to hers. "You're mine forever now. Don't you know that?"

She sobered and met my gaze. "You promise?"

"I already did. Do you want to hear it again?" She nodded. I grinned, and began kissing her all over as I repeated my vows. "I, Matthew...take thee, Ruby...to be my wife...forever...and ever...and ever."

I didn't want our time together to end, but I knew I'd have to get her back to camp before dark, and there were important matters to discuss. So despite myself I pulled back from her lips, and pushed up to a seated position. I reached out for her hand. "Come on, I can't think straight when you're looking at me like that. Let's sit up and talk for a few minutes."

"Uh oh," she said, sitting up and crawling over beside me. "This sounds serious." She crossed her legs Indian-style, and straightened her back, her eyes wide and bright. Draped only in her camisole, she was radiant, and my heart pounded just looking at her.

"Ruby, I need you to make me a promise."

"But I already did," she said, grinning. "I, Ruby, take thee, Matthew—"

"I'm serious, baby." I took her hand, and she stopped. "You have to swear to me that if the chance comes for you to escape this island, no matter what happens, you'll take it."

She dropped her gaze and picked at the grass beside her legs. "Have you heard from Mike? Is that what this is about?"

"No. We haven't heard from him. I've just been thinking about things. And it will be a lot easier to get you off the island than it will be for me. You're a civilian. An officer's wife. I'm a soldier. And I have a duty. I might not be able to go with you."

Abruptly she stood, folded her arms over her chest, and walked several paces away. "I know what you're getting at. And I'm telling you right now, I won't leave you here."

I figured she'd say something like that. *That's my Ruby.* "Things are different now. You're my wife. And it's my job to protect you. To provide for you. To give my life for you if I have to. And I wasn't kidding around before. I know it's not something that comes naturally to you, but I hope you'll pray about it and see that I'm right. We're married now. And as your husband, I have to make difficult decisions—"

She shook her head vehemently and turned away. "No. I'm not leaving you again. Not like before. Just because I married you doesn't mean I don't have a say in my own life. And leaving you was the dumbest thing I ever did. I won't do it again."

I rose to my feet and walked over to her, turning her to face me. "This is nothing like before. Like I said, you're mine forever. And I'm yours. Nothing can come between us like that ever again. No matter what happens, even if we're separated for a while, I'll find you. God will always bring us back together. I know it. I feel in it my deepest spirit. He will keep our hearts together. One heart. One flesh. You just have to trust Him...and me."

I cupped her sweet face in my hands and kissed her forehead, hoping she'd agree. But her eyes hardened, and I knew what was coming. "I will make you a promise." She pushed her finger into my chest. "I won't leave you again, Matthew. Not ever."

Ruby

March 10, 1942

After the rush and excitement of our secret wedding, Matthew and I had a difficult time going more than a day or so without seeing each other. I discovered Henry had somehow found a burned-out truck on the side of a road, traded for parts, and fixed it enough to run. He and Matthew had been driving that beat-up truck through the jungle nearly every evening after the four-thirty mess to meet Janine and me at the river.

For now, the fighting appeared to have reached an unsettled impasse and the Japanese were hardly even making a sound, except for the occasional distant bombings, so stealing away for an evening rendezvous wasn't difficult. In fact, Janine and I learned that we weren't the only ones doing so when we'd happened upon a young soldier and a nurse named Margaret not too far from where we'd been meeting our husbands.

Margaret had blushed deeply and straightened her clothing. She'd stammered an excuse, but Janine and I were just glad she was too embarrassed to realize we were out doing the same thing. In fact, all over the camp, people were doing their best to forget their troubles and make a bit of merriment. There were nightly gatherings at various quarters throughout the camp, and with the substantial break in the conflict, the atmosphere bordered on a giddy euphoria.

Every few nights or so, some of the male doctors and medics tacked a blanket over a bamboo floor. Someone had a vinyl record player and had managed to get hold of a few records. Couples would dance long into the night, despite their exhaustion. I reckoned, even for the sick and wounded, a good bit of dancing did the soul a whole heap of good.

All this newfound jollity in the evenings meant it was easier to stay out longer and go unnoticed. I found myself staying later and later wrapped in Matthew's arms, returning to my bed well after midnight most of the time. Many of the girls would be asleep, but some flashed Janine and me knowing grins. Thankfully, Natalie was never one of them. She seemed to be growing more and more unwell, and she retired to bed each evening before dark.

Each morning, Natalie would approach me at the breakfast table, and I'd hand her everything but my toast. We didn't say much to each other.

But one morning, she sat down across from me and launched into a long description of all her medical troubles, claiming a touch of malaria—which I knew to be impossible since it would have put her on her back already—and a bout with dysentery. She even suspected she had beriberi, which was entirely possible given the state of our nutrition.

"My stomach hurts all the time," she said as she shoveled another bite of my oatmeal into her mouth. Her face was pale and damp with sweat. Her eyes had begun to bug out just a bit, and sometimes when she was eating, I could see her gums had been bleeding. As much as I couldn't stand her, I actually felt sorry for her.

"Maybe you should ask Mrs. Fincher for a few days off to rest," I said. "We're not as busy now anyway. I'm sure she'd let you."

She shook her head. "I'm not going to let the other girls think I can't pull my weight around here." She dug her spoon further into the oatmeal and groaned. "Oh, that's just disgusting. There's worms in here!"

She pushed the cup away from her, and I did my best not to smile. "You should definitely eat it, then. The cooking sterilized them, and you probably need the protein."

She glared at me. "What I need is some quinine."

"Aren't you taking your daily dose?"

"Yes, but the ration isn't even half of what we should be taking. I need more."

"Don't you think the soldiers should be getting what they need first?"

Natalie's eyes narrowed. "I think those of us in the military should be getting it first." Then she leaned forward onto the table. "You need to give me your quinine. You shouldn't even be getting any. You're a civilian. And a criminal at that."

"I'm not giving you my quinine. I'll get malaria for sure!"

"Don't think I haven't noticed you and your little friend sneaking off every night. What are you two doing? Are you stealing food? Medicine? You certainly look healthier than the rest of us, and there's no way that should be happening."

I leaned onto the table as well. "Because you're taking half my food, right?"

"I knew it. You are stealing! Admit it!"

"I am not. And I won't give you my quinine. You'll have to take the same amount as everyone else."

She sat back and studied me. "Is that so? Well, maybe once Mrs. Fincher hears that a convicted murderer is in our midst, sneaking around and stealing supplies, I'm sure she'll agree that the quinine should not be wasted on the likes of you."

I wasn't about to give in, but I had no idea what might happen if Natalie told Mrs. Fincher about me. Although I'd sworn I'd take no more of Natalie's blackmail, now Janine was involved and would be linked to me, as well as Matthew and Henry. "Fine," I said, sighing as I gave in against my better judgment. "You can have it." And I pushed away from the table so I wouldn't have to look at her hideous face again.

***

Later that evening, Janine, Matthew, Henry, and I decided to go for a swim in the river near our meeting place. The days were getting hotter and hotter, and the evenings were sticky with humidity. The cool water was invigorating, although my stomach turned at the sight of the mosquitos dancing on the surface, knowing that my body's defenses would soon be lowered without my daily dose of quinine. Afterward, Janine and Henry stole away for a while, and Matthew and I lay sprawled on the riverbank, my head on his chest, our legs entwined. I listened to his heartbeat and ran my fingers along his smooth chest.

I could never have imagined that I could love him more, but somehow I did. Every moment—with every kiss, every touch of his hands, every prayer we shared—a new bud of my love bloomed from a branch inside of me. It was wonderful, and yet terrifying at the same time. He'd tried nearly every day to get me to promise I'd leave him if I had the chance. Even thinking of that scenario made my chest tighten with fear.

As if he felt my body tense, Matthew took my hand in his. "What's on your mind?" he said.

The bombings had started again. Only a few in the distance today, but enough to remind me of what was to come. "This isn't going to last, is it? This lull in the fighting. The Japanese are still coming."

"They're still coming," he replied quietly. "Do you still have the gun I gave you?"

I sat up quickly. "Matthew…I'm so sorry. I had it when we crossed the bay, but as we were getting off the boat we were attacked. It was hit by a bullet and destroyed."

He frowned. "Well, at least the bullet didn't hit you. That's all that matters. I'll see if I can get you another one."

"There's really no need. I don't think I could actually *shoot* anyone."

He put his finger beneath my chin and tilted my face until I was look-ing into his eyes. "You can do it. And let's face it, you may have to. Just breathe and squeeze." He kissed me and pulled my body tighter into his. "Breathe…and squeeze."

It felt like our love might swallow us whole right there. I almost wished it would somehow, that we could escape the sickness and the war and the unthinkable threat of approaching troops. If we could exist in only our small bubble, life would be perfect. I wrapped myself around him and willed my mind to forget everything else for the moment. There was no death, no hunger, no gut-wrenching sickness.

Until there was.

***

A week later I awoke and could barely get out of bed. When I stood, my stomach swam, and I ran into the trees to vomit. I couldn't walk back to my bed, so I sank to the jungle floor and closed my eyes, resting my back against a large tree trunk. Janine found me a few minutes later and helped me back to my bed.

"I need to get to my ward," I said, forgetting momentarily to which ward I was assigned at present.

"You need to rest," Janine said. She pressed down on my shoulder when I tried to stand, which was enough to keep me planted where I sat. "I'll get a doctor to come check you out, but from what I can tell, it looks like you have malaria."

I wanted to curse Natalie for blackmailing me for my quinine doses, but I was too delirious to form the words in my mind. "No, I can make it. I just need a bit of coffee to get me going. Could you see if there's any to spare?"

She eyed me with disapproval, but then she stood and helped me to my feet. "I reckon we can go see if there's any at mess area #3. I heard they had some a few days ago."

She tried to help me put myself together, but I pushed her hands away. I could brush my own hair. At least, I thought I could. After a few strokes, my arms felt so heavy I couldn't lift them again. Janine scolded me and grabbed the brush.

She helped me walk slowly to camp, grumbling the whole way that I should've stayed in bed. I was thankful to finally make it to the mess area where I could sit down at a table. I was also glad it was a different mess area than where Natalie ate breakfast with the other nurses. Maybe I could get enough food down today to get me through the morning.

Janine came back with a small cup of coffee and a plate of oatmeal. I remembered the worms from the week before, and my stomach swam again. I pushed it away and sipped on the coffee instead. It was weak, and it tasted terrible, but I could tell instantly it was exactly what I need-ed. Feeling a small kick of energy, I told Janine I was fine, even demon-strated I could walk on my own, and headed for my assigned ward.

When I arrived for duty, Roberta Jacobs, the army nurse in charge of the ward, met me with a concerned expression. She stuck her wrist to

210 | JENNIFER H. WESTALL

my forehead and asked me if I was all right. I straightened the best I could and told her I was well enough. I had to admit, she looked pretty ill herself.

"We've had three nurses come down with malaria since yesterday," she said. "All of 'em are laid up. I'd be much obliged if you could hang in there for a while until I can get some help."

"I'll do my best," I said.

She thanked me and made her way back over to a chair near the center of the ward. Then she plopped down and leaned her head back. Closing her eyes, she breathed deeply for a minute, and then abruptly grabbed a bag off the ground and vomited into it.

I steeled myself against the fatigue threatening to take over, and I made my rounds. I had to stop frequently, and I had to sit down with my head between my legs a few times. Once, I noticed Roberta had fastened her arm with a sling and attached it to a table beside her. That seemed to be the only thing holding her up and keeping her from tumbling to the ground.

Near midday, I'd had about all I could take. The heat beat down on me, and I had reached the point where I needed to sit down between every single patient. The men with shredded bodies and missing limbs were actually looking on me with pity. I had begun to shake, and did my best to quell the tremors.

I came to the end of the row where I was working, and I was about to clean the dressing of a young man who'd been sprayed by bullets, when the whole earth swayed beneath me. My vision went dark around the edges, and I felt like I was turning topsy-turvy. My head hit something hard, and pain shot through my neck. Then everything went black.

I awoke some time later on a cot in the ward where I'd been working. I tried to sit up, but I couldn't. I was completely done. No matter what I tried to tell my body to do, it simply would not move. I managed to somehow roll my head to the side, and could just make out a nurse wending her way through the ward. My vision was too fuzzy to see who it was. And I couldn't hold my eyes open any longer, so I drifted off to sleep.

CHAPTER FOURTEEN

Matthew

March 17, 1942

I paced along the riverbank with my boots squishing in the damp grass and mud, trying to make heads or tails of Henry's news. It had rained earlier, and every piece of my clothing stuck to me like it was glued on. My pacing had set me to sweating, which wasn't helping matters. Henry sat on the fallen tree trunk smoking a cigarette like he didn't have a care in the world.

"So, you're sure you can trust this Mike guy?" I asked for the third time since Henry had told me about Mike's message.

He took a long drag on the cigarette. "Yep. Known him since we played ball together in San Diego. He's a good fella. If he says they're getting planes and subs through the blockade, then they certainly are."

"And you trust him to get the girls through the blockade?"

"I do. Ole Dugout Doug made it through. And I trust Mike a heckuva lot more than I trust him."

I grimaced at the mention of MacArthur's escape to Australia. I'd done my best to give the general the benefit of the doubt, but my opinion of him sank every day this debacle of a war continued.

213

"And he's certain there's no way he can fly over here to the peninsula to get the girls?" I asked. "Only way we get them on the plane is from Corregidor?"

Henry let out a deep sigh. "I done told ya; he says any evacuations are coming from Corregidor. We gotta get there first. He said if there's an evacuation, he's pretty sure he can squeeze two more bodies on board."

"And you trust him?"

"Again. Yes, I trust him. Now can we please focus on getting to Corregidor? Ain't nobody going nowhere if we can't do that."

I glanced at my watch. The girls were late. I was already uneasy from my discussion with Henry, but something else was gnawing at me too. I still hadn't gotten a solid promise from Ruby that she'd even get on the plane. How was I going to convince her to go?

Henry jumped down from the tree trunk and moved swiftly toward the path behind me. As I turned, he met Janine running toward us. My heart raced when I saw Ruby wasn't with her. And from Janine's expression, I could tell something was wrong.

As I came over to them, I heard her explaining to Henry that Ruby had taken ill. "She just wouldn't listen to me. I tried to get her to stay in bed today and rest, but she insisted on working, and now she's being treated at the ward."

"What for?" I asked. "What's wrong with her?"

"It's malaria," she said. "I'm sure of it."

"Which ward?"

"The one near the dental clinic."

I set out along the trail, determined to see her for myself. Janine ran up beside me, and I could hear Henry's boots clomping along behind. "Remember to be discreet," she pleaded. "Natalie's been hovering around like a fly. I think she's been using Ruby to get more than just a bit of breakfast."

"What do you mean?" I asked.

"I've seen Ruby giving Natalie her quinine dose a few times."

I shouldn't have been surprised, but this news sent my blood to boiling. By the time I reached the ward, I was good and worked up, but once I found Ruby, I almost lost my composure altogether. That Joseph fella was seated beside her, watching her sleep like he had some claim on her.

I went to her side, and Joseph looked up at me, startled. "She's just fallen asleep," he said quietly.

"What are you doing here?" I asked. "Don't you have patients to attend to?"

His dark features hardened as he glanced over my shoulder at Henry and Janine making their way toward us. "Why don't we step over here and talk?"

He gestured toward a cluster of mango and palm trees a few feet away, and I followed him. I felt like decking him right there, but I kept my composure and forced myself to listen to him. He crossed his arms and set a defensive stance, as if somehow I was the one trying to steal his wife.

"Look," he said, "Ruby's fever is much higher than it should be. She's nauseous and her blood pressure is significantly raised. She needs rest."

"What can we do to help?" Henry said.

"We're very low on quinine. Do you have access to any at your camp?"

"Are you her doctor?" I asked.

"Not exactly," Joseph said with a hint of annoyance. "But I offered to help out in the ward during my break. I wanted to make sure she was all right."

"That's my job."

"Then maybe you should do it. She's wasting away, in case you haven't noticed." His eyes narrowed with unspoken accusations.

Henry cleared his throat. "Hey, we're all doing the best we can. No one's exactly thriving out here."

Joseph took a deep breath and turned away for a moment. Then he turned back to Henry, visibly forcing himself to relax. "I get that. I really do. And I know how she is. She'd give all her food away to some poor local family and starve herself if she had half the chance. I'm just worried about her."

It struck me in the oddest way that he would know her so well. I had to wonder what else he knew. "Look, I appreciate that you're doing your best to care for her. I'm sorry if I came on a little strong."

Henry coughed, and Janine smiled. I didn't have the patience for those two right now. For any of this, actually. I needed to figure out a way to get Ruby to Corregidor. But she wasn't going anywhere in this condition. I turned to Henry. "So what do we do now?"

"We wait for her to get better," he said.

"How long before she can travel?" I asked Joseph.

He lifted a brow. "Where is she going?"

"Don't worry about that part. How long?"

He hesitated, then looked at Henry. "No less than a week. More like two most likely. Henry, where is she going?"

Henry glanced at me before he answered. "We might have a way to get her and Janine to Australia. But we got to get them to Corregidor first."

"Wait a minute," Janine said. "What's this? I'm not leaving my patients. Or you, for that matter."

Henry rolled his eyes. "It's nothing definite yet."

"Uh, uh. No way." Janine crossed her arms and shifted her weight. "If the other nurses aren't leaving, and the soldiers aren't leaving, then I'm not leaving."

Henry glanced at me for support. I shrugged, and he pulled Janine away to finish their conversation in private. I headed back to Ruby's bed and crouched down beside her. Sweat trickled down her temples, and I could see in her neck that her pulse was racing. I was so helpless to do anything for her; it made me crazy inside. I reached over and pushed a few strands of hair away from her face. Her skin was hot as fire.

Over by the dental building, I could see Henry and Janine arguing. She was clearly not budging. Looked like Henry and I both had our jobs cut out for us. I was wondering just what I could possibly say to convince Ruby to leave, when I noticed someone moving through the trees between the dental building and the ward. A figure I recognized, and despised. Natalie snaked through the rows of beds toward us. I didn't think she'd seen me yet, so I headed out of the ward in the other direction. If I stuck around, I'd surely confront her on this business of taking Ruby's quinine. I had to keep it together a little longer.

Just a little longer.

Ruby

March 24, 1942

I knew that days were passing, but I couldn't tell how many, and I couldn't tell the difference between my dreams and reality. Once, I crept along the ground and stole fresh cabbage from the mess hall. Another time, I came across a pile of bananas on the ground and dove into eating them; only, after a few bites, I realized that they were rotten and filled with maggots. Sometimes, I saw Natalie's face bending over me, studying me closely before moving away. Those were the worst dreams.

Other times, I found Matthew sitting beside me, holding my hand and whispering prayers. He'd tell me how much he loved me, about all the wonderful things we were going to do together once I was better, and how we were going to make our way to Australia to live out our lives in peace. I'd never been to Australia, but in my mind it was beautiful. Beaches, the ocean, and all kinds of flowers. When I pictured us walking hand in hand across the sand, it was so real I almost cried.

Janine checked on me every day it seemed. Sometimes Henry came with her. She'd check my temperature, my pulse, and get me some fluids. She and Henry spoke quietly nearby, sometimes whispering of their own future plans, sometimes fussing over my lack of recovery, and a few times arguing over her stubborn refusal to leave if the opportunity for escape were to come.

At one point, I finally awoke with enough clarity and energy to sit up in bed and take a little food. I couldn't taste it though, and I could barely swallow. I only got down a couple of bites. Joseph came by to check on me, looking concerned.

"I just don't understand why your recovery's so slow," he said, pushing my hair back to feel my forehead. "You should be at least a little better by now. Have you been able to eat anything?"

I shook my head. "I can't seem to swallow anything."

The world still seemed a bit unsteady. I had the strangest sensation that I was about to fall out of my bed. Joseph took his hand away and made a note on the papers he held. Then he sighed and looked down at me again. "I wish I could do more for you. If I could get you out of here, I would. I should've sent you into the mountains with my mother."

I managed a weak smile. "You're a good doctor, Joseph. And an even better friend. Thank you."

He gave my hand a pat and assured me he'd return after supper. Then he said goodbye and headed toward the main surgery building. I closed my eyes for a moment to try to steady the dizziness. When I opened them again, I saw Natalie making her way through the rows of beds toward me. I actually hoped I was having another nightmare.

But I was definitely awake. She stopped beside my bed and took my wrist in her hand. "Thought he'd never leave," she muttered. "Why does everyone in the world fuss so much over you? Got 'em all fooled, don't ya?"

I pulled my arm away from her grip. My head pounded, and all I wanted was for her to go away. "What do you want, Natalie? I don't have anything I can give you right now."

She put on a fake smile and nodded toward another nurse a few rows away from us. "So," she said loud enough for others to hear. "How are we feeling today?"

"We?" Just for a split second, I wished I needed to vomit. Then she'd see just how we were feeling.

She eyed me with a hint of triumph as she felt my forehead. "Still a touch of fever I see. And your pulse...very fast." She handed me a small cup of water, along with something in her hand. "Here's your quinine." She placed her hand over mine, but didn't release the pills. Then she handed me the cup of water as she slid the pills into her pocket. "Drink up," she said.

I put the cup to my lips and took a sip while she wrote something on my chart, probably the fake quinine dosage. She smiled at me and took the cup. I expected her to turn and leave at that point, but instead, she plopped down onto the end of my bed and frowned at me with a look of disappointment.

"Just can't figure out why you're not recovering faster. Reckon it's God's judgment? You know, this arrangement of ours could've worked in both our favors if you'd have stuck to your end of the deal. But you just couldn't do it, could you?"

My head swam, and my stomach churned. She had that look in her eye. She was determined to get something more from me. But I couldn't think of one thing more I could give her. "I have no idea what you're talking about," I said.

"Yes, you do." Natalie's tone was icy. "You think I'm a fool? I see what's going on. I see Matthew here with you. I've heard your brother and his girlfriend arguing. And it isn't right. You—a dangerous criminal, a convicted murderer who runs around with negroes—you steal my boyfriend, who you swore you'd stay away from, and now you have some plan concocted to escape justice once again."

Gingerly I scooted back down the bed until I was flat on my back again, then I rolled onto my side so that I wouldn't have to look at her. "Natalie, I don't know what delusions you have in your head, but I don't feel like playing games. I assure you, I am not escaping anything."

"Then what's all this talk about a plane to Australia?"

"That's just a lot of wishful thinking. Like everyone else around here. How many times have we heard rumors of convoys headed across the Pacific? Or supplies that will arrive any day now?" I looked over my shoulder and into her cold eyes. "There's no one coming but the Japanese. And none of us are getting out of here."

I didn't think her face could get any paler, but somehow she looked even more sickened when I said that. Some part of me went cold inside as well. It wasn't until that moment, when I said it out loud, that I realized how true that statement was.

Natalie stood, her hands shaking. "No. You're lying again. That's all you know how to do. I'm going to find Mrs. Fincher and tell her everything. Right now."

She turned and stomped a few steps away, and desperation rose inside of me. "Wait!" She turned around, and I saw a brief chance to stall her just a little longer. "What do you want from me?"

She walked back to my bed, looking around to see if anyone was listening. But it seemed that each soldier in the beds around mine was struggling with their own special kind of hell. No one cared about mine. Natalie leaned down and lowered her voice. "I want off this godforsaken island! I want food, and real clothes. I want my life back!"

In her eyes I saw my own desperate desires for home and safety. I could almost sympathize with her. She was going about it in the worst possible way, but I could understand how she felt. "Look, I know this is hard. It's hard on everyone. I can't guarantee that there's a plan to escape. I've been out of it for a while. But if there is, if a chance comes up to get off the island, a real one, not just a rumor, then you can go too."

She eyed me with suspicion, stepping away to consider this. "You swear?"

"I'm sure there will be enough room for one more."

"How can I be sure you're not lying just to keep me quiet?"

I was, and I prayed to God he'd forgive me for one more untruth. "Because if you turn me in, then you have no chance at all of escaping. I'm your only hope."

***

Within a couple of days, I was sent to recover in my own bed in the nurses' quarters. When I could manage to walk well enough, Janine and I made our way back to our meeting place to see Matthew and Henry. I was so happy to see Matthew again, but I was also still weak from the malaria. I nearly collapsed as soon as I arrived.

Matthew sat beside me, our backs against the tree trunk, my head resting on his shoulder. And Henry and Janine sat leaning into each other on a large rock protruding from the bank. When I'd caught my breath, I told them everything that had happened with Natalie. I could feel Matthew's body tense when I told them I'd promised her a place on the plane.

"Ruby, we can't do that," he said. "Mike said he could get two people on. No more. That's you and Janine."

"I know that, but I didn't know what else to say. She was going to tell Mrs. Fincher who I really am."

"So what if she does?" he said. "At this point, I can't see what Mrs. Fincher could do to you. The army has much bigger problems than a wild story from Natalie that she can't prove."

"It's not just about me anymore. All three of you could get in big trouble. Courts-martial? Prison? Who knows what could happen to you? I love all three of you, and I won't put any of you in that position."

"Not that anyone seems to notice," Janine said, "but I think I've made myself clear on this. I'm not leaving Henry or my patients. And Ruby's been just as clear on the same point. So all this discussion about us hopping on a plane to Australia is meaningless. Natalie can have it."

Henry removed the cigarette from his mouth and blew out smoke. I hated that he'd taken up smoking in the past few months, but it seemed like such a silly thing to be worried about when he was dodging bombs and bullets. He pulled away from Janine so he could get a good look at her.

"Listen here. You have to be reasonable. I ain't talking about sneaking you away from your duty in the middle of the night. We're talking about a legitimate evacuation. No one's getting court-martialed. I'm just asking you to be ready and willing if the opportunity presents itself."

Janine jumped off the rock and pointed a finger at him. "No, you're talking about making my decisions for me 'cause you think you know better than I do."

She turned and stomped away with Henry jogging to catch up. I could hear them arguing as they headed for the shelter they'd been using as a ramshackle honeymoon getaway. They'd be making up soon enough.

"Sounds like a familiar conversation," Matthew said, grinning down at me.

"She has a point."

"So does he."

I didn't have the energy for arguing, so for once I let him have the last word on the matter. I shuffled down until my head rested on his lap, and he ran his hands through my hair. I closed my eyes and wished I could block out the sounds of bombing in the distance. Every day, it seemed to be getting closer. And just the day before, Radio Tokyo had announced that a large convoy from the U.S. had been obliterated. Every one of us had known it was propaganda, and yet, it was more discouraging than anything else we'd heard so far. Just that morning, five of the nurses didn't even try to get out of bed, while others returned immediately after their shifts. Morale had sunk to new depths.

"The bombs are getting closer," I said. "Won't be long till the Japanese break through the line."

"Are you frightened?"

"A little, but not really about the Japanese."

His hand stopped for a moment. "What are you afraid of?"

I paused. I hadn't fully admitted my fears to myself, and here I was sharing them out loud. "I'm not sure how to explain it. God doesn't speak to me anymore. He doesn't fill me with His peace. He hasn't healed through me since the day of our accident. Instead, I'm filled with this vague anxiousness about the future. When I read my Bible, when I pray, there's this emptiness inside me, and I don't know why. I want desperately for God to come near me, to feel His presence with me again. That's what I'm afraid of. That God's left me."

Matthew was quiet. He'd gone back to stroking my hair, and as he listened, he stared toward the river. Was he disappointed in me? He'd never been comfortable with God's healing work through me, and I had no idea what he was thinking. But I'd released some invisible wall that had been holding me up, and all my fears came tumbling out of me.

"I keep reading the same Bible verses, over and over, and they're stuck in my head. From Psalm 18. It says, 'How long wilt thou forget me, O Lord? For ever? How long wilt thou hide thy face from me? How long shall I take counsel in my soul, having sorrow in my heart daily? How long shall mine enemy be exalted over me?'"

By this time, I was crying, and I couldn't make it stop. Matthew pulled me up and held me against his chest. "Oh, Ruby. I had no idea you were struggling so much with your faith. Don't you know how much God loves you? He's blessed us over and above what we deserve. He'll restore you in His time, at exactly the right moment. He'll use you again. He will bless us even more."

"Bless us?" I sobbed into his chest. "I've done my best to remain faithful through every trial I've faced. Losing Daddy and our home. Almost losing you to T.B. and Brother Cass's relentless campaign against me. Every person in Cullman, and maybe even the whole state, believing I was a murderer. Sitting in that courtroom, listening to the judge sen-

224 | JENNIFER H. WESTALL

tence me to the chair. Having to leave you behind." I took in a shaky breath, trying to keep my composure. "And the worst of all was living these past years without you. Knowing I'd broken your heart. But through all of that, I prayed for courage and faith. That God would direct my steps, and that He would be glorified. And now, where has all of that gotten me?" I sat up and looked him in the eyes. "I'm trapped on an island with starvation and malaria all around me, the Japanese coming at me from one direction, and Natalie coming at me from the other. I am surrounded by enemies. And I don't see the blessings."

He cradled me against him while I wept, kissing my forehead. "It's all right. All of those things happened for reasons we can't completely understand. But God does love us, and all those struggles you went through, those were my struggles too. And facing them has made me into a man that can trust God. You know, I've been meditating on some verses as well. Psalm 34 says, 'This poor man cried, and the Lord heard him, and saved him out of all his troubles.' That poor man was me. I cried out to God every day after I lost you. And not once was it out of faith. But in time, I felt His hands surrounding me, caring for me, putting people in my path that showed me He still loved me. And now..." His eyes looked on me with wonder and joy. "Now, you're my wife. Part of my soul forever. And I meant it when I said nothing could break that. Not Natalie, not the Japanese, not separation...not even death. That's how I know that I'll find you again if you go to Australia." He kissed me, wiping my tears with his thumbs. "My heart will always find yours, Ruby. Always."

March 30, 1942

My strength grew over the next two days, and I was able to resume my duties. Matthew's words of encouragement stayed with me, giving me hope that God would protect us. After all, we'd managed to survive this far without either of us getting seriously hurt. Considering all the suffering around us, I counted that as a blessing.

On the morning of March 30, I was making my rounds in the ward near mess #4 when I noticed Joseph standing about twenty yards off, watching me. I waved, and he headed over. "I'm so glad to see you," I said, smiling and hugging him. "I haven't had a chance to thank you for taking such good care of me when I was sick."

He looked me over and stuck his hand to my forehead. "How are you feeling? It's a little soon to be back on duty."

"I'm no worse off than any of the other girls working. And I was tired of lying about all day. It's not in my nature."

"No truer words were ever spoken." He rubbed the back of his neck and let out a deep sigh. "I miss this, you know? I miss you."

Warmth spread up my neck and into my face. "Joseph, I'm married—
"

"Oh, I know," he interrupted. "And I don't mean...well, I just mean...I miss arguing with you over patients, and taking you to dinner, and dancing with you." He smiled. "You're a lovely dancer." I didn't know what to say, so I stood there blushing like a little girl. "I just miss our friendship, that's all," he finished.

"Don't say that like we're not friends anymore," I said.

"Look, I haven't gone anywhere. I'm here. You're the one who's slipping away. And I understand. But tell me the truth. Does this Matthew fella make you happy?"

"Yes. He's...he's the only man I've ever truly loved." I could see how much that hurt him, but it had to be better to tell him the truth. "I'm sorry."

His dark eyes looked down on me with such sorrow that I felt my heart ache for him. He managed a small smile. "I am glad you found such a love. Hold on to it with all your might."

Something in his words seemed final, and they sent a rush of fear through me. As he turned to go, I threw my arms around his waist and hugged him close. He pulled me tight against him, and then he kissed the top of my head. "You're a wonderful doctor," I said. "I don't know what I wouldv'e done without you."

He let go of me, so I stepped back and let him walk away. I turned back to my patients, praying God would bring someone into Joseph's life who would love him for the amazing man he was. I leaned over to pick up the clipboard for my next patient. That was when I heard the high-pitched squeal. And another second later, everything around me exploded.

***

I thought my eyes were going to come right out of their sockets from the pressure of the blast, and my lungs were instantly raw from the smoke. I couldn't see, and all I could hear was a loud ringing in my ears. I crawled a few feet and felt the bamboo shoot of what used to be a bed. My vision began to clear. There was a body lying beneath a pile of rubble. I moved the rubble around, fumbling in the dirt, and realized the arm I'd grabbed wasn't attached to a body.

I dropped to all fours and vomited up bile.

The earth beneath me shook, but I still couldn't hear anything. I tried to stand, but I stumbled again. Pushing myself forward, I gripped a mangled bed in front of me for support. The entire ward was in disarray. People ran in every direction. Beds were overturned or simply blown away. Bodies lay strewn about, some moving and moaning, many deathly still.

I stumbled out of the ward as gradually the ringing in my ears was replaced by screaming. And the blasts from more bombs. I searched for a trench, but I didn't see one. I half-ran, half-stumbled to the next ward over. People hurried to take cover. A nurse and a medic crawled under a desk.

Two more concussions sounded nearby, and I hit the dirt. Another bomb dropped right on top of the ward. I watched in horror as the nurse and medic underneath the desk were thrown into the air. As the shrapnel rained down around me, I covered my head.

I couldn't think straight. I needed to find shelter. Desperately I looked around again and spotted the edge of a trench through the smoke just a few feet away. I crawled over to it and fell inside.

CHAPTER FIFTEEN

Ruby

March 30, 1942

When the bombing finally ceased, it seemed like everything went still for a long minute before chaos erupted. I lay on the ground inside the trench along with other terrified soldiers and nurses. Some climbed out when the bombing stopped. Two others, including the young nurse named Laura who I'd met in Manila and slept three cots away from mine, clung to a medic in silent terror. Her eyes were wide, and her whole body shook. The medic seemed to be clinging to her too.

Our gazes met, and he asked me if I was all right. "I...I think so," I said. "I just need a moment."

I felt around my body to see if everything was still intact. I had a few minor cuts, probably from flying shrapnel, but otherwise I was free from injury. My heart thundered, my head ached, and my ears felt like cotton had been shoved inside them. I pulled myself out of the trench to a ghastly sight.

Some personnel worked furiously to uncover bodies buried beneath debris. Others carried casualties toward the surgical building, which thankfully, appeared to have escaped a direct hit. I wasn't sure where to jump in, and the destruction was overwhelming. I nearly fell to my knees right there, my legs buckling in shock, but I knew I had to keep it together so I could help others.

Outside the surgical building, nurses and medics triaged the incoming. I ran in that direction, noticing Mrs. Fincher off to one side directing them on where to place the injured, and where to lay the dead. She had a nasty gash along her forehead, and she was holding her side, but she was barking orders with as much command as any general. I rushed up to her and asked where I could help.

"Triage is most critical at the moment. Over there." She pointed to a clearing where writhing bodies already littered the jungle floor.

"Are you all right?" I asked. "You look like you need medical attention as well."

"I'm perfectly fine," she growled. "Now stop gabbing and get to work!"

I raced for the clearing, pausing briefly at a supply station to stuff my pockets full of gauze, morphine, and clean rags. Then I bolted for the far side and began with the first person I reached. I worked my way from one moaning, ravaged body to the next, trying to focus on their immediate needs. Arms and legs were missing, chests were sliced open, and blood seeped into the ground. Before long I ran out of morphine and had to race back to the supply station. On my way back, I saw Joseph being laid among the injured.

My stomach dropped, and I rushed over to him. I grabbed the arm of the medic who had laid him there before he could disappear. "What happened? How badly is he injured?"

The medic looked back at me with panic-stricken eyes. He was covered in blood, maybe even his own. I couldn't tell. "I don't know. I have to go back and carry more of them here."

I let go of his arm and dropped beside Joseph, immediately seeing the trouble. Shrapnel. Everywhere. And a large chunk was lodged in his right collarbone, slicing him from neck to chest. Blood was everywhere. I looked around for a doctor, but all I saw were nurses and medics. So I took off for the surgical unit. I sprinted into the building, searching frantically for someone who could help. Every doctor I saw was standing at a table, cutting into patients.

"I need help!" I screamed, not knowing what else to do.

Roberta, who'd supervised my ward the past few weeks, came over and put a hand on my arm. "What's the trouble, Grace? Are you hurt?"

"No, it's not me," I said. "It's Dr. Grant. He's critically injured. He needs surgery right away."

"Take me to him," she said. "I'll see what I can do."

Together we dashed back into the clearing to Joseph's lifeless body. I knelt beside him and checked his pulse. It was faint, but still there. Roberta went to the other side and examined the wounds. "Oh, Grace," she said. "He's...he isn't..." She met my gaze and shook her head slightly.

"No! He's still alive. He needs surgery, now."

"I'll see what I can do." She jumped up and ran back into the building.

I leaned over Joseph and prayed with all my might. "Lord, please help him! I can heal him! Just let me!" I sobbed as I did my best to clean his wounds and stop the bleeding. But I could see his life was pouring out of him. "Please, God. Please. Let me heal him."

I closed my eyes and stilled my racing mind. I searched for the calm spirit that would come over me in the past, the pool of peace that would wash over me when He healed someone. *Lord, send Your presence here. Joseph is a faithful servant, who only wants to help others and give You glory. Please, save him!*

I waited and waited. But nothing came. I opened my eyes and took Joseph's hand in mine. "Joseph, I'm so sorry," I whispered. "I'm so sorry." I bent over and kissed his cheek. His eyes never opened. And his body lay perfectly still.

I felt along his neck, then his wrist. Nothing. I checked for breathing, but he was gone. This amazing man, who deserved to be loved and cared for, who had loved me when I'd felt so lost, was just...gone. I pushed myself up from the ground and surveyed all the other dying men around me. I couldn't do anything to help them. Why? Why was God withholding His healing? Why was He allowing this suffering?

I couldn't take it anymore. I had to get out of there. Had to breathe. I turned to run, with no destination in mind other than some place as far away as possible. But I only took three steps before I ran into someone. Strong arms enveloped me, and immediately I knew I was in Matthew's embrace.

"Ruby! Are you all right?" He pressed my head into his chest, and I let go of the anguish inside of me.

"He's dead! He's dead!" I held onto him with all my strength. "I couldn't save him!"

We stood there in the middle of the destruction, clinging to each other. I knew I needed to gain control of myself, that I should be helping others. But I was so useless. God wouldn't allow me to heal anyone. And all I could do was try to comfort them as their life slipped away. What good was I to anyone?

Matthew held onto me, but pulled my face back to look into my eyes. "I was so worried when I heard the bombs go off. Thank God you're all right."

"I couldn't save him," I cried. "Why can't I save anyone?"

Carefully stepping over all the debris, Matthew walked me over to a more secluded spot in the trees. He held me close and did his best to comfort me. "What happened?"

"Joseph is dead! I tried to heal him. I prayed, and I begged God to let me heal him. But nothing happened, and he just died right there on the ground! Like...like his life meant nothing!"

He pulled me against him again and tried to quiet the rising storm inside of me. "You aren't the Savior, Ruby. You know that. You always told me it wasn't your power, it was God's. I know it doesn't make any sense, and you want to blame yourself, but you didn't fail Joseph. You did everything you could. It's going to be all right, baby. You'll see. It's all right. We're still here, and God's watching over us. Don't lose hope."

But I had. I was all out of faith, all out of energy, all out of hope. What more was there to hope for? Death?

Matthew

April 1, 1942

I stayed at the hospital well into the next day helping to put things in order, along with many other volunteers from Cabcaben and neighboring camps. The worst part was gathering the dead bodies, many of them in pieces. Henry actually had to climb a tree to retrieve a corpse. It was the stuff of nightmares.

Ruby went about helping the wounded in a daze. I worried about her state of mind, and I prayed for her every chance I got. She seemed lower than I'd ever seen her, even more so than when she was sentenced to execution. It was as if something inside her had broken. I had to find a way to get her off that island and away from all this. But the chances were growing slimmer every day.

Just two days before, Henry and I had climbed a ridge not far from Cabcaben and watched as Japanese planes bombarded Corregidor. My hopes had fallen as I realized there was no way we'd survive a boat ride across the bay. Henry still thought a night crossing was possible, but my faith was stalling. Seeing Ruby in such a state made me realize that I'd have to be strong for both of us somehow. I prayed for God to strengthen my faith, 'cause things were looking bleak.

The next day, I held onto Ruby a little longer than usual when I said goodbye. Seemed we both had dispensed of trying to hide our relationship, even from Natalie. What did it matter at that point? I kissed her goodbye and told her to keep her chin up.

She lifted her face to mine without even attempting to smile. "Please be careful. I love you."

"I love you too," I said. "I'll be back as soon as I can. If they evacuate the nurses to Corregidor, don't worry about getting word to me. Just go. Understand?"

She nodded and closed her eyes, but not before a tear slipped by. "I don't want you to go. I know you have to. But I don't want to be away from you anymore."

I pulled her into my chest again. "Don't lose faith. God is with us. It may be hard to feel His presence right now, but He's here. He's guarding our souls. Remember what Paul said to the Romans? 'Who shall separate us from the love of Christ?...In all these things we are more than conquerors through him that loved us. For I am persuaded, that neither death, nor life, nor angels, nor principalities, nor powers, nor things present, nor things to come, nor height nor depth nor any other creature, shall be able to separate us from the love of God.'"

The words of the Bible flowed out of me as if someone else were saying them. I took comfort in their message of hope, and I prayed Ruby did as well. I squeezed her one final time, and kissed her goodbye. She did her best to hold back her tears, but I could see she was struggling.

"I'll see you soon," I said.

Then I hopped into the truck with Henry, and we made the short drive back to Cabcaben.

***

When we arrived, the camp was buzzing with news. Doug came over to me before I'd even climbed out of the truck. "We got orders coming. Rumor has it they're moving us to the front line."

"Is this like the convoy rumors, or is this real?" I asked.

"I think this is real. We have a meeting at eighteen hundred with Captain Prescott and some other bigwigs."

Henry came around the truck and leaned against it. "I reckon it's about time we got to kill some Japs. I'm tired of sitting on my rear waiting for 'em to come after me."

"We'll need to get word to the girls," I said.

"Don't know if there's time," Doug said. "Sounds like they're moving us out tonight."

"Tonight?" I said.

"Japs broke through the line," Doug said. "Every division is falling back."

I glanced down at my watch. If Doug was right, we only had half an hour before the meeting, and that wasn't enough time to get word to Ruby. I'd just have to pray that she listened to me and would stay with the nurses.

***

For once, a rumor had proven true, and we were indeed heading to the front line that night. After the initial meeting, Captain Prescott called me into his quarters, where he had a large map stretched across a table. "Lieutenant, you've done an excellent job around here. Your battalion has maintained an excellent airstrip, and the barracks project was completed ahead of schedule, despite many of the men being weakened and ill."

"Thank you, sir," I said.

He pointed to the map. "As I stated earlier, we're being called to the front line, right here." I took a closer look as he continued. "Now, this spot between a division of Filipino Scouts and the 57th Infantry has been held up to this point by an entire division. The Nips overran them, and it's our job to push them back."

An entire division was overrun? "Sir, with all the illness in our ranks, you realize we're only at about a hundred men. And many of them are not infantry. Does Headquarters know this?"

He frowned, the lines in his face deepening. "Yes. They know."

"With all due respect, I understand the logic of sending us in there. I mean, I'm all for facing the enemy. I'm not afraid to fight. I just don't understand how this is a winnable situation."

"Winning isn't the objective anymore, Lieutenant."

"Then what is?"

"Survival. We hold off the Japs long enough for the rest to retreat to Corregidor."

"I see." So the mission was doomed. But if the plan was a retreat to Corregidor, then that meant Ruby would be moved there too. And if I could play a small part in making that possible, even if it meant certain death, then I would face it. "What can I do to help, sir?"

He walked around the table and handed me a piece of paper. "You're being promoted to Captain. I've been promoted to Major. I'll be coordinating with the other divisions, the Scouts and the 57th, as we arrive. Your job is to move this ragtag group through the jungle and fill the gap. Then kill as many Nips as you lay your eyes on."

Ruby

April 8, 1942

Days passed, and Matthew and Henry had disappeared. Janine and I visited our meeting place a few times, but we could hear the sounds of small arms fighting drawing closer, and eventually decided it was too dangerous to venture away from camp. I prayed Matthew and Henry were safe, but a gnawing feeling in my gut told me they were in danger. But what could I do? So I prayed nearly every moment of every day. I even carried Daddy's Bible with me to my ward.

I had plenty to keep me busy. Over the week following the bombing, soldiers came pouring into the hospital, wide-eyed and full of horrific stories. The Japanese were overrunning our lines, slaughtering thousands. First a few, and then by the dozen, men would wander through the hospital, emerging from the jungle in a daze. Many of them had gotten separated from their units and had no idea where they were. Some continued on their way after a meal, but many were so ill or wounded, they wound up in a bed in the latest ward. I found myself ministering as much to their spirits as I did to their broken bodies. Sometimes, I was able to read from Daddy's Bible out loud. This, more than anything else, seemed to bring a small measure of comfort.

Dread filled the entire staff. At mess, Janine and I tried not to talk about it because we were so afraid for our husbands, but the nurses around us couldn't seem to help it. The Japanese were closing in fast, and imaginations ran wild with the possible tortures that might be on the horizon. About a week after the bombing, we were sitting at a table finishing our pitiful rations of rice and tomatoes when Natalie seemed to lose it.

"What if they execute all of us?" she asked, panic rising in her voice. "Or worse?"

"If they do, I can only hope it's quick," Roberta said. "After that business in Nanking—"

"Roberta!" Janine shouted. "Now isn't the time to frighten everyone."

Roberta shrugged and went back to eating. Gail Downing, one of the higher-ranking nurses, came running across the clearing toward us and waved another group of nurses to come near. We all crowded around as she caught her breath.

"We just got orders to evacuate to Corregidor. They're moving all the nurses out in less than an hour!"

"What?"

"No!"

"We can't leave now!"

The grumbling erupted, with almost everyone objecting to the move. "What about our patients?" Roberta asked. "We can't just leave them."

Gail quieted everyone down. "Mrs. Fincher is meeting with Colonel Lansing right now. He said they don't want any women in the camp when the Japs come through. I overheard her arguing with him. Apparently, the orders are for all military nurses to be evacuated, and only the military nurses."

My heart pounded. As a civilian, I would be left behind. Where would I go? I glanced at Janine, who furrowed her brow. "Don't worry, I'm not leaving you here," she said, as if she could read my mind.

Gail shushed everyone again. "No, listen. Mrs. Fincher flew into a hot rage and told Colonel Lansing he had to evacuate *all* her nurses—American, Filipino, and civilians. He said he couldn't 'cause his orders were only for the military nurses. But then she said, 'If you don't evacuate all of the nurses, then I won't go!'"

The murmurings started up again, with most of the nurses agreeing with Mrs. Fincher. I was relieved to know my comrades weren't so eager to ditch me.

"Well, I won't go," one of the nurses called out. "I mean, can they make us go?"

"That's right," called another. "We took a pledge, and I don't intend to abandon my patients."

"And what about the doctors and medics? If they have to stay here and face the enemy, then so should we."

I glanced over at Natalie, who sat hunched in her seat. Clearly she was unnerved by all this talk of staying. "Don't we have to obey orders?" she asked no one in particular.

"Hush!" Gail said. "Mrs. Fincher's coming this way. Guess we'll find out soon enough."

Mrs. Fincher marched across the clearing like she was ready to take on the Japs herself. I figured Colonel Lansing got an earful of what she thought about his orders. She stopped at our gathering and surveyed everyone.

"Well, I suppose you've heard the news. But just to make it official, we are being evacuated to Corregidor tonight. You will have less than an hour to gather your belongings. As of right now, the order is for military personnel only, but I guarantee that will change to include all of you nurses shortly. So, go ahead and gather your things as well. Everyone will report to the surgical building to be loaded onto buses and trucks, and we will then make our way to Mariveles to catch a boat across the bay. Ladies, the situation on Bataan is grave. Do not delay."

Many of the girls jumped up and hurried off toward their quarters. Some stayed behind to plead their case to stay with their patients. But Mrs. Fincher would hear none of it. She shooed everyone off to gather their belongings. I approached her with a certain amount of trepidation.

"Mrs. Fincher, thank you for standing up for the civilian nurses—"

"Grace, that's all fine and dandy for later. For now, get moving. I'll send final word of the decision for the Filipinos and civilians."

"Yes, ma'am." I took off for my quarters wondering what I would do if Headquarters refused her. As tough as she was, this was the military, and you couldn't just go around defying orders.

***

The nurses' quarters were ablaze with activity. Many of the nurses were crying as they rushed to pack, worrying over their patients and who would care for them. None of us had much in the way of belongings, especially those whose suitcases had gone down with the *Mc E. Hyde* on Christmas. But over the months on Bataan, Mrs. Fincher had worked tirelessly to get us the more feminine supplies necessary to keep our spirits up. It was amazing how precious bobby pins and bit of makeup had become, but those small items kept us from feeling completely cut-off from the world. Sally Carpenter hadn't been at the mess area with us, so she was only now being told the news. She had just come back from bathing in the river, and her hair was still in curlers as she struggled to get ready.

It didn't take me long to finish since, even with my salvaged suitcase, I had so little to my name. Having recently washed my undergarments and a dress, I pulled the still damp clothes from the line and threw them into my suitcase along with Daddy's Bible. Then I stood and looked at my bed with a sudden inexplicable sadness. This tiny little corner of the jungle had been my home for over three months, the place where I'd married Matthew, and where I'd buried Joseph. A piece of me would always remain here.

But there was no time to ponder my thoughts, so I grabbed my suitcase and found Janine. "I'm heading over to my ward to check on a few fellas one last time. I want to make sure the medics and doctors know what's going on with the most critical cases."

"I should do that too," she said.

Several others agreed, and we all took our bags and ran for the hospital. I was out of breath by the time I reached the ward I'd been assigned all week. It wasn't too far from the nurses' quarters, but it was a good distance from the surgical building. I'd been handling mostly the medical cases, those with various illnesses and some with shell shock. But of course, many had multiple issues. Illness on top of injury. I walked through the rows of beds, checking temperatures and dressings. Some needed changing, so I worked quickly to dress the wounds with fresh gauze.

For most, I simply prayed over them and said goodbye. I did my best to stay strong, but looking into the eyes of the men who had suffered so much already and were terrified at what lay ahead, sent waves of guilt through me. Why should I get the chance to escape, when they would not? How many of them would be dead within days? Maybe hours?

I called over a medic named George. He was good with the patients, kind and gentle. He hurried over and looked at me with surprise. "Grace, you should get going. You'll miss the bus!"

"I just want to make sure you know—"

"I'll take care of them, I promise. But you have to get moving. Don't worry about these guys. They're tough."

I took a moment to meet the gaze of each patient nearby, not one of them seeming in the least bit resentful. "Go on, Grace," Harold called. "You get to safety. We can handle a few Nips."

The others nodded. "Hurry on, now. We'll be all right."

"I love all of you," I said through my tears. "I'm so sorry."

George put a hand on my shoulder. "You girls have been as brave and strong as any soldier out here. It's been an honor to serve with you."

I hugged him and waved goodbye to the others. Then I picked up my suitcase and ran for the surgical building. As I got closer, I realized I was the only woman still in the camp. A few of the men encouraged me to hurry 'cause the bus and trucks were already pulling out. I rounded the dental clinic and ran along the path toward the main road.

Dust kicked up in the air as the bus pulled forward. I ran as hard as I could, waving my hand in the air and yelling for the bus to stop. It kept moving, picking up speed. As I neared the bus, I saw a face turn to look at me out of a window. It was Natalie. She made eye contact with me, and I hollered for the bus to stop. But then she turned her face forward and sunk low in her seat. The bus continued on without stopping.

I couldn't keep up, nearly collapsing as I watched it head along the main road for Mariveles. Could I catch another ride? Should I walk? How many kilometers was it? I caught my breath for a moment, then turned back to camp. In the distance, gunfire erupted, and something exploded. Something akin to fireworks shot into the air in the distance back toward Cabcaben.

Mrs. Fincher had said the situation was grave. She was right. And I had no idea what to do next except to pray for mercy.

CHAPTER SIXTEEN

Matthew

April 8, 1942

The heat and humidity nearly suffocated me as I climbed the final few feet to a ridge overlooking a small creek that snaked through the jungle. I dropped to one knee and held onto a vine for support while I caught my breath, keeping my eyes peeled for Japanese patrols. Henry and Doug climbed up beside me. Henry fell onto his back and pulled a cigarette from his pocket. He gave one to Doug, and then lit them both. Within minutes, the rest of our unit made it to the top, and they all took a seat along the ridge.

Our scant group of one hundred had been reduced to fifteen over the course of the week. We'd held our position at the front for nearly eighteen hours—less than a day—before the Japanese scattered us like flies. I had no idea how many of my men were dead, injured, or lost. My first week as a captain, and I was a miserable failure.

"Where are we?" Doug asked.

"I'm pretty sure we're somewhere in the Bataan jungle," I said. "Beyond that, it's just a guess."

Henry chuckled. "That's encouraging."

In the chaos of getting separated from our unit, I tried to form a decent strategy. It seemed like moving south was the best idea, toward the bay. We'd run into other stragglers from various units, some had stuck with us, some had continued wandering through the jungle like ghostly skeletons. My own body was wasting away to nothing. I'd had to cut several notches in my belt to hold up my pants, and my shirt hung on me like like it was three sizes too large. What I wouldn't give for a hot shower and a steak.

"Our best bet is to continue south and get to Headquarters," I said. "Hopefully we can regroup with other units there."

I waited for the men to finish their smokes, then stood to try to rally them into making a few more kilometers. But a hail of gunfire shattered the air, and bullets whizzed past my head. My training kicked in and I dropped to my stomach. "Hit the deck!" I yelled.

"They're behind us!" Henry pointed down the slope we'd just climbed.

Men ran through the vines and trees near the bottom, stopping to fire up at us. We were exposed and needed to take cover. I started to order the men to the other side of the hill, but I saw movement there as well. The Japs were trying to surround us. "Let's move!" I yelled again.

Pushing myself up, I ran along the south side of the ridge, having seen fewer Japs on that side. Bullets streaked past, splintering the trees and leaves around me. The ridge curved around to the right and descended toward the creek. I stumbled and rolled down the hill before regaining my footing. Glancing over my shoulder, I saw to my horror that the men were still in pursuit: ducking and tumbling down the hill.

Toward the bottom, I noticed a fence made out of bamboo, and I dove behind it. My men landed all around me, and we crawled along the ground behind the fence. I could hear the Japs shouting to our right and to our left. It occurred to me that bamboo would be very poor protection from bullets, so I signaled to Henry to keep moving, and pressed on toward the creek.

The fence ended once I reached the water. I took a quick look around and didn't see any Japanese soldiers, so I signaled for the rest to follow me, and jumped into the shallow creek. I ran as low to the ground as I could, trying to keep my head lower than the bank on either side. We followed the creek until there was no more shouting or gunfire. Only then did we crawl out onto dry ground.

I waited for the men to catch up and took a head count. Fourteen. "Who are we missing?" I asked.

"Henderson," Doug said, panting. He shook his head. "He didn't make it."

I noticed Doug's shirt was ripped at the shoulder, blood seeping into it. "You hit?"

He shrugged. "Just a bit."

"Anyone else hurt?" I asked the group.

There were gashes and bruises, and another fella with a bullet hole through his forearm. All in all, we were still in decent shape. Except for Henderson.

"Let's put a little more distance between us and that Jap patrol," I said. "If we get separated, just keep moving south until you get to the coastal road. That will take us into Mariveles. We can regroup and get orders there."

Barely speaking, we walked another hour south until we finally found a small road. It seemed to be heading in the right direction, so we stayed on it for another hour or so. By then it was late afternoon, and most of us hadn't slept for nearly two days. I wondered just how long I could keep moving, but knew, as Captain, the men were looking to me for leadership. I could not stop.

"Look," Henry said from beside me. It occurred to me then just how well he was doing keeping up with our enforced march, considering his leg had barely finished healing. He pointed ahead of us to a charred truck on the side of the road.

246 JENNIFER H. WESTALL

I hurried over to inspect it. Very little remained unburned. "Must have taken a mortar bomb," I said.

"Whoa!" Doug shouted. "It's the mother lode!"

I ran around back to where he and the others stood sifting through the supplies. C-rations, probably meant for the front line, and they'd never made it. Doug used his rifle to push a can away from the pile. He touched it and pulled his hand away. "Still hot," he said.

"I don't know about the rest of you, but I'm ready for dinner," said Kyle Sanders. He'd joined our group three days before after getting separated from his unit. He was eager, but like the rest of us, quickly running out of steam.

"I reckon there's no point in letting it rot here," I said.

"And it's already cooked!" Henry added.

We grabbed as much as we could handle and moved a few feet off the road to dig in. My stomach cramped and my mouth watered as I opened a can of spam. I must have eaten ten cans, even knowing I'd pay for it later. I threw about twelve more cans of spam and corned beef into my rucksack for later, and went over to Doug to check on his shoulder. It was still bleeding heavily. I helped him clean it with an emergency kit, and we bandaged him up best we could.

"All right," I said, making my way back to the road. "We better get moving."

Just then, I heard gunfire ahead of us, and mortar bombs landed not far ahead. While we'd been eating, the Japs had flanked us. "We better stay off the road," I said. "Come on."

We moved into the jungle, walking parallel to the road. The food had given me a bit more energy, but I was still exhausted, especially after the sun set. Thankfully, once darkness fell, the Japanese quit bombing the road, so we made our way back to it. That was at least easier going on our feet and legs. But nightfall seemed to have brought out every American left on the entire peninsula.

The road was even more congested than it had been at Christmas, and completely unorganized. As trucks, buses, and cars loaded down with soldiers and civilians passed us, droves of equally haggard soldiers emerged from the jungle and lined the road, marching toward Mariveles as well. It suddenly became quite clear to me that we were not falling back to regroup and attack again. We were retreating. We were running for our lives.

***

Sometime later, we came upon a Philippine camp flying a white flag. It was mostly abandoned but for one officer who stood at an oil drum, burning documents. "Pardon me, Sergeant," I said. "What's going on here?"

"General King surrendered Bataan a few hours ago," he said. "Everyone's heading to Mariveles to figure out what to do next."

"Surrender?" I couldn't believe it, especially after MacArthur had been adamant that there'd be no surrender.

"Makes sense," Doug said. "Better than a mass slaughter of our boys."

Kyle huffed and shook his head. "Ole Dugout Doug slipped away to Australia to leave the rest of us to get captured by the dirty Nips."

"General King only relinquished his command of Bataan," the sergeant said. "He left it up to every man to decide for himself what's best to do. You're free to surrender or continue fighting. A lot of guys are trying to catch boats over to Corregidor. Some are fleeing into the jungle rather than be captured. Many are just too weak to continue."

I turned to our weary group. "You heard him. Every man's free to decide for himself. I'm heading to Mariveles and then for Corregidor. Any of you are welcome to come along."

"Well, you know I'm with ya," Henry said.

Doug agreed, as did the others. No one was ready to surrender. "So, we keep going then," I said, a sudden flush of pride for these brave men spreading across my chest. "Let's get back on the road and try to make it to Mariveles tonight."

The road had grown even more congested, though I hadn't thought that to be possible. Now the trucks were crawling past us. I waved down one, and then another, getting one or two of my guys on board to continue the journey. The last truck I flagged down, I jumped on with Henry and Doug. Despite the ruckus of honking horns, people shouting, and the constant jarring of holes in the road, I dozed off.

***

Sometime near midnight, I awoke to a loud explosion. I looked around the end of the truck up ahead of us and saw that we were no longer moving. Sparks flew into the sky, like a huge roman candle.

"Engineers are blowing the ammunition dumps," Doug said.

"Good idea," I said. "But won't that tell the Japs exactly where we are?"

"I don't think it's much of a secret at this point," Henry said.

I closed my eyes and tried to go back to sleep, but every time I drifted off, another explosion woke me. I finally gave up. Since we were barely moving, I suggested we hop off the truck and walk the rest of the way. The others agreed, and most of the soldiers emptied into the road. The driver said Mariveles was less than a kilometer ahead, so we pressed on rather than making camp.

As we arrived at the docks, it became painfully clear there was no Headquarters in charge of anything. Groups of soldiers and civilians, American and Filipino, were scattered along the beach, waiting for a chance to crowd into a boat. At the dock, one of the boats nearly capsized from the people swarming it. The captain had to pull his weapon to tell the mob to get back.

I scanned the beach for familiar faces, and saw some nurses. Relief hit me knowing that Ruby would be evacuated with them. I figured the chances of actually finding her were slim in this chaos, but I told Henry I was going to look for her.

"I'm coming too," Henry said. "Janine's bound to be with her."

We found a group of nurses huddled together near the road, so I went over and asked if they'd come from Hospital #2. A tall woman with curlers still in her hair nodded at me. "Yeah, we're supposed to be heading to Corregidor, but by the time our bus got here the boat was gone."

"Do you know if Grace Miller was on your bus?"

She shook her head. "I didn't see Grace get on or off."

"How about Janine Langston?" Henry asked.

"She was on a truck ahead of us. Pretty sure they made it. Haven't seen anyone from that group here."

I didn't like the sound of any of that, but I wasn't sure what to make of it yet. Doug was looking pretty poor, and I knew Henry and I would need to find the girls quickly. "Hey, any of you girls mind taking a look at my friend's injury here?" I patted Doug gently on the back, taking care to avoid his shoulder. "He was wounded on our way here."

"Sure," said the tall one with the curlers. "Leave him with us. We'll look after him."

Doug actually smiled, and the nurse blushed. What a time to make a connection with someone. I bid Doug goodbye and set off with Henry to see if we could find out more. Another group of nurses were standing near the docks, and this time I recognized Natalie. I hated the idea of even trying to speak politely to her, but I willed myself to approach her.

"Hey, Natalie. Have you seen Janine or Grace?"

Her grime-streaked face broke into a broad smile and she moved to hug me. "Matthew! You made it. I heard your whole camp was sent to the front. I was sure I'd never see you again."

I figured the quickest way to the information I needed was to appease her, though when my arms went around her, I had to force myself not to imagine squeezing the life right out of her.

"I'm all right," I said. "But I really need to find Janine and Grace. Have you seen them?"

She pointed toward the docks. "Janine got on a boat already."

"Thank the Lord," Henry said. He covered his mouth with his hand and closed his eyes for a moment.

"What about Grace?" I said.

Natalie looked from me to Henry, and back to me again. "She didn't get on the bus."

"What?" I said. "She didn't get on the bus?"

"She said she wanted to stay with her patients. And since she wasn't army, she wasn't forced to leave."

"So you're telling me she's still at the hospital site?" I thought my head was going to explode right off my body. "How is that possible? Why on earth would they leave her there?"

Henry strode toward Natalie and leaned down until his face was level with hers. "Natalie, are you absolutely sure she told you she was staying behind?"

She lifted her chin and glared back at him. "Of course I'm sure. She's a stubborn mule. I don't understand why everybody makes such a fuss about her. You know she's a liar and a—"

"You're going to want to stop talking now," I said, marching over and taking her shoulders in my hands.

Her eyes widened in fear. "Don't you lay your hands on me!"

"What's going on here?" one of the other nurses said, rushing to Natalie's side. "Sir, you need to step back."

I released Natalie and turned away from her, panic replacing my anger. I had to get to Ruby, but how could I be certain Natalie was telling the truth? Henry and I walked back toward the road, and I did my best to stay calm.

"What should we do?" I asked him. "She could be lying. Ruby could be on Corregidor right now for all we know."

"Look," Henry said. "She probably got on a truck and is already on a boat. We can't trust Natalie."

"But if she's telling the truth, and Ruby is still at the hospital, then she'll be captured by the Japs." My heart thundered at the thought of what they might do to her. "I have to go back to the hospital. If she's there, I'll get her. If not, then she's probably safe on Corregidor."

Henry turned and stared out over the water. "I should go with you. It's just..." He turned back to me. "I can't imagine Janine getting on the bus without Ruby."

"You think Natalie's lying about her catching a boat?"

"I just wish there was some way to know for sure."

"I reckon if Janine evacuated with the others, and made it onto a boat, then she's safe on Corregidor. If Natalie was lying, and she stayed behind with Ruby, then they're both in danger."

He nodded. "Let's head back to the hospital. That seems to be our best option."

"All right," I said. "Let's start walking. I doubt there are any trucks heading in the other direction. And I have a feeling there will be plenty of Japanese patrols to get through somehow."

Ruby

April 10, 1942

I peeked out of the opening of my tent to watch the Japanese soldiers move through the ward nearby. They looted everything they could get their hands on—watches, rings, sunglasses, medicine. I was glad I'd buried my belongings in my suitcase the night before.

As soon as Colonel Lansing had learned that I'd been left behind, he ordered me moved into my own tent just a few yards away from the ward I was working in. At around five the night before, some Japanese infantrymen had wandered into the main hospital area looking for water to drink. They'd continued on their way, but two hours later, two Japanese officers and twenty more enlisted men had arrived. The officers had met with Colonel Lansing, commanding that all personnel remain within the hospital grounds. Anyone found outside the perimeter would be shot on sight.

The next morning, the Japanese had ordered all Filipino patients be released immediately. I'd watched as they'd all hobbled off toward East Road. I had wondered for a moment if I should try to join them, but something in my spirit stopped me. A warning maybe. That was not the way to go.

So I'd quietly gone about caring for the Americans left behind, keeping out of sight of the Japanese as much as possible. Around noon, I'd taken a break and gone to my tent for a drink of water and to rest. But I'd heard a commotion near the ward, so I'd peeked outside. Thankfully, the Japanese were only taking belongings so far. No lives. Yet.

Across the clearing and near the main surgical building, the Japanese mechanics were busy stripping the generators of everything usable. Other Japanese soldiers were examining and transporting water from the filtration system our engineers had built.

Once the Japanese soldiers were done moving throughout the ward, I scurried out of my tent and went to each patient to check on his condition. Some were visibly upset at the violation. Others grateful it had only been "stuff" that they'd lost. One soldier in particular was heartbroken over having his father's watch taken. "It was all I had left of him," he sobbed.

I had no idea what to do. There were very few supplies left, so we'd buried what we could the night before. I had nothing to offer these men except my prayers, so that was what I did. I walked around to each of them, asking about their families back home, and asking them how I could pray for them. Not one refused me. They all wanted to pray.

As I was praying with a young man from Texas named Charles, I heard a commotion near the barracks. One of the doctors, Captain Sawyer, who had been in charge of patient care, was arguing with a Japanese officer.

"These men need food!" Captain Sawyer growled. "You can't allow your men to come in here and steal whatever they want."

The officer's response was quiet but clear. "No one is stealing anything," he said in perfect English. "These are but the spoils of war."

"These men are not combatants. They are patients in need of medical care. They have to have food and water."

"You will provide the Japanese army with whatever we deem necessary. There will be no further discussion on the matter."

The officer started to walk away, but Captain Sawyer grabbed his arm. "Now, wait just a min—"

In an instant, the officer whipped out a pistol and shot Captain Sawyer right in the chest. I gasped and started to run to him, but George, who'd come up beside me during the exchange, grabbed me and held me in place.

"No, Grace," he said. "You'll only get yourself killed. I'll see to Captain Sawyer. You tend to the boys here, and keep your head down."

I watched from among the patients as George walked toward Captain Sawyer with his hands held high. The Japanese officer looked at George and put his gun back on his waist. "You there," called the officer. "Take care of this."

George went over to Captain Sawyer's lifeless body and placed his hand on his neck. Then he looked over at me and shook his head. A few of the patients behind me muttered curses, others promised revenge. All I could do was go back to praying. So I continued my rounds.

***

Just after nightfall, I was sitting in my tent reading Daddy's Bible by a lantern, when a group of four Japanese soldiers came through the entrance. Two of them approached me, while the others stood near the flap at the front. My heart raced as all the horrible possibilities of what was about to happen flashed through my mind. I set the Bible on my cot and slowly stood.

"What is your name?" asked the soldier closest to me. He was the shortest of the group, with a wide-set face and a slight build.

"Grace," I said.

He turned and said something to the others in Japanese. Then he turned back to me. "Why are you here? War is for men, not a woman. You...ah...toy for men to play with?"

Heat rushed up my cheeks, and I wrapped my arms around my stomach. "I'm a nurse. I care for the sick and wounded."

He spoke Japanese over his shoulder, and all four of them snickered. Then the one to his right, the tallest of the group, bent over and sifted through my things. All I had was a cot, a blanket, and my Bible. He picked up the book and looked it over. Then he said something in Japanese. The shorter one said something that I thought sounded like "Jesus". The tall one wrinkled his mouth up like he was disgusted and tossed the Bible onto the ground.

He examined me from head to foot. There was such a chilling look in his eyes that an involuntary shudder skittered down my spine, and I could barely stop myself shaking as he stepped over and stood uncomfortably close. Slowly he ran a finger along my neckline, and I thought I was going to come out of my skin. He felt inside the pockets of my coveralls. Then he lifted my hand and slipped my wedding ring off my finger. He dropped it into his pocket.

The taller soldier walked around behind me where I couldn't see him, but I could feel his eyes on me. I kept my gaze on the shorter one, who'd spoken English. "I have nothing of any value."

"This is not true," he said. "You...very beautiful for American girl. You have plenty value for now."

The sneer on his lips made my stomach crawl. What would I do if they attacked me? If I fought back, would they kill me? Maybe it would be better to die. If only I still had Matthew's gun. I closed my eyes and prayed for courage.

"What are you doing?" the one in front of me asked. "Why you close your eyes? You...afraid?"

I opened my eyes and looked directly into his black soul. "The Lord is my rock, and my fortress, and my deliverer; the God of my rock; in Him will I trust: He is my shield, and the horn of my salvation."

His eyes narrowed. "I see. You call on your god to save you."

"I will call on the Lord, who is worthy to be praised: so shall I be saved from mine enemies."

He stepped toward me and lowered his voice. "Your god cannot save you from me tonight. No one can save you."

He nodded to the other soldier behind me, who grabbed me by the shoulders and forced me to the ground. Instead of fighting back, I dropped to my knees and began to shout.

"The Lord is my rock and my fortress and my deliverer! My God! My rock, in whom I take refuge, my shield, and the horn of my salvation!"

The hands that had grabbed me now pulled me up again, and I saw genuine confusion on the short one's face. He stepped closer to me and shook his finger. "You make too much noise, Grace. You will get hurt if you are not quiet."

I heard someone shout something outside, and one of the guards near the entrance slipped out. There was more murmuring outside. *Lord, please help me. Give me courage. Come near and show Your power to these men.*

The guard stepped back inside and nodded to the leader. He turned back to me and smiled. Then he spoke something in Japanese, and the guard holding me from behind brought a knife around near my throat. "Be very still, Grace," said the one in front. "We don't want to hurt you." The soldier standing just outside my field of vision laughed nastily.

The knife moved down to my coveralls, and he began to cut them open. Hot tears streamed down my cheeks, despite my best efforts to remain calm. I looked the soldier in the eyes again and steeled myself for the inevitable.

And at that moment, a gentle peace came over me. Something wonderful, and terrifying, filled the entire tent. The hair on my arms prickled, and my racing heart slowed. I saw that poor, broken soldier for what he truly was: a lost sinner with no idea of mercy. And no matter what he did to me, he could not take my soul.

I closed my eyes again. "You, O Lord, are a shield about me, my glory, and the lifter of my head."

"Stop it!" he yelled.

My voice rose again, as if it were no longer me speaking. "Fear not, for I am with you; be not dismayed, for I am your God; I will strengthen you, I will help you, I will uphold you with my righteous right hand!"

He slapped me across the face, and my cheek stung. "Stop it! You will stop that now!"

I brought my gaze back to his furious eyes, knowing now I was no longer speaking from my own lips, but delivering a message from the Lord. "The wicked draw the sword and bend their bows to bring down the poor and needy, to slay those whose way is upright; their sword shall enter their own heart, and their bows shall be broken."

He grabbed me by my shoulders and flung me to the cot. As I fell onto my back, my head striking something hard, I closed my eyes and prayed for mercy.

Matthew

Henry and I had maneuvered around several enemy patrols on our way back east, so we'd concluded that the hospital would be under Japanese control by the time we reached it. We decided to head back to Cabcaben, and follow the path we'd been taking to see the girls each week. And the first of many miracles that night greeted us as we circled around Cabcaben. Our beat-up shell of a truck we'd used to travel through the jungle was still sitting right where we'd left it.

"You know, Henry," I said as he turned the ignition. "Salvaging this might have been the smartest thing you've ever done."

He eased the truck along the path we'd carved out over the weeks and grinned at me. "Nah, you ain't seen nothing yet."

We bumped along at a snail's pace in the fading sunlight. I'd been worn completely out up to that point, but knowing we were so close to the hospital had sent a shot of adrenaline through me. I prayed all the way to the river that Janine was safe on Corregidor and that we'd be able to sneak Ruby away from the hospital.

At the river, we climbed out and crossed the fallen tree, then we snuck along parallel to the path leading to the nurses' quarters. I hadn't actually expected to find Ruby there, but I was disappointed all the same. That would've been the easiest thing in the world. But clearly all the nurses were gone. A few random items still hung on clotheslines, undergarments and such. The sun had almost set by then, but we decided we could see well enough to cut through the jungle.

As we neared the main hospital clearing, we saw patrols monitoring the perimeter in certain areas, but the hospital was so large that they were spread pretty thin. Most of the Japanese stood around talking and laughing, while the Americans went about their business caring for the patients.

I knelt beside Henry and whispered. "Any idea where Ruby might be?"

"Ain't too sure. Bet they moved her close by to keep an eye on her, though. That's what I'd do."

"Let's make our way along the outside of the main wards. Maybe over by the barracks."

He agreed, and we crept through the foliage as quietly as we could. I remembered helping to build the barracks, so I was able to find my way there in the fading light. Once we were in sight of them, I lowered my-

258 | JENNIFER H. WESTALL

self to a crawl, and slid beneath low hanging palm leaves. Henry crawled up beneath the large leaves of a tree to my left, and together we scanned the area.

"There," I whispered, pointing to a tent about twenty yards from the barracks, and about ten yards from a ward. "Bet that's where she's staying."

We crawled along the ground with the bugs and spiders until we were positioned just off the left side, and about ten yards behind the tent. "Let's wait till it's dark," I said. "Then we'll see if she's in there."

"What if it ain't her?" Henry whispered. "We'll scare the holy hell outta some poor soul."

"It's her," I said. "I know it's her."

My gut was uneasy. Something didn't feel right, something beyond the normal thrill of sneaking up on the enemy. Ruby was in danger here. Something dark was lurking around this place. Something evil.

I watched the tent for a few minutes as the final rays of sunshine disappeared behind the tree line, waiting to see if Ruby entered or exited the tent. But there was no sign. A few of the doctors and medics went into the barracks, but not much else stirred. I was about to tell Henry to prepare to move toward the tent, when I saw a group of four Japanese soldiers coming our way.

They stopped outside the tent, spoke for a moment, and then all four slipped inside. My heart raced, and my first thought was to rush in. "We gotta get in there," I said.

"What if it ain't her tent?" Henry whispered. "What if it's their tent?"

I knew it wasn't, though. My chest constricted, and my mind raced through all the options. If we rushed into the tent, what could we do? We'd be killed for sure. We'd have to go in there with the intent to kill those soldiers. Could I do that? Sure, I'd fired a gun at an enemy dozens of yards away, but this would be close quarters. I'd have to look them in the eye as I killed them.

"Let's wait and see what happens," Henry said. "Maybe it's nothing."

At that moment, loud voices came from inside the tent. A female voice floated out over deeper murmurings and laughter. Was it distressed? "I have to get closer," I said. "You keep an eye out for any more Japs." I removed the bayonet from my rifle, gripping it as I crawled out into the clearing and ducked behind a large tree. Holding my breath, I sat with my back against it. Someone was approaching the tent from the direction of the barracks. I couldn't see who it was because the tent was blocking my view.

"What's going on in there?" a male American voice called.

I crawled around to the side of the tent. I heard the sound of rustling as the entrance flap opened. Another voice spoke up with a thick Japanese accent. "Nothing. You go."

There was a pause. "There's a nurse in there," the American said. "She sounds upset."

That had to be Ruby for sure. There was some kind of shuffling at the front. "Go!" The Japanese voice ordered. "No business!"

Footsteps moved away from the tent. Low voices murmured inside. Then the female spoke again. My heart thundered, as I knew without a doubt that this was Ruby's voice. I couldn't hear the exact words, but I heard her fear, and my body tensed all over. And then she shouted, clear as a bell.

"Fear not, for I am with you; be not dismayed, for I am your God; I will strengthen you, I will help you, I will uphold you with my righteous right hand!"

I looked around again. No one was coming. This was my chance. I prayed the Lord would give me swift hands, and a decisive mind. I motioned for Henry to crawl around the opposite side of the tent. Then I crawled around to the front entrance. I could see just beneath the front flap two sets of boots. Guards. Two of them. How would I get them out of the way?

Quickly and soundlessly I slipped the flap back just enough to peek at them from the ground. They were watching something at the rear of the tent. I tried not to think about it. I had to focus on these two first. They were distracted. I could get one for sure, but not both.

Henry crawled around the other side of the tent and signaled he was with me. I showed him two fingers, and then I showed him my bayonet. He nodded and flashed his bayonet back at me. Slowly we rose to our feet on opposite sides of the tent opening. There was scuffling around inside. I prayed the Lord would keep anyone else away. Then I used my fingers to count to three.

Simultaneously, Henry and I pulled back the flap and stabbed up into the kidney of each guard. Both dropped to the ground, almost at the same time. We stepped into the tent, and what I saw sent hot fire through my entire body. Ruby lay on the cot, exposed, the front of her coveralls flung open while one of the apes gripped her hands above her head. Another Jap was bent over her, fighting to grab hold of her as she kicked her legs around. He punched her in the stomach, and she gasped. It was the last thing he ever did.

I flew at him with all my might, driving the bayonet up into his abdomen, under the ribcage, and into his heart, just like I'd been trained to do. But there was no remorse, no hesitation in taking his life. His black eyes met mine, and the life drained out of them. I dropped him to the ground and turned to find Henry pulling his bayonet out of the back of the other one. Blood spilled everywhere, all over the ground. And Ruby sat up, gasping for air.

I went to her and pulled her into my arms. "Are you all right?"

She wept into my chest, unable to speak for a long while. I wanted to hold her, to comfort her, but I knew we had precious little time to get out of there safely. I glanced over her head at Henry, who was wiping the blood off his bayonet on the Jap he'd just killed.

"What do we do now?" I asked.

Henry took a look around. "We put as much distance between us and this tent as possible before dawn."

Ruby pushed away from me. "No, wait. When they're found in the morning, the others in camp will pay for this. We can't let others die because of me."

"It's not because of you," I said. "They decided to assault you. They deserve exactly what they got."

"But the doctors here, the medics, they don't deserve what they'll get."

I pulled the blanket off her cot and wrapped it around her shaking shoulders. "Ruby, this is war. People fight. Soldiers die. There's nothing wrong with doing everything you can to survive. We did what we had to in order to protect you."

"Fellas?" came a low voice from outside the tent.

The three of us froze.

"Y'all need some help in there?"

"I know that voice," Ruby whispered. "It's okay."

Henry pushed open the flap and let in a large, fair-skinned medic covered in freckles. "You all right, Grace?" he asked.

"Y-yes, George," she stammered, a faint smile warming her pale cheeks. "Can you help us?"

"Most certainly," he said, taking in the scene around him. "Looks like we got us a burial detail."

CHAPTER SEVENTEEN

Ruby

April 10, 1942

While I kept watch for patrols, George helped Matthew and Henry bury the dead about a hundred feet into the jungle, before straightening my tent and removing as much of the blood as possible. Matthew wiped spatters of blood from Daddy's Bible and pushed it into his rucksack, but decided we didn't have time to locate and dig up my suitcase. I did, however, retrieve my ring from the pocket of the dead Japanese soldier.

George brought me a new set of coveralls from the barracks. They nearly swallowed my emaciated frame. My heart thundered the whole time, but it was as if God had put some kind of protective shield around us, and no one came near that section of the hospital that night. I prayed none of the Americans would suffer once I was discovered to be missing, along with four Japanese soldiers. Guilt weighed heavy on my mind as we said goodbye to George.

"You're a good friend," I said, hugging his neck in gratitude. "Thank you for everything. I'll pray for you every day until I see you again."

"Don't worry about me at all," he said. "You get somewhere safe and stick with your brother and husband."

I thanked him again, and he shook hands with Matthew and Henry. We crept out of the tent, and I followed them into the dark jungle, barely able to see Matthew's form ahead of me in the moonlight. We hiked silently for what seemed like hours, circling around the northwest edge of the hospital, crossing the Real River, and then turning south for a long stretch. Every once in a while, Matthew would freeze and listen carefully for a few minutes before moving on again. I could sometimes hear voices nearby, but mostly I heard the chatter of monkeys and other creatures, like they were cheering us on. Or maybe alerting the enemy.

Just as the sky was turning a light gray, we reached the East Road. We didn't dare approach it, as we could make out multitudes of American soldiers trudging past in columns four across toward Lamao, away from Mariveles, with Japanese guards prodding them on like cattle. As the day wore on, we spotted Filipinos mixed in with the Americans. There were thousands of them. My heart broke, even as I cowered beneath the foliage. I couldn't hold back my tears as I watched gaunt men limp by, some having to be supported by others. The Japanese guards were ruthless, striking the prisoners with fists, elbows, and rifle butts as they walked, for no apparent reasons.

One American fell to his knees as he was hit, which seemed to bring even more emphatic strikes. I watched in horror as two Japanese soldiers beat the man until he was no longer moving, and then commanded that no one help him. If any Americans even looked like they were moving toward him, they too were beaten. Then I watched in horror as a Japanese truck drove over the motionless body.

I met Matthew's gaze and saw a rage in his eyes I'd never seen before. I felt it too. How could anyone be so cruel? I couldn't watch any more of it, so I quietly slipped further away from the road. Eventually Matthew and Henry joined me, and we made a shelter beneath a group of low hanging palm leaves. No one spoke of the chilling sights we'd witnessed. Matthew pulled out two cans of spam from his rucksack and handed them to me.

"Here, you need to eat something," he said, barely looking at me.

I dug into the meat despite the trouble I had swallowing. My stomach seemed conflicted over the sudden introduction of something substantial, as though it had forgotten how to function properly. Matthew handed me a canteen of water, and I drank it down.

"What's the plan?" Henry asked.

Matthew took the canteen from my outstretched hand and took a long gulp. "Can't cross over here. At least not until dark. If I remember correctly, there's a wharf not too far north of here. We might be able to get a boat across the bay."

"So we're still heading to Corregidor?" I asked. "Why?"

"Why wouldn't we?" Matthew answered. "That's where evacuations are going to happen. That's your best chance to get away from this nightmare."

"Not anymore," I said. "Don't you hear that?" I paused so they could hear the erratic blasts I'd noticed in the distance. "They're bombing Corregidor. The Japanese were setting up huge guns around the hospital pointed out to that island. It won't last long."

"Then we'd better hurry," Henry said.

I shook my head and tried to stay calm as I thought of leaving Matthew again. "I don't think we should separate. What if we find our own way to Australia? All three of us?"

"What about Janine?" Henry asked. "I'm not leaving her here with those...those animals."

"He's right," Matthew said. "We go to Corregidor first. Then we make contact with Mike and get you and Janine to Australia." He dropped his chin and eyed me with a hint of defiance. "That's the plan. And we're sticking to it."

I didn't say anything more, knowing it would be useless. Besides, I could barely keep my eyes open any longer. I crawled across the grass to a spot next to Matthew, and curled up next to him. He slid his rucksack beneath his head and lay down behind me.

"Guess I'll keep watch for a while," Henry said. Then he moved a few feet away and turned his back to us.

I craved the safety of Matthew's body surrounding mine, but I could feel so much tension in him, it was difficult to relax. He slid his arm along my waist, tucking me a bit closer. Then he leaned down and spoke into my ear.

"Why are you so determined to make me crazy?"

"I'm not," I said. "Why are you so determined to control me?"

"I'm not trying to control you, Ruby. I just want to protect you. Do you have any idea what it was like for me to see that, that animal, trying to...to hurt you? I nearly lost my mind." He turned me onto my back, and his voice thickened as he looked down at me in anguish. "I love you more than my own life. But I don't know how to be a soldier and a husband at the same time. I mean, I can order men to climb a mountain, or charge into a battle that they may not survive, but I can't even persuade my own wife to get on a plane to safety."

I reached for his face, and he covered my hand with his own. He kissed my palm, placing my hand back on his cheek. "Don't you understand me at all?" I asked. "Don't you see how much I love you? That the nightmare, for me, is being apart from you?"

He leaned down and kissed me, sending warmth down my chest, rippling into my belly. "Ruby, please. Do this for me. If I can make arrangements with Mike, you have to get on the plane. Promise." He slid his hand around my waist, kissing me deeper. "Promise," he said again. "I need to know. I need to be able to trust that you'll get to safety. If you love me, you'll get on that plane."

My chest felt like it would split open. How could I say no? How could I promise to leave him? I couldn't stop my tears, and I had no idea what to say. But my spirit knew. And a small quiet voice whispered inside my mind. *Submit.*

"I promise," I whispered, my throat aching. "I'll get on the plane."

"No matter what?"

"No matter what."

He pressed his forehead to mine. "Don't cry," he said, wiping my cheek with his thumb. "It'll be all right. God will protect you. He'll be our mighty fortress. Our shield. Our safe harbor. Have faith, Ruby."

I grabbed hold of those words and buried them in my heart, memorizing everything about that moment as if it were an anchor. His arms around me, the promises between us, and my pounding heart.

***

I slept in Matthew's arms until it was his turn to take watch, and then Henry was able to rest until dark. I ate four more helpings of canned meat, and I paid for it less than an hour later. My stomach churned, and I had to find a large tree to hide behind for a while. It was about the most embarrassing thing I'd ever done. But Matthew did his best to keep his distance without letting me out of his sight. It wasn't far enough.

After darkness fell, we gathered our things and made our way quietly back to the road. It was still fairly busy, with trucks moving south toward Mariveles, as well as Japanese troops. But it wasn't a constant flow like it had been earlier. There were breaks in the traffic, and Matthew figured if we moved north to some bends in the road, we could find a place to cross where we wouldn't be seen.

Steeling ourselves, we turned north and crept along parallel to the road for more than two hours. Finally, we got to a sharp curve and waited for a break. I raced across the road with my heart nearly coming out of my throat. I was certain a Japanese truck would come around that curve, and we'd be shot dead on sight. But we made it across without being seen. I doubled over when we were in the clear.

"You all right?" Henry asked.

I nodded. My pitiful little body was having a hard time keeping up with theirs, even though they were pretty emaciated themselves. "I'm fine," I said. "Just give me a second to catch my breath."

"Want me to carry you for a while?" Matthew asked.

"No, no. Save your strength."

Henry grimaced as he looked up and down the shoreline through the trees. "Yeah, you may need it for rowing. Or worse, swimming."

"There's a dock just a little ways north of here," Matthew said. "There's gotta be a boat."

"What makes you so sure?" Henry asked.

Matthew shrugged. "The Lord's just worked everything out so far. I mean, think about it. If that truck hadn't been where we left it, we wouldn't have made it in time to save Ruby. Then we were able to bury those dirty Japs in the jungle without being discovered. And haven't you noticed how few patrols we've encountered? God's clearing our path. And he'll have a boat for us. You watch and see."

Henry looked over at me with an exasperated smirk. "He's been married to you for what—a month—and you've already got him talking like you."

Matthew and I locked gazes for a moment, and he smiled at me. It reminded me of the days when he'd been so sick with T.B. that he couldn't get out of bed, and I would sit in the chair opposite, listening to the high-pitched whistle of each breath he took. He'd sometimes lock eyes with me, just like now, and he'd smile at me as though we were the only two people on earth, and he was just fine with it. That smile still stirred me, just as it had when I was barely fourteen.

"Well, let's go find this boat God's gonna have ready for us," Henry said.

We headed north between the road and the coast, ducking down each time a vehicle passed. Eventually, we saw the dock up ahead, and a tiny rowboat floating beside it.

Henry stopped and turned incredulous eyes to Matthew. "You have to be kidding me." He turned his eyes toward the sky. "After everything You've managed to pull off over the past few days, You're going to leave us to cross the bay in that?"

I was just grateful that even one small boat was there, but I was concerned about getting across the bay before we were spotted by Japanese planes. And how would any of us find the strength to row that far? Maybe if we weren't starved near to death, it would be possible. But there was no way we'd make it in the few short hours before daybreak.

We picked our way down to the dock and looked the boat over. Matthew rubbed the back of his neck, looking at the boat skeptically. "It's the best we can do for now. I say we go for it."

"Just take it?" I said. "You mean steal it?"

"Ruby," Henry said, rolling his eyes. "Now's not the time to worry about a measly little boat. Apparently, according to your husband, God put this here for us to use. So use it we must."

I didn't like the idea of taking something that didn't belong to us, even if it was war, and even if we were running for our lives. I turned my back on them while they discussed the best route to take across the bay. But only about a hundred yards away was another small dock, and it had a motorboat tied to it.

"What about the motorboat?" I asked. "If we're going to steal something, wouldn't that be faster?"

"Of course, but what motorboat?" Henry asked, turning around.

"That one." I pointed at the other dock.

"Now, see," Henry said, turning to face Matthew. "She's much better at finding God's gifts than you are."

***

It turned out that the boat belonged to an old Filipino man who was camped out in the trees near the dock. He was taking a group of other stragglers over to Corregidor just before dawn, and for five pesos, we could go as well. I wondered where these other passengers were, but since we were hiding in the dense foliage along the coast, I figured they were too.

Around five in the morning, we went back to the dock, and paid our five pesos to the old man. Then we stepped on board what had to be the oldest boat on the entire island, with a huge hole in the left side near the front and just above the water line.

"Please stand on right side," the old man said. "Keep from sinking."

"I don't know about this," I said to Matthew.

Henry had a good laugh. "Figures. Guess we might be swimming some after all."

We climbed on top of the cabin, figuring it was furthest from the water, and sat and waited for the rest to get on board. Seven American soldiers slipped out of the trees and loaded up, looking every bit as gaunt and exhausted as we must have appeared. A Filipino man, his wife, and their four kids got on. And last came two Filipino men: one older and gray-haired, the other probably in his twenties. Each of them carried sacks that they held close to their chests.

Henry called down to them. "Hey, whatchya got in the sacks?"

They looked up at him, then at each other. The younger one answered. "Canned fruit. Mangos. Peaches. Pineapple."

That sparked interest from all the starving Americans on board. "What'll you take for them?" Henry asked.

"What you got?" the young one said.

Henry dug through his pockets and pulled out some papers. "Twenty pesos."

"Not enough!" The older man answered.

Henry looked at Matthew, who dug around and found ten more pesos in his rucksack. "How about thirty pesos? And some canned meat?"

"Not enough!"

Henry took the money from Matthew and jumped down to the deck. He walked over to the seven other Americans, and each of them dug through their pockets as well. "Forty pesos!" Henry said.

"No. Not enough!"

Henry grimaced, looked up at me where I sat on the edge of the cabin and shook his head. He walked over to the older Filipino and shoved the money into his shirt pocket. Then he grabbed the sack from the younger one, who stepped back with wide, frightened eyes.

Henry tossed several cans to the seven soldiers, then he climbed back onto the cabin and sat beside me. I didn't bother scolding him. What good would it do? And that pineapple was so delicious; I couldn't bring myself to feel bad. We feasted on the fruit as the boat pulled away from the dock and slid along the coastline toward a spot of land that jutted out into the bay. From that point, we turned directly toward Corregidor.

As we chugged away from shore, I looked back at the jungle I was leaving. The place where so many had suffered and died. The place where I'd buried friends and colleagues, and my dress from Daddy, still hidden beneath the dirt outside my tent at the hospital. It was where I'd married Matthew, where we'd played in the river and loved each other more deeply than I'd ever imagined possible. As much as I wanted to escape the horrors on that peninsula, the moment was bittersweet. I was leaving a part of myself behind. That part of myself that believed people were essentially good, and that hope was enough to carry me through to the next day.

***

Morning broke as we neared the middle of our journey, and tension rose along with the sun. Corregidor lay in front of us, teasing with its safety that was just out of reach. I felt so exposed and vulnerable. I prayed the boat would move faster, but it chugged along at the same speed, with the distance to the shore seemingly unchanging.

I lay back on the cabin roof, hoping that when I sat up, the island would be closer. Matthew sat beside me, keeping watch on the sky. "We need to decide what we're going to do about Natalie," he said. "She'll be there when we arrive, and she'll expect to be a part of any attempt to get to Australia."

I recalled her blank stare as I'd run after the bus. "We'll do our best to appease her and keep our plans quiet. I don't know what else we can do."

"Does she know we're married?" he asked.

"I don't know. She knows we're together. That seems to be enough to incite her anger toward me."

He gazed out over the water for a long minute before speaking again. "You saw us, didn't you? At Fort Stotsenburg, after I taught you to shoot. You saw me kiss her, didn't you?"

My chest ached at the memory. "Yes."

"I'm sorry," he said. "That was...that was stupid, and cruel of me. I knew it would hurt you. I wasn't thinking."

I sat up and took his hand in mine. "That's in the past, along with everything else painful between us. Let's just leave it there, all right?"

He nodded and squeezed my hand. Corregidor was finally drawing closer. But as I glanced to the east, I noticed the unmistakable outline of Japanese bombers approaching from over Manila. "Matthew, look!"

By then, others had seen the planes and were shouting at the captain. "Speed up! Speed up!"

"She's sailing as fast as she can!" The captain called back.

Matthew and I jumped off the cabin roof, and moved to the front of the boat, still careful to stay on the right side. Water slopped around our ankles. Everyone onboard stared helplessly at the approaching planes. I looked again at Corregidor. I could see a dock, or at least the remnants of one. We might just make it.

"We're not going to make it!" Henry shouted.

"Yes, we will!" Matthew said.

Wind and water stung my face. My heart pounded. The planes were lined up directly with the island. I grabbed Matthew's arm.

"When we get to the shore," he yelled, "don't wait for me. Just run. Find shelter. I'll be right behind you."

"Move back!" the captain called. "Don't weigh down the front!"

All the passengers stretched along the right side of the boat, preparing to jump as soon as the shore was in reach. The Filipino woman and her children moved to the front, and Matthew pushed me in line behind them. I still had Matthew's arm in a vice grip, but he squeezed my hand and spoke into my ear. "It's all right. Let go. You'll be fine."

The planes were nearly on us now. Shiny flashes of silver fluttered down like leaflets. For a moment, I thought maybe the Japanese were just dropping more propaganda on us, as they'd done throughout our time on Bataan. But Matthew shattered that hope.

"Bombs are away! Move as quickly as you can and get into the cement building there just off the right side of the dock!"

The boat never slowed down, barreling up to the wreckage that had once been a dock and onto the shore. The Filipino woman jumped first, then Henry followed. Matthew and the other soldiers handed the children to the woman and Henry while I jumped into the waves. I ran and stumbled up to more solid ground. The first bomb exploded at the other end of the island, followed by another. The ground shook as I ran with every ounce of energy I could muster, my eyes set on the small cement building Matthew had pointed to. *Run! Run!* I screamed at myself. My legs burned, and I could've sworn I was running through quicksand.

Another bomb exploded. Closer. I stumbled and fell forward, my face hitting the sand. Another concussion made my whole body feel like it was ripping apart. Feet flew past me. The snatched sound of children screaming. I pushed myself up and ran again. More bodies passed, running into the building. Then I was on my face again. I was finished. My legs gave out.

But then strong hands grabbed under both my arms, and I was carried the last few feet into the building. The door closed behind us, and we dropped to our knees. I felt Matthew's body surround me from behind, his arms tightening around my shoulders. More explosions, more pain in my ears and head. I wanted to scream, but nothing came out. It went on like that for another few minutes. Then there was silence. The kind that's unsure, waiting for the death blow. But it didn't come this time. We were safe. For now.

Someone pushed the door open, and light streamed inside the small shed. The sudden brightness made me dizzy. Matthew stood and helped me up. My legs were weak, and they buckled. He scooped me up into his arms. "Are you all right?" he asked.

I could barely breathe, much less talk. So I nodded instead. He carried me up the hill, following Henry as he and the other soldiers from the boat led our little procession around to a huge cement entrance to Malinta Tunnel. I could barely move, so I rested my head against Matthew's shoulder as he carried me into the belly of Corregidor. All I could think about was how grateful I was to have cement and rock above me rather than open sky.

"Let's find the hospital," Matthew said to Henry. "I think she's going into shock."

Shock. That was what it was. I hadn't recognized the symptoms in my own body. The shivering. The disorientation. I closed my eyes as Matthew carried me deeper and deeper into the tunnel complex. When he stopped, I heard familiar voices and opened my eyes as he laid me on a bed.

Several of the nurses from the hospital on Bataan came over to us, relieved to discover I'd made it. Janine pushed her way through and wrapped her arms around me, sobbing an apology for leaving me behind. "I thought you were on the bus! I'm so sorry!"

Before long, Matthew herded the group away from me so that I could be examined. A medic came over to check my vitals. "Can you answer a few questions?" he asked.

I nodded. "I'll d-do my best."

"Can you tell me your name?"

My name? "M-maybe you should start with something easier."

He placed two fingers on my neck, concern coming into his eyes as he checked my pulse. "You don't know your name?"

Matthew came up beside him and took my hand. I gazed into his weary, bloodshot eyes and spoke the honest truth. "It's Ruby Grace Doyle." The words felt lovely rolling off my tongue.

Matthew grinned. The medic took no notice of my declaration. "Well, Miss Doyle—"

"It's *Mrs.* Doyle," Matthew interrupted.

"All right, Mrs. Doyle, are you in pain?"

"No."

"Any injuries?"

"No."

The medic made a note on a clipboard and said he'd return to check on me after I'd had some food and rest. Janine brought over some rations, which I practically inhaled. Matthew sat in a chair beside the bed, looking completely spent. "I'm all right now," I said, concern for him flickering at the edge of my dwindling consciousness as the darkness crept closer. "You should go...get some rest...too..."

He leaned onto my bed and kissed my forehead. "I'll go once you're asleep. Now close your eyes."

I wanted to keep looking into his eyes, but I couldn't hold mine open any longer. The combination of a full stomach and the safety of the tunnel worked its magic quickly, and I was soon asleep.

***

I slept for almost two days straight, vaguely aware of the muffled sounds of bombs and the occasional rattle when one hit directly above our section. When I awoke and was able to get around, Mrs. Fincher walked me through the various tunnels that branched off Malinta's main tunnel, showing me the hospital laterals, the mess, the pharmacy, and the quarters where the nurses slept.

"You can take any bed that's open," Mrs. Fincher said. She gestured toward Janine, who had volunteered to get me settled. "Janine will show you where you can get the basic items you'll need. And I'm sure she'll cover the expectations we've set in place for making the best out of our situation. You're welcome to continue working in a nursing capacity with the others, or I can assign you to civilian duties."

"I'm happy to do whatever is necessary, but I would prefer to continue working with patients," I replied.

Mrs. Fincher gave me the closest thing she had to a smile. "You're a fine nurse, and we appreciate your skills. When you get settled here, report to me and I'll assign you to a ward." She began to leave, before turning back to us with a more serious expression. "And one more thing. Janine has informed me of your nuptials in the jungle. There are strict policies in place here to protect the integrity of the nursing corps. I will expect you two to be discreet."

"Yes, ma'am," I said. She bustled away as I turned to Janine. "What was that all about?"

"Since we arrived here, the servicemen have been frequenting this area of the tunnel more often than she'd like. She called us all together and laid down some rules. No more coveralls, for example. She had some Chinese women in another section of the tunnel sew everyone khaki skirts and regulation shirts. Hair has to be pinned up off the collar. Guess she thinks returning to shipshape standards will keep everyone in line. And no fraternizing with the soldiers."

"Why did you decide to tell her about the wedding?"

Janine walked over to a shelf and grabbed a white sheet and blanket, bringing them back over to my bed. "I guess I was a little emotional when Henry showed up here. I just couldn't help myself. I was so happy to see him. I made quite a scene, and she was none too happy about it. I had to explain."

We made the bed, and then headed over to the supply depot to gather my basic toiletries. I never realized how happy I could be to have a bit of soap and a comb. I could hardly wait to take a shower. "There's a barber in the tunnel too," Janine said as we walked back to quarters. "You can get your hair cut if you like."

"This is like a little city down here," I said.

"Oh yes. This is so much better than the jungle, even with the bombings every day. These tunnels are impregnable. I imagine if we had enough food, we could all stay down here until the war was over."

"But we don't, do we? Have enough food?"

She shook her head. "Rations here are much better than on Bataan, but they're dwindling fast. Especially with all the sudden evacuees being added. The rumor is that we might be able to last another six weeks. If that."

"And then what?"

We'd made it back to my bed by then, and Janine stared back at me with anxious eyes. "Surrender."

***

Over the course of the next couple of weeks, my appreciation for the safety of the tunnel wore off. The stale air became filled with more and more dust as the bombs shook everything around us. Respiratory problems increased dramatically. It seemed like everyone was coughing. And when the bombs fell, which sometimes seemed constant, the air pressure made my head ache so badly I could barely see. Rations were cut again. I thought about food to the point of obsession.

Then there was Natalie. She hadn't said much when I first arrived, watching from afar with a disgusted expression as I was cared for and instructed in my duties. But it only took a couple of days before she insisted on claiming my rations again. This time I refused. When she threatened to tell Mrs. Fincher about me, I almost laughed.

"Do you not understand anything?" I said. "We're all facing a death sentence here. Even you. No one cares about what you have to say."

Her face paled before she pressed her mouth into a thin line. "I suppose this means your promise to get me on a plane out of here was a lie as well. I shouldn't be surprised."

"Perhaps I'd be more inclined to help you if you hadn't left me to be attacked and nearly raped by Japanese soldiers on Bataan."

"*I* didn't leave you!"

"You looked right at me from your seat on the bus. I saw you."

She huffed and narrowed her eyes. "This isn't over, you know. You're going to get what you deserve. All of you will." With that, she stormed away.

I went back to my duties, vowing never give her another thought. There was such precious little time left before Corregidor would also fall.

***

Matthew and Henry had been assigned to the artillery unit, managing some of the huge guns along the coast. They took direct hits from the Japanese on a daily basis, setting my nerves on edge all day. I was in a constant state of prayer, imagining each concussion to be the one that would take either one or both of them away from me. Every evening, after my duties were complete, I waited at the tunnel entrance with Janine as if I were waiting for oxygen. When Matthew and Henry finally appeared, I could breathe again.

Gathering at the entrance became a social occasion for many, including the four of us. Someone set up a radio, and most would gather to smoke and visit while 'The Yellow Rose of Texas' or some other reminder of home played in the background. Sometimes, a couple or two might sway along. A few solitary types wrote letters. Most simply wanted a moment away from the oppression of the tunnel.

A few civilians, like myself, had wound up on The Rock either by choice or by fate. One of the better-known civilians was Homer Freeman, a journalist with *Time* magazine who'd been sending back army-approved stories of our courageous boys holding out against the heinous enemy. I hadn't read any of the stories, of course, but he was rumored to be a fair reporter, despite a flare for embellishment. I sometimes saw him strolling the laterals inside, but he was usually at the tunnel entrance in the evenings, leaning back in his chair against the cement wall, chatting with anyone nearby and scribbling in his notebook.

One evening as I waited with Janine, Mr. Freeman made eye contact with me and smiled. He was probably in his mid-thirties, though it was hard to tell how old anyone was at that point with so much disease and stress adding years to our bodies. His smile was friendly, and he motioned with his head for us to join him. We weaved around a few people and I took a chair next to him, while Janine rested against the wall beside me.

Mr. Freeman leaned forward and offered his hand. "Homer Freeman."

I shook his hand. "Grace Doyle. This is Janine Graves." It was the first time I'd used her married name, and it sounded a bit strange on my tongue.

"You ladies come over from Bataan?" he asked.

"Yes, sir," I said.

His eyebrows shot up. "None of that 'sir' stuff. Just call me Homer."

"All right."

He leaned back against the wall again and jotted down something in his notebook. "You going to write about us in one of your stories?" Janine asked.

"Depends," he said without looking up. "You got anything interesting to tell?"

I glanced up and met Janine's gaze, giving a slight shake of my head. It hit me that talking to a reporter wasn't the smartest choice of pastime. So I answered instead. "We're just here to serve the brave men out there in harm's way. They're the ones whose stories you should tell."

He looked up at me then and nodded. "That's mighty humble, Grace. But I've heard some of the other nurses' stories, and I know for certain you all are just as brave as the men. What was it like over there on Bataan?"

"Well, if you've talked to the other nurses, I imagine you've gotten a pretty good picture already," I said. "I doubt we'd have anything to add."

He bit the end of his pen and studied me for a long, uncomfortable moment. "I see." His eyes slid to Janine. "See any Japanese on your way over here?"

"Nope," Janine said. "Just their planes and mortar fire."

I knew I should remain quiet for my own sake, but something in me also wanted to let the world know what was going on across the bay. "I saw them," I said quietly.

Mr. Freeman plopped his chair legs on the ground as he leaned forward. "What did you see?"

I told him about the never-ending columns of broken American and Filipino soldiers marching along the coastal road, about the brutality of the Japanese, and their complete disregard for the lives of the men who'd surrendered. He was quiet for a while afterward, scribbling furiously with his pen.

"And you saw them do these things with your own eyes?" he asked.

I nodded.

"Can I quote you on that?"

"I'd rather you didn't."

Just then, Matthew and Henry walked up, and as soon as Matthew saw whom I was talking with, his expression darkened. I excused myself and went to him, wrapping my arms around him.

"That's a reporter you're talking to," he whispered into my ear.

I released him from my embrace and stepped back. "I know. I didn't say anything I shouldn't have."

He eyed Mr. Freeman, who I noticed was still watching us. "All the same, probably best to steer clear of him."

Artie Shaw's 'Dancing in the Dark' began playing behind me, a reminder that I was determined not to waste a moment of our time together. So I smiled up at Matthew. "Want to dance?"

His eyes softened, and he smiled down at me as he slipped his arm around my waist and pulled me close. "Absolutely, Mrs. Doyle."

***

Matthew and I did our best to be discreet—Henry and Janine less so—as Mrs. Fincher had requested. Most evenings we'd steal away to a bunker Matthew shared with several Marines during the day's bombings, and we'd have a few solitary moments to forget the nightmare we were living. They'd even found a mattress in an abandoned house down the hill, making our accommodation just a bit more comfortable.

Some evenings, we would imagine ourselves in some far off, mysterious corner of the world. Matthew would pretend to serve me the most wonderful meal, describing it in such detail my mouth would water. Sometimes, we imagined being in our own home, a quiet little bungalow on the coast of Australia. If I closed my eyes while his hands roamed over me, I could imagine it perfectly.

But even our momentary escapes couldn't last. The Japanese grew more persistent in bombarding The Rock, and casualties mounted every day. They were even firing from Bataan throughout the night, and it was becoming ever more dangerous to even try to slip out to the bunker. On April 26th, Matthew and I were making our way back to the tunnel when we heard the booming sound of the huge shells being fired. We raced back to the bunker, and were spared the atrocity that followed. But many of our friends were not.

The first shell was a dud, but the second landed right at the main entrance to Malinta Tunnel. Matthew and I sped to the entrance, only to find a scene right out of a horror movie. Those who had been gathered for a few moments of music and laughter, fresh air, and a bit of hope, had instead taken a direct hit. I skidded to a stop as soon as the devastation came into view and dropped to my knees.

The massive iron gate had been slammed shut by the explosion, crushing bodies in its path, and mangled limbs were strewn between the slats. Slowly, medics and other servicemen were able to push it open, and they stared open-mouthed at the slaughter. After a moment of pure shock, everyone jumped into motion.

Matthew and I began checking for anyone who might have survived. Screams echoed into the tunnel, reverberating off the walls and down my spine. At least a dozen were dead on impact, and as many as fifty or more were wounded to various degrees. I went to work triaging the wounded, sending the most urgent to immediate surgery. I had almost cleared the area of the entrance where I'd been working, when I saw Henry sitting on the ground, holding Janine in his arms.

He cradled her like a baby and sobbed as he kissed her hair. They were both covered in blood. I ran to him to help, kneeling in front of him.

"Henry! Let me help her." He wouldn't release his grip on her. "Henry, please."

I took her wrist and felt for a pulse. Nothing. I slid my hand along her shoulder and up to her neck. I couldn't look at Henry. I was sure he already knew. She was dead.

CHAPTER EIGHTEEN

Matthew

There were no funerals for the dead. Just a somber goodbye as the bodies were stacked outside the south entrance to the tunnel. The Japanese assault had grown so intense and so frequent, there was no time for burials, not even time to mourn. Sometimes a single assault would last for hours, with bullets and mortar bombs launching from Bataan to the north and Cavite to the south, and bombers dropping their payloads from the sky.

I'd gone back to the .50 caliber machine gun battery just up the hill from the south docks. I hated leaving Ruby when she was so upset, but there were enough casualties to keep her busy, and I was needed to help man the gun. Every time I turned around, another marine was injured. I made two trips to the tunnel to help carry the wounded. But there was no time to do more than make eye contact with Ruby.

She was so thin, so frail and desperate-looking. Being unable to give her the life she deserved was maddening. I had to wonder if maybe the quiet life we dreamed of was never really meant for us. But somewhere in my mind, I knew I couldn't lose hope. So I kept praying the Lord would find some way, somehow, to get her out of this torment. And finally, after months of prayers, He sent an answer.

As I was leaving the hospital ward a couple of days after the entrance bombing, I nearly ran smack into Major Prescott. I was shocked to see him, and he seemed just as surprised to see me.

"Major Prescott!" I exclaimed. "Why, I thought...forgive me, sir, but I thought you'd been killed."

He shook my hand vigorously. "Captain Doyle, my goodness. I feared your entire unit had been destroyed on Bataan. Good to see you, son. And it's Colonel now." He tapped the insignia on his shoulder.

"Congratulations," I said.

"Well, I wish it were under better circumstances. I replaced a brave fellow who took a hit from a mortar bomb while he was outside the tunnel." He frowned as if a thought had just occurred to him. "Say, where are you stationed?"

"On a .50 calibre machine gun above the south docks."

He shook his head. "Listen, I can't guarantee anything, but Wainwright has gotten word of two PBY planes coming in the next day or so. They're going to evacuate key personnel and some of the nurses."

My heart jumped. *Finally, a chance to get Ruby away.*

"They're going to need engineers," he continued. "MacArthur is specifically requesting officers to plan the reconquering of all the Pacific islands taken by the Japanese, and they'll need airstrips, bridges, barracks. You name it. I'd be happy to put your name up for consideration."

"I do appreciate that, sir, and would happily accept such a position. However, it would be more important to me to get my wife evacuated first."

"Your wife?" he said. "I had no idea you even had a wife, much less one on the island. My God, man. Why didn't you evacuate her sooner?"

"We just married on Bataan, sir. During the lull in the fighting. She's a civilian who's been working with the nurse corps."

"By all means, I'll put in a word for her, and for you as well."

I shook his hand, trying not to explode with gratitude. "Thank you so much, Colonel. I can't tell you what that would mean to me."

***

I returned to my gun battery with renewed hope. Maybe that dream of a life together was still possible. I thanked God continuously as I ran along the side of the hill, forgetting altogether that shells could drop on me at any moment. I climbed up the side of the cliff and around to the pit where we were dug in, and I jumped down into the trench where Henry sat waiting on me.

"There are two PBYs coming in. They're going to evacuate some personnel and some of the nurses. This could be our chance to get Ruby out of here."

Henry sat with his back against the wall, his eyes closed, puffing on a cigarette. He didn't move as he answered. "Good. It's about time."

I hadn't been a good friend the past two days. I had no idea what to say. When I'd thought Ruby was dead, there was nothing in the world anyone could've said to make things better. But Henry had tried. I owed it to him to try to get him out of here as well.

"Prescott says MacArthur is looking for key personnel for planning a counter attack on all the Pacific islands. Says he'll put in a good word for me. I'm sure they'll need pilots too."

"Don't worry about me," he said. "Get yourself and Ruby out of here. I can handle a few Japs."

"Henry, I know you must be devastated. I understand, believe me."

He turned his head and met my gaze with dark, despairing eyes. "Yes, I know. But Janine isn't coming back to me. I don't get another chance like you did."

I squatted next to him and put a hand on his shoulder. "You've been like a brother to me out here, man. I ain't planning on leaving you behind. We should stick together. Help me get Ruby out of here."

He didn't say anything for a long moment. Just puffed on his cigarette. Then he tossed it out in front of him and stomped it into the dust.
"You'll get Ruby out. I know you will. As for me, I'm going to stay here
and kill me as many of them dirty Nips as I can. Till I kill every last one
of 'em."

Ruby

April 29, 1942

I hadn't known Janine for long, just a little over half a year, but I felt her
loss all around me. Despite the relentless bombings, and the unending
procession of injured through the hospital laterals, I found a few moments to grieve my friend and sister-in-law. I went to her bed and gathered her personal effects, placing them in a small box. I took them over
to my bed and prayed over them. Then I cried for a little while as I
thought of Henry. How many more friends and family members did we
have to lose in this living hell?

While I was sitting on the bed, Roberta came over to offer her con-
dolences, and before she left, she handed me a note. I was to report to
the dining lateral at sundown. It contained no more information than
that, and Roberta had nothing to add. So I went back to my duties,
dressing wounds and praying over dying souls. It all seemed so hopeless.
And I was so tired.

As I made my way to the dining lateral, Matthew caught up to me
from behind and swept me into a big hug. "Didn't I tell you not to lose
faith?" he said in an excited whisper. "We're getting out of here. Tonight."

"What?"

"Keep moving. Go to the dining lateral. You'll find out everything."
Then he kissed me and stopped at the headquarters laterals. "I have a
meeting too. I'll find you afterward. I love you so much."

He looked almost giddy. Was it true? I walked into the dining area and took a seat among several other nurses. Despite my curiosity I was exhausted, so I laid my head on the table and waited for whatever was to come.

Shortly, Mrs. Fincher marched over and stood before us with a grave expression. "Ladies, I will get right to the point. We've been presented with an opportunity to evacuate you all immediately."

So Matthew had been right. Mrs. Fincher handed each of us a piece of paper as she continued. "You have each been relieved from your present assignment and duty and will proceed by first available transport to Melbourne, Australia, reporting upon arrival to the Commander in Chief, Southwest Pacific Area, G.H.Q., for further disposition."

Murmuring filled the room as the girls began to ask questions. How soon would we leave? What about the others? What about the patients?

Mrs. Fincher quieted them down quickly. "There simply isn't enough time to discuss all the details. There are exactly twenty spots for nurses. No more. There will be no time for goodbyes. Gather your things, and prepare to leave immediately. You may take one bag that weighs less than ten pounds. And for the sake of everyone, especially those left behind, you will speak of this to no one."

I surveyed the others, all of us stunned by this sudden turn in our course. Some seemed reluctant to go.

"This feels like desertion," someone said.

"I'll stay. Someone else should go in my place," said another.

The questions were endless, but time was not. We were hurried away, and I went to my bed to decide on what to take with me.

Some things were easy. Daddy's Bible, a few toiletries, and a camera I'd found in Janine's locker. I put the Bible and camera into my small bag, then went to gather some clothing.

When I turned to pick up a skirt, I spied Natalie stomping toward me, stopping with her hands on her hips. "Is it true?" she demanded. "Are you leaving?"

I had been so overcome with the excitement of the announcement that I had failed to notice Natalie's absence from the room. Yet I had no fear left inside of me over what she might do. I gave her a moment's glance, and resumed packing. This seemed to anger her even more.

"I asked you a question! Are you on the list to be evacuated?"

In answer, I put another skirt into my bag before zipping it up.

"Why would they pick you? That doesn't make any sense. You're a...a *nobody*. You're a liar...and...and a murderer!"

I placed my bag at the end of the bed and pushed past her.

"You promised!" she screamed, almost hysterical. "You said if a chance came to escape, that I could go too! You liar!"

"Look," I said. "I had no idea any of this was going on. We just found out about it a few minutes ago. Had I known, I would have asked that you be included—"

"Then ask now! Or give your seat to me!"

I'd had enough. I charged at her, raising my voice. "And then what, Natalie? You want my husband? You want my firstborn? Should I give you all my money? I have nothing more to give you, and I won't be controlled by you any longer! Go tell your little story to whomever you like. At this point, you'll just sound like a lunatic. No one cares!"

Natalie's face grew red as she noticed a couple of other nurses nearby who were outright staring at us. Then she pointed her finger at me. "You won't get away, Ruby Graves...Doyle...Grace Miller...oh, whoever you are. I know your true identity. And everyone else is going to know too."

Matthew

I stood in the background, my back pressed up against the cement wall of the lateral that housed General Wainwright's offices. Several higher-ranking officers stood around a table pointing at a map of the thousands of islands that made up the Philippines. The main focus was the safest route to navigate around the islands that were already under Japanese control in order to reach Mindanao, where the PBY planes would be waiting.

Once the route was settled on, the generals and colonels were dismissed, and Major Prescott brought a marine named Hank Stringer and me over to the map. He pointed at the south dock. "You'll each be in charge of a group of evacuees. You'll lead them down to the dock, load them onto the two boats waiting, and secure their transitions to the PBY planes here, just east of Cabayan." He pointed to a small cove on the northern tip of Mindanao. "It will be important to keep everyone calm, quiet, and most importantly, moving. Help the civilians as best you can. They haven't been trained for things like this. Come to think of it, the nurses probably haven't been either. Identify the most cool-headed of the nurses in each group to help with leading the women. Hopefully none of them will be given to hysterics."

I nodded along as he finished the instructions, still wondering how this had all happened so quickly. I didn't want to analyze it too much. God had obviously worked to make it possible, just as He'd been guiding us all along.

"You understand everything?" Prescott asked.

I studied the path leading down to the docks. That area had taken heavy fire all morning, but for some reason no one could explain, the Japs had backed off later in the day. They hadn't bombed the southern side of the island since the morning. Another intervention by God, I was sure.

"I've got it," I said to Prescott. "I'm ready."

Stringer concurred. He'd obviously once been in great shape, a real athlete. Like all the marines, he still had the confidence and stance of someone who had mastered the pain that comes with pushing your body to its limits. But starvation had taken its toll, as it had on everyone. Dark circles framed his eyes, and I noticed several bandages along his arms. Shrapnel. Stringer was one tough cookie.

So what was I doing there? I was a newly appointed captain, and I'd lost most of my men in the jungles of Bataan. What had Prescott seen in me?

Prescott shook our hands and dismissed us. We were to report down to the south tunnel entrance in one hour. I headed out of the headquarters laterals, coming out near the main lateral of the hospital section. I'd planned on finding Ruby and making sure she was ready to go, when I turned a corner and found Natalie waiting for me instead.

She looked terrible. I couldn't believe I'd ever found her attractive. She'd wasted away to skin and bones, and her angry eyes bulged as she practically spat at me. "You promised to get me on a plane."

"I didn't promise you anything, Natalie." I started to continue past her, but she stepped into my path.

"She did. She promised me I could go too. That was the only reason I kept my mouth shut."

"That, and you didn't want to kill the goose that was laying your golden eggs. Who else would you have stolen rations and medicine from?"

Anger flashed in her dull eyes, and she stepped toward me, pushing her needle-like finger into my chest. "If you don't figure out a way to get me on one of those planes, I swear, I will—"

"You'll what? Tell Fincher who she really is? So what? We'll deny it. And given your state of mind, no one will believe you."

"Maybe not. But do you know who else is in this tunnel? Homer Freeman."

"Who?" I feigned ignorance, but my nerves tightened.

"The journalist, Homer Freeman. Works for *Time*. He's been reporting on everything going on here. I bet he'd love to know there was an escaped convicted murderer posing as a nurse. That she was taking the place of some poor, brave *real* nurse who deserved to escape this hell. What a story that would be."

"If he's about to be captured by the Japanese, I doubt he'll be concerned with your little tale."

"He isn't going to be captured. He's in the group that's about to be evacuated. So you and your *wife* might reach Australia, but I doubt you'll go anywhere else."

I didn't have time for all this. "What do you want me to do? I have no say in whose name is on the list to go."

"That's a lie! *Grace's* name is on the list. You must have had something to do with it."

"Official policy. The wife of an officer can be evacuated. You don't qualify, unless you can get some poor sucker to marry you in less than an hour."

"Then think of something. You think of something right now, or I'm going to shout from the rooftops who Ruby really is."

Everything in me wanted to challenge her to do just that, if nothing but to end the threat. But I couldn't take that chance. Not with Ruby's future. I threw my hands up. "All right, all right! I'll think of something. Go get your belongings." Then I stepped over and lowered my voice to a growl. "And stay away from Ruby."

She studied me for a long moment as if she wasn't sure if she could believe me. "I have your word?"

I sighed, resigned to what I was about to do. "Yes. I swear to you before God, that I will do everything I can, not that you deserve it."

She seemed to relax, almost smiling. "Good. And I swear to you, when we land in Australia, I'll forget everything I know about Ruby."

"Sure you will," I said, not hiding my sarcasm. "Now you better hurry if you want to make it. I'll do what I can, but I will not hold up everyone else for you."

She turned on her heels and ran down the main lateral of the hospital, disappearing into the dark. I asked around until I found Mrs. Fincher seated at a desk in a small branch off the main lateral. She looked up from her paperwork as I approached. "How can I help you, Captain Doyle?"

I sat down opposite her and set my mind to the task at hand. "I need to speak with you about the list of evacuees."

Ruby

I left just before midnight ahead of the other nurses to go to the entrance where we were to meet. I was hoping to catch Matthew, and I wasn't disappointed. He smiled as I came to him, kissing my cheek. He was heavily armed, along with another fellow I'd never met before. Matthew gestured toward him. "This is Captain Stringer with the 4th Marines. He'll be leading the other group of evacuees. Captain Stringer, this is my wife, Ruby."

His expression registered surprise when Matthew called me his wife. Then he smiled at me and shook my hand. "Nice to meet you, ma'am," he said with the drawl of a cowboy.

"Will you excuse us for one moment?" Matthew said. He took my hand and led me around the edge of the entrance and onto the path that led down to the road. Setting his rifle down, he pulled me into his embrace, holding onto me without saying anything for a long moment. Then he kissed me deeply.

"I don't want you to worry about anything, all right?" he said. "This is all going to happen fast, and we might not get a chance to talk again until after it's all over. Just stick with your group and stay calm. And know that I love you more than anything in this whole world."

"You sound like you're saying goodbye," I said, my heart thumping.

"No, of course not. It's just...this is a dangerous mission, and anything can happen. I just want you to know that I love you and that I'll do anything to protect you."

He kissed me again, sliding his hand around my neck and holding on like it might be the last time. The desperation in his kiss gave me pause. "Matthew, is something wrong?"

He pressed his forehead to mine and took a deep breath. "No, everything will be fine. Just remember, you promised. No matter what happens, you get to safety in Australia."

The uneasiness in my stomach grew. "What do you mean? What's going to happen?"

"I don't know. The Japs could attack us. The boats could get separated in the open water. The plane could stall. We could take anti-aircraft fire as we take off. I don't want to worry you. I just want you to promise me you'll stay on that plane and get to Australia, no matter what else happens. Promise me again."

"I promise."

He hugged me close, gently swaying in the breeze. I couldn't shake the feeling that something was wrong. That he was saying goodbye. I pushed the feeling down the best I could, knowing there was nothing more I could do. Maybe Matthew was just nervous about the plan. Maybe he was afraid for me.

"What about Henry?" I asked. "Are we just leaving him here? He'll be captured."

"I have a feeling Henry will take care of himself."

I pulled back slightly and looked up at him. "Is he...is he all right? I haven't seen him since..."

"He'll be all right. He wants you to get to safety. I'm sure he'd come say goodbye to you if he could, but there just isn't time."

I peered out over the bay at the dark horizon, wondering what lay ahead. Down below, I could make out two small lights bobbing in the blackness of the bay. So much darkness.

"Do you remember when you and Henry came into my father's furniture store looking for a table and a bed for your mother?" he said.

The memory made me smile. "Yes. I was so nervous."

"You were adorable. All a mess and barely able to look at me."

"Did you know, even back then? Did you know how hopelessly in love I was?"

He grinned and gave a little shrug. "Well, not at first. When Henry and I went back to get the extra chairs, he hinted around that I should walk you to get some ice cream. That it would give you a thrill."

"That scoundrel!" I couldn't keep myself from laughing. "After he abandoned me and everything."

Matthew laughed along with me. "You were something else. I was so turned around and inside out, not knowing whether to love you or leave you alone. Seemed like I made you mad at me at every turn."

"You were turned around? You? I was sure you'd never love me back. All I did was tell myself how ridiculous I was."

He kissed me gently. "Doesn't seem so ridiculous now, does it?"

"No," I said, soaking in the feeling of his arms around my back, my hands on his chest, our hearts so close. "It feels like...like I've loved you forever."

"You have. And I've loved you forever. Remember, nothing can come between us. God will always bring us together. Have faith in that." He took a quick look around. "Let's get you back to the group."

He took my hand again, and we walked back to the entrance where the rest of the evacuees were gathering. There were twenty nurses selected to go, along with some civilians whom I knew to be the mistresses of several high-ranking officials. Some of the men included older officers who looked like they might not make the trek to the docks, let alone withstand captivity. Mr. Freeman also joined the group, scribbling furiously on a small notepad. General Wainwright stood among us, shaking hands and wishing each person well. Mrs. Fincher stood just behind him and off to the left, looking as stoic as ever.

As we gathered around, General Wainwright thanked us for our bravery and our service to our country. He told us to pray for those left behind, as they would pray for our safe travels. And he hoped we would all meet again someday soon. As he spoke I glanced around at the group of about fifty souls, praying for each person. Until I saw Natalie.

My heart was already racing with nerves, and now it dropped into my stomach. What was she doing? She hadn't been on the list. Mrs. Fincher had specifically said there was only room for twenty nurses. I scanned the group and did a quick headcount. Twenty-one nurses. What was going on? Had she meant twenty *army* nurses? Maybe she'd originally counted me as part of the twenty.

Matthew was speaking to the group, giving instructions on how to proceed. "Keep moving at all times. No matter what happens. We may take fire from the Japanese, but keep your hand on the shoulder in front of you, and keep moving. If you stop, you stop everyone behind you."

I tried to focus on his words, but couldn't shake the dread that Natalie's presence brought over me. How had she gotten added to the group? Could I never, ever escape that wretched woman?

"Everyone form two lines of twenty five," Matthew continued. "When we reach the docks, you'll be loaded into two boats. The line on the left will board the boat on the left. Line on the right, the boat on the right."

We began separating into two lines. I stepped behind another nurse, one of the older ladies who'd been ill most of the time since we'd arrived on Corregidor. But I kept my eyes on Matthew up front.

"The boats will take you to a cove on an island south of here. Should be there by morning. Two PBY planes will then transport you to Australia. Stay calm, and keep moving. The voyage along the water might be rough, so find a sturdy position. Everyone ready?"

There was nodding and several calls of "Yes!"

"Follow me!"

CHAPTER NINETEEN

Ruby

April 29, 1942

I kept my hand firmly on the shoulder of the nurse in front of me as we walked out the entrance and down a short path to the dirt road that wound along the southern coast of the island. Although we moved along at a steady pace, there were times we had to veer off the road to get around fallen trees and debris, and we slowed down for a bit. As we approached the bottom of the slope, we circled around a huge crater, and the nurse in front of me lost her footing. She stumbled, and I reached to steady her.

She turned her head to the side, thanking me between heaving breaths. "I'm too old for this," she gasped.

"You can do it," I said. "One step at a time. We're all here to help you."

"I have to slow down."

"Just a little bit further. Look, we're almost to the dock."

We reached the bottom of the hill and moved quickly along the wooden dock out over the lapping water. The boards shook with our combined weight. Ahead of us, I could see two boats on either side. When Matthew reached the boats, he turned and directed each line into them, helping the older evacuees climb aboard. When the lady in front of me reached the edge, she hesitated.

Matthew stepped over and took her hand. "What's your name?"

"Beckett. Captain Laura Beckett." Her voice shook.

"Let me help you, Captain Beckett," he said.

I took her right elbow and together, Matthew and I eased her over the side of the boat. Then we shared a quick glance before I jumped on board. I took a seat on the side and held on, my heart thumping fit to burst. Soon, everyone was loaded, and Matthew jumped in as well. He gave the captain a thumbs-up, and the engine revved to life.

Water misted around my face; a cool, refreshing spray after so long in the oppressive tunnels. I kept my eyes on the dark land mass to the southeast, where Cavite lay in the hands of the Japanese. Could we really sneak away undetected?

I only worried about the Japanese until we were out of the bay, because that was when the sea grew angry. The further away from Corregidor we sailed, the higher the waves rolled, and the more nauseous I became. The sting of the water spraying against my face was no longer refreshing, and each time we crested a wave, I thought I might vomit all over Matthew, who held onto me as if I might fly overboard at any moment. Once again, I couldn't help but think of Jonah, but unlike him, I wasn't about to ask anyone to throw me overboard.

April 30, 1942

Just after dawn, the boat coasted into a cove along the coast, and taxied up to a long dock. The beach was short, and the area near the dock was covered in mangroves, providing some cover for the two PBY planes waiting nearby. When we climbed out onto the dock, I saw the crew of one of the planes anxiously standing around, leaning in various directions and studying the fuselage.

"Hit a rock or something as we were coasting in," one of the men said to Matthew as we approached. "Ripped a hole in the fuselage. Water's leaking in."

"Oh, no," I said. "Can it be repaired?"

He shrugged. "We're working on it. Got a salvage expert coming over with a boat crew from the Naval base nearby. But they said there's Japs all in this area. Best to keep your heads down and stay hidden until we get it repaired."

Matthew and Captain Stringer herded everyone onto shore. "Ladies and gentleman, there's a slight problem with one of the planes, but the crew is doing their best to repair it. Stay close by, get something to eat, and rest up. We have a long night ahead of us."

There was much anxious grumbling, and loud whining from Natalie's direction. Matthew did his best to keep the group calm. "Listen everyone, these are very capable flight crews who handle similar situations all the time. I'm sure the plane will be repaired and ready to go soon."

One of the colonels stepped forward. "Captain Doyle, I've been at this game quite a long time. You're right about the capabilities of the crew. However, with the limits on their resources, there most likely isn't anything they can do. I think we'd better have a backup plan."

Agreement sounded from various group members. Matthew turned to the colonel and nodded. "Colonel Higgins, maybe you and some of the more senior staff here could discuss a plan while we wait for more information."

"I'm familiar with this area," the colonel said. "There's a hotel a few kilometers inland, where we can hide out until MacArthur can send another plane."

I noticed Natalie's expression change from worry to downright terror. "But the plane could still be repaired, right?" she said.

"I say we give the crew some time to fix the problem," Matthew said. "If it appears the plane won't be ready, we'll seek shelter at the hotel this afternoon."

"The entire group?" someone called out from the back. "What about the other plane? Half of us can still leave."

Several more group members began talking, and quickly their voices blended into a cacophony of suggestions and concerns. Overall, most of the evacuees wanted to stay together. Only a few seemed desperate to leave, despite the fate of their comrades. I had mixed feelings myself, and imagined even the most outspoken patriots did as well. Would we really give up our chance to escape as a sign of support? How was it in any-one's interest to get captured? But how could we leave our fellow travel-ers, those who'd suffered the same hardships and loss, in such peril?

Gradually the group splintered into smaller groups as we waited to see what would happen. The navy boat crew arrived to work on the re-pairs while the other plane was refueled. Matthew and I found a quiet spot up the side of a slope, shaded by a tree and within sight of the planes. We ate some of the rations we'd been given, and then I lay down in the grass to sleep, Matthew returning to the action below.

The servicemen scattered out into a perimeter to keep a lookout for Japanese patrols, rotating after an hour. Matthew came over to where I lay and was finally able to stretch out and get some rest as well. A chorus of parrots roused us an hour later to a beautiful day drenched with sun-shine. There were just enough clouds to provide occasional shade, and the steady breeze kept us from getting too hot.

As we dug out some of our rations, I spotted a familiar form ap-proaching up the hill. I shaded my eyes to be certain, then smiled at Mike Sawyer as he stopped in front of me. "Well, I'll be," he said. "If it ain't Grace Miller!"

I stood and went to hug his neck. I was amazed at how healthy and strong he looked compared to the skeletons I'd gotten used to seeing. "Mike! Are you flying one of the planes?"

"Yes, ma'am." He looked me over as I stepped back, a look of concern coming over his expression.

I turned to introduce Matthew, who'd stood behind me. "This is Matthew Doyle. We grew up together, and he and Henry used to play ball for our school team. He's...he's my husband."

Mike's eyes widened, but then he broke out into a huge grin. He took Matthew's extended hand, shaking it vigorously. "Well, my stars! Glad to meet you Matthew. Henry didn't mention anything about Grace getting married when he contacted me. Say, where is that son of a gun, anyway?"

Matthew and I shared a tense glance. He gestured for Mike to take a seat with us. "Come have a bite with us. We'll fill you in."

Matthew sat down with his back against a tree, and I sat next to him, leaning into his shoulder. Mike took a seat on a rock a few feet away. I let Matthew explain everything that happened to us on Bataan and Corregidor, while Mike's friendly smile faded to sorrow, especially when he learned of Janine's death.

Mike shook his head. "I sure do hate that for him. I didn't think that boy would ever settle down. How's he taking it?"

"Not well," Matthew said, and that appeared to be all that was needed by way of explanation.

We sat in uncomfortable silence for a bit before Matthew nodded his head toward the docks and the damaged plane. "How does it look for the repairs?" Matthew asked.

"I'm not sure," he answered. "They're still working on it."

"What do you think we should do?" I asked.

He sighed and leaned onto his elbows, resting on his knees. "Hard to say. I think we should get as many as possible on my plane and get out of here. According to the boat crew, the line has basically broken. There are Japs all over the place. Better to get as many out of here as possible rather than have all of you captured."

"My sentiments exactly," Matthew said. He cursed the Japanese with words I'd never heard from him before.

"Sounds like things got rough for you all," Mike said.

"You look well," I said. "Where have you been stationed?"

"I've been working out of Australia with MacArthur's bunch. They've really been rooting for Corregidor to hold out."

"Should've been doing more than that," Matthew said, not hiding his resentment. "Our boys need reinforcements. Ammo. Supplies. It's a dirty shame to just leave us all there to suffer and die."

"The whole Pacific's reeling," Mike said. "No one was ready for the Nips. They've taken over everything from the Dutch East Indies to Hong Kong, and now they appear to be setting their sights on the Aleutians. If they get a bridge to Canada and the U.S., there's no telling how far they'll get before we can stop them. Nobody wanted to give up the Philippines, least of all MacArthur, but I think he's doing his best to regroup and form a plan to recapture everything. But it's going to take time."

"Well, from what we saw leaving Bataan, it'll be too late," Matthew said. "There won't be any soldiers left alive."

Mike shook his head. "Nips really caught us with our pants down, didn't they?"

"Partly, but seems to me we didn't respond like we could have. I saw Clark Field. I saw all the bombers and fighter planes there. We could've taken out the Japs at Formosa, and no one lifted a finger. Not MacArthur, not Sutherland. No one."

I could feel Matthew tensing beside me and decided to change the subject. We were so close to escaping this nightmare. "So what's the plan for getting out of here?" I asked.

Mike looked over his shoulder toward the rest of the evacuees gathered down the slope. Some had taken off their shoes, rolled up their pants, and were wading in the water. If I didn't know any better, we might look like a group on holiday at the beach.

"Talk to the colonels," Mike said. "They'll make the final call. But decide something soon. I don't recommend trying to get inland. I'd stay near the plane and hope for the best with the repairs."

"Thanks, Mike," Matthew said. He pushed himself away from the tree and stood. "I'll walk back down with you and get the colonels together."

He pulled his pistol out of its holster and handed it to me. "Here, Ruby. You remember what to do if anything untoward happens? Breathe...and squeeze." Then he gave me a playful smirk. "I'll be back soon. Don't go anywhere. And stay out of trouble."

***

After Matthew and Mike left, I knelt beside the tree and shut out everything around me that was contributing to my fear. I focused on the songs of the parrots and other colorful birds, on the bright blue sky above me, and tried to quiet my racing mind. I needed to hear from the Lord, and part of a Psalm came to mind.

Why art thou cast down, O my soul? And why art thou disquieted in me? Hope thou in God: for I shall yet praise Him for the help of His countenance.

The words were a soothing balm for my soul, reminding me of who held my faith and hope. Not Matthew, not the flight crews, not anyone but the Creator of heaven and earth Himself. "Thank You, Lord," I whispered, looking to the sky. "Thank You for Your peace. You are the rock upon whom I build my home. All other ground is sinking sand."

I turned my gaze on the people just down the slope from me. Matthew and Captain Stringer had joined the colonels, engaged in intense planning. The others were gathered in small groups of various numbers. My eyes fell on Natalie as she sat on the ground, talking with some of the nurses and Mr. Freeman, who was scribbling on his notepad, as usual. Immediately I felt the Spirit of God convict me. It was time to forgive. For my sake, if not for hers. So I prayed that God would grant Natalie peace, and that she would no longer hold any sway over me.

When I'd finished my prayer, my stomach sent a violent reminder that it was not fully recovered from the dysentery I'd struggled with since Bataan. I looked around for a private spot to relieve myself, but nothing seemed suitable. I was not about to do my business in sight of the others. I knew Matthew would be angry, but I was desperate, and I had to find a place immediately.

I grabbed the pistol he'd left for my protection and went a short ways deeper into the tall grass. I made sure I was out of range of the group, and then I dug a small hole in the ground behind a tree.

Matthew

Although there was a slight disagreement on the details, the colonels agreed that it wasn't looking likely the damaged plane would be repaired soon, and they wanted to seek out a place less vulnerable. Colonel Higgins made the final call. "The group that came over on captain Doyle's boat will board and leave as soon as the plane is ready. Those of us on the damaged plane will set out for the hotel." He pointed through the woods behind him. "Captain Stringer and Colonel Johnson, we'll head southeast until we reach a road that runs to a small village near Madamba. You two will clear the path ahead of us, making sure we don't run up on any Jap patrols. I'll lead the rest just behind you."

Everyone agreed to the plan, and we headed back toward the group to explain. No one argued, but I could see the panic on Natalie's face. She met my gaze, and I knew I was in for trouble. The group headed for the hotel and began gathering their things, but Natalie headed straight for me.

"I already know what you're going to say, and it's not possible," I said.

"Then figure out how to make it possible," she hissed. "I am not staying on this island one minute longer than I have to."

"Natalie, don't you understand? If you go with the other plane, then everyone else will want to do the same." I could only imagine the chaos it would cause to have everyone clamoring to board the undamaged plane. But she was incapable of reason.

"I don't care how you do it, but you better get me on that plane."

"Or what?"

She narrowed her hateful eyes, and then she turned on her heels and headed straight for Homer Freeman. "Excuse me, Mr. Freeman!" she called. "Have I got a story for you!"

I stomped after her and grabbed her by the elbow. "That isn't going to work anymore."

"Then why are you trying to stop me?"

"You know what? It doesn't matter." I released her arm. "Do what you have to do. And I'll do what I have to do. But if you don't go with the group to the hotel, you *will* be left here on your own. There's no room for you on the first plane."

"We'll see about that," she said, turning away and marching toward the journalist.

I realized there was nothing more I could do to stop her. It was in God's hands now. Maybe Mr. Freeman wouldn't believe her. Maybe he would. But I couldn't worry about that anymore. I glanced up the slope to find Ruby and warn her, but I didn't see her beneath the tree where I'd left her.

Of course she wasn't there. Because I'd told her precisely to *stay* there. So naturally, she didn't. When was she ever going to learn? To that matter, when was I?

I climbed the slope and searched the area near the tree. She'd taken the gun, at least. I looked back down at the groups of people getting ready to move out. Natalie was talking animatedly with Homer Freeman, whose face looked utterly fascinated. She pointed up the slope at me, and he glanced my way. I waved and smiled. He managed a confused wave and turned back to Natalie.

Lord, please make her sound like a raving lunatic. And please help me find Ruby.

Ruby

The minutes passed in agonizing fashion. I did my best to clean up and bury the evidence of my dysentery. I figured I needed to return quickly before Matthew noticed my absence, so I grabbed the gun from the ground and shoved it into the waist of my pants.

When I reached the tree where we'd been sitting earlier, Matthew was waiting on me like someone had lit him on fire. "Didn't I tell you to stay put?"

"I just went a little ways into the trees—"

"Why can't you ever just listen to me?"

"Why are you so worked up?"

He paced back and forth just below the line of trees. "Natalie's down there, telling that reporter all about you."

"What?" I couldn't believe I was just trying to forgive her.

"She's determined to be on the first plane out, but there's no way."

"How does telling Mr. Freeman about me accomplish anything?"

He shrugged. "I have no idea. I reckon we're about to find out. But I swear, you are going to be on that plane."

I walked over to him and wrapped my hands around his neck, kissing him gently. "Haven't we learned our lesson yet? God will take care of us, and He'll figure out what to do with Natalie. Maybe Mr. Freeman won't believe her."

Matthew touched his forehead to mine and closed his eyes. "I love you so much."

"I love you, too."

He took my hand. "Come on. We need to get everyone on the plane soon."

We took a few more steps down the slope into the clearing, but soon juddered to a halt. The familiar sound of buzzing overhead sent chills down my spine. The people down the hill from us had stopped also, some pointing to the sky. A plane approached from the south, and though I hoped it was American, I knew in my gut it was not.

"Take cover!" someone yelled, and everyone scattered up the hill and into the trees.

Matthew and I ran in the direction we'd come from, into the cover of the dense forest. We watched the plane fly over the cove some distance away. I prayed the pilot hadn't seen us.

"They'll have seen the planes next to the dock," Matthew said.

"Maybe not," I answered, not ready for my hopes to be dashed. "It was pretty far away."

"We can't risk it. If he saw the planes, then we'll be swarmed in a matter of minutes."

"Minutes?" I suddenly felt dizzy.

"Depends on how far away they are. We can't afford to wait any longer."

Once the plane was out of sight, we ran back down the hill to the rest of the group. As people came out of the trees, everyone was anxious. Colonel Higgins and Matthew did their best to keep everyone calm. "I think we'd better get going," Colonel Higgins said. "Those of you going with us inland to the hotel, gather over here to my right."

"But, what about the second plane?" Natalie said. "Is it fixed?"

"No," Matthew answered.

Natalie huffed and pointed her finger at me. "She shouldn't even be here! Did you all know that woman is an escaped convicted murderer?" Heat flooded my face as all eyes turned to me. "That's right," Natalie continued, her excitement mounting. "She was convicted of murdering a man in cold blood and sentenced to the electric chair! She faked her own death and has been pretending to be a nurse this whole time!"

For a moment Colonel Higgins seemed at a loss for words, but he swiftly recovered, doing his best to regain control of the situation. "Young lady, you are a lieutenant in the United States Army. This irrational, cowardly conduct is unbecoming. Now we are leaving to find a place of safety. Get your act together, or you will be facing a court martial."

Natalie's face went white. "*Me?* A court martial? What about him?" She pointed at Matthew. "He's aiding an escaped murderer!"

Colonel Higgins regarded Matthew with an impatient scowl. "I'm sorry about all this, Captain Doyle. You have performed your duties honorably. I'll be taking Lieutenant Williams with me, and I'll be certain her behavior is dealt with."

Natalie sounded like she was choking. "But...but...I'm telling the truth!"

"*Lieutenant!*" Colonel Higgins roared. "In case you are unaware, we could be captured by Japanese soldiers at any moment. Perhaps you could focus your attention on staying quiet and following orders. Now fall in line with the others!"

Matthew met my gaze, and I thought he would burst out laughing right there. It wasn't exactly funny. But it was deeply satisfying. Colonel Higgins commanded the group to get moving, and then apologized to Matthew and me before turning to go. Natalie followed like a whipped puppy behind.

Matthew addressed Mike and his crew. "All right boys, let's get that plane in the air!"

CHAPTER TWENTY

Matthew

While Mike and his crew went through the final plane checks, I organized the evacuees on the dock. Ruby hung toward the back of the line, her face still flushed from the attention. I overheard two of the other nurses talking quietly. "What in the world got into Natalie? Did you have any idea what that was about?"

I walked up to Mr. Freeman and leaned toward him as I lowered my voice. "You didn't really take any of that nonsense seriously, did you?"

He looked down the line at Ruby, then back at me. "I'm always interested in a good story, son. But right now, I'm just interested in staying alive."

It wasn't what I was hoping for, but it would have to do. I made my way down the line until I got to Ruby. I couldn't help but smile. "Well, that was interesting."

She nodded. "It certainly was. What do you think will come of it?"

"I think Natalie will get exactly what's coming to her. And if the Japs catch her, so will they."

A sharp whistle sounded from shore, catching my attention. Colonel Franklin, who'd been keeping watch near the trees, jogged down the slope. I ran to the end of the dock to meet him.

"We've got a Jap patrol," he said. "They're coming down the hill. Be here any moment."

"Let's head 'em off," I said. I turned and called to the group. "Anyone want to kill some Japs?"

"I'm in!" yelled an older colonel.

"Oh yeah!" said another.

Two of the crew members joined them, and they ran down the dock with their rifles. From the corner of my eye I noticed Ruby coming as well. I sent the men forward to take position above the tree line, then met Ruby at the end of the dock. I could see the determination in her eyes that I'd grown to both love and detest.

"Go back with the others," I said.

"What's going on?"

"Ruby, you promised. No matter what happens, you get on that plane."

Understanding dawned on her face. "I can't...I'll come with you!"

"No! You get on the plane. We'll be right behind you." I gave her a quick kiss and ran off the dock.

"Matthew, wait!" she cried. "Here, take this." With that, she tossed me the pistol I'd left for her protection.

There was no time for me to argue. "Now don't forget your promise!" I yelled over my shoulder. "Get on that plane! I'll be right behind you!" I glimpsed back one more time to make sure she was returning to the plane. She was, but slowly. *Lord, get her on that plane.*

I found the others spreading out about fifty yards into the tree line and took a position just beneath a small ridge of rocks jutting out of the hill. To my right, Colonel Franklin and one of the crew from the plane lay on the ground behind some trees. To my left, the other crew member and the two colonels had taken up positions crouched behind foliage. I waited, my eyes darting through the trees as I held my breath.

I saw movement about twenty yards away, but I couldn't be sure of what it was. The trees and vines were so dense; it was difficult to see more than five yards or so. I looked down our line of defense to the left, then to the right. Everyone's rifles were trained and ready. The entire forest seemed to go silent. Like a balloon about to burst.

And then it did. Shots rang out, and bullets whizzed through the air past my head. I returned fire, though I still hadn't seen the enemy. But I heard them. Shouts in Japanese. More bullets zipped past, slamming into the trees and earth around me. One of the crew members to my left took a hit and tumbled down the hill. I kept firing and firing, until I needed to reload.

Colonel Franklin called out to me, asking if I was all right. Before I could reply, he too took a shot to the torso and dropped to his knees. He moaned and rolled over, cursing. I finished reloading and propped my rifle on the top of the ridge. A bullet hit the ground right beside it. I finally saw them. They were advancing down the hill. I hit one. Then another. They were getting too close.

"Fall back!" I called to the crew member to my right. "Get Colonel Franklin and get to the plane!"

He ran in a crouched position over to the colonel, propping him up beneath the arm.

"I'll cover you! Get to the plane!" I shouted.

He nodded and began moving down the hill. I fired into the woods at the approaching Japanese, forcing them to take cover. But the line to my left was still moving forward. Soon they'd have me surrounded. I swung my rifle to the left and fired again, halting that side of the line.

"Get to the plane!" I yelled at the two remaining men.

The one closest to me ran to a nearby tree, dropped into a crouch and fired into the line of Japanese to my right. "You can't hold them off by yourself!" he said.

I paused to reload my rifle one last time, because I would have no more ammunition after that. Then I unloaded into the line, dropping two more soldiers. Only a handful remained. "Go!" I yelled at him again. "I need you to give my wife a message!"

Ruby

I watched the end of the dock anxiously for Matthew to return. When the gunfire broke out, I nearly dropped to my knees. "Lord," I cried. "Put a hedge of protection around him. Bring him back! Bring him back!"

"Grace!"

I took a few steps toward the end of the dock. Two men were running out of the woods and through the clearing. One was supporting the other.

"Grace!"

I turned to the voice calling my name. It was Captain Beckett, the older nurse I'd helped when she'd stumbled. She waved her hand, signaling for me to get on the plane. I turned away. The two men were running down the dock now. Neither of them was Matthew.

Get on the plane. I'll be right behind you.

"Grace!" Mrs. Beckett called again. "Get on the plane!"

The two men had nearly reached me. "Where's Matthew?" I yelled.

The soldier helped his injured comrade into the plane. Then he turned to me with an outstretched hand. "It's time to go!"

"Where's Matthew?"

"He's right behind us. Come on!"

I looked at the end of the dock. No one was coming. *Get on the plane.*

"Grace! Come on!" Several people were yelling at me now. I took the crew member's hand and stepped aboard, my heart thundering. I hurried to the front of the fuselage where a small hole opened into the cockpit. "Mike! Wait for Matthew! He's coming!"

"Grace, we have to go!" Mike yelled over the roar of the engine.

"Please! Just wait!"

"We have incoming!" the co-pilot shouted.

I looked ahead and saw two planes heading directly for us from the other side of the lake. I ran back to the door of the plane. One of the crew was about to close it. I grabbed his arm. "Wait! Give him one more minute!"

"*Grace!*" The desperation in Mike's voice chilled me to the bone. "We have to go *now!*"

"One more minute! Or I am getting off this plane!" I thought my heart would come right out of my chest. I looked out the side door at the end of the dock. "There's two more coming!" I shouted.

"Stay inside, ma'am," the crew member at the door said. He stepped out onto the dock to help the others inside.

I darted to the front again. The Japanese planes were lower now, coming straight at us. The men handed the body of an injured crew member through the door. The nurses took him to the back with the other injured colonel and began working on him. Then two more men came through the door. Neither one was Matthew.

"Everyone take cover, now!" Mike yelled.

The zeros roared over us as bullets streaked through the fuselage. I jumped up as soon as they passed and flew to the door again, looking to the end of the dock. One last figure was running toward us. It had to be Matthew, but I could see from his build that it wasn't. I looked past him to the woods. Nothing. *Lord, he said You'd always bring us back together. Do it again. Bring him down that dock!*

The plane began to move, sending a surge of panic through me. "No! Wait for Matthew!"

The next man through the door jumped in as the plane was already moving. I flew to him and grabbed his shirt. "Where is Matthew?"

"He told me to give you a message!"

My heart thudded. I felt dizzy.

"He said to tell you that you promised him something, and that I was not, under any circumstances to let you get off this plane."

I couldn't breathe. "But he's coming," I choked out. "Mike! Don't leave him here!"

"The zeros are coming for another pass. We have to go!"

My throat tightened. My chest ached. I went to the door again. We were moving steadily along the dock now. The colonel near the door put a hand on my arm, as if to remind me of his orders. I stretched my neck to look once more. He would be there. He would be coming. I knew it.

And then I saw him. He was running along the dock. I screamed at Mike. "I see him! He's coming! Slow down!"

I pulled my arm away from the colonel's grip, and leaned out the door. But it wasn't Matthew running along the dock. It was Natalie. And my heart dropped.

She waved her arms frantically, crying for us to wait for her. The plane continued picking up speed. I saw the terror in her eyes, and I had just a moment's thought of reaching up and closing the door. I'd stared into those cold eyes as she'd let the bus pull away from me. Now was my chance to finally be rid of her. Her steps pounded on the dock. The Zeros were turning in the sky behind us.

Grace.

I stretched my arm out toward her. "Come on! You can make it!"

She pumped her skinny arms and ran harder. The zeros straightened out and headed for us again. Natalie was close enough now. I reached out as far as I could without falling out of the plane. "Come on! You have to jump!"

"I can't!" she screamed.

"Jump! I'll catch you!" We'd nearly reached the end of the dock. "Jump!"

She leaped into the air from the dock, getting her right foot to the plane, but she didn't quite get her upper body there, and the left half of her torso slammed into the side. I grabbed her right arm, slipping as I did. I fell to my bottom, and her leg slipped out the door and into the water. She screamed and grasped the side of the door and my hand.

Someone from inside the plane grabbed onto my waist and hauled me back into the plane. I tugged on Natalie until she was finally inside as well. The crew member slammed the door, and the plane began to taxi in earnest. I sat on the floor in shock as the others around me attended to Natalie and the injured men who'd been with Matthew. Then most of the passengers moved to the front of the fuselage to balance the weight and once again took cover.

I could barely move. Could hardly breathe. My chest felt like it was cracked wide open. Matthew was still back there.

***

As we soared further away from Mindanao and Matthew, it felt like my heart was unraveling, as if it were a line anchored to him. If I could just turn the plane around somehow. He was right there. *Right there.* I should have jumped out of the plane. I should've broken my promise. Because keeping it was breaking me into a thousand pieces.

When we were clear of the zeros, and everyone found a place to sit, I went over to the colonel who'd been the last to see Matthew. He looked up at me with sympathetic eyes and gestured for me to take a seat next to him.

It took everything within me to keep my composure. "Was he alive when you left him?"

"Yes."

"Why didn't he come?"

"He was holding off the Japanese patrol so we could take off. He made an incredible sacrifice to save all of us."

Sacrifice. Would they capture him, or kill him, or worse? "Do you think...was there even a chance he got away?"

316 | JENNIFER H. WESTALL

"Of course," he said, at least his mouth did. But his eyes darted away from mine.

I dropped my head, unable to stop my tears. The colonel's heavy hand rested on my back. *Lord, please protect him. Send Your angels, send Your Holy Spirit over him. Give him strength.* And then my words ran out, and all I could manage were groans of gut-wrenching heartache.

***

When we landed on the waters of Port Darwin, I set my mind to getting back in the air immediately. I stood by the door as we approached the docks, shifting my weight from right to left. As soon as everyone was off the plane, I'd get Mike to fly back for Matthew and the others left behind. But it was taking an eternity to get into position.

When the hatch finally opened, I plowed out of the plane and immediately began pacing along the dock. The nurses came after me, and were greeted by high-ranking officials. I marveled at how everyone could so calmly salute and shake hands while Matthew and the others in our group were in mortal danger.

When Mike finally showed himself, he sighed as our eyes met. I rushed over to him, and he immediately put his hands up in defense. "Now, Grace—"

"When can we go back for them?" I demanded.

"I have to get orders for that mission first—"

"How could you just leave him there?" I shouted, barely giving him a moment to answer before I blasted him again. "He was...he was in danger! And you just left him there!"

"He told me to, Grace."

That made me pause. "What?"

"He told me if it came down to it, he would fight off any Japanese we encountered, and I was to get everyone in the air. It was as if he knew what would happen. And he knew you'd go nuts."

I stepped closer and pointed my finger at him. "You haven't even seen me go *nuts* yet."

Someone put their hands on my shoulders from behind. A soft-spoken voice tried to calm me. "Grace, honey. Come with us."

I turned to see Mrs. Beckett holding onto me, her weary eyes brimming with tears. "I have to go back and get him," I pleaded.

"Look, we're here for you. We're going to do everything we can to get all our friends and colleagues back. But first, *first,* you have to take care of yourself."

She pulled me into a hug, and I wept on her shoulder. Behind us, I heard some of the others trying to explain to the officials what had happened. They'd been expecting a joyful return, an occasion for celebration. But half the group was still stranded on Mindanao.

I pulled away from Captain Beckett and approached the nearest official with an insignia that looked high enough to get something done. "When will you go back for the others?"

"Miss...I don't...That's not my call," he stuttered.

"Well, whose call is it?" another nurse demanded.

Several others showed their support. "Yeah! Who's going after the rest of them?"

"We can't just leave them there!"

The officials looked at each other with wide eyes and then looked back at us. "Girls, let's get your medical needs attended to first. Then we'll see about retrieving the others."

I knew we weren't getting anywhere. They probably had no say in any decisions made. If we were going to get anything done, we'd have to get to headquarters. So even though it nearly killed me to do so, I went along with the others to the hospital to get checked out.

***

I lay on a bed at the Darwin Army hospital, going through the motions of getting an exam. I knew my condition was deplorable. I didn't need an exam to tell me I was still battling the effects of malaria, malnutrition, and dysentery. That my weight was dangerously low. That I hadn't had my "monthlies" in months due to the stress of the ordeal I'd been through. But I supposed my body needed to tell its story.

I'd tried to close my eyes in between visits from the doctor, but my mind was clouded with terrifying visions of Matthew alone in the woods, fighting hordes of Japanese soldiers as they closed in on him. And there I was, on a comfortable mattress with a warm blanket, clean water on a tray beside my bed. All of it was so enticing, so temptingly soothing. But it had come at too high a cost, and all I felt was shame. *I shouldn't be here.*

I wandered along from the physical exam to the mess hall in a daze. I had no desire for food, but my stomach cramped when the aromas hit me. I sat down at a table across from Captain Beckett, who tilted her head in sympathy. "How are you holding up?" she asked.

"I don't know," I said. "I pray for mercy every moment. For Matthew, for me, for all those we left behind. For Henry. I know that the only reason I'm still breathing, is that God Himself is doing it for me."

She reached across the table and covered my hand with her own. "I know this is terrible. It's heartbreaking beyond measure. But I said that we'd support you, honey, and I meant it. You've been right there with us all along, right in the thick of the most gruesome moments of our lives. We're going to speak to whoever we have to in order to get our fellow nurses and your husband rescued."

My heart overflowed. "Thank you so much," I said, somehow keeping myself pulled together.

The food was served: steak and potatoes, with carrots and buttered rolls. The girls at the table gaped in amazement as it had been so long since they'd seen any food that hadn't come out of a can, and then they fell silent as they shoveled it down. I did my best to eat, but I couldn't seem to swallow. Everyone was so hungry; the meal was over in a few short minutes. I gave most of my steak to Roberta, who finished it off in less than two minutes.

I was so exhausted, so spent and overwhelmed. I propped my head in my hands and closed my eyes, hoping I could make it to a quiet room of my own soon so that I could completely break down. *Lord, I'm begging You once more to keep Matthew alive and safe in Your hands. Guard him with Your angels of mercy and power. Give me the strength to speak for him. Show me what to do.*

The chatter of the women around me went quiet, and the hair on my arm prickled. A gentle, quiet voice whispered in my mind.

My grace is sufficient for you, for my power is made perfect in weakness.

My heart swelled, and I almost cried out with the prick of joy that came with the scripture. It was only a moment, a reprieve from the burden of my grief. But it gave me hope.

Through many dangers, toils and snares, I have already come. 'Twas grace that brought me safe thus far, and grace will lead me home.

I opened my eyes with a small measure of peace in my heart that hadn't been there before. Across the mess hall, at a table by herself, Natalie sat staring out of a window. No one had spoken to her much, and she hadn't said a word. My spirit stirred me to take pity on her, so I walked over to her and sat down at the table.

She turned to glance at me, surprise registering in the dullness of her eyes. She dropped her gaze to the empty plate in front of her. "What are you doing?"

"I wanted to speak with you," I said.

She shook her head and turned back to the windows. "Please leave me alone."

I wanted to. I wanted to leave her in her misery. It was what she deserved. But the small voice inside me was insistent. *Grace.*

"Natalie, I want you to know that I forgive you."

Tears ran down her cheeks, and she swiped at them immediately. She turned to me, almost in frustration. "Who are you?"

"I don't know what you mean."

"Why did you help me? On the dock. When I was running. You could have just left me there. Why did you help me?"

"Because God told me to."

"What?"

"God told me to help you."

Her eyes darted around the mess hall in bewilderment. "But I...I didn't help you. I didn't tell the bus to stop."

"Believe me, if it were up to me, I would have left you there. That's exactly what you deserved. But I know in my heart that God has given me immeasurable, wonderful grace that covers all my sin. And He wants to offer you the same. An abundant grace that fills you with joy and love. *He* saved you, Natalie. Not me. He did it. The question is: what are you going to do about it?"

This time she made no attempt to stop the tears from flowing. "I'm so sorry for everything. I was so terrible to you. I don't know how you can ever forgive me."

"God's grace is sufficient for both of us. It's overflowing. It covers me; it will cover you." *And it's covering Matthew too.*

CHAPTER TWENTY-ONE

Ruby

May, 1942

We were flown on a B-17 bomber from Darwin to Melbourne on May 5th, moving me even further away from transportation back to Matthew. But I realized my best chance would lie with officials at Headquarters, so I resigned myself to staying there as long as necessary.

As the plane climbed above the small town of Darwin, I viewed the devastation of a recent Japanese bombing, and I wondered if there was any place on earth left untouched by war. For the first time since I'd left, I longed for Hanceville, Alabama. What I wouldn't give to see my Mother's face, to talk with Asa again and have him set my feet back on the path God chose for me. To play with little Abner and hear his laughter.

But I couldn't go home. Not without Matthew and Henry. And not with the threat of execution hanging over me. I tried desperately to think of a plan during the flight to Melbourne, but I knew nothing about the structure of the military beyond my limited exposure. I knew I needed to get someone influential on my side. I needed to figure out where Matthew might be—there was no thought in my mind that he was anything other than alive somewhere on Mindanao. And I needed someone in authority, possibly MacArthur himself, to order a rescue mission. By the time I arrived at Headquarters with the rest of the nurses, I was certain I could find a way to bring Matthew and the other stranded evacuees to Australia. I just needed someone to listen.

At first, we were treated for our various medical conditions at the base hospital. Already, I could feel the effects of the full doses of quinine. My stomach was still unsure of things and reminded me of its ordeal frequently, but even that was improving. The shocking part was my appearance. I'd lost over twenty pounds, and as I gazed at myself in a full-length mirror for the first time in months, I got a complete view of how war had ravaged my body. I looked ten years older.

My hair was as rough as a mule's tail; my cheeks were sunken, and my skin dull. I had no meat left on my bones, no curves to speak of. I looked a fright, indeed. But it mattered so little, I barely attempted to right myself. A hot shower and a dab of makeup were all I managed before making my way to a meeting room on base where we were to be questioned by Army officials. I was looking forward to this, because I had a few questions of my own.

As soon as the young man from Military Intelligence sat down across from me, I laid into him. "Is the Army doing anything to get the other group out?"

His blue eyes widened at my sudden question. He couldn't have been much older than I was, and I could tell from his uniform he wasn't very high in the rank structure. "Um, well, Miss..." He glanced down at the papers in his hands. "Miss Miller—"

"It's *Mrs.* Doyle. My husband is Captain Matthew Doyle, who was among the group that was left behind. I want to know if any effort is being made to retrieve them."

"Ma'am, that's not...I'm just supposed to ask you some questions. I don't—"

"Then who does?" I leaned onto the table separating us and bore my gaze into his. "Who do I have to talk to that knows what's going on over there?"

He looked around the room as if he needed help. "Ma'am...Mrs. Doyle, I would like to help you out, but I really need to do my job."

"Then do it! Find out if the Army is going to bring my husband home."

"I will do everything I can to help you, but first, I just need you to answer a few questions."

I sat back in my chair and huffed. "All right then. Let's make this quick."

He glanced down at the papers in the folder on the table. "Okay, let's make sure I have the correct information. Your name is..."

"Grace Doyle."

"I have Grace Miller."

"I married Captain Doyle on Bataan."

He wrote that down. "And you're an American citizen?"

"Yes, sir."

"Where were you born?"

I sighed. "What does that have to do with anything?"

"I'm just supposed to ask the questions."

"Alabama. Hanceville, Alabama." It was the first time I'd answered that question honestly in over five years. What was I thinking?

He wrote that down too. Then he proceeded to ask me the details of how I'd come to be on Bataan with the Army Nurse Corps. I did my best to keep my answers short and to the point. When we'd finished, I asked him again whom I should speak with to get more information. He pointed to a broad, older man who appeared to be observing the questioning from the front of the room. "I'd start with Colonel Dorsey over there," he said. "He might be able to help you out."

I thanked him and headed over to the front of the room where Colonel Dorsey sat reading over the notes already delivered to him from other officers. "May I speak with you, Colonel Dorsey?" I asked, as patiently as my anxious heart would allow.

He glanced up at me as if I were a fly buzzing around his meal. "What's that?"

"May I speak with you for a moment?"

As he took in my ravaged appearance, his demeanor softened. "What can I do for you?"

I took a seat across from him and prayed he would know something. "Sir, my husband, Captain Matthew Doyle, was left behind on Mindanao, along with other nurses and officers. I was wondering if there's been any attempt to go back for them?"

"You're Captain Doyle's wife?"

The way he said that made my stomach swim. I nodded, and he dropped his gaze to the table for a long moment before he looked at me again. "Mrs. Doyle, I'm aware of no mission to return for the other evacuees. Mindanao fell into Japanese hands the day your party arrived on the island. You were lucky to escape with your lives."

My eyes stung. "So...what? The army just gives up on them? They're left to fend for themselves?"

"At this point, there is no air base in the region for a plane to land on. It would be a suicide mission."

I swiped at my tears, refusing to give up. "You're in the Intelligence Service, right?"

"Yes, ma'am."

"So you get reports about what's happening over there, right?"

"I have access to most of them, yes."

"Has there been any word...about what happened to the other group? About what happened to Matthew? Do you know where they are?"

He looked like he'd rather be anywhere else but seated across from me. "Mrs. Doyle, I can't speak to you about classified information; however, what I can tell you is this. Captain Doyle was last seen by Colonel Nathan Hanson, who boarded the plane with you and delivered a message to you from Captain Doyle."

"How do you know about that?"

"We've already debriefed the crew and the other passengers." He sighed. "There's been no word from Captain Doyle, but at least we know the last sighting of him puts him as still possibly alive. And his actions were of the highest valor. I know this isn't any comfort right now, but his sacrifice will not be in vain. General MacArthur is fully committed to turning the tide of this war and liberating those left behind in enemy hands."

He was right. It was no comfort. None at all.

***

I spent the rest of the day in a fog, wondering what I should do next. The other nurses offered their support, but none of them really knew me, and they knew nothing of what Matthew and I had already been through years before arriving in the Philippines. How could they possibly understand the depth of my sorrow?

So I went to the only One who could. That night, I sobbed into my mattress as I knelt beside the bed, my chest sore from heaving. I was spent, and still the tears flowed. My anger had finally hit a boiling point, and I turned my face to heaven and yelled, "Where are You?"

It came up out of me with an anger in my spirit I'd never felt before. "I've begged You! I've pleaded with You! All I've asked for is Your presence and comfort. I'm not asking for a miracle! I don't understand what's happened, but I can accept that You are Lord. Just...please...please...don't leave me here. I only need You." I pounded my fist into the mattress, sobs wracking my body. "I only need You. I only need *You*. Everything else can fade away. I can face whatever lies ahead. But I need You. Lord, please, come near to me."

The room was so still, so quiet. And so empty. I hadn't felt so alone in all my life. Where was God when I needed Him most? And then, like a procession of images through my mind, God showed me.

Henry. He'd been there for me when I was alone and terrified after the car accident. He'd stayed with me, despite all his instincts to run from trouble. He'd never left me.

Joseph. He'd taken me in when I had no purpose, no path to redemption. And he'd given me a chance to serve others again. With no strings attached, and all his love.

Janine. She'd loved me like a sister, and she had believed in me. She had loved my brother with all her heart, and had joined our family without reservation.

Matthew. God had brought us back together, and despite the pain and suffering around us, He'd given us precious moments together I'd never forget. And in the end, God had placed Matthew in the perfect place to save the lives of all of us on that plane.

Maybe I hadn't felt His presence, but He'd been there all the same. He hadn't left me, and He wouldn't leave me now. He had given me my new name, and His grace would sustain me in whatever lay ahead.

I am God, and there is no other;

I am God, and there is none like me.

I crawled under the covers and for the first time since we'd left Mindanao, I was able to fall asleep with hope in my heart.

***

The next day, the nurses and I got word that Corregidor had surrendered to the Japanese, and we spent the morning quietly thinking of all those we'd left behind. All those patients. What would become of them? The soldiers? Our friends and comrades? Henry? Some of the girls went to their rooms and didn't come out again the rest of the day.

I went to the mess hall at lunchtime, and found a table near the windows where I could take in the scenery while I prayed for Henry and Matthew. I figured until I knew one way or the other, I would assume they were both alive, and I would trust God to keep them safe. What else could I do?

I'd gotten about halfway through my meal, when Mr. Freeman approached me and asked if he could sit down. "Sure," I said. "What can I do for you?"

He leaned back in his chair, his intense eyes studying me closely. "I spoke with Natalie Williams earlier this morning."

"Oh?" I did my best to sound nonchalant.

"She's singing a different tune." I took another bite of my sandwich as an excuse not to answer. So he continued. "She says she was confused and afraid. That she just wanted to get away from the Japanese, so she made up that whole story about you."

I swallowed and gave him a shaky smile. "Yes, she apologized to me as well. All's been forgiven."

"Funny thing is, I rang my editor back in the States as soon as we arrived. Told him about some of the stories I was working on. Profiles of the nurses and such. And on a whim, I told him to check out the story Natalie had told me on the island."

The bottom dropped out of my stomach. He seemed to be waiting for me to respond, but I didn't know what to say. I couldn't hold his gaze, so I turned my face to the window. The game was up. I knew it. And I'd be shipped back home to face the electric chair.

"You want to know what he said?" Mr. Freeman asked.

"Sure," I said. "Should be interesting."

"He confirmed everything. Said there was indeed a young Alabama woman named Ruby Graves convicted of murder back in '36 and sentenced to the electric chair. Lots of debate over whether or not she really did it. She claimed the guy was attacking her, and she was only defending herself." He paused and raised an eyebrow. I kept quiet. "Anyway, turns out when the cops were transporting her to the state prison, there was an escape attempt, and she was killed in a car accident." His mouth tipped into a wry smile. "Well, at least they *declared* her dead. Never found the body."

I cleared my throat. "That's a tragic story."

"If she was innocent, yes. If she was guilty, I'd say justice was served."

I stared back into his eyes, which were still slightly sunken from malnutrition. "What do you think?"

He leaned up on his elbows and lowered his voice. "I think, this girl...Ruby...she's probably one of the most honest, caring, and brave people on earth." Then he smiled mischievously. "No way she killed anyone."

My shoulders relaxed, and I let out a long breath.

"It's really too bad she died," he finished, leaning back again. "I bet she has the most interesting stories to tell."

I couldn't help but smile a little. "Guess you'll never know."

He shrugged. "I'm all right with that. I'll have plenty to keep me busy for a long time. The nurses, the doctors over there, and the soldiers—they deserve to have their stories told. The world needs to know what the Japanese are doing to our boys. And I'm determined to make sure it happens."

He stood and pushed his chair back under the table, his expression turning thoughtful. "I am curious, though. I can't help but wonder if she did it. Ruby, I mean. If she really killed that man. I'm having trouble with that." He waited for a moment, and then shrugged. "I guess it doesn't matter. You have a nice day, Mrs. Doyle. You deserve it."

He took a few steps, and something irrational came over me. "Mr. Freeman," I called. He turned around and suddenly it was as if there were only two of us in the mess hall. Accused and Judge. "She didn't."

He grinned. "I didn't think so." He waved a final goodbye and headed out the doors, leaving me to wonder how, in a world overcome by war, I'd managed to avoid that particular bomb going off.

***

A couple of weeks later, after being cared for and given leave to rest as much as they liked, the Army nurses were ordered back to the States. As usual, it was a mad dash to gather them all and pack their things. Captain Beckett had convinced her superiors to allow her to stay. She wanted to be in the first group back to the Philippines as soon as it was recaptured. I was grateful, because I was sticking around as well.

If Matthew and Henry were alive, then Melbourne was the closest I could stay to them, and it was where Matthew had told me to wait for him. So I would. I would wait forever if I had to.

I found a job as a waitress in a small café, and I was able to rent an apartment nearby. I called Colonel Dorsey every day, asking if there was any word. He never once refused to take my call, and if he was busy, he always returned the call. Although he was tight-lipped about it, he hinted that a handful of Americans had refused to surrender on the various islands in the Philippines, and that the Communications officers were trying to establish contact with some of them.

I kept my hope alive that Matthew was somewhere on Mindanao, fighting to stay alive, and fighting to come back to me. At night, in my bed, I would remember the feeling of him lying next to me, holding me close. And I'd hear his words, promising that God would always bring us back together.

Until that day, I would lift up every soul I could think of by name that was still trapped in the Philippines. That would be my new mission. To pray unceasingly, until they were home.

The End

AUTHOR'S NOTE

In my efforts to create a fictional story that takes place during an actual historic event, I did a great deal of research into the events that occurred on the Philippine Islands during the time period leading up to and during the invasion by Japan. I've done my very best to keep this fictional story as close to the actual events as possible, as well as reflect the courage of the men and women who suffered greatly during this time. There were a few occasions where I combined several events into one, or altered the event slightly for the sake of keeping the story moving along in a succinct manner. For example, there were two jungle hospitals set up on Bataan, Hospital #1 and Hospital #2. I chose to have Ruby located at Hospital #2 because its setup and location provided the best stage for the story I wanted to tell. However, I've included one or two events that actually happened at Hospital #1 (such as the direct bombing of the hospital that killed Joseph). I also altered the escape of the nurses and personnel from Corregidor in order to fit in some story elements that were needed in order to wrap things up. In the actual escape from Corregidor, the evacuees flew to Mindanao rather than traveling by boat. One group was in fact left behind on Mindanao because of a hole in the plane. However, the plane that did take off was not under direct fire at the time. I hope the reader will understand and forgive any slight altering of history.

If you've found this story intriguing, I encourage you to read any of the number of non-fiction books out there detailing the actual events that took place. I have included the ones I found most helpful in my research in a recommended reading section following this note. I am in awe of the nurses on Bataan, often referred to as the Angels of Bataan. Their selfless acts of heroism were in simply doing their job every day no matter what trials they faced. And I doubt you could find even one of them that would have considered themselves to be heroic. I have tried to capture as much of that spirit as possible within this story. I have come to a newfound admiration for nurses through my research. This is a group of people committed to pouring themselves out for others, people who often go unnoticed and receive very little thanks. They deserve our gratitude.

Lastly, I want to thank all the men and women who have served in the armed forces in any capacity. I am in awe of what my fellow citizens have done so that my family and I can sleep safely in our beds at night. They deserve our gratitude and our prayers. May God bless them and keep them.

RECOMMENDED READING

The titles below aided me greatly in my research of the events leading up to and during the attack on the Philippines. There are many, many more books available that I simply don't have the room to list. If you're looking for stories to amaze you, this is a great beginning.

We Band of Angels by Elizabeth M. Norman

Bataan: A Survivor's Story by Lt. Gene Boyt with David L. Burch

Resolve by Bob Welch

Tears in the Darkness by Michael Norman and Elizabeth M. Norman

Undefeated: America's Heroic Fight for Bataan and Corregidor by Bill Sloan

Escape from Corregidor by Edgar D. Whitcomb

MORE FROM JENNIFER H. WESTALL

Historical Fiction:

Healing Ruby, Volume One of the *Healing Ruby* series

Breaking Matthew, Volume Two of the *Healing Ruby* series

Saving Grace, Volume Three of the *Healing Ruby* series (Coming 2016)

Contemporary Christian Romance:

Love's Providence

ACKNOWLEDGEMENTS

As always, I must first thank my family for their support and encouragement. My kids try to keep the guilt trips to a minimum, only occasionally implying that I love writing more than I love them. My husband has been a real trooper, taking them on outings and keeping them busy so I could bang away at my computer. I'm forever grateful.

I have to once again sing the praises of my amazing editor, Bryony Sutherland, who knows my heart and encourages me through every panicked email filled with self-doubt. And I owe so much thanks to my beautiful cousin, Amy Hobbs, who has once again created a cover I can't stop admiring. Thanks also goes to my cousin Morgan Kimbrough for letting me dress her up so that Amy could take her picture over and over. She has now posed for two covers in the Healing Ruby series, and she makes such an amazing "Ruby."

I also want to thank the enthusiastic readers who continue to email me or send me messages through Facebook. You've all become such an encouragement to me, and I love interacting with all of you. I have to personally thank those of you who volunteered your time to help comb through the early manuscript for errors and typos: Elaine Ream, Charmaine Fray, Rose Kooi, Rebecca Kolb, Loretta Phillips, Donna Dvorshock, Lanell Harrington, Lucy Harvey, Jaime Chapman, Melissa Billiot, Beth Poly, April McAnally, Dana Gray, Melody Reynolds, Melissa Sanford, Karen Richards, Elaina Sharron, Judy Juenger, Tammy Collins, Tanya Hays, Rebecca Spencer, Marie Kohl, Beverly Welsh, Lucy Flenner, Kris Gillen, and Barbara Bennett. Thank you from the bottom of my heart!

And most importantly, I must give thanks to God for His inspiration and comfort through all my self-doubt and fear. It's still amazing to look through a story I've written and see His hand throughout. I'm so grateful He called me to writing.

Jennifer Westall loves writing Christian fiction as a way of exploring her own faith journey. Saving Grace (2016) is the third installment in the Healing Ruby series, the first of which was inspired by events in the life of her grandmother and explores the mysteries of faith healing. She's also the author of Love's Providence (2012), a contemporary Christian romance novel that navigates the minefield of dating and temptation. She resides in northern Virginia with her husband and two boys, where she homeschools by day and writes by night, thus explaining those pesky bags under her eyes. Readers can connect with her at jenniferhwestall.com or find her on Facebook and Twitter.

72702480R00209

Made in the USA
Lexington, KY
05 December 2017